The
Coffin Trail

Novels by Martin Edwards

All the Lonely People
Suspicious Minds
I Remember You
Yesterday's Papers
Eve of Destruction
The Devil in Disguise
First Cut Is the Deepest
Take My Breath Away
The Lazarus Widow (with Bill Knox)
The Coffin Trail
The Cipher Garden
The Arsenic Labyrinth

Collected short stories
Where Do You Find Your Ideas? and other stories

Dedicated to Helena

Dedicated to Helena

Author's Note

I could not have written this book without help from a great many people. Too many, in fact, to acknowledge each of them individually. I would like, though, to single out my family, Roger Forsdyke, Alan McDonald, Ted Brown, Gill Longford, Ann Cleeves and Ian Peacock, all of whom provided particular assistance with my researches, together with my agent Mandy Little, my publishers David Shelley and Robert Rosenwald and everyone at Allison & Busby and Poisoned Pen Press who helped in bringing this book to publication. Representatives of Cumbria Constabulary, Merseyside Police and Cumbria Tourist Board provided invaluable assistance. At the risk of stating the obvious, I should add that although some of the people in the novel have surnames often found in Cumbria, all the characters, businesses and incidents depicted are fictitious.

Martin Edwards

OLD SCAR FELL

PRIEST EDGE

SACRIFICE STONE

COFFIN TRAIL

TARN COTTAGE

BRACK HALL FARM

BRACK HALL

BRACK CHURCH

THE MOON UNDER WATER

BRACKDALE

QUARRY WORKINGS

BRACK VILLAGE

Prologue

Barrie could see the woman stretched out on top of the Sacrifice Stone. Moonlight played upon her pale skin and long fair hair.

She is waiting for me.

He broke into a run. The trail was steep. Usually he counted every pace up to the top of the fell. *Safety in numbers.* But tonight he wasn't counting, tonight he could do anything. His shirt was damp and the cotton stuck to his chest. In the night sky, an owl's wings flapped. Breathing hard, he halted. The moon dipped behind a cloud. In the distance he could hear the waters of Brack Force slapping the rocks. Straining his eyes in the gloom, he made out the slender motionless form of the woman. She was so patient.

'I kept my word,' he said.

His throat was parched and his voice sounded scratchy. He'd never had much to do with pretty women, but he knew that they liked to be wooed. Petted. They treated it as a game. Paying compliments didn't come naturally to him. He'd never bought anyone flowers in his life: what was the point? All the same, he'd been rehearsing words of admiration over and over in his mind. If you wanted to win, you had to play by the rules, even if they didn't make sense.

Pebbles crunched under his feet. Even now, she remained perfectly still. Most people baffled him, but young women were the worst. They never behaved as he expected. He whispered her name, then called it aloud. Nothing. The only sound, the only movement, came from a fox that had ventured far from its lair. Perhaps she was testing him, maybe she wanted to see whether his desire would overcome his nerves, but it wasn't what she'd promised.

She should be waving me on.

He caught a whiff of sourness in the air.

This isn't right.

Two strides brought him close to the Sacrifice Stone. Just then, the moon gleamed and he glimpsed bare flesh. At once he saw that something terrible, something beyond words, had been done to her. His stomach was strong, but the sight made him retch.

He reached out—he could not help himself—and his fingertips brushed against her. The skin was chill and sticky and wet. He stepped back hastily, as if bitten by an adder, and wiped his fingers on his sleeve. She was covered with blood and now so was he.

'But you said…'

Of course she didn't reply. She was dead and everyone would say that he had done it. That he had killed her. He didn't understand anything, except that he was in danger. Panic began to choke him. Who would believe that she had begged him to come? A teacher had once said he lacked imagination, but he could see the future unfolding with the vividness of colour pictures in a horror comic strip. He had been a fool. He had been betrayed.

Tears stinging his eyes, he stumbled along the rocky ridge. In blind haste, he clipped a cross-wall built to shelter visitors to the summit and cut his knee, but he hurried on. Time was short. The wind smacked his skin as if punishing him for stupidity, but he paid it no heed. He couldn't go home. Home was where people would come to find him. To escape, he must find a safe way down. He was aiming for a dip between the crags and the chance of shelter in the next valley.

His breath came in short gasps. Spots of rain greased his hair. The ground was like glue under his feet. Ahead, a familiar squat cairn loomed out of the darkness and he yelped in frustration. He was exhausted, yet so far he had covered little more than a mile. Not far enough, not nearly far enough. His cheeks were moist and he knew he was crying for himself, not for the dead woman. Soon people would be chasing after him. Whenever something bad happened, he was blamed. What could be worse than this?

No one knew Tarn Fell better, he thought of it as his back yard, and yet in his distress he was unsure which downward track to take. As the ground fell away, his foot slid. For a moment he thought he'd turned his ankle, but it was all right. Facts, he would cling to hard facts. People mocked him for his love of facts, but facts weren't like women. They were safe—and they never let you down.

Four, five, seven, ten. *Safety in numbers.* He paused. There was so much that he knew by heart and yet the shock of finding the woman's body had emptied his brain. No, it was all right. Fourteen, seventeen, nineteen, eighteen, fifteen, eleven, seven and six. Those were the average daily temperatures in the Lakes, from January to December inclusive.

He stopped to peer over the precipice. Darkness, punctured only by a light in the lonely farmhouse far below. Thunder rumbled and he counted three seconds until the lightning flashed. The rain began to sheet down, sharp and unforgiving. He was close to the heart of the storm.

Now—the four highest mountains, in order of height. Feet, not metres. Scafell Pike 3210. Scafell 3162, Helvellyn 3118. Skiddaw 3053. The numbers soothed his brain. Lists and figures were a comfort, you always knew where you were with them. As a child, when his mother had shouted at him, he'd taken refuge in his bed and pulled the blankets over his face, reciting to himself the latest data he'd stowed away. He started to pick his way down the narrow path. Wait—he'd blundered on to the Devil's Elbow, a zigzag route winding between two deep fissures carved by frost and rain.

No point in tears. In a downpour so fierce he could see nothing. The fells were safe, Wainwright used to say, as long as you watched where you put your feet. Suddenly the path convulsed over a mass of shattered rock. The rain had made it more dangerous and he found himself slipping. He threw out an arm and grabbed a clump of heather, striving in vain to break his fall.

A phrase his mother used came spinning into his mind. *Rolling down the hill,* she liked to say, *Barrie's always rolling down the hill.* It was her way of describing what he was like when he went on and on about trivial things that meant nothing to her. Now he was rolling down the hill for real.

The ravine gaped in front of his eyes, a cruel mouth waiting to swallow him. He pitched into it, arms and legs smashing against stone as he fell. His forehead caught on a ledge which gouged his flesh. The pain was cruel. He screamed for help, but there was nobody to hear. He didn't pray—he'd never been able to imagine God—but he told himself that he would survive the drop. Even if his body was wrecked beyond repair, he was going to live. People would be searching for him. *Safety in numbers.* He would be rescued. He could not simply be left until he starved. Or froze to death.

Chapter One

Forget about the murder. It's history.

Daniel tightened his grip on the steering wheel as the Audi jolted over potholes in the winding lane, his palms sweating. Miranda thought he was so cool, so relaxed, but it was an illusion. Might a conjurer feel like this when walking onto the stage? Fearing that his magic wouldn't work, that when he whipped the cloak away, his audience wouldn't gasp, but merely yawn? The car eased over the top of the fell and Daniel held his breath. At last Brackdale revealed itself. Unfolding below them, luxuriating in the sunshine.

'A hidden valley!'

Miranda's delight made him shiver with relief. This was the moment he'd yearned for. Out of the corner of his eye, he saw her leaning forward in the passenger seat, craning her long neck so as to drink in the scene. Stone buildings squeezed around a spired church and its lush graveyard, and on the other side of the village, a jigsaw puzzle of fields and copses spread out across the hollow. Quarry workings, deserted and melancholy, pockmarked the far end of the valley, yet he wouldn't have loved Brackdale as much without its scars. Steep surrounding crags closed in together beyond the dead industrial remains. There was no through road. Miranda was right: a casual visitor would never guess that the valley existed. Tarn Cottage was concealed from view, as if by pale plumes of smoke. But Daniel knew that no fire burned, it was only the blossom of damson trees.

'Look over there!' Miranda was excited, he was aware of her tensing beside him. 'That weird stone on the summit.'

The boulder was shaped like an anvil, stark against the sky. Even on this innocent spring morning, its grey bulk loomed dour and secretive. Without thinking, he said, 'I climbed up there once. People round here call it the Sacrifice Stone.'

'Really?' Her voice rose. 'Go on, tell me more.'

He'd said too much. That was the trouble with the valley; it seduced you into betraying what was on your mind. Laughing, he changed the subject. He must focus on the here and now, not let anything darken a perfect day.

They shuddered over a cattle grid; it would be a miracle if the car's suspension survived the weekend, but who cared? As they joined the road on the far side of the village, dry stone walls gave way to hedgerows smudged by the gold of willow catkins. A mile further on stood a wooden sign with worn lettering. He could barely make out the words *Tarn Fold*. Next to it a gleaming estate agent's sign pointed towards the woodland: *Cottage for sale by private treaty*.

It must be Tarn Cottage. Had to be. There was no other dwelling down the track. His skin tingled: soon he would see the old place again. He parked on a square of turf where the asphalted lane became an unmade track. Miranda leaned towards him, eyes closing as they always did when she was aroused. Her perfume had a heady jasmine fragrance. They kissed and he put the cottage out of his mind until she pulled away.

'Time to explore.'

As he led her across an old packhorse bridge, they heard the faint splash of a fish in the beck. Past a ruined corn-mill, the route forked, and without hesitation, he headed towards a coppice of beech and ash. Wrens murmured in the trees. He'd read that birdsong is quieter in the countryside: no need to compete with city noise. Above the track, sinuous branches arched to form a green tunnel. He had a sudden fancy that he and Miranda were people in a story for children, passing through a portal into another world.

A breeze set the trees swaying, as if to the rhythms of a samba that only they could hear, and he glimpsed the whitewashed walls of the cottage. Beyond, he remembered, lay the barn and the bothy. When they reached the clearing, they stopped a few yards from the gateway at the end of the track, taking in the luscious air. A board freshly painted in a blinding shade of yellow bragged that Tarn Cottage "presented outstanding potential for sensitive refurbishment."

Ground elder and nettles had colonised the gravel path that curved towards a front door from which green paint was peeling. At least the tracery of the mullioned windows was intact. Moving closer, they could see the slope of the garden down to a reed-fringed tarn. Sunlight glinted on the water. Further on, the land rose towards the lower reaches of the fell. They paused, no longer able to hear the rushing of the beck. The breeze had dropped, the birds had lost their voice.

For a long time, neither of them broke the silence. Daniel slipped his arm around Miranda's waist and felt her trembling. It wasn't in her nature to be uncertain. Perhaps, like him, she felt as if she had arrived at a sort of holy place. The two of us are worshippers, he thought, we're here to make our devotions. And now we are overcome by awe.

'How could anyone live here and not be at peace?' She was whispering, even though no one could hear.

'Maybe we ought to put in a bid.'

'Oh God, yes,' she murmured. 'Let's do it.'

Her smile was dreamy. He'd seen it before, in her flat in London, moments after they made love for the first time. She could ask for anything, he would give it gladly. Seizing his hand, she gripped it tight.

'Let's do it,' she said again.

'But...'

'No buts, Daniel. I mean it.'

'You're not serious.'

Her eyes opened wide. 'Believe me, I am.'

He tried being logical, though this was no time for rational argument. 'You work in London. I'm in Oxford. It takes almost as long to drive up here as to fly the Atlantic.'

'You weren't talking like that a couple of days ago.'

'You weren't talking about buying a holiday home then.'

'Not a holiday home.' She pinched his arm. 'Listen, remember when I read out my horoscope last night, that stuff about making a new start? We could make it here. Sell up everything and move into Tarn Cottage.'

'You're joking.' His mouth was dry. 'Aren't you?'

'I've never been more serious,' she said. 'I hate my job, and the college is stifling you. Listen to me, Daniel. Life is short, we don't get second chances. Let's escape from it all, make a fresh beginning together. We could be so happy here.'

He took a step away and stared at her flushed cheeks. Once such intensity would have scared him, now it made him giddy with desire. She lived by instinct and he adored her for it. For too long he'd played the sober academic, weighing evidence with cool scholarship before proceeding to a measured judgement. But reason was a ball and chain. Even though he'd never been able to get Brackdale—and Barrie Gilpin—out of his mind, it had taken him twenty years to return. Miranda was different. From the moment she'd seen the cottage, she had fallen head over heels.

'It's not exactly Islington.'

'Thank God.'

'Didn't you once tell me that anywhere north of the Wash was like a foreign country? You've never even lived in a small town. You're a Londoner, the city's part of you.'

'Parts of it I hate. The greed, the dirt, the crime. The newspaper placards screaming *Murder of Woman—Witnesses Sought.*'

'But…'

'Hey, I thought you'd understand, that you'd want this as much as me.'

A gust caught the damson petals. Daniel watched them flutter in the air like crystals of snow before they merged with the wood anemone carpeting the ground beyond the little wood.

'Well?' she asked. 'Are you up for it?'

If I say no, he thought, will things ever be the same between us? I mustn't mess up, the way I messed up with Aimee.

He swallowed hard. 'Sure.'

Flinging her arms around him, she kissed him with a fierce hunger. Unbuttoning his shirt, unbuckling his belt, pushing him backwards and down. The grass smelled damp but they didn't care. The two of them were drunk with passion for each other. Her skin tasted sweet. He'd never experienced this before Miranda: not such abandonment. Surrendering to the will of another human being. Until now he'd always kept control.

Later, stroking his chest with warm fingertips, she said, 'You've never been able to get this place out of your mind, have you? I love that. That kind of obsession.'

Obsession? Yes, he supposed she was right. He ought to tell her that once, in this quiet and lovely place, a woman had been savagely murdered. But this moment was too precious. He would never forgive himself if she took fright and fled, vowing never to return. She was impulsive, he could never quite be sure how she would respond. He could tell her later.

Their pilgrimage had come out of the blue. Miranda had been trying for a late booking at a hotel on the Riviera that a friend claimed was the last word in luxury. She was desperate to take a break from London. At a party a few weeks back, Tamzin, her editor at the magazine, had made a pass following too many glasses of wine. Perhaps Miranda's rebuff had been scathing, she really couldn't remember. Ever since then, Tamzin had subtly set about making her life hell. When told that the hotel was full, Miranda burst into tears. Daniel threw out a suggestion, scarcely imagining that she'd say yes.

'Why go abroad? We could stay in England, off the beaten track. How about the Lakes?'

'Windermere?' she asked, making it sound as remote as the Sea of Azov.

'Too many tourists. But there are plenty of out of the way places. I stayed up there as a boy, it's where we had our last family holiday before my father left us. I always wanted to go back.'

'You mean—you'd like us to take a break up north?'

'It's not the Arctic Circle. Who wants to spend fifteen hours at an airport when air traffic controllers go out on strike? Even with all the motorway jams, the Lakes are only a few hours' drive away. Where better to get away from it all?'

'Doesn't it rain a lot?'

'You know what they say in the Lakes? There's no such thing as bad weather. Only bad clothing.'

She laughed. 'Okay, you win. I've never been there before, not even as a kid. My parents used to take us to France every year. Besides, I was never keen on Wordsworth and all that. We had daffodils in our front garden at home, they were my mother's pride and joy. I never saw any need to visit Grasmere to see them in their thousands.'

'There's more to the Lakes than rain and daffodils. Forget Wordsworth and Beatrix Potter. Think Coleridge, think De Quincey, think…'

'All right, all right, any moment now you'll be reliving battle scenes from *Swallows and Amazons*.' She was laughing already and he knew he'd persuaded her. 'Okay, I admit it. When I was a kid, I couldn't help liking Arthur Ransome's books. And it's silly, travelling the world and ignoring your own back doorstep. Even if I don't get the chance of a tan. Let's do it.'

Now here they were in Tarn Fold. Talking about junking their jobs, their homes, and moving up here. Unreal, but so was the whole of their affair. They had fallen for each other in the course of a single evening. He'd met her at a party thrown by his publishers at Soho House. At seven that evening they were strangers; they parted next morning as lovers. Her spontaneity was a gift. It turned him on, the way she let herself be swept by a tide of passion.

'I just can't believe…"

'You must believe,' she said quickly. 'Swear to me you won't change your mind?'

'I swear,' he said. 'You know I wanted you to share this place with me.'

She put her head on one side, as though trying to decipher an inscription in Sanskrit. 'I've never seen you like this before.'

'You've never come here with me before.'

Taking a pen out of the pocket of her Levis, she scrawled the estate agent's name and number on the back of her hand. 'Fine, we'll call at the branch and arrange to view.'

He couldn't help grinning. 'You really are set on this, aren't you?'

'Once I start on something,' she said, 'nothing will stop me.'

It wasn't precisely true. A month ago, she'd begun to write a novel, about some other young journalist who lived in Islington and suffered from lesbian harassment, but she'd never made it beyond chapter one. Last night in the hotel she'd talked of pitching a feature to a broadsheet about alternative therapies. Over breakfast, she wondered about yet another variation on a favourite theme: *Diana: how she taught us to get in touch with our emotions.*

'Hey,' she said, 'we'd better get a move on. We mustn't lose out.'

She skipped off towards the car and he tramped after her in a blissed-out daze. Anyone would think they were both high on something.

'This whole valley is a Shangri-La,' she said as they left Tarn Fold behind. 'If only the people here were immortal too. It's too beautiful a place to die in.'

He switched on the CD player and started humming to Norah Jones. Anything to avoid talk of death. A lane led off to a squat pele tower that formed the centrepiece of Brack Hall; another curved towards the hall farm and the fell beyond. As they passed through Brack, he pointed to a window above the front door of a large pub on the main street. The Moon under Water. From it hung a 'bed and breakfast' sign.

'That was my room,' he said. 'I shared it with my sister Louise. She kept me awake, telling me stories from a book my parents bought us. *Legends of Lakeland*, it was called. Tales about stone circles that came to life and rivers that wept.'

Beyond the church, the road narrowed. Purple aubretia and white alyssum spilled from cracks in the walls. On the verges, poppies were starting to bloom. He remembered clambering halfway up to Priest Edge with his father to an embankment within which an irregular pattern of marked-out footways was all that remained of a hut village constructed by ancient Britons. According to Ben Kind's books, fewer folk lived in the valley now than during the years BC.

'My father and I used to roam around here while my mother and sister went into the town to shop.'

'Your old man was a policeman, you told me. Was that difficult?'

'Not for me,' he said. 'I was fascinated by the stories he told.'

'But your mother, did she have a tough time?'

He hesitated. 'The week we came home, he told mum that he was seeing someone else. The affair had been going on for some time, but she didn't have a clue. He might have walked out sooner, but the holiday was booked and he didn't want to wreck it for all of us.'

'And you never saw him again?'

'No, my mother would have regarded it as a betrayal. Louise backed her to the hilt. We both had to promise never to speak to him again. It was a long time before I broke my word.'

By evening, Miranda's plans for the cottage were well advanced. They were staying in a hotel on the outskirts of Keswick, halfway between shimmery Derwentwater and the brooding heights of Skiddaw and Blencathra. The restaurant occupied an airy conservatory and over their meal they'd watched the sunlight streaking the lake, then marvelled at a sky so red as to delight even the gloomiest of shepherds. The dinner would have had Egon Ronay drooling. As they drank a final glass of Chablis in the low-beamed bar, Daniel felt light-headed, as if a hypnotist had put him in a trance of happiness. Viewing was scheduled for half-nine tomorrow. No one else had put in a bid. For Miranda that meant the cottage was as good as theirs.

'Did I ever tell you I've written for home magazines about interior design? The importance of lighting and colour and stuff.'

He waved at the 'to-do' list she'd scrawled on the hotel notepaper, and her lavish sketch of their redesigned living accommodation. Already everything was planned out in her mind. The bothy could provide additional guest accommodation, and she'd decided the barn could be split into two offices: his and hers. In their new lives they could work from home and be together all the time.

'You saw how rundown the place is,' he said. So far words of caution had blown away like leaves in a gale, but he dreaded her distress if it all fell through. She cared so much about everything. In her vulnerability, if nothing else, she reminded him of Aimee. 'The garden's bad enough; who knows what a survey might show?'

'Come on, loosen up. Anything can be fixed.'

'It'll cost a small fortune.'

'Have you checked house prices here? You could buy a mansion for the cost of a terrace in Islington. Well, almost. Anyway, we'll have plenty of cash to spare when we sell our old homes. Money isn't a problem.'

He swung back on his chair and tried another tack. 'Country living is different. Winters are hard. Ever tried unblocking a septic tank?'

She giggled. 'I'll learn to love it. Hey Daniel, relax. This is going to be wonderful. Trust me.'

◇◇◇

The ruddy-faced estate agent smelled of bacon and burned toast and looked like a prime candidate for a coronary. Tubby and panting and over-dressed in tweed suit and camel coat, he was yet naked in his desperation to earn commission on the sale. A fast man with a superlative, he didn't seem to realise that all he needed to do was to let the cottage and its setting sell themselves. The sun gatecrashing through the faded blinds was so strong that Daniel needed to shade his eyes. The cottage hadn't been occupied for months; although the windows were flung open, a mustiness hung in the air. Who cared? One glance at Miranda's face was enough to tell him that Tarn Cottage was everything she'd yearned for. *It's going to be all right*, he said to himself. *We can make it happen.*

Wherever they looked, work needed to be done. The window-frames were rotten and the cellar was a damp dungeon cluttered with chunks of coal. The bedrooms were dingy, the bathroom a claustrophobe's nightmare. Doors creaked and the staircase railing twitched neurotically at a touch.

'Character!' the agent declared, as the rusty handle of a kitchen drawer came away in his hand. 'You won't find anywhere like this in—where was it, again?'

'Islington,' Miranda said. 'You're right. I live in a flat opposite an all-night diner. This is very different.'

'And you're from Oxford, Mr. Kind?' The agent tried to shove the handle surreptitiously inside the drawer whilst he was speaking, but he lacked legerdemain and it clattered on to the uneven slate floor. 'This is a marvellous place for getting away from it all. And if you need someone to keep an eye on your bolt-hole while you're away, we can arrange it for a modest fee.'

'We want to live here permanently,' Miranda said. 'Forever.'

'Even better!' The agent beamed. 'It's all the rage nowadays. Downshifting. Well, there's nowhere lovelier on God's earth than the Lakes. And Brackdale's very much off the beaten track, as you can see. Yet you're not cut off. You can be on the motorway inside twenty minutes. Think about that!'

'Thanks, but I'd rather not,' Miranda said, glancing through the kitchen window that overlooked the tarn. 'My God! That's a heron by the water's edge—Daniel, do you see?'

The estate agent's head jerked, as if on a string. 'Where? Oh dear, I must have missed it. Never mind. They're like London buses, there'll be another along in a minute! You're rubbing shoulders with Mother Nature here, make no mistake! The water's fresh from a spring on the hillside. Marvellous!'

They went out to look at the barn. It had double doors, high beams, and a wooden ladder that led to the old hayloft. In his enthusiasm, the agent climbed up a couple of rungs, clutching at the frayed rope to steady himself, before descending rapidly when the ladder shivered under his weight. 'Couple of loose brackets,' he said, mopping his brow. 'Nothing to worry about. The thrill of starting from scratch. The world's your oyster. You can design everything exactly the way you want it. No need to put up with someone else's tastes.'

Daniel shrugged. It didn't matter: the spell was unbroken. No stopping now, they had gone too far. He'd make an offer even if the outbuildings were a jumble of stones.

Misunderstanding, the agent gabbled. 'As I said, there's a healthy discount factored into the asking price to allow for renovation expenses. You'll have realised that already, if you've been looking around in the area. Tarn Cottage is exceptionally competitive. Oh yes, we're expecting a lot of interest. A very great deal of interest indeed. The basic structure's as sound as a bell. All the place needs is a bit of fine tuning. You're lucky to have spotted it so soon after it came on to the market.'

They stood outside the bothy, under the shade of a damson tree. Daniel remembered telling Barrie Gilpin a story from the guidebook he'd been studying conscientiously. Supposedly, damsons were named by the Crusaders, who brought them back to England from Damascus. He could still recall Barrie's shrugging: *so what?* Whatever they'd shared, it wasn't a fascination with history.

The path to the tarn was criss-crossed with brambles and the long grass cried out for a scythe. The layout of the grounds was bizarre. As a boy, Daniel had taken its charm for granted; now its eccentricity intrigued him. Paths wound aimlessly, with no obvious destination, and at one point the picket fencing inexplicably changed into a stretch of dry stone wall. Two spiky monkey puzzle trees thrust out of a tangle of ferns, and an old cracked mirror was nailed to an ivy-clad trellis with an arch that gave onto the waterside. Everything seemed to lack rhyme and reason, yet it struck Daniel that the garden must have been planned like this for a purpose. He could not guess what it might be.

'You say the lady who owned the cottage died recently?'

'Yes, it's been in her family for generations. In the end she finished up in a nursing home. Cancer. Dreadful business. She left it to a distant cousin who is settled in Yorkshire. She gave us instructions to sell a week ago, so you've timed your enquiry to perfection. There aren't many homes in Brackdale, and a little gem like this comes on to the market only once in a Preston Guild.'

'So what can you tell us about Tarn Cottage?' Miranda asked idly.

The agent cleared his throat noisily. Daniel guessed that the man intended to be economical with the truth. He wouldn't want to risk the sale, not with two people up from the soft South who wanted to live the dream.

'Well.' The agent ran a pink tongue over fat lips, choosing his words with a cabinet minister's care, 'I never knew the family that lived here, but I suppose they were just ordinary folk. It's very quiet, you can see for yourself. Can't imagine anything out of the ordinary happening in a sleepy spot like Tarn Fold, can you?'

Except murder, Daniel thought. Of course it was history, but he still couldn't get it out of his mind. He of all people knew how much the past mattered.

Chapter Two

'Daniel, is this wise?' the Master asked.

'Unlikely.'

'But you intend to go ahead anyway?'

'That's right, Theo.'

Theo Bellairs sighed. They were taking Lapsang Souchong upstairs in the Master's lodgings, just as they had done on the day of Aimee's death. Daniel had always had a sneaking affection for the sitting room and its atmosphere of sinful, old-fashioned luxury. To be enfolded by the vast leather armchairs was like succumbing to the embrace of comely if ageing courtesans. The room smelled of old Morocco-bound books and the tang of finest Spanish sherry; he associated it with learned conversation about Swinburne and Gerard Manley Hopkins and with slyly obscene jokes veiled by elaborate aphorisms.

Since Theo's election as Master, the room also reeked of his cats, a pair of promiscuous Persians called Cesare and Lucrezia. Daniel had first come here as a shy undergraduate, to a cocktail party thrown by one of Theo's predecessors, and to submit to the ritual of 'handshaking', when Theo, as his tutor, gave the Master an end of term report on his progress. Now he had succeeded Theo as Blenkiron Fellow in Modern History. They were colleagues, if hardly equals in the hierarchy of academe. Yet his stomach had lurched as he climbed up the worn stone steps to the Master's door, as it had on his very first visit. He needed no reminding that he was embarking on an eccentric adventure. On something like a whim, he was giving up academic tenure, and an accompanying level of job security that most people would kill for.

Theo put down his cup with the reverence that Crown Derby deserved and strode to the seat in the bay window overlooking the spreading oaks of the Great Quadrangle. Settling himself on the velvet cushion, he folded one long skinny leg over the other. He was only a year away from retiring to the villa in Nice that he shared with his partner, a mediaevalist called Edgar, yet every movement was invested with a youthful grace. He was wearing one of the white suits for which he was renowned. Daniel had always wondered how Theo managed to keep them so clean; if he'd risked dressing in anything similar, it would be filthy within an hour. Grubbiness was alien to Theo; he was never besmirched by so much as a single cat hair.

He beckoned Daniel to join him. Down in the quad, a group of rugby players was heading for the Buttery bar, and a young man in a college scarf was running after a girl with red-rimmed eyes who was blowing her nose and pretending not to notice him.

'Look at them, Daniel. Do you recall how it felt to be eighteen? Your early struggles with Tocqueville stick in my mind. Remember telling me that you intended to change subjects, that you wanted to study…ah, Politics, Philosophy, and Economics?'

He rolled the words out as if they were exotic profanities. Daniel couldn't help smiling. 'And I remember your telling me to have patience.'

'And I was right, was I not?'

Conversing with Theo was like playing chess with Capablanca. You always had to anticipate the move after the move after next to have a prayer of staying in the game. In his mind, Daniel heard Miranda's words.

'Yes, but life is short.'

'It may feel longer for those who fritter away the opportunities that it affords.'

'Sorry, but I didn't come here to be talked round. You gave me time to think over my decision. I'm grateful, but my mind's made up.'

Incapable of crude exasperation, Theo fingered his cravat. 'You always had a streak of stubbornness.'

He'd once employed the same tone to criticise a truncated account of the coal mining industry's role in Britain's industrial development that Daniel had dashed off during an essay crisis prompted by a hectic affair with a girl from St Catz. That was the first time Daniel had heard the advice that Theo gave to all his disciples: *to quote from one source is plagiarism, to quote from several is scholarship.*

'And it's no good telling me that a man who's tired of Oxford is tired of life.'

'Yet of course it is true. Oxford is unique. Look out of the window, Daniel.' Theo's tone became warm although he was not, Daniel thought, a warm man. For all his many acts of personal kindness and his unfailing manners, he always seemed remote from the quotidian. *Quotidian* was, Daniel thought, the right word: very Theo. Theo simply did not do emotion; according to Edgar, he loved his cats more than any human being, and Daniel wasn't sure that Edgar was joking. 'The brightest and the best come here to learn from us. We owe it to them to give them what they seek.'

'They seemed to manage well enough when I was away.'

'We are about to start Trinity Term, Daniel. As you well know, the custom is to give notice during Michaelmas, so that interviews for a replacement may be conducted during Hilary with a view to an appointment commencing at the start of the new academic year.'

'Sorry, Theo, but you won't be short of strong candidates available at short notice. Have a word with Pederson, he's chafing to move back from Wales. Or how about…'

Theo put up a mottled hand. It was more like a claw, these days, Daniel thought. 'Enough. I hope this isn't a delayed reaction to Ernst Walter's boorishness?'

Last summer, an argument had raged in the Senior Common Room about Daniel's entitlement to a sabbatical. The guiding principle was that one was eligible for a term away from college after completing six years as a tutorial fellow. Daniel had spent his sixth year as a visiting fellow on the other side of the Atlantic. A law don called Ernst Walter Immel had complained that a year's absence from Oxford should not be permitted to count towards the entitlement to yet more leave, but Theo had ruled in Daniel's favour. The deal was that he'd continue teaching until the end of Hilary. By giving notice now, Daniel could honour his side of the bargain and still leave college at Easter.

'Much as I hate college politics, I promise that wasn't the reason.'

'What of the response to your television series? Petty jealousies are always vexing.'

Daniel's scripts had been edited by ratings-driven zealots. The book on which they were based proclaimed a parallel between historical research and the work of a detective; the rewrites transformed it from a light academic essay into a quasi-crime show. The producer said this made the programmes more accessible, and the viewer figures left him salivating with delight. A couple of reviewers from rival faculties of history, on the other hand, had frothed with rage. The focus on history as popular entertainment was symptomatic of collapsing educational standards, and they made it pretty clear that Daniel was personally to blame.

'By the time the editors had done their worst, the series didn't feel as though it had much to do with me.'

'Don't tell me you're planning a new career as a—' Theo's cough became a choke, as if at the horror of it, '—a *celebrity?*'

'Been there, done that. Never again.'

Theo's saurian eyes narrowed. 'Do tell me, then. How is the new book progressing?'

'So-so.' *Not at all* was the truth, but he refused to allow Theo to score too many points. Time to score one himself. 'You know how it is.'

'Indeed.'

A rival from Cambridge had savaged Theo's last book in *The Times Literary Supplement*. Although he had brushed off the assault with his customary suavity, during the past decade he had published nothing but a handful of articles in obscure journals. No ego, Daniel knew, is as easily bruised as an academic's.

'But will pursuing this rural idyll provide fresh inspiration?'

Put with such urbane irony, the idea sounded absurd. 'I want to make a new start, simple as that.'

'There was a dreadful rumour—scurrilous, I'm sure—that you might be moving to Harvard.'

'Your grapevine's as efficient as ever. God only knows why you were never recruited by the security services.'

'How do you know that I wasn't?' Theo's eyebrows might have been designed to be arched. 'So—Harvard?'

Daniel shook his head. His series had been shown in the States and picked up a couple of awards, although to his chagrin one of them came in the category of Best Docu-Crime. For a few weeks Harvard's extravagant offer lingered in his mind, until he met Miranda and everything changed. Only yesterday he'd received a chaser from the Americans, but at once he'd scribbled a reply saying how flattered he was, but no thanks. He was going to extend his break from teaching for a while. Stay in England and write another book. Perhaps they might come back, putting even more dollars on the table, but it would make no difference.

'So you said no?'

'This really isn't about money.'

Theo sniffed. 'Have I ever mentioned that your famously vague, rather dishevelled charm can be a little wearisome on occasion? When it acts as a cloak for intransigence, for instance?'

'Thanks for pointing that out, Theo,' Daniel said easily. 'I'll bear it in mind.'

There was a scuffing at the door and Lucrezia made an entrance, heading for Theo's lap. 'There, there, my pretty. Now look, Daniel, you don't have to resign. Why not get the best of both worlds? Pursue your rural dream and remain on the Faculty.

Keep the flat. Rent it out, become a filthy capitalist. If you come back in Michaelmas, you won't have to do much teaching. For goodness' sake, sixteen lectures for the university over the space of a year are scarcely going to wreck your work-life balance. You're hardly likely to succumb to occupational stress on the—'

'It's not about the teaching, either.' Daniel couldn't ever recall interrupting Theo before. It simply wasn't done, it was worse than singing bawdy songs during a sermon from the Archbishop of Canterbury. 'It wouldn't be fair to you or to the students if my heart wasn't in my work. I just want a break, end of story.'

'The sabbatical wasn't long enough for you?'

'Don't worry, I'm well aware that I've not done enough for college lately. Better to resign than deprive a worthier candidate of a place at high table.'

Theo kept probing, like a dentist seeking evidence of decay. 'I'm glad you want to write. But with the greatest of respect to the libraries of Cumbria, they can scarcely match the resources of the Bodleian. Why not research your book here?'

'I've spent almost half my life in Oxford. I'm stale. Believe it or not, I'll be a better historian when I'm living in the Lakes.'

'*Recharging the batteries?*' Theo winced at the cliché even as he uttered it. 'Well, it is not for me to suggest that you're being self-indulgent, but you might spare a thought for the college. We've lost Quiggin and Kersley this year already.'

'Sorry, but we've bought the cottage. I never realised conveyancers could move so quickly. Miranda is up there already.'

'You're sacrificing a great deal for her. I hope she's worth it.'

Daniel was supposed to be laid-back, the newspapers said that was his style, but Theo knew better than anyone how to get under his skin.

'Thanks for your concern, but yes.'

Theo stroked his cat, spoke softly to it. 'He doesn't love us any more, Lucrezia. He'd prefer to run off to the back of beyond with some girl he's picked up. He met her on the rebound and now his heart is ruling his head. Or if not his heart, some other part of his anatomy.'

'It's not on the rebound.'

'No?' Theo flicked an imaginary spot of dust from his immaculate cuff. 'Are you sure about that, Daniel? Can you put your hand on your heart and say that this—this *frolic* has nothing to do with what happened to poor Aimee Durose?'

The question stung like a wasp. 'Aimee has nothing to do with this.'

'You're going into hiding.'

'I want to do something different.'

'It's the same thing.'

Daniel shook his head, not trusting himself to speak.

'The truth is that you blame yourself, isn't that right?' Theo's voice was barely audible now, but Daniel had never known it to sound so harsh. 'Be honest, admit it. All this nonsense about recharging batteries may fool your new girl, but it doesn't fool me. This is all about you and Aimee and your ridiculous guilty conscience.'

'I've never known a place as quiet as this,' Miranda said.

'Can't I hear someone drilling in the background?' Daniel said into his mobile. He was draped over an armchair in his college room, on the top floor of staircase fourteen. Below in the Great Quadrangle, a lawnmower roared. In his mind he pictured the grounds of Tarn Cottage, untamed and yet oddly suggestive of an elaborate and long-forgotten design.

'Too right. The builders are working upstairs and any minute now, I expect them to smash through the bedroom wall. I should have bought ear-muffs. At least the electrician has sorted the wiring now and the shower's working too. I must have sluiced myself under the jet for a quarter of an hour this morning. It was just like washing away my old life. But—you should have been here last night.'

'Wish I had been.'

She giggled. 'It was as silent as—well, a graveyard. In the evening, I went out for a walk, just a ramble around the tarn. It was so eerie, with an owl hooting and twigs cracking. This sounds silly, but I felt nervous, knowing there wasn't another person within a mile of the cottage.'

'Sounds like heaven. Remember when the woman in the flat upstairs from you was burgled? And the boy stabbed by the racists while you went out to the kebab house?'

'Of course you're right,' she said. 'Funny thing is, I've never felt as alone as I did last night.'

'You won't be alone for long,' he said. 'The sooner I pack up here the better. Theo's cutting up rough and I can't really blame him. I didn't make a good job of explaining myself to him.'

'Maybe you should have been cryptic,' she said. 'It worked for me.'

He laughed. 'I suppose you're right.'

When Miranda had announced that she was leaving the job, Tamzin had jumped to the conclusion that she was planning to bring a claim for sexual harassment. Without any prompting, the company offered a severance payment, 'in full and final settlement.' Her response didn't mask her contempt, and senior management, in panic mode, increased the golden handshake by fifty per cent. Better than winning the lottery. 'Anyway, I'll have said my last goodbyes by the time you get back here.'

'I can't wait to see you again,' she said softly. 'This really is a different world, you don't realise until you spend a few days here. It's not just that you can't drive fast down the lanes and that the hills mess up the TV reception. I keep thinking I'm a different person. When I called the plumber on the phone, I was tempted to make up a new name for myself. A new identity for a new life.'

'Please don't change,' he said. 'It's you I want, no one else.'

During a break from the tedium of packing books, he glanced through the *Oxford Mail* and an article about people-smugglers caught his eye. It was so easy these days to buy a new identity. With a few keystrokes, an internet surfer could acquire a fake driver's licence, eulogistic job references, a sheaf of utility bills for a false address. Miranda's fantasy had lodged in his brain.

What it would be like, to take on a different name? How did it affect the way you felt inside, pretending to be someone that you were not?

He was jerked out of his reverie by a fierce knocking at the door. The caller strode in without awaiting a response. Gwynfor Ellis seemed to fill the poky room. No one could doubt that his hefty frame and battered features belonged to a veteran rugby player. Few who did not know him would guess at his unrivalled knowledge of Celtic history or at the delicacy with which he pored over ancient texts.

'Thought I'd better come and see for myself,' he said, nodding at the boxes of books piled high on either side of the window. 'See whether you'd change your mind before you succumb forever to the embrace of Satan, masquerading as The Good Life. I was looking out from the library window and saw you leaving Theo's. He's pissed off with you, that's for sure.'

Daniel spread his arms. 'He thinks I've let him down. Possibly he's right and I should have hung around longer. I owe him a lot, no question.'

'I'd say you've repaid the debt over the years. Of course, opinion in the SCR is divided. You've replaced the new building programme as the hot topic in college. It's just as well you've been lying low. Most of the fogies think you've lost your marbles, giving up your fellowship in return for a lifetime's servitude of doing-it-yourself.'

Daniel groaned. The scions of the Senior Common Room loved nothing better than trashing the reputations of absent friends over tea and scones. Whenever he thought of them—which wasn't often—he not only remembered that Lewis Carroll had been an Oxford don, but also guessed what inspired the Mad Hatter's tea party.

'What they don't realise is that Miranda loves nothing better than slapping paint on walls. She's in her element already, organising the tradesmen. With any luck, the makeover will be half-finished by the time I move up there.'

'You'll be lucky. It took Debbie and me six months to get one small bathroom sorted.' Gwynfor hesitated. 'Tell me it's none of my business—but…is Miranda running away from something—or someone?'

'Of course, it's none of your business,' Daniel said calmly. 'Listen, she was in a relationship for a few years. He was married with three kids. Eventually his wife found out and gave him a her-or-me ultimatum. He chose to stay married. My lucky break, but it shattered Miranda's confidence for a while. I understand what you're thinking. But you're wrong.'

'Question is, do you really need to make a complete break? Why can't you leave yourself a bit of wriggle room?'

'Sorry, it's like a Mills and Boon romance, but we want to make a commitment to this.'

Gwynfor stared. '*Commitment?* Daniel Kind? Am I hearing right?'

Daniel grinned. 'Past performance is no guide to the future, as the investment folk say. Wriggling's off the agenda. Miranda had enough of that with the married man and all the reasons why the time was never right for him to pack his bags and leave his family.'

'But in case things don't work out up north?'

'Cumbria isn't on the other side of the globe.'

'It's further away than you think. And I'm not talking miles on the clock.'

'I suppose you're right. But it's something I have to do.'

'Well, Miranda is a gorgeous lady.'

'Yes,' Daniel said. 'She is.'

'Think of all those disappointed fans of yours. The porters were complaining they couldn't cram all the mail into your pigeon-hole. And what will the two of you do for money?'

'I'll start writing again, when I'm ready. A proper book, not a TV script. And I've sold the house in Summertown for twice the price that the two of us are paying for this cottage. Miranda's flat is still on the market, but we haven't even needed a huge loan. So the cash won't run out in a hurry. It's not as if I earn a fortune as a college fellow.'

'Tell me about it. All the same, you're committed and she isn't?'

Daniel shook his head. 'You're wrong. We're going into this together, the cottage is ours in equal shares. She's passionate about Brackdale, the move was her idea. I tried to talk her out of it.'

'But you've changed your mind.'

'The more I think about it, this isn't so much getting away from it all. It's more like going back home.'

Gwynfor stabbed a thick index finger at the wall posters advertising a musical at the Playhouse, a performance of *The Real Inspector Hound* in the Newman Rooms, a Balliol concert. Daniel had taken Aimee to each of them.

'This is where you belong. Oxford gets inside you, there's no resisting it. You're part of the place and it's part of you.'

'That's what I used to think,' Daniel said. 'But now I'm breaking free.'

◇◇◇

'Something I need to tell you,' Daniel said, switching off the car radio. 'I should have mentioned it before, but the time never seemed quite right.'

After a final weekend in Oxford, they were caught in a tail-back on the Thelwall Viaduct, on the way back to their new home. Three lines of vehicles stretched ahead of them, as far as the eye could see. In a minibus in the adjoining lane, a group of teenage girls were waving their arms in the air and singing to pass the time. Rudimentary lip-reading suggested a tribute to Abba's greatest hits.

Miranda took a breath. 'If it's about Aimee, you don't need to say any more, okay? That's all in the past. What went on between you and her—it's private. It doesn't affect you and me.'

'It's not about Aimee.'

With a wicked grin, she said, 'Listen, I already worked out that you weren't dressing down for the benefit of the TV ratings. No image consultant required, you really *are* that scruffy.'

'Lucky that unkempt was fashionable at just the right time. No, it's about the cottage.'

'Oh, is that all? Break it to me gently. Does the roof need replacing? Some bad news in a secret codicil to the survey that I wasn't allowed to see?'

'The roof's fine. This is to do with the cottage's history.'

'You've been investigating?' She smiled. 'Does it have a ghost? The spirit of an old farmer's wife who fell in the tarn and was too plump to climb out?'

'No ghost,' he said. 'At least—not exactly.'

'What, then?'

He swallowed. 'All those years ago, when we took a holiday in Brackdale, I made friends with a murderer. He lived at Tarn Cottage.'

'Jesus.'

'But he was only thirteen years old. He'd never done anyone any harm in his life. What's more, I've never believed he was capable of murdering anyone.'

'A miscarriage of justice?' She was at once sympathetic, ready to be outraged. Her research for a series of articles about women falsely accused of killing their children had robbed her of faith in the judicial system. She cared passionately for life's victims; it was one of the things he loved about her.

'He was suspected of murdering a young woman, a tourist. But the case never came to court. He and I met while my dad and I were out walking. Our first full day in the Lakes. His name was Barrie Gilpin and he lived in Tarn Cottage with his widowed mother. We talked and started playing together. I could tell he was different, but I didn't know quite why. I'd never heard of autism and he had a mild form of it. We were two loners who sort of hit it off together. We saw each other every day, he became part of our family for a fortnight. When we were leaving, I made a promise to write, to stay in touch. Then my father left home and our world fell apart. I let Barrie down. I never wrote that letter.'

'You can't take the blame for that. Don't always be so hard on yourself.'

The car was stuffy, the windows were misting up. He turned down the heater and said, 'There's more. Like I told you, I swore to my mother that I wouldn't make contact with my father. Louise never exchanged a word with him from the day he walked out until the day he died. But I did. He'd fallen for a civilian worker at police headquarters and they moved up to Cumbria together. He'd always loved the Lakes, wanted to settle there, but my mother was Mancunian, through and through. The Lakes weren't far away, but she insisted on sticking close to her roots. We never travelled much, for me going up to Oxford was a great adventure. All the time, I wanted to get back in touch with my father. I must have written *him* a hundred letters, over the years, but I never sent a single one. I just couldn't do that to my mother, it would have been worse than his infidelity.'

Miranda squeezed his hand. 'But he was your flesh and blood. She didn't have the right…'

'She didn't have very much at all after Dad abandoned her,' Daniel said. 'He was never mean over money, but the divorce was bitter. There were rows over his right of access to Louise and me. In the end he simply gave up. That made me feel he'd written me off, but as the years drifted by, I wondered if there was another side to the story. Then one day I saw my father's name in the newspaper. Inspector Ben Kind of the Cumbria Constabulary, quoted in connection with a murder inquiry. A woman had been killed and her body left on the Sacrifice Stone. Remember it?'

'The strange boulder, perched on the summit of the fell.'

'Yes, Barrie was in awe of the Stone. The story was that every year in pagan times, the community used to sacrifice a virgin. To make sure the gods were appeased and the lakes didn't run dry. I'd forgotten all about it until I read that report in *The Guardian*. Then I started to wonder if it had rung a bell in my father's memory.'

'Did your father arrest Barrie?'

Daniel shook his head. 'He never got the chance. Barrie's body was found not far from the victim's. He'd fallen into a ravine and died. Case closed, as far as the police were concerned. I couldn't help thinking about his mother. Poor Mrs. Gilpin, he must have caused her plenty of grief, but she still worshipped him.'

'And she's the lady whose cousin is selling the cottage?'

Ahead of them, traffic was edging forward. Daniel touched the accelerator and switched the tape back on. Carole King, singing "It's Too Late".

'So there you have it. Tarn Cottage was once home to a murderer, if the police were to be believed. Barrie spent his whole life there. He would never have moved away. Sorry, I should have told you before. But…'

He hadn't known how she would react, but she surprised him with her calm. 'It's not a problem. You didn't want to upset me, to put me off after I'd set my heart on the cottage. That was sweet of you. Just like your trust in your old friend.'

'Barrie may have seemed odd, but he was a gentle soul.'

'You and he were only kids. Time passes. People change.'

'Not that much. There wasn't a violent bone in his body. My father knew Barrie, he entertained him one wet afternoon with the card tricks he used to amuse Louise and me with. Barrie lapped it up, the two of them got along famously. That should have counted for something with the old man.'

'You discussed it with him?'

'Not for a long time. I was too furious. It seemed to me that they'd found a convenient scapegoat. But eventually I made the call. He'd retired by then and he nearly had a seizure when he realised it was me on the line. He wasn't good at articulating his feelings, but that was what I suppose I wanted. When it didn't happen, I felt frustrated. I'd had a couple of beers, I said a few harsh things. When I rang again to apologise, he said he'd done a lot of thinking. He wanted to call my mother and apologise for the hurt he'd caused her. Louise too.'

'And did he?'

Daniel kept his eyes fixed on the line of cars ahead. 'No, but it wasn't his fault. I—I didn't encourage him. I said they were both still bitter, even after so many years. Knowing them as I did, I couldn't imagine them letting bygones be bygones. They were too proud.'

'Did you discuss Barrie Gilpin?'

'It was a one-sided conversation. He clammed up on me. I had the feeling that there was plenty he wanted to say, but he didn't know how to say it. Not long after that, while I was speaking at a conference in Philadelphia, he died. Killed one night in a hit and run accident. They never found the driver, I suppose it was some idiot who was way over the limit. I didn't even find out he was dead until after the funeral. My mother had a stroke a month later and never regained consciousness.'

'What did you think he'd wanted to tell you?'

He hesitated. 'It's probably wishful thinking.'

'Go on.'

'Something in his manner made me believe that he agreed with me. He didn't believe Barrie Gilpin was a murderer.'

Chapter Three

'Think of it as an opportunity, a new start.' The Assistant Chief Constable had spent six months on a management training programme in the United States and she'd come back with the tooth-whitened smile and relentless self-confidence of a seasoned television evangelist. 'A fresh challenge.'

Hannah Scarlett said through gritted teeth, 'Yes, ma'am.'

'You're not happy, Hannah,' the ACC said gently.

Not a question, but a statement with a subtext: the difficulty lay with Hannah and not with the job she'd been offered. Lauren Self liked to think of herself as adept at psychology. Her rapid rise to high office was proof, so far as the dinosaurs in the Cumbria Constabulary were concerned, that in the modern police force, people management skills mattered more than mere detective work—what mattered was whether you could talk a good game.

'Not really, ma'am.'

The ACC topped up their tumblers of sparkling water. 'Shall we chat about it?'

They were both sitting on the same low, semi-circular leather sofa. The faintest tang of citrus hung in the air. Abstract oil paintings, splashes of blue and gold, decorated the walls. It was so cosy not even the most sceptical diehard in the Police Federation could complain about a confrontational management style. The ACC simply didn't do confrontation, it wasn't in her vocabulary. She was a passionate believer in talking through problems, in seeking consensus. Faced with a complaint, she preferred to kill it with kindness. If the worst came to the worst, she might resort to mediation.

Hannah took a breath. 'It just doesn't seem right.'

'Hannah, I do understand.'

The ACC spoke as though soothing a juvenile martyr to period pains. She had three children and their bright-eyed pictures stood on top of a bookcase crammed with tomes covering every aspect of staff relations and the measurement of key performance indicators in the modern police service. Raising children was, Hannah thought, ideal training for a woman who had to deal with rebellious or intransigent police officers. Hannah didn't have any kids herself, although occasionally she wondered if she'd spent the last seven years sleeping with one.

She took a sip of water. 'This is all about the collapse of the Patel trial, isn't it?'

'I wouldn't say that, Hannah.'

You might not *say* it, Hannah thought. But it's true. When a murder prosecution falls apart in such spectacular fashion, someone has to take to take the blame. Where there's a PR disaster, there must be a scapegoat. This time, it's me.

'I know you had reservations, ma'am.' Somehow she managed to resist the urge to say: *you sat on the fence, waiting to see if we'd drop lucky.* 'But the case was sound enough to take to court.'

'Mmmmm.' The ACC could pack a wealth of meaning into the simplest sound. A mere clearing of the throat could express a gamut of emotions, and a reproving cough sufficed where others would rant and swear.

'Sudhakar Rao was murdered ten years ago. It's a long time. Sometimes it just isn't possible to find corroboration.'

'Well…' The ACC looked disappointed that Hannah couldn't come up with a better excuse.

'Of course there was risk.' Hannah hated herself for sounding defensive, but the ACC had that effect upon people; it was another of the qualities that had secured her high office. 'There's always risk when you rely on a criminal's word. But Golac was adamant that Patel hired him. The cuckolded husband, wanting his wife's lover dead. Golac's story fitted the facts. We couldn't find a single hole in his statement.'

'Or a single piece of evidence to support it.'

'Ivan Golac is an old man, his heart's weak. He faces spending the rest of his life in prison. He'd kept his mouth shut for long enough. Like he said to me, now he has nothing to lose by telling the truth. And nothing to gain by lying.'

'Fifteen minutes of fame,' the ACC suggested. 'He liked being the centre of attention, it gave him something to fill his days. Being seen as hard. He's spent all his life as a second-rate villain. He'd be walking the streets now if the security guard he clubbed had a thicker skull. But—a hitman? That's very different. Dangerous, someone that nobody in their right mind messes with. A Premier League killer.'

The ACC liked to throw the occasional soccer metaphor into her conversations, just to show that she was really one of the lads. It made no difference if she were speaking to a female subordinate like Hannah who didn't have a clue what she meant.

Hannah said, 'You think it was just a robbery gone wrong? That Golac simply panicked and Sudhakar Rao was in the wrong corner shop at the wrong time?'

The ACC frowned. 'I really can't say, Hannah. The judge may have been caustic, but I rather go along with his old-fashioned idea that before a man's convicted of murder, it helps for the court to see his guilt proved beyond reasonable doubt.'

She had to be taking the piss—surely? Hannah counted to ten, then to fifteen just to be on the safe side, before saying, 'You've seen Golac's witness statement. It had the ring of truth.'

'You heard the judge,' the ACC said. 'Once Golac refused to testify, the statement couldn't be read in place of sworn evidence. Sandeep Patel walked away without a stain on his character. The way he's talking to the press, he's another victim.'

Hannah leaned forward. 'I still think he's a murderer.'

The ACC pursed her lips, adopting the more-in-sorrow-than-in-anger expression that she'd perfected. 'Well, anyway. No one's ever going to prove it now. We need to look forward. And that's why I wanted to share this new project with you.'

'It's a backwater. We both know that.'

'Not at all.' The ACC winced at such blasphemy. 'The Cumbria Constabulary Cold Case Review Team will be a flagship unit, a sign of our commitment to making sure that no serious crime in the county goes unsolved.'

'And the murder of Sudhakar Rao?'

'Already detected,' the ACC said, folding her arms to preclude argument. 'Golac had a fair trial and was properly convicted. He's served nine years and he'll be dead before the year's out. Most people would say that justice has been served.'

'Not if they'd listened to Golac describing how Patel hired him, the conversations that they had, all the...'

'I really think you should leave it, Hannah. The team will have enough on its plate to keep it occupied from the word go, I'm quite sure.'

Digging her teeth into her tongue, Hannah muttered, 'Yes, ma'am.'

'Now, let me give you an outline of what we have in mind. Tonight you can see what your husband says. I've absolutely no doubt that once you've thought it over and had a chat with Marc, you'll be excited by the whole idea. This is a once in a lifetime chance for any ambitious police officer, Hannah. Trust me.'

'She might just be telling you the truth,' Marc said as they lounged on their living room sofa, after washing down a microwaved Bird's Eye dinner with a bottle of supermarket Chardonnay whose high alcohol content compensated for any lack of subtlety. 'It could be a great opportunity.'

Lauren Self had remembered Marc's name correctly, that was one of her skills, but she had made one small mistake. Marc wasn't Hannah's husband. Marriage was, she'd understood from day one, a commitment too deep for him. He maintained that if a relationship was strong enough, who needed a piece of paper to document it? If the bond wasn't strong enough without the official seal of approval, then there wasn't much hope for it anyway.

'The ACC's a politician, and who trusts politicians?'

'You always swore you wouldn't let the job turn you into a cynic.'

'Right now I feel more like I'm in a maze, and I've turned into a dead end. Word's got out already. Albie Kelsen couldn't wipe that smug smile off his face when he asked if the rumours were true, that I was stepping back from front-line detective work. God, I could have slapped him.'

Marc cast a glance at the television screen. An elderly contestant on a quiz show was agonising over the answer to a question that might win him a villa in the South of France. In the studio audience, his wife covered her face with a knobbly, age-spotted hand.

'You worry too much.'

He spoke absently and she didn't know whether he was offering a considered analysis of her reaction to the new job, or merely chanting a mantra that had become over-familiar. He reckoned that she cared too much about the job. She'd worked so hard to earn her stripes. It had paid off; she'd reached the rank of Chief Inspector at an absurdly young age, thanks to the accelerated promotion scheme. Not so long ago, gossips reckoned she was marked down for stardom. But then Ivan Golac had failed to show up in court to give the testimony that would have convicted Sandeep Patel.

'Reviewing cold cases is a job for old men. Lauren is even going to dig some superannuated detective superintendent out of retirement to contribute his wisdom. And harp on about how much better police work was in the good old days.'

'So you'll be reporting to him?'

She shifted on the sofa. They'd bought it a couple of years ago from a Scandinavian store that offered designer living on a budget. It was blue and elegant and looked wonderful in the catalogue. It was also astonishingly uncomfortable. 'No, retired officers don't have full police powers. Nominally, I'll be in charge.'

'What's the problem, then?' he murmured. 'Sounds fascinating to me. Go for it. It could be just the change you need.'

Could it? Hannah had feared that she'd been lucky in her career. What if her luck had run out? Was the collapse of the Patel trial her fault? Of course, witnesses fail to turn up every day of the week. Talk to any officer who has worked in Merseyside or the Met, they'll say it's an occupational hazard. In any city, intimidation of people due to give evidence is a way of life.

But this was a high-profile murder and she'd been sure that Golac would see it through. Of course, she should have sat on the fence with the ACC. If the investigation had been allowed to die quietly once further enquiries drew a blank, no one would have complained. No one mourned Sudhakar Rao. His widow had remarried and his two daughters had been so young at the time of his death that they could barely remember him. Would it really have mattered if Sandeep Patel had been allowed to escape prosecution? Hannah thought it would. Even after ten years in the police, she still wasn't cynical enough to abandon all belief in doing the right thing simply because it was the right thing. But, clearly naïve. Her efforts had come to nothing and Patel had been allowed to put two fingers up to justice.

'Even if this new team isn't just a rest home for detectives who have screwed up,' she said, 'it isn't…'

'Oh, don't you know anything, for God's sake? It's Gerard Manley Hopkins! Any fool should know that.'

Hannah blinked and then realised that Marc was shouting at the hapless quiz show contestant. The man on the small screen had developed a nervous tic. The questionmaster's trademark sarcasm wasn't helping.

'Tennyson?' the man enquired, with a mixture of hope and panic.

'Doh!' Marc flicked the remote so that the crushed features of the ignoramus vanished. 'Imagine Tennyson writing "The Windhover". I mean…'

'Sorry, was I distracting you?'

'All right. Don't start.' Marc put his hands up in mock surrender. 'You've had a bad day, a miserable experience, and it's a shame. Just don't take it out on me, okay?'

'I wasn't…'

'Look,' he said, stretching a bony arm around her, 'I was listening to you, honest. Just remember, you're not the only one who has bad days. The bank manager was telling me this afternoon to carry less stock. The accounts aren't looking too clever at the moment. All the same, I try not to bring these things home, right? Trouble is, you let that woman get to you. Has it crossed your mind she could be right?'

'There's a first time for everything,' Hannah said bitchily. 'I just have this sneaking feeling that I'm being set up to fail. Or not to succeed, which is just as bad.'

'Listen, cold cases are sexy at the moment.' His hand strayed to her breast. 'Journalists love them. Maybe she thinks she's doing you a kindness.'

'Moving me out of the firing line? Perhaps. But she's also taking away my best chance of redeeming myself after Sandeep Patel. *Outcomes*, that's the name of the game. The police authority loves to see them. Budgets are fixed, reputations won and lost, all because of outcomes. Any progress I've made so far has been because I've delivered the right outcomes. And then came the Patel trial, and a shedload of negative publicity.'

He began to nibble at her ear. 'You'll get over it.'

'Sure,' she said, wriggling away, 'but if I'm shuffled into reviewing cold cases, it won't only be Kelsen who sees it as a sort of demotion. And far worse, I won't be able to do much to claw back my credibility. Let's face it, there's often a very good reason why cases go cold. It's because they're bloody difficult to solve.'

'But running a small team, you can be hands-on, conduct key interviews yourself if you want to.'

'I suppose.'

With infinite care and patience, he undid a couple of buttons on her blouse. 'So what are you going to do at make-your-mind-up time? Resist—or submit?'

He put on such a comically lascivious expression as he unbuckled his jeans that she couldn't help laughing. 'Submit, of course.' She leaned back against the sofa. The TV remote was digging into her thigh and she threw it on to the floor. As he eased himself on top of her, she whispered, 'You never know, miracles happen. I may find I enjoy it.'

In bed that night, she rolled over and turned to face him. They had switched off the light, but the moon was shining in through a gap in the curtains. The fair hair was flopping over his face, the way she'd always loved, and she couldn't resist giving his cheek a kiss. His skin was smooth and warm and smelled of lemon soap. He was a fastidiously clean man; that was something she'd liked about him early on, though now it counted for less. His eyelids were drooping and she almost let him slip out of consciousness, but there was something she wanted to get out in the open before it created a barrier between them.

'Marc, I've been thinking. Suppose I accept this job…'

'You should,' he said sleepily. 'It'll be fine.'

She took a breath and summoned up her courage. 'Okay, *when* I say yes, I'll be asking the ACC if I can have Nick Lowther on the team.'

Marc lifted himself up and pushed the hair out of his eyes. He leaned on his elbows, staring at her. When he spoke, his voice was tight. 'Why do you need him?'

'He knows me, I know him. We can trust each other. That's important, in a unit like this. God knows what the retired guru will be like. I don't just want any old sergeant. I need someone who's on my side.'

Marc grunted. 'Just as long as…'

'What?'

'Oh, nothing.'

He turned away. She put her hand on his bony shoulder. His whole body was taut with suppressed anger.

'Marc, listen, you've got the wrong idea about Nick Lowther. We're friends, that's all. It's never been any more than that.'

No answer.

She felt as though a rope had been pulled tight around her midriff, squeezing the breath out of her. She didn't want to be trussed up, she had to break free.

'Marc,' she said, 'talk to me. I know you're awake.'

'Friends?' he muttered. 'He'd like to be more than that.'

'He's a married man.'

'Ah, but is he a *happily* married man?'

'Oh God, Marc. I can't imagine why you're so...so...'

He turned over again. 'Jealous?'

The rope slackened a bit, now that the word was out in the open. Usually it lingered unspoken, somewhere in the air between them.

'Protective.' She was willing to compromise, but it took two.

'He'd love to get into your knickers.'

'You're imagining it.'

Marc put his arm around her, started to caress her rump. 'I'm sorry, darling. It's not that I don't trust you...'

Even as she closed her eyes, her thoughts were racing.

But that's not true, you've never trusted me. Not altogether, not with Nick, not with any other man I admit a liking for. After all these years, why can't you?

'You've made the right decision, Hannah.' The ACC beamed, magnanimous in triumph. Another tricky people problem resolved, another box about to be ticked. 'I'm absolutely sure you won't regret it.'

On a wet and windy morning, the breakfast TV weathergirl had warned of ridges of low pressure sweeping in from the west. The ACC's room offered a temperate, climate-controlled refuge. Through the colour-coordinated blinds Hannah could see the rain slanting down on to the overflowing bins in the yard at the back of the headquarters building. This room was an oasis of calm, far removed from the incoherence of the world outside. A world where—yes, even in Cumbria, so proud of its modest rate of criminal activity—old people were mugged for the price of a shot of heroin, where men in anoraks hid in bushes beside lonely paths, waiting for young women to walk by in the twilight.

'So where do we go from here, ma'am?'

Her tone was all brisk efficiency. When giving in, no point in doing so with a bad grace.

The ACC straightened the papers in her folder. She hated anything to be out of place. 'We've already agreed on a start date and that you can have Lowther as your sergeant.'

Hannah had briefly contemplated making a sacrifice for Marc's sake. Why not forget about recruiting Nick for the Cold Case Review Team? But that would be absurd. Nick was perfect for the job; she couldn't overlook him simply to please her partner. Marc would have to grow up. She wouldn't cave in.

'I've already sounded him out, ma'am, and I'm sure he'd be interested.' Hannah paused, groping for suitable Lauren-speak. '*Motivated* by the *opportunity*.'

'Marvellous. You'll have four constables, working in a couple of teams so that you make best use of resources. Obviously you won't want a group of idle uniform-carriers.'

'So can I choose who I want?'

'Provided they are available and happy to sign up. And then there's your consultant. We've trawled through NROD.'

The National Retired Officers Database listed men (they usually were men) who had opted to leave the police and pick up their pension, only to weary of the prospect of watching daytime television until they dropped dead of boredom. Hannah supposed that they hankered after the camaraderie of the job, to say nothing of the chance of a bit more cash.

'And?'

'I've offered a contract to Les Bryant. Until a couple of years ago he was a Detective Superintendent with North Yorkshire Police. He's headed several high profile murder inquiries over the years. The Whitby caravan shootings, yes? I'm sure we'll benefit greatly from his experience.'

So he's to keep an eye on me, Hannah thought, to make sure I don't mess up like I did with Sandeep Patel.

'I'm sure he will, ma'am.'

'Very good.' The ACC took a sheaf of correspondence from her in-tray to indicate that the meeting was at an end. 'One more point, Hannah. With this kind of project, public profile is all-important.'

'Yes, ma'am.' Hannah wondered what was coming. A warning not to screw up again, on pain of being transferred to traffic control and enduring career gridlock?

'The press office will be issuing a news release and we're planning a media conference.' The ACC put on a smile, as if rehearsing for the cameras. 'I'm hoping for extensive press, radio and regional TV coverage. It may stir a few memories about cases of the past, and, just as important, we could do with all the positive publicity we can get after…recent events. So please, whatever you do, don't walk out on the assembled media the way you did when the questioning over Patel got rather sharp. Everyone's allowed one mistake, but two PR disasters in quick succession are simply unaffordable. Do we understand each other? Lovely. That will be all, Hannah. And please accept my congratulations on your appointment.'

'Dream Policing,' Nick Lowther murmured the next morning, over coffee in Hannah's office. 'Isn't that what the ACPOs call it when they blend a team of serving officers with someone from NROD? Taking advantage of expertise that would otherwise be lost forever. Tapping into the investigative skills of senior officers who retired while still at their peak. Combining the talents of…'

Hannah grinned. 'Or, to put it another way…'

Nick Lowther accepted the feed-line gleefully. 'Alternatively, we're being lumbered with some wrinkly has-been whose old lady is sick of him getting under her feet and who thinks that fingerprinting and grainy photo-fits are the last word in forensic detection.'

'I don't know much about Bryant. Except that he's a Yorkshireman.'

'So we can look forward to an open-minded, forward-thinking colleague who's always first to buy a round at the bar and the last to venture a controversial statement, for fear of giving offence to those who might disagree. And is that a pig I see flying past the window?'

Hannah laughed. 'And you reckon *Yorkshiremen* are bigoted! Be fair. We ought to give him a chance before we write him off.'

'When did being fair ever have anything to do with police work? Did they teach you nothing at police college?'

Nick gave her a mischievous grin. He had untidy black hair and easy charm. Whenever people described him, the adjective of choice was *laid-back*. Only the absentminded way he gnawed at his fingernails made Hannah wonder if he was really as relaxed as everyone thought.

'On second thoughts, you're right.' She leaned back in her chair and stretched her arms out wide. 'Anyway, you've taken the ACC's shilling now. You're spoken for. There's no going back.'

'Fine by me.' He yawned and said, 'Better this than a transfer to Millom. And to tell you the truth, I was ready for a change.'

'Me too.' She'd never thought so until that moment, but as soon as Nick said it, she knew he was right. 'Patel was such a sickener. But the first time I spoke to you about reviewing cold cases, you gave me the impression it was taking a step down.'

'That was before I heard that the ACC had arranged for us to tell the world how good we are before we actually do a lick of work.'

She giggled. 'Kelsen's sure I've been shown a yellow card. One more mistake and I'll be out of his life forever.'

Nick made a gesture that gave a graphic indication of his opinion of Detective Inspector Albie Kelsen. 'Yeah, he's as happy as a dog with two dicks. It's what he wants to believe, that your career's gone off the rails. None of it's about you, it would be the same with any younger woman who climbed the ladder faster than him. Don't take any notice.'

'Honestly, I try not to. But can you remember, as a kid, trying to ignore chicken pox? You know what you shouldn't do, but the irritation's so great that you simply can't resist...'

Of course Nick was right. Generous, too. Both of them knew that he was just as good a detective as she was. Yet, smart as he was, he'd never had much luck with promotion boards and exams. Perhaps he didn't want it enough, perhaps he preferred to be one of life's sidekicks. The two of them had worked together for a couple of years and not once had he ever given her a moment's trouble. Marc maintained it was because he wanted to sleep with her, but she refused to believe that. Nick never flirted and she never caught him giving her a sidelong glance. She told herself that she was almost entitled to feel peeved by his lack of interest. All that grief from Marc and not a thing to show for it.

Chapter Four

'To Tarn Cottage,' Miranda said, raising her glass.

'To Tarn Cottage—and us.'

Daniel took a sip of Bollinger and leaned back gingerly in his chair. His back was creaking like the cellar door after a long afternoon spent laying carpets in the hall and living room while the plumber fitted a wash basin and the builders put finishing touches to the new airing cupboard. No matter how many times it was vacuumed, the cottage never seemed free of dust, and he and Miranda were always glad of a chance to get some fresh air into their lungs. They escaped to the paved area outside the living room as soon as the last of the workmen left. The York stone flags were uneven and some were half-hidden by creeping dandelions, but until the sun sank out of sight they could escape the wood shavings and the smell of new carpets and look out at the tarn. In the chill evening air, he felt another twinge: an unexpected sense of loss. One day, would he regret abandoning the career he'd striven for, simply to fulfil a fantasy of a new life with a woman he still hardly knew?

The moment she stretched her arms and yawned elaborately, allowing him to admire the way she filled the navy blue overall, he knew the answer. How could he ever tire of Miranda?

'Oh, I do love sloshing paint on walls.' Her overall was covered with splashes. 'Wonderful therapy.'

'I never suspected you of this insatiable appetite for do-it-yourself.'

'It's not my only insatiable appetite,' she said, sneaking a hand inside his shirt. 'At least there are one or two things you're still good for. But I'm not having you use your lack of expertise with drill and chisel as an excuse for fiddling with a new book just yet.'

'Spoilsport.'

'Did you hear the forecast for tomorrow? It isn't bad. Why don't you get out from under my feet and leave me to be lusted after by that nice young builder with the unicorn tattoo? You can go into the village and run a couple of errands. Afterwards, you could make a start on clearing the grounds.'

'Aren't you supposed to wait a year in a new house before making any drastic changes to a garden? So you can work out exactly what is growing, and where.'

She removed her hand and waved at the thick undergrowth spreading out from the patio all the way down to the pool. 'Does it take an Einstein? The brambles have to go. Same with the ground elder. Weeding isn't enough. It needs digging out, so not a trace of it is left. Otherwise we'll never be rid of it.'

He savoured the flinty taste of the champagne. It crossed his mind that she wanted rid of more than the ground elder. She was determined to transform the cottage in a matter of weeks, to make it unrecognisable as the house that a supposed murderer and his mother had shared. A sort of exorcism. But Mrs. Gilpin had left no trace of her personality here, nothing to show that she had ever existed. It was as if she had withdrawn from the world after the death and disgrace of her son, determined to wipe away all evidence of his life or hers, even in her own home.

'You're a ruthless woman.'

'I know what I want.'

'Me too,' he said, reaching towards her.

She shivered. 'It's freezing. I think I'll take my drink inside.'

He put his arm around her. 'Good idea. I'll help you to warm you up.'

'Twenty minutes ago you were dog-tired and your back was killing you.'

'A chance for you to try out that massage technique you wrote about last month.'

'But the bedroom stinks of paint, even with the windows open.'

'There was another reason I bought that sheepskin rug for the living room. Come on, let's test it for comfort.'

'Daniel?'

'Mmmmm?'

'You were talking in your sleep.'

His head was hurting after too much Bollinger and his back still ached. Miranda always made love with an intensity that he'd never before experienced, not even with Aimee. Exhilarating, but she'd left him drained. He forced his eyes open. The living room was in darkness.

'What time is it?'

'Half past four.'

'Too early.'

'No, Daniel, don't drop off again. This is important.'

They were curled up together under a duvet on the massive new rug. He felt a spasm of pain in his vertebrae as he propped himself up on his elbows and looked into her anxious face.

'What's the matter?'

'I woke up ages ago and couldn't get back to sleep again. Then I heard you muttering to yourself.'

'What was I saying?'

'*Aimee.* You kept repeating her name, over and over again.'

Guilt knifed him. 'Oh Christ, Miranda, I'm so sorry.'

'You were dreaming of her.'

'No, no. It's just that…'

But he was lying and they both knew it. He'd had the same dream many times before, although this was the first time he'd woken her with it. Each time he was running through the streets of Oxford, pounding the pavements, heart thumping, desperate to find Aimee before it was too late. Always the same panic, the same sick feeling in his stomach. No matter how many times he had that dream, it always ended in precisely the same way. He failed to save her, he was always too late.

Miranda dozed off, but sleep continued to elude him. In the recesses of his brain, a scratchy voice echoed. It belonged to the woman who had lived here for so long.

'Barrie! *Barrie!* Now look what you've done!'

Daniel remembered Mrs. Gilpin shouting out to her son, scolding him for coming into the cottage without bothering to wipe his muddy feet. It was the wettest morning of the holiday and the two of them had been right here in the front room, playing with a Monopoly set that Daniel had brought. Barrie was unfamiliar with the rules but found the names of the London roads and stations fascinating. Soon he could recite them by heart, even though his strategy in zooming around the board was closer to anarchy than capitalism. It was great fun and their hoots of glee attracted the attention of his mum, who had been out in the barn, chopping firewood. She always needed to be occupied. He never actually heard her say that the devil finds work for idle hands, but he was sure she believed it.

'It was my fault, Mrs. Gilpin, not Barrie's,' he said, as she appeared in the doorway, red-faced and scowling. 'I got caught in the cloudburst and dashed in the moment Barrie opened the door. Sorry, I forgot…'

'You mustn't cover up for him,' she said, her cheeks red with temper. 'He has to take responsibility for his own actions. He's not a little child any more.'

Daniel opened his mouth to protest but a glance at Barrie kept him quiet. His friend was shaking his head, as if to say *It's not worth it, she won't listen to you. Everything's always my fault.*

In the end he gave up the struggle for sleep and padded into the front room. It was a mess, with hundreds of his files crammed into cardboard storage boxes piled into dangerously leaning towers. He tiptoed around them, searching out the sheaf of press cuttings he'd collected about Barrie Gilpin's crime, before retreating into the soon-to-be-tiled kitchen to study them by the warmth of the stove.

The murdered woman was called Gabrielle Anders and she'd been in her twenties. Not much seemed to be known about her. She came from London, not Cumbria, but she'd lived in the States for years. She had been staying in Brackdale for a few days while she toured around and visited friends. One night someone had slashed her throat so viciously as almost to sever her head. After stripping off her clothes, the killer laid her ruined body on the Sacrifice Stone.

A young woman found dead on an ancient boulder mentioned in legends about pagan rituals. Journalists loved it and treated their readers to lurid descriptions of human sacrifice through the ages. A popular historian from Bristol University contributed an excitable feature claiming that the instinct to shed the blood of innocents as a means of self-preservation remains just below the surface of every supposedly civilised society. Early reports added that a local man was missing from home. The police gave his name as Barrie Gilpin and revealed that he was known to the victim. With a red pen, Daniel had highlighted the quote from Detective Chief Inspector Ben Kind of Cumbria Constabulary that had first caught his eye. His father said that the missing man might be able to help with their inquiries. A smudged photograph of Barrie scowling at the camera illustrated more vividly than any words that he was the sort who preyed on pretty and defenceless young women. Even the laziest reader would deduce his guilt. The hunt did not last long. Forty-eight hours after the killing, a walker peered into a narrow ravine and caught sight of a crumpled body at the bottom of the cleft. Barrie had not travelled far.

Suicide or accident? A quick death or a lingering end in a rocky tomb? Who cared? The reports implied a poetic justice about his death. The final cutting carried another comment from Ben Kind. It said little, but was pregnant with implications.

He announced that the police investigation into the murder of Gabrielle Anders was being scaled down.

Same old story, Daniel thought, as he slipped the scraps of paper back into the buff folder. Everything was always Barrie's fault.

◇◇◇

After daybreak, he went out for a walk. Dew glistened on the grass and gusts of wind whipped his hair. After circling the tarn, he followed the track that meandered up the side of the fell to a small cairn that marked the halfway point. Above the tree-line, the terrain was patched with heather and scrub. In the sun, he had to screw up his eyes as he took in the view. The serenity of the valley was a perfect cure for a troubled night. The village slept, but he could hear plaintive cries from sheep in the fields surrounding Brack Hall.

I mustn't let the murder take me over.

Rather than continue on the steep path to the Sacrifice Stone, he turned back. When he reached the cottage and looked in the living room, he saw Miranda's shape under the duvet.

A tousled head appeared. 'Where did you get to?'

'Just getting some fresh air.'

He bent over and began to kiss her. She squealed, protesting that his cheeks were cold, and he said that she would have to warm him up. Hungrily, he undressed again and wrapped himself around her.

An hour and a half later, after breakfasting on scrambled eggs and scalding coffee, he jumped in his car and drove along the tree-fringed lanes towards the village. When he switched on the radio, Isaac Hayes was crooning "Walk On By", followed by Sandie Shaw with "There's Always Something There to Remind Me". He couldn't help laughing at himself. There was no escape.

What exactly had happened to Gabrielle Anders up on the heights? Unable to resist temptation any longer, he glanced over his shoulder. High on the hillside stood the Sacrifice Stone. Melancholy even on a spring day, it preserved its mysteries in sombre silence.

He turned his head back just in time to see an oncoming tractor. Putting his foot on the brakes and squeezing against the hawthorn hedge, he reminded himself that even in this pretty lane, unexpected dangers could lurk around the corner. Taking more care, he arrived at the first row of cottages that marked the entrance to Brack. The village was full of nooks and crannies. Over the centuries it had grown in higgledy-piggledy fashion, artless and appealing. The main street curved over the stream before running past the church. It divided around a small square boasting a general store and The Moon under Water before narrowing as it left the settlement and heading for the world beyond the valley. Behind the square wound a maze of paths and lanes, the homes of a couple of hundred people and a handful of barns, small businesses, and workshops.

Daniel was still accustoming himself to the transition from the busy malls of Oxford to this quiet backwater. In Brackdale, people relished the chance to linger over gossip. Everyone knew everyone else and no transaction was ever hurried; he was having to learn to relax and stop rushing at everything. And he was loving it.

Brack's principal store was called Tasker's; it doubled as a post office and he had a parcel of books to send back to the London Library. The local newspaper regularly chronicled the continuing struggle between the Royal Mail, wishing to increase efficiency and cut overheads through centralisation, and local people who campaigned against plans to compel them to travel miles to collect their pensions and BBC licences. In the end, economic realities would prevail and the community would lose its battle, but Daniel was sure it was worth going down fighting.

A sporty yellow Alfa 156 was parked opposite the entrance to the shop, a garish contrast to the rusting Fiestas and mud-splashed 4x4s on either side, and as unlikely a sight in a Cumbrian hamlet as a lumbering Hackney cab. Tasker's was a double-fronted Aladdin's cave, with narrow aisles leading between overflowing shelves that reached up to the ceiling. If you couldn't find it in Tasker's, the odds were you wouldn't find it anywhere north of Manchester and south of Carlisle. Behind the main shop counter were rows of chunky toffee jars, the kind that Daniel had seldom seen since childhood. A girl was serving a small boy with liquorice and blackcurrant chews and it took an effort of will for Daniel to tear himself away from the sweet aroma and join the queue stretching back from the post office grill.

Half a dozen people were ahead of him. At the front, a shrivelled pensioner in a vast brown overcoat smelling of mothballs was arguing with a baffled teenage assistant. Daniel took his place behind a tall woman with blonde hair falling on to the shoulders of her wax cotton Barbour. After window-shopping at a pricy country-wear shop in Kendal the other day, he recognised her walking boots as top-of-range Le Chameau. She was clutching a packet of headache tablets. Turning, she smiled at him and towards the cantankerous old man.

'I hope you're not in a hurry to send that parcel. If you are, please do go before me. I'm not rushing off anywhere.'

She wasn't wearing make-up and didn't need to. Her lightly tanned skin was close to flawless, her cheekbones high, almost Slavic. Although he didn't recognise her subtle fragrance, he had no doubt that it was expensive. No prizes for guessing that she owned the sporty Alfa outside.

'Thanks, but I've all the time in the world.'

'You may need it,' she said. 'Once Derek gets a bee in his bonnet…'

The old man raised his voice, blaming the assistant's youth for her incompetence. Tiring of the wait, a couple of women in the post office queue drifted away to pick up milk and provisions. A burly man in shirtsleeves, presumably Mr. Tasker, appeared behind the counter and joined in the debate with his dissatisfied customer.

Daniel grinned. 'Regular occurrence, is it?'

'It's uncanny,' she said. 'Whatever time I call in, he always seems to be in front of me, making some sort of complaint.'

'You live locally?'

'Not far away. You?'

'We've just moved here.'

'I thought we hadn't met. Do you live in Brack?'

'Further down the valley. A little place called Tarn Cottage.'

Her eyebrows lifted. Whenever the cottage was mentioned, people seemed to take a step back. Everyone in the valley associated it with the Gilpins, which was natural enough after so many years, but they regarded it as inextricably linked to the murder of Gabrielle Anders.

'How lovely. So we're more or less neighbours. My husband and I live on the way out to your new home.'

'Brack Hall?'

She laughed. 'How did you guess? On second thoughts, don't answer that. Maybe it's better if I don't know. Anyway, my name's Tash Dumelow. Tash as in short for Natasha. Pleased to meet you…'

'Daniel Kind,' he said as they shook.

'Kind?' She frowned. 'The name rings a bell.'

This kept happening, thanks to the television series. He'd never quite realised until the first programme was broadcast how many people spent their time with eyes glued to the screen. His ratings had scarcely rivalled the soaps, but people kept recognising his face or name. He decided not to enlighten her and instead said something anodyne about the pleasures of country living. She gave a vigorous nod of agreement.

'You're absolutely right. I was a city girl, but now I'd never want to live anywhere else. As Wordsworth nearly said, this is the loveliest spot that woman hath ever found.'

When Daniel explained that he'd moved up from Oxford and Miranda from London, Tash said, 'So you don't know people in this part of the world?'

'Not unless you count the fact that in the last few weeks we've had half the tradesmen in Cumbria helping us renovate the cottage.'

She smiled. 'Will you let me give you a tip, as one off-comer to another?'

'Please.'

She lowered her voice, one conspirator briefing another. 'If you ever hope of being accepted by the locals, you'll need to get the details right. People like the Taskers don't talk about *Cumbria*. That's an administrative creation. Dating back to the seventies, admittedly, but in a place like this, that's only yesterday. The powers-that-be patched together Cumberland, Westmoreland, and a bit of Lancashire. If you're a native, you talk about the Lakes. Or the Lake District.'

He grinned. 'Thanks, I'll try to remember.'

She patted him on the back. Her hand felt warm. 'Now, you must come for dinner. My husband will be delighted to meet you both. We'll be four off-comers together. Simon is a property developer from Skipton and I was born in Moscow, would you believe?'

'I'd never have guessed you weren't a native.'

'Oh, I moved to England in my teens and I like to pretend I'm a native. Anyway, we've lived at the Hall for ten years and people are only now starting to believe that—oh, I don't know, that Simon really isn't about to concrete over Kentmere or build a shopping arcade or multi-storey car park in Longsleddale. That's one thing you'll soon discover, Daniel. They are a suspicious lot round here.'

'I'll bear it in mind,' he promised. 'And thanks for the invitation. We'd love to come sometime.'

'Let's make a date now,' she said. 'Would Saturday evening be too soon?'

◇◇◇

By the evening, as he lazed outside with Miranda and a glass of Sancerre, listening to the soft sounds in the trees and watching the fading amber of the sun colour the fell-side, he'd started having second thoughts about dining out at Brack Hall.

'We could make an excuse. Remember, we did come up here to get away from it all.'

'We ought to get to know our neighbours,' she said, waving a cloud of midges from her face. 'This is our home now. Besides,

I'm intrigued. Last time I was in the shop, I overheard Mrs. Tasker chatting about the Dumelows.'

'Don't tell me. She's a trophy wife. He's a rich businessman who's away a lot.'

Miranda chortled. 'Mrs. Tasker, a trophy wife? She must be size eighteen at the very least.'

He feigned to cuff her ear. 'I suppose she's torn between a Brackdale native's instinctive loathing of excessively rich off-comers and fervent gratitude for their continuing custom. It'll take a long time for us to gain acceptance in a place like this.'

'You're telling me. I asked at the shop if there was a gym in the valley and Mrs. Tasker looked at me as though I wanted to celebrate a black Mass. In the end, she admitted there were a few places. Apparently Tash works out at a fitness centre in Kendal.'

'I suppose she's bored out of her skull, that's why she was so quick to invite us around.'

'She paints watercolours, she gives time and money to good causes. Does her best to fit into the community. But her husband's away a lot—a tenant farmer looks after the estate.'

'So let's hear the gossip. Tales of wild debauchery up at the Hall?'

'No mention of orgies, sorry. You'll have to make do with me. The Dumelows seem popular enough. Mrs. Tasker said they'd agreed to sponsor an arts festival in the village hall and to throw their grounds open for charity in the summer. But she and her friend were badmouthing the farmer. He's not popular, even though his family have lived in Brackdale for generations. Apparently, he has a vile temper, and last week he blacked his wife's eye after a row. They were both wondering why she puts up with it.'

'Probably the same reason women have put up with bullying for centuries. Lack of options.'

'At least we don't have to schmooze with him when we visit the Dumelows. Maybe I'll wear my little black dress. Just as well I didn't throw it out to make more room for Aran sweaters and dungarees. Mind you, I get the feeling that whatever I wear, I won't be able to compete with the lady of the manor.'

He reached out for her. 'You don't need to compete with Tash Dumelow.'

As she leaned towards him, a loud shot cracked the silence, transfixing them both for a second until they realised that no one was shooting at them. The noise had come from the other side of the woodland.

'Jesus.' Miranda's face was white. 'Was that a rifle? Who would be shooting around here?'

'A farmer,' Daniel said. 'Presumably the tenant of Brack Hall Farm. Hope he wasn't aiming at his wife.'

'You don't think…?'

'No, no.' It hadn't been a good joke; her hands were shaking. 'Happens all the time in places like this. Farmers shooting vermin.'

She frowned. 'You mean—foxes?'

A current of air stirred the trees, otherwise everything was quiet again. But the mood was shattered and Miranda picked up her glass and trudged back to the cottage. Daniel stayed outside, wondering about the fox. Dead, presumably. The farmer must be a skilled marksman. He'd only required a single shot.

Chapter Five

'I thought I'd look up my father's second wife this morning.'

Daniel was clearing the breakfast things while the Adonis with the unicorn tattoo and his colleagues competed in the hall to see whether an electric drill could drown out the noise of the hammering. He spoke casually, not wanting Miranda to guess how much this mattered to him, this attempt to make a connection with his old man, trying to figure out whatever had made him tick.

The previous evening she'd been tense and fidgety, even after dosing up with paracetamol because the shock of the rifle shot had given her a headache. A good night's sleep was the best medicine. Now she was perched on a high stool, engrossed in a paperback about getting in touch with one's inner self, learning how to tap into her spiritual chi and tune in to her seven chakras. It wasn't entirely an indulgence: self-help manuals often sparked ideas for magazine articles; Miranda could do jokey as well as introspective, whatever was required. Editors loved pieces like 'Men Are from Margate, Women Are from Venice' or 'Don't Settle for the Small Stuff'. Half the time she wrote about how to get more done and pack one's life with achievement, the other half about the work-life balance and techniques for cutting down on stress.

'You're going to see her right now?' She put the book down. 'What do you expect her to tell you?'

'Not sure.' He poured more coffee from the filter machine. 'I suppose I want to fill in some of the gaps. Learn about what he was really like, find out what I missed. I was so young when he went away.'

Her brow furrowed. 'It's different, of course, but I never wanted…'

'I know,' he said as her voice faltered. Miranda was adopted, but she'd never attempted to trace her birth mother. She'd once said that she'd never come to terms with the idea of being given up. Her horror of rejection explained a lot. Why her ex-lover's decision to stay married had hit her so hard, why she was so angry that Tamzin hadn't hired her simply because of her literary gifts. 'But what's the worst that can happen?'

'She might slam the door in your face.'

'Fine, at least I'll know where I stand. I don't want to upset her. But I'd like to hear his side of the story.'

'What makes you so sure she'd be willing to tell it?' Miranda shook her head. 'You know your trouble, Daniel? You're too fair, you see two sides to every argument. What's wrong with a bit of good old-fashioned one-eyed prejudice?'

He laughed. 'I came across enough of that in Oxford to last a lifetime. Listen, if Cheryl doesn't want to talk to me, that's fine.'

'Yes, but what if she talks and you hate what she has to say?'

The address he had for Cheryl—Cheryl Kind, as he ought to think of her, although he'd never associated her with his own name—was in Oxenholme. Spots of rain were smudging his windscreen as he arrived at his destination, a grey semi-detached at the end of a cul-de-sac crowded with sycamores. Painstakingly striped lawn, a bed of precisely spaced pink and white impatiens on either side of the front path, crisp floral curtains at the bay window. Disappointment stabbed him, although he wasn't sure why. Perhaps he'd expected a house with more character and found it hard to credit that that his father would have deserted his family for somewhere so utterly devoid of personality.

A 'for sale' sign stood next to the front wall. Presumably Cheryl was moving on. Understandable, after a bereavement. She must want somewhere easier to manage. A flat, maybe, although he reminded himself that she was much younger than his father. He'd conjured up unflattering mental images of her a thousand times, but he'd never even seen so much as a photograph of her. His sister reckoned that Cheryl was much younger than their father; she wouldn't even be close to retirement age. Striding up to the door, he told himself to keep calm. This unknown woman had cast a shadow over his life, but his father had loved her, he had to remember that.

As he pressed the doorbell, someone called to him from next door. 'You won't find anybody in!'

A short bespectacled man in his late sixties, clad in a purple cardigan and grubby old corduroy trousers, had bustled out of the back garden of the adjoining semi. Rain had plastered strands of grey hair to his scalp. He had a garden trowel in his hand and he pointed it at Daniel, rather as a sheriff might threaten a snake oil salesman with his revolver.

'Do you happen to know when Cheryl might be back?'

The neighbour scowled. 'Said she'd be away for a few days. Left the key with us, asked us to water the plants if there was a dry spell. Fat chance of that in this country. Whatever happened to global warming?'

'So she's gone on holiday?'

'I suppose you could call it that.' The man's tone was disapproving, for a reason Daniel could not understand. 'Why do you want to know?'

'Her husband was my father.'

The old man coughed; it seemed to be his way of showing astonishment. 'You're Ben's son?'

'Yes.'

'Daniel? Good God.' He stared fiercely. 'I can see the likeness now. The eyes, anyway. Of course, he was burlier to start with and he did put on a few pounds after he retired. Who would have thought it? He used to talk about you. You've had a programme on the television, isn't that right? Historical stuff, not my cup of tea. Gardening's my thing. My wife watched it after Ben told us it was on.'

Daniel blinked. Somehow he'd never imagined that his father would have mentioned his name to anyone up here. He'd presumed that Ben Kind would have been determined to keep his first marriage a secret, too ashamed ever to reveal the existence of the family he'd deserted for the hedonistic pleasures of life in Oxenholme.

The rain was drumming against the roofs. The man took off his spectacles and wiped them with his handkerchief. 'What did I say? Now then, you'd better come inside, have a cup of tea and a scone. You can say hello to Edna, she'll shoot me if I let you go without introducing you. It isn't every day that a celebrity turns up on our doorstep.'

◇◇◇

'The only mercy is that it was quick,' Edna Whiston said. She was a dainty little woman whom Daniel and her husband had interrupted in the middle of knitting a Postman Pat jumper for an infant grandchild. 'Another scone?'

Daniel put down his tea cup on a coaster depicting a view of the harbour at Whitby. The only word for the Whistons' living room was *cosy*. It smelled faintly of roast beef and gravy. Photographs of beaming family members covered the tops of the sideboard and a nest of occasional tables. A magazine rack bulged with copies of *The Radio Times* and *Bella*. In the background, the James Last Orchestra blasted out non-stop hits on an aged Bush stereo system.

'Thanks, but I'd better be going soon. You have been very kind.'

'Well, as I say, we were very fond of your father and it was a dreadful tragedy when he died. Such an active chap, loved his garden. You can see how carefully he tended it, even though nothing much has been done since he passed away. Cheryl has a man in one afternoon a week, to keep up appearances. Of course, she doesn't spend much time around here nowadays.'

'I see that she's selling the house. Staying in the area?'

'Moving to Grange-over-Sands, she said.'

Edna pursed her lips, rather as if Cheryl had decided to relocate to Gomorrah. The Whistons had evidently enjoyed Ben Kind's company, but it was apparent that they cared less for his second wife. Daniel caught the couple exchanging a look and wondered what it might signify.

'I should have given her a ring. Perhaps I'll do that when she's back.'

George Whiston cleared his throat noisily, like a 1950s father preparing to tell his son the facts of life. 'Um, it's none of our business, young man, but you might want to think over whether it's such a good idea.'

'You think she won't want to talk to me? I realise it's not so long since Dad died, but…'

'This is a bit difficult for Edna and me, lad. We don't care to interfere, like. But between you and me, Cheryl has a gentleman friend. He has a house in Grange-over-Sands and that's where she is now.'

'Oh, right.' All was becoming clear. 'Thanks for telling me, I'll be discreet. Obviously I don't begrudge her a new relationship.'

'Right you are. But there is one thing…' George Whiston coughed in noisy embarrassment and took a sudden interest in his shoes, '…it's not a new relationship at all.'

'So your father got a taste of his own medicine?' Miranda asked.

They were snacking while the cottage echoed to the beat of Status Quo, thanks to the muscular builder who had brought a portable CD player along. At least the music drowned out the rain, which was bouncing off the paving stones outside the kitchen window. This was the fiercest downpour since they had moved in.

'Sounds like it. According to Edna and George, she'd been having a long-term affair with her boss. They'd seen him call at the house when my father was out. He wouldn't leave for hours. In the meantime, she drew the bedroom curtains.'

Miranda clicked her tongue. 'Scandalising the neighbourhood. Not a good idea.'

'Especially when your neighbours don't care for you and have a soft spot for the husband you're cuckolding.'

'Did they give him any hints about what was happening?'

'No need. He and George were in the same pub quiz team. One night, after a few pints, he confided in George. He'd had his suspicions for a while and when he confronted her, she didn't deny it. He gave her an ultimatum, said she had to choose. Her boyfriend was married but his wife had cancer and he wouldn't leave her, in fact he had retired from work to spend his time caring for her. Cheryl promised Dad that she'd finish with him. It never happened, she couldn't let go. The boyfriend's wife died a month before Dad. Now Cheryl's in the process of moving in with him.'

'Presumably you don't want to see her any longer?'

He finished his tuna sandwich. The act of putting his plate and tumbler in the new dishwasher gave him time to compose a reply. 'This makes no difference. She broke up my parents' marriage, then her own, but there's no changing the facts. She lived with my father for the past twenty years. If anyone can tell me about him, she can.'

'Yes, but how much more do you want to know about him?'

He hesitated. 'I—I need a clearer picture of him than the old blurry snaps in the family photo album.'

'How can you be sure that Cheryl would be a reliable witness?'

'I can't. But she's the best that I have.'

Despite failing to find her at Oxenholme, Daniel remained unwilling to phone Cheryl and give her advance warning of his arrival. That would give her the chance of making an excuse, or refusing outright to have anything to do with him. Judging by what the Whistons had said about her, this was more than likely. He'd rather take the risk that she was out.

Even if she eluded him, his journey would not be in vain. He planned to stop off en route. Like a child husbanding a special treat for a rainy day, Daniel had been saving up his first visit to Amos Books. The shop was supposed to be something special, an Elysium for seekers after secondhand and antiquarian books. There was even a café which earned high marks in the guidebooks for value and atmosphere. Best of all, the shop was only a short drive from Brack.

He found it without difficulty, one of half a dozen small businesses grouped around a large yard. Most of the units produced and sold crafts of one sort or another: wall hangings decorated with Lakeland themes, pottery and wooden gifts, hand-made greetings cards, and teddy bears with large, beseeching eyes. The bookshop occupied a section of a converted mill, the rear of which overlooked a weir. Rain was rattling on the gravel and although Daniel ran from his car, his sweatshirt was soaked by the time he was inside. The rich aroma of Kenyan coffee blended with the smell of old books and he recognised the *andante* movement of Hanson's Romantic Symphony coming from discreet speakers near the entrance. The front part of the lower floor was devoted to fiction and the rear to the café, which spilled out on to an elevated area of decking from which on a fine day customers could sit out and watch the beck rushing past.

This afternoon an elderly couple taking shelter from the weather were pretending to interest themselves in slip-cased effusions of the Folio Society while a pair of earnest back-packers studied a glassed cabinet containing a complete set of Wainwright first editions as if glimpsing the Crown Jewels. A quick reconnaissance established that one of the upstairs rooms had a stock of historical titles that many libraries might envy. A yellowing pamphlet called *Ancient Corpse Ways of Cumberland and Westmoreland* caught his eye and he started leafing through it.

'Looking for anything in particular?' A man with floppy fair hair paused in the act of filling a box with dog-eared *National Geographics* and gave him an amiable grin.

'Just browsing.'

'Fine. Have a browse over a latte, if you like. No obligation to buy. It's not a bad way to spend a few minutes drying off until this downpour eases.'

'You've talked me into it. Do I gather that you're Mr. Amos?'

'That's me.' The man extended a slim, well-manicured hand. 'Now tell me, why is your face familiar? I don't think we've met…'

'My name's Daniel Kind.'

'The historian? Good Lord, quite an honour.' He squinted at the pamphlet Daniel was reading. 'Don't tell me you're planning a programme about corpse roads?'

Daniel shook his head. 'The editor of *Contemporary Historian* called a couple of days ago and asked if I'd like to contribute an article. I thought that corpse roads might be a suitable subject. But television—no. One or two of my colleagues seem to think I've done enough harm already, creating a generation of historical illiterates. From now on I'll be writing, not presenting.'

'We have one of your books here, as it happens. Not just the TV tie-in, but your very first.'

'So I see. Like all authors, I can't resist checking in any bookshop whether it stocks a title of mine. I see you're asking a good price.'

'It's a sought-after book, especially in such a pretty dustjacket. Maybe I can persuade you to sign it for me, make it even more special? Don't worry, I won't sell it for an even more vastly inflated sum. It will go into my private collection. However hard I try, it keeps growing. My bibliomania is pretty acute.'

'Worrying in a bookseller,' Daniel said. 'Like trying to diet when you own a chocolate shop.'

As Daniel inscribed the book, Amos asked, 'You're up here on holiday?'

'We've bought a cottage over in Brackdale.'

'My favourite spot, I've walked every fell in the valley. Hope to see you dropping in here more often, then.'

'You won't be able to keep me away. Especially if the coffee's as good as the stock.'

'No worries on that account. When you've finished browsing, come and meet Leigh Moffat. She runs the café.'

Amos led the way back down the steps. They creaked just as, Daniel believed, all floorboards in secondhand bookshops should creak. It was an essential part of the ambience, like the giddy sense of claustrophobia that came from squeezing between tottering towers of books and the clouds of dust that had to be blown from the ancient volumes lingering in the darkest recesses. In the other half of the old mill, the cafeteria was fresh and airy, with seductive cakes arrayed beneath a transparent cover. A pretty woman with shiny auburn hair in a neat bob was washing up behind the counter.

'Leigh is a near-neighbour of yours,' Amos announced after making introductions. 'Brackdale born and bred.'

'I live opposite the lychgate at the side of the church.' Her voice was husky and the aroma of orange cake that clung to her appealed to Daniel just as much. 'Where are you?'

'The cottage at the end of Tarn Fold.'

She glanced sharply at the bookseller. 'I know it, of course. The story I heard was that Mrs. Gilpin's relatives had sold it to a couple from down South.'

'Word gets around.'

'You know the history of the place?'

'I've heard what happened to Barrie Gilpin.'

'Poor boy.' She sighed. 'We were at school together.'

'You liked him?'

'We were never close. There was no harm in him, but I remember the way he prowled round the playground, day after day. He always followed exactly the same routine, patting the same railings on the wall, as if to prove everything was where it should be.'

Amos stared. 'There was no harm in him?'

Daniel said quickly, 'You lost touch with Barrie later on?'

'You never lose touch completely, not in Brackdale. It's too small for that. But I'm sure his mother found him a handful. As he grew older, he became more and more of an outsider, even though he'd spent the whole of his life in the valley. Not a recluse, but not "one of us". I felt sorry for him. Most of all after he died and people nodded and winked and hinted that he'd killed a woman.'

'Come off it.' Amos was brusque. 'There wasn't any doubt that he killed her.'

'Innocent until proved guilty,' her tone defiant. 'Whatever the police may believe.'

She held Marc Amos's gaze until he looked away and changed the subject. Something lay unspoken between them, but Daniel could not guess what it was.

Grange-over-Sands lay just outside the National Park, perched above the shores of Morecambe Bay, a last resort for the over-sixties. Daniel remembered a childhood trip to Grange, and the accompanying sense of disappointment. At twelve, he'd associated English seaside towns with the raffish seediness of Blackpool or Brighton, but anyone in search of big dippers or louche entertainment at the end of the pier would, he discovered, be wise to skip Grange. It might have been sheltered by the fells and warmed by the Gulf Stream, it might even have boasted an improbable palm tree and a promenade, but it didn't possess a pier. The only thing he'd enjoyed about his visit was his father's quip that the town's demographic profile had earned it the nickname of 'God's waiting room'. As the rain thinned, the gentle slopes of Grange still didn't set his pulse racing, but as he paused at a red light, a glance over to the bay startled him. As a boy, he hadn't paid any attention to the view but now, even in steady drizzle, the panorama took his breath away.

The address the Whistons had given him was a substantial thirties detached house, set back from the road leading out to Cartmel. By moving in with her boss, Cheryl had scrambled up several rungs of the property ladder. She'd been personal assistant to the company's finance director and it was a safe bet that her lover's remuneration package was a good deal healthier than Ben Kind's police pension.

The door opened and a small woman in a lime green trouser suit appeared. Her heart-shaped face was immaculately made up, mascara and lipstick applied with painstaking care. His first thought was that he'd seen her before. As he trawled through his memory, he introduced himself. He'd been expecting surprise rather than instant, naked hostility, but as soon as she realised that her ex-husband's son had shown up on the doorstep, she glared as if the Boston Strangler had paid a call.

'Why have you come?' Her tone was combative, her whole body trembling with barely suppressed anger. 'What do you want here?'

'I drove over to Oxenholme this morning and the Whistons told me I might find you here. I won't take up much of your time, Cheryl. I just want to talk.'

Her cheeks reddened, as if she found his use of her forename an offensive act of enforced intimacy. She folded her arms, one more barrier between them. 'You and I don't have anything to talk about.'

'Sorry if it's a shock, my turning up out of the blue. I don't want to cause any trouble or disturb you and your…friend.'

'My fiancé, you mean?'

With a snort of defiance, she flourished her ring finger with its winking diamond. Suddenly he remembered who she reminded him of. His father had always had a soft spot for Elaine Paige, had owned most of her albums and played them interminably. Even now Daniel could remember the lyrics to her greatest hits by heart. Twenty years ago, Cheryl must have looked like Elaine playing Evita, and she still had a feisty prettiness. Daniel pictured Cheryl opening her lungs and bursting into "Don't Cry for Me Argentina" and even with his nerves stretched taut, he had to suppress the urge to laugh out loud.

'Dad is dead,' he said. 'What you make of your life now is none of my business.'

'Very generous of you, I'm sure.'

'Please. I don't want a quarrel. You meant a lot to him, he told me so. I tried to explain in my letter.'

It had never occurred to him to blame Cheryl for the delay in getting the news of his father's death to him, but he wondered now if she felt a pang of guilt. Maybe she hadn't wanted him at the funeral. It didn't matter: he'd written to her afterwards, a short, civil letter of sympathy. He hadn't expected a reply. Why would she want to mend fences with a family she'd never met?

She tapped her heel on the doorstep, waiting for him to give up and walk away. 'No point in raking over the past. I really don't have anything to say to you.'

'If you could just spare me a few minutes.'

From inside the house came the sound of a door opening. Looking past Cheryl, Daniel could see into a long hallway with a highly polished parquet floor. Framed photographs of brooding mountains covered the walls. At the far end of the hall a stooped, bespectacled figure appeared.

'Have you seen my golf clubs?' the man called. 'Surely you wouldn't have moved them again after what I said before?' His voice had a grumbling, disconsolate note that Daniel guessed was habitual. Unexpectedly, he felt a pin-prick of sympathy for Cheryl.

'Not today,' she said hurriedly, glancing over her shoulder to offer a tense smile of apology. 'I'll look for them in a minute.'

The man shuffled out of sight, muttering to himself.

'Look,' Daniel murmured, 'I'm sorry if it's a bad time…'

She compressed her lips. 'No point in saying you'll be back another day. It would always be a bad time.'

Daniel wouldn't give up. 'He investigated a case. The woman who was found on the Sacrifice Stone. I wondered…'

'He and I never talked much about the job.' She spoke so quickly that he felt sure she was fibbing.

'You worked for the police.'

'Only as a civilian, and not after we moved up here and got married. When he came home, it was better for him to forget about all the crime and squalor. I tried to make the house nice for him, help him to unwind. He worried too much about his cases, he could never let them go. I hated that, hated the way his work mattered more than…'

She bit the sentence off, as if regretting that she had said so much.

'Did he ever…?'

'Listen,' she said, 'I'll have to go. Sorry if you've had a wasted journey. If you're that keen to rake up the past, you'd have done better to talk to that bloody sergeant of his.'

'Which sergeant?'

She was closing the door on him, her face a powdered mask even as she replied. 'Hannah Scarlett. That was her name. She thought the sun shone out of your father's backside.'

Chapter Six

'Hannah, Nick, there you are!' The ACC, practising for the media scrum, flashed a maximum-wattage smile as she beckoned them over. 'Can I introduce Les Bryant?'

Hannah had walked into the ante-room ready, willing and able to take a serious dislike to her new colleague. First impressions were not encouraging. She'd never liked the smell of tobacco and he reeked of it. His weather-beaten features were moulded in a look of dour scepticism, as though he were about to caution her that anything she might say would be taken down and might be used in evidence.

'Pleased to meet you.'

Bryant's flat Yorkshire vowels gave no clue to his true feelings. But then, how thrilled was he likely to be that, after years of his own command, the senior serving officer in this new team was a woman? Plenty of policemen, not all of them veterans, found it hard to cope with female superiors. Given her experience of Lauren Self, Hannah was tempted to sympathise.

'This is a truly exciting project,' the ACC said. She spoke with deliberation, and Hannah guessed that she was rehearsing her lines for the conference. 'Too many families of too many murder victims have had to wait too long for justice. Now we have an opportunity to tackle the mysteries that baffled a previous generation of investigators.'

'What if they ask about resources?' Bryant asked. 'Are the figures finalised?'

Nick coughed. Hannah guessed that he was trying to suppress a snigger. *Trust a Yorkshireman to focus on the money.* Bryant had a point, nonetheless. There was a lot of talk at the moment about Government money being redistributed from rural forces to the metropolitan areas with higher crime rates. If this unit wasn't properly funded, her fear of being set up to fail would prove prophetic.

'Well,' the ACC said, colour rising into her cheeks. 'The Head of CID's initial budget proposals have been approved by the police authority.'

'I was only thinking, my contract is for six months at four days a week. Not exactly a long time to see justice done.'

The ACC flushed. 'Yes, but don't forget that your contract has an option to extend, if both parties wish it.'

Bryant thrust his hands in his pockets. A small pony-tailed girl from the press office put her head round the door and said in a breathless tone, 'We'll start in two minutes, ma'am, if that's all right.'

'Thanks, Sally-Ann, that's great. Are we all set?'

'Absolutely. The BBC crew is here and the room's full to bursting, but I thought you'd like to keep them waiting for a few moments. Make a bit of an entrance. Build the excitement.'

Hannah caught Bryant wince at that last phrase, but the ACC was too busy checking her cue cards to notice. She lifted her head and squared her shoulders, her momentary discomfiture already forgotten. 'Marvellous, absolutely marvellous. This could kick-start our project in the best possible way. Nothing like wall-to-wall media coverage for regenerating interest in an inquiry that's gone cold. Don't you think so, Les?'

'Two-edged sword,' he said bluntly, slouching towards the door. 'We could find ourselves knee-deep in rubbish. Time-wasters and clairvoyants. It's all about sorting the wheat from the chaff.'

'Of course, you're right, but...'

The ACC hesitated. For once she was lost for words. And for once Hannah actually felt sorry for her.

◇◇◇

'So now the circus is over,' Les Bryant said as they trooped into the room that Headquarters had allocated for the team briefing, 'where do we go from here?'

'The pub?' Bob Swindell stayed true to form. He would be the unit's self-appointed joker. Every team had to have one.

Hannah waited until everyone had settled down and Bob had stopped pretending to shiver. Or perhaps he wasn't pretending. The room was light and airy and freezing. Some problem with the radiators; they always malfunctioned during a cold snap. At least the media conference had gone as well as could be hoped. The ACC was thrilled with all the photo opportunities and the fact that nobody had asked penetrating questions about budgets. She was currently giving an in-depth interview to a local journo who needed to fill a page in a slack news week.

'All right, where *do* we go from here?' Hannah asked. 'Well, we start by having to make choices. The resources allocated to us are limited. Our aim has to be to make an impact, fast. The ACC has been told to make an interim assessment of our work after six months. Not much time, not much cash.'

'No change there, then.' Lindsey Waller crossed her long legs and her skirt rode higher than ever. Hannah had already noticed that eyes kept straying to admire her. No change there, either. Linz was an object of almost universal desire and also one of the sharpest young detectives in the county. When the pressure was on, her sceptical sense of humour kept everybody grounded.

'Too right. Six serving officers plus Les here as consultant, to cover all three regions of the county, all unsolved murders and rapes in Cumbria over, say, the past thirty years. That's enough for a start.'

Bryant rocked on his chair and said, 'More than enough, don't you think, ma'am? Better make it fifteen years.'

The *ma'am* nettled Hannah even more than the hint that she was biting off more than she could chew. A small team needed to operate with maximum cohesion, minimum formality—she had little doubt that he was taking the piss. She'd retaliate by killing him with courtesy.

'Excellent idea, Les. Spot on. Fifteen years it is. As for you four,' she nodded at the detective constables, 'I'd like you to split into two teams. Linz, you're with Bob. Maggie, I'm pairing you with Gul.'

Bob Swindell nodded with enthusiasm and Maggie Eyre seemed happy enough, but DC Gul Khan wasn't much of an actor and his flicker of disappointment was noticeable. A renowned ladies' man, he'd obviously fancied taking the chance to bond with Linz Waller. Maggie had the rosy cheeks and ample proportions of a true farmer's daughter, but glamorous she wasn't. Anyway, she'd recently fallen for a young car mechanic from Keswick. Gul's parents ran a convenience store in Workington; he and Maggie might not be soul-mates, but they could share experiences about escaping the clutches of a family business without becoming distracted from the grunt work of cold case review.

'We need to take a look at each case, focusing on the evidence that might be improved with a little help from our friends in the Forensic Service. Then we can prioritise in order of re-examination for more detailed work. Looking at the statements that were taken at the time, the exhibits…'

'*If* they've been retained,' Bryant said.

'Obviously it won't help if stuff's gone missing. We'll have to take our chances on that. But as we all know, there's scope for identifying minute quantities of DNA these days, in contexts where investigators a few years back didn't have a prayer. We can consider the tests made originally and whether we can improve on them.'

'Finance permitting,' Bryant said.

'Absolutely right, Les.' She wouldn't let him knock her off her stride. Above all, she couldn't allow a negative attitude to take root in the team. A unit like this needed to be highly motivated. It would be so easy to despair of ever achieving a result. 'Because cash is tight, it's all the more important to take good care to use it to maximum effect. Maybe you'd like to give us the benefit of your experience? Anything to add?'

Les Bryant grimaced. His trousers seemed tight; Hannah guessed that he'd put on weight since he'd last worn a suit. Had he already spent too long in cardigan and slippers? Maybe he'd lost it and meant to cover up by seeking out for a chance to make her look a fool. Hannah realised she was holding her breath, waiting to gauge his response.

'Take nothing on trust,' he said finally.

As was her habit, Linz said what everyone else was thinking. 'Meaning what, specifically?'

'Yes,' Hannah said. Seize the moment. 'Would you like to elaborate, Les?'

Bryant contemplated Linz's legs wistfully. For a moment, Hannah thought he was going to crack a locker-room joke, just to see how she handled it. Then he cleared his throat and began to talk in a drab monotone that she found oddly hypnotic.

'You need to remember, cold case review is different from a typical murder inquiry. There you start with a body and nothing else. Right? In this game, you have a whole load of stuff on your plate from day one. Photo-fits, e-fits, exhibits, a thousand and one facts. Things are simpler when you don't have too many facts getting in the way.'

'You can say that again,' Bob Swindell murmured, but Maggie hushed him with a fierce look.

Bryant didn't seem to notice the interruption. It was almost as if he was talking to himself, as he defined the nature of the challenge that the ACC had set. 'You see, a lot of those facts are going to be useless. Worse than that, they'll lead you astray if you let them. Facts are like ideas, you can have too much of a good thing. We're walking in old footsteps, ladies and gentlemen, dealing with other detectives' preconceived ideas. Sure, we're playing catch-up with the past, but don't let it get you down. There's always a reason why a murder inquiry fails to get a result and it's mostly down to cock-up, not conspiracy. Was a bit of evidence overlooked, a statement not checked? We can't assume that any of the original work was sound. Maybe all but one per cent of it was—but we don't know which particular one per cent it might be.' He folded his arms and looked at Linz, the faintest hint of a cynical smile on his seen-it-all features. 'That's why I say—take nothing on trust.'

'So what do you make of him?' Hannah asked.

Nick stirred his coffee with a plastic spoon. They were sitting in a corner of the canteen while the four constables sifted through the first calls responding to the press office's publicity blitz. Les Bryant was upstairs with the ACC, wrangling about the procedure for claiming his expenses.

'I was hoping for Gandalf. Looks like we finished up with Eeyore.'

She laughed. 'Under pressure, he did talk a bit of sense.'

'Pity it had to be dragged out of him. See what I mean? Stereotypical Yorkshireman.' He put on a cod Leeds accent. '*If tha does owt for nowt, do it for thissen.*'

'He's supposed to have all the right experience.'

'Meaning that he knows just which buttons to press if he wants to be a pain.'

'You could be right. I can't see him joining my fan club, somehow.'

Nick gave her a cheeky grin. 'That's a pretty select grouping anyway, isn't it? Never mind, solve a couple of cold cases and everyone will love you. Above all, Lauren Self will love you.'

It was on the tip of her tongue to say *I don't care about being loved.* So far as her work as a detective was concerned, it was the unembroidered truth. Yet she realised that if she said it to Nick, she'd feel uncomfortable. Would he infer a dig at Marc, even though she didn't mean it like that? She didn't want to risk being misinterpreted. Not by Nick, not about her feelings for Marc.

When she got home that evening, the lights were on upstairs. Marc had converted the loft into an office and he spent hours alone there, revising his stock catalogues and checking prices charged by American book-dealers on the internet. They lived in a sprawling old house with a cellar and out-buildings and he'd been assiduous in filling every inch of available space with books. Books everywhere. Books in boxes, books on shelves. Books lurking behind table lamps, books propping up plant pots, books crammed into racks intended for magazines and videotapes.

Until she'd met Marc, she'd thought herself a book-lover, but now she was not so sure. He was so well-read as to make her feel half-educated, but it was more than that. He worshipped books in a way she had never experienced before. For Marc, books were far more than mere texts to be read. He protected their jackets with archival Brodart sleeves and cosseted those with unwrappered spines for fear that they might split. When there was dampness in the air, he would prowl the cellar feverishly, fearing that moisture in the atmosphere would cause bindings to bulge and pages to curl, rendering the books valueless. Condition was crucial, content seldom came into the equation. An ex-library reading copy of *Anna Karenina* was worthless, a first edition in a fine wrapper of *The Curious Mr. Tarrant* by the late C. Daly King (whoever he might be) was worth its weight in gold. All this was a mystery to Hannah. When provoked, she would tell their friends that it left her slightly foxed.

She hurried into the kitchen and turned on the coffee machine. As it began to burble, she called out that she was home. Soon, Marc came tramping down the stairs. Head shaking, brow corrugated, footfalls so heavy that they might have belonged to an unhappy policeman.

'You'll never believe this,' he said and recounted the iniquities of the day's dealings with an especially finicky collector of nineteenth century Cumbrian guide books. After delivering the punch-line, he had an afterthought. 'By the way, how did your thing go?'

'My thing?' she asked, without expression.

'You know, the press conference. Cold cases and stuff.'

'Oh, all right.'

'Great.' He gave a brisk nod. 'Told you so.'

As she climbed into bed, he said, 'Forgot to mention. We had a celebrity visitor at the shop today.'

'Oh yes?' From his over-casual tone, she sensed that he hadn't forgotten, he'd just been biding his time to mention it.

'He was just looking round, but when I spotted him, I persuaded him to sign his book for me.'

'Salman Rushdie? Terry Pratchett?'

'Not even warm.' He put his hand on her bare shoulder and tugged casually at the strap of her night-dress. 'I'll give you a clue. He's a historian.'

'David Starkey? Simon Schama? One of the other guys you watch on the box?'

'You're not being serious,' he said. 'No, the answer is Daniel Kind.'

She sat up at once. 'You're kidding.'

'As true as I'm lying here. Daniel the scruffy don, expert in horrible history. Son of your old boss.'

'What on earth is Daniel doing up here? It's rather late in the day to be taking a look round his father's haunts.'

'Oh, I think there's more to it than simple sight-seeing. He's bought a cottage in Brackdale.'

'He's *what?*'

'Thought you'd be surprised,' Marc said complacently. 'And he hasn't just bought it for the occasional weekend break. Seems as though he and his partner have decided they want a new way of life, and they want it here in the Lakes.'

'What about his job? He was one of Oxford's shining stars.'

'As far as I can gather, he's walked out on his college. What's more, he doesn't have any more television scripts in the works. He simply wants to sit in his cottage and do a bit of writing. When he comes up for a breath of air, with any luck he'll drop in at the shop and treat himself to a couple of first editions.'

Hannah shook her head. 'I don't get it.'

'It's not that unusual. We know plenty of people who came here to live the dream.'

'But *Daniel*. It's—very strange.'

'Trust me, it gets stranger. You'll never believe which house he's bought.'

'Go on, nothing can surprise me now.'

'Don't be so sure,' he said, slipping his hand inside her nightdress and stroking her nipple. 'He's become the proud owner of Tarn Cottage.'

She pulled his hand away. 'You can't be serious?'

'Never more so.'

For all the warmth of the bed, Hannah had gooseflesh. 'Ben was never convinced that Barrie killed the girl.'

'Perhaps it helped him to feel better about failing to lock Barrie up.'

'It wasn't like that at all,' she said angrily. 'Ben was bigger than that.'

Marc grunted and Hannah cursed herself for falling into a trap. Long before Nick Lowther, Marc had been jealous of Ben Kind. She'd taken pains to convince her lover that she and Ben used to talk about nothing but work, work, work. But she and Ben both cared so much about the job that work always become something more, something intensely personal. Maybe that was why Marc suspected that their relationship was not merely platonic. Or maybe he just liked having someone of whom to be jealous.

'My guess is, the son's like the father,' Marc muttered. 'He simply can't bear to let things go.'

Chapter Seven

'Daniel, tell me about Barrie.'

Daniel was sitting with Miranda in the kitchen, nursing a mug of coffee. When he'd arrived back from his encounter with Cheryl, the cottage had been filled by a cacophony of drilling and sanding, but at last the workmen had finished for the day and the place was still.

Forget about the murder. He remembered his injunction to himself that first morning as they drove over the fell and into Brackdale. He should have known better. Even if you wanted to, you couldn't forget history.

'Why do you want to know?'

'I'm curious.' Miranda gestured at their surroundings. 'I mean—he spent the whole of his life here, this was the only home he ever knew. You were fond of him, but most people think he was responsible for a shocking crime.'

He sneezed. Unexpectedly, and yet it kept happening. It was the dust from the builders' work, the dust that was everywhere; sometimes he feared his sinuses would never be rid of it.

'I suppose you think I'm crazy, to imagine for a moment that he was innocent. Probably it *is* crazy. After all, we were only together for a few days, a long time ago.'

'Why do you believe in Barrie? In his innocence, I mean?'

'Because people don't change, that's what I believe. They learn, they make mistakes, they grow, they get older—but their *nature* doesn't change. And the Barrie I knew was kind, not cruel.'

He left the room for a few moments. When he returned, he was carrying an aged Revelation suitcase. He opened it up and took out a thick photograph album, thumbing through the pages. Each picture was carefully pasted in, and carried a brief caption in careful, immature script. On the final page, he came to a snapshot of two boys, leaning against a beech tree. In neat childish handwriting the shot was labelled *Barrie and me, in his garden.*

'There,' he said. 'The very last photograph my father took for the family album. Recognise the scene? Dad took this, he was standing outside this window. Barrie used to help his mother in the garden, but you can see it was wild even then.'

Miranda studied the photo. 'Neither of you believed in combing your hair for the camera.'

He grinned. 'Like I said, people don't change.'

'How did you meet?'

'I bumped into him at the start of the holiday, after Dad decided we'd climb to Priest Edge while the girls looked round Brack. Barrie was coming in the opposite direction. He said hello—abruptly, he had a jerky way of talking, but I didn't mind. Soon we were in deep conversation. My father went on ahead, but Barrie showed me a short-cut along the coffin trail.'

She knitted her brow. 'The coffin trail?'

He pointed through the window, towards the hillside. 'See the stony track in the distance, disappearing behind the trees? That's the coffin trail.'

'So it's a path?'

'Yes, there are several in the Lakes. Often called corpse roads. Years ago, the trail was the route that mourners took when they buried their dead. There was no church in the next valley in those days, so a packhorse carried the body over the top of the hill and then down to St Helen's in Brack.'

Miranda's eyes widened. 'They loaded a dead person onto a horse?'

'Having first blindfolded it. When the funeral party was ready to start the journey, they put on blinkers.'

She shivered. 'Poor creature.'

'What amazes me is how those ponies managed to pick their way up and down the fells with such a burden on their back. The coffin trail is steep, although it makes a terrific short-cut. My father was a fit man, but Barrie and I reached the Sacrifice Stone first. From that moment on, we were firm friends. I'm not sure that Barrie had ever made a friend before. The fact that I came from outside made a difference. He could show me places, be in charge. I didn't have any preconceived ideas, I just took him at face value. I think he liked that.'

'What about Mrs. Gilpin?'

'She made me nervous. Barrie was in awe of her. He might have been clumsy, but even at that age he was big and strong. Nothing seemed to make him afraid—not swinging from a tree branch, not picking up an adder and wrapping it over his hand. But he was terrified of his mother's wrath. She was small and fragile, but when she went on the warpath, he would cower in a corner and make noises like a stuck pig.'

'But he wasn't violent?'

He shook his head. 'Let me tell you a story. A couple of days before the end of my holiday, Barrie persuaded me to follow his lead. He loved to swing from the tree, over the tarn. I kept waiting for the branch to snap, but it never happened. He assured me it was perfectly safe and in the end I accepted his dare.'

'Don't tell me—the branch broke.'

'No, more embarrassing than that. I lost my grip and fell into the tarn. The shock of the cold water nearly stopped my heart. It was choked with weeds and when I went under I was afraid I'd never get back to the surface. For a few seconds I was sure I was about to drown.'

'What happened?'

'Barrie jumped in and rescued me. He picked me up and put me under his arm and seconds later he'd laid me out on dry land. I was crying from the shock, but he calmed me down. When his mother came out to see the cause of the commotion, he made up a story. I was embarrassed by my own foolishness, but he didn't let me down. I never told anyone except my father what he did for me that day. If my mother had found out, she would have panicked. So it was our little secret.'

'Which you've never forgotten?'

'How could I?' Daniel paused. 'I bet my father never forgot it, either. Barrie saved me from the consequences of my own bravado. More than that, he saved my life.'

An hour later, they headed out to The Moon under Water for an evening meal. The original building was a couple of hundred years old and had been much extended. It boasted beamed ceilings, uneven floors and décor with a Hitchcock movie poster theme. Miranda amused herself by picking a table where Daniel had to sit beneath a picture of James Stewart from *The Man Who Knew Too Much*.

'So is it the way you remember?' she asked as they studied the menu chalked up over the counter.

'It's doesn't seem as busy and the air's not as thick with smoke. Maybe it's less of a pub, more of a restaurant than it used to be. The bar was always packed to the rafters with locals and fell-walkers. Louise and I were kept awake every night by the drinkers downstairs in the bar. She complained endlessly about the raucous laughter and the stink of beer. But I liked the twisting staircases and tucked-away alcoves. We whiled away time by telling each other the legends of Lakeland.'

He ordered their food from a young woman whose carelessly buttoned cheesecloth shirt revealed more than it concealed, then moved along the counter to buy the drinks. The landlord had a perma-tan and highlights, along with a receding hairline and a designer shirt that had been the height of fashion a few years back. His pinched, quizzical face reminded Daniel of a fox, but of a fox with an especially high opinion of himself. As he pulled a pint, he introduced himself as Joe Dowling. When he learned that Daniel and Miranda were the new owners of Tarn Cottage, his eyebrows wiggled.

'So you're the television star, then?'

'Never a star, I'm afraid. Anyway, I've given all that up.'

Dowling stashed his money in the till and said, 'So what brought you to Brackdale? Most people drive straight past on their way to the Lakes. They don't even know the valley exists. Thank God for that, I say, even though a bit more passing trade would put a smile on my bank manager's face.'

'I stayed here on holiday as a boy. We had a room in this pub, matter of fact.'

'You're kidding! In the days of old Dick Hubbard?'

'My sister and I used to call his wife Old Mother Hubbard. Predictable to a fault. I didn't expect they'd still be around. They both looked about one hundred even then.'

'Dick passed on seven years back, and Millie followed soon after.'

'I see you still advertise bed and breakfast.'

'You wouldn't recognise the rooms if you haven't been here for twenty years. En-suite, tea and coffee making facilities, Corby trouser press, you name it. I know three star hotels in Windermere with less to offer. The wife and I built on at the back as well as refurbishing. Ex-wife, I should say. Glenda and I split up a while ago.' The landlord cast a proprietorial glance at the milky white cleavage of the young woman taking food orders. As if trying to recapture his youth, he pulled his stomach in. 'Lynsey and I are tying the knot in the summer.'

'So that's what you call it?' said a man standing next to Daniel. 'Now if you've finished bragging about your love life, mine's a pint of best.'

'You'll have to excuse my friend,' the landlord said. 'Very uncouth, but I suppose if you've settled in the valley, I'd better introduce you. This is Tom Allardyce. Tom, meet Daniel Kind. He and his other half have just bought the cottage up in Tarn Fold.'

Allardyce nodded, but his expression was as welcoming as a shower of sleet. His brown hair was cropped to the scalp, his complexion weathered by years out of doors. His hands were callused, the nails short and dirty. The sleeves of his ancient Black Sabbath tee shirt were rolled up to the elbows. On each hairy forearm, dragons breathed fire.

'I've heard your name.'

'News travels fast round here,' Daniel said. 'You live in the valley too?'

'I'm the tenant of Brack Hall Farm. Mr. Dumelow may be a property tycoon, but I look after his own land.'

'If you ask me,' Joe Dowling said, 'the man's more interested in the tax losses. Tom's family has looked after that farm for generations, Mr. Kind. He's forgotten more about farming than Simon Dumelow will ever learn.'

'No skin off my nose, as long as his lordship leaves me to it. It's when he starts interfering that I get hot under the collar.'

'And does he interfere?' Daniel asked.

Allardyce snorted. 'Just a bit. We had a few sheep get out a while back. Sort of thing that's always happened, always will, but he went apeshit because the fence was broken. Just as well my lease is watertight, or he'd have me out on my arse. Though her ladyship might have something to say about that. She and the wife are as thick as thieves.'

'Your wife helps on the farm as well?'

'Jean takes care of the Hall, she's head cook and bottle-washer. She's already got her orders for your dinner at the weekend. The lovely Tash doesn't like to dirty her pretty hands with cooking or cleaning. It might interfere with pretending to be an artist.'

'She's a bonny-looking woman.' Joe Dowling smacked his lips in a parody of lust.

'Out of your league, my friend,' Allardyce said. 'So, Mr. Kind, you've bought Cissie Gilpin's cottage?'

'It was a stroke of luck,' Daniel said. 'Miranda and I were taking a break up here and we saw that Tarn Cottage was up for sale. I remembered it from my first visit, on holiday twenty years back. That was when I met Barrie Gilpin.'

'You knew Barrie?' The landlord seemed taken aback. 'Bloody hell, it's a small world.'

'We bumped into each other on my first day here and became friends,' Daniel said. 'Most days, we played together.'

'That must have been a first,' Allardyce said. 'He never had any friends as I can remember. Not right in the head. That was the excuse they always gave for him being such a bad-mannered bastard. You'd be in the middle of a conversation with him and he'd walk away, just like that, for no reason.'

'Asperger's Syndrome, they call it,' Joe Dowling said.

'Is that right?' Allardyce scoffed. 'They've got a name for everything these days.'

His derision provoked Daniel. 'I liked him a lot.'

'Then you won't know what happened?' Joe Dowling said.

'I know he's supposed to have murdered a tourist.'

'No suppose about it,' Allardyce muttered. 'He battered her face and cut her throat so she was as good as beheaded.'

'Stripped her naked,' Joe Dowling added. The prurient gleam in his eyes made Daniel's flesh creep.

'Then he laid her out on the Sacrifice Stone, high above your own little cottage. So much for your boyhood pal, Mr. Kind. Not that likeable after all, eh?'

'He was never charged with a crime, let alone tried and convicted.'

'You can't prosecute a corpse.'

Daniel took a sip of beer. 'Maybe his death was convenient for someone.'

Allardyce scowled. 'And who might that be?'

'Whoever really killed Gabrielle Anders.'

'You serious?' Allardyce demanded. As his voice rose, the bar area fell quiet. People turned to look, then quickly turned away again. Daniel guessed that locals didn't fancy making eye contact with the farmer when he was in a temper.

'That girl's death caused a lot of upset round here,' Joe Dowling said quickly.

'Everyone agrees, Barrie Gilpin was as guilty as hell.'

Daniel glanced over his shoulder and caught Miranda's eye. She gave a pointed glance at the glass of white wine he'd bought her, then mimicked downing it in a single gulp.

'What if everyone was wrong?' he asked. 'Suppose Barrie was innocent, that in more ways than one, *he* was the fall guy.'

'I never heard such a load of crap.' With a contemptuous snort, Tom Allardyce banged his tankard down on the bar. Some of the beer sloshed on to the counter and trickled over the edge on to the floor.

Joe Dowling frowned. 'Barrie Gilpin must have killed that girl. Who else could it have been?'

Daniel shrugged and picked up the drinks. As he wove through the crowd, a woman in an alcove looked up from her meal and smiled. Leigh Moffat. She was having dinner with a woman with shoulder-length auburn hair whose cast of features resembled Leigh's so closely that she had to be a younger sister. He paused by her side, breathing in the rich aroma of a steak and kidney pie drenched in onion gravy.

'I suppose that after serving food to your customers all day long, the last thing you want to do at night is stay at home and cook.'

Leigh smiled. 'Joe Dowling doesn't have any greater pretensions to *haute cuisine* than me. But I wouldn't like you to think I spend all my evenings pigging myself with pub meals. My sister and I only come here once a fortnight, don't we? Dale, this is Daniel Kind. I mentioned him to you, remember?'

'How could I forget?' Dale gave him a teasing grin and offered a small ringless hand. 'Pleased to meet you, Daniel. In fact, the food in the pub down the road is at least as good as this, but The Moon has a nostalgic pull for us. We both used to work here.'

'For Joe Dowling?'

Dale giggled and put her hand over her mouth as hiccups threatened. Where Leigh's manner was thoughtful, considered,

Dale seemed to have a mischievous instinct. She'd opted for a seat next to a poster depicting Ingrid Bergman getting up close and personal with Cary Grant in *Notorious*.

'Casanova himself, yes.'

Leigh gave her sister a reproving glance. 'I saw you, talking to Tom Allardyce.'

'You make it sound like a hazardous sport.'

The sisters exchanged looks and Dale said, 'Let's just say he isn't someone you'd want to meet in an alley on a dark night.'

'I bet. We heard a rifle shot in the woods, or the fields beyond. Might that be Allardyce?'

'Uh-huh. His trouble is, he still thinks he's in the army.'

'He was a soldier?'

'In Northern Ireland, yes. His father and granddad farmed all their lives, but Tom joined up after school. He's a rebel by nature. But Brackdale never prepared him for Belfast during the bombings. He saw some pretty grim things, so the story goes. One night he beat up a Republican suspect, and the powers-that-be kicked him out. So back he went to farming.' Dale forked in a mouthful of beef bourgignon. 'Even he decided there's no point in fighting against Fate, I suppose. He likes animals right enough, better than people actually, but that doesn't stop him shooting those that get in his way.'

When Daniel told her about the rifle shot he and Miranda had heard, Dale nodded. 'That would be Tom. He likes letting the foxes know who's boss. Tom's not someone you'd want to fall foul of.'

'Frankly,' her sister said, 'most people round here give him a wide berth.'

'Except mine host?'

Dale smirked. 'Tom's wife is Joe's cousin, but even Joe's scared of Tom. See him quiver when Tom shouted at you? Not wishing to be nosy, but if you've never met the man before, what was that all about?'

In a few sentences he explained about his doubts over Barrie's guilt. 'It's a long time ago, of course, but I just can't imagine him as a murderer.'

Dale shrugged. 'It's not much to go on.'

'The police didn't look any further,' Leigh said. 'Hannah's old boss was in charge of the enquiry. I don't know whether her new job will cause her to re-open the case.'

Daniel caught Miranda's eye. She looked with theatrical despair at her watch and he offered an apologetic smile. A waitress emerged from the kitchen, carrying their meals. But there was one more question he had to ask.

'Hannah?'

Leigh nodded. 'Marc Amos' partner, Hannah Scarlett. She's a police officer, one of the team that investigated Gabrielle Anders' murder. Didn't you catch her on the regional news the other night? She's in charge of a team that's been set up to investigate cold cases. You know, unsolved crimes.'

Chapter Eight

The renovation of the cottage was proceeding at a pace Daniel had believed impossible outside the fantasy world of TV make-over programmes. Surely it was too much to hope that their luck could last? Joiners, plasterers, plumbers and electricians came and went more or less as per timetable, and the gleaming new kitchen equipment functioned with supernatural efficiency. Yet somehow there were always more jobs to be done.

Miranda presided over the activity with irresistible enthusiasm and was forever locked in earnest debate with the self-appointed foreman. Eddie was a shrunken fellow in his fifties with a piratical patch covering a glass eye that was presumably the legacy of some long ago breach of health and safety legislation. He didn't disguise his appreciation of Miranda's tight tops and even tighter jeans and took voluble pride in making sure that her every wish was the builders' command. His younger colleague, the hunky Wayne, didn't say much. Daniel suspected that talking, and probably thinking, took up effort better devoted to ogling.

They were counting the days to the start of work on the bothy. On the rare occasions when either of them found time and energy for writing, they shared a laptop, but the plan was for each of them to have a dedicated office. The secret of homeworking, Miranda explained, was to separate business activity from space devoted to domestic life. She'd once written an article about it.

Early on the morning after his visit to Grange, Daniel was pouring cornflakes into his bowl when he became aware of water dripping on to the breakfast bar. He glanced upwards and saw a patch of damp by the light fitting. Above was the new bathroom. Miranda was taking a shower and the seal had failed. One problem swiftly followed another. Within hours, they suffered a power cut and a van delivered the wrong kitchen blinds. Miranda was in her element. She had a flair for domestic crises, Daniel discovered, making frantic phone calls to beg for help and threatening legal action against unreliable suppliers. His own coping strategy when all else failed was to seek refuge in a book. He'd acquired a paperback RSPB guide and could now almost tell the difference between a coot and a moorhen. He'd also started battling through *Walden* by Henry David Thoreau, a parting gift from Gwynfor Ellis. Not the lightest read, Gwynfor admitted, but highly appropriate. Thoreau too had tried to live the dream.

'Any good?' Miranda asked. She was on her way upstairs, carrying mugs of steaming tea for Eddie and Wayne. They both took so much sugar that it was a wonder either of them had any teeth left.

'I'm picking up tips,' he said. 'Thoreau opted out of corporate America a century and a half ago and made his home in a log cabin in the backwoods of Massachusetts.'

'A role model, then?'

'Not exactly. He only stuck it for a couple of years.'

'And after that?'

'Back to the city. The simple life wasn't quite as simple as he hoped.'

'What happened?'

'He tried to cook a fish for supper and ended up burning down three hundred acres of woodland. Some people called him the Sage of Walden. To the locals, he was the fool who set fire to the forest.'

◇◇◇

He wanted to learn more about the murder, but the tradesmen came from Kendal or further afield and none seemed to know anything of the Gilpins or the history of the cottage. Even in this day and age, Brackdale kept itself to itself. People in the village spoke of Carlisle as though it were as distant as Cairo. Few tourists seemed aware of the valley's existence, although one morning Daniel had to slam on his brakes as he turned out of Tarn Fold. A huge coach full of Japanese Beatrix Potter fans was executing a perilous about-turn between sharp-edged stone walls. The driver had not realised how badly he had lost his way until the lane leading to the quarry workings narrowed to such an extent that he found further progress impossible. There was only one way in to Brackdale, only one way out.

Daniel followed the coach all the way to the village. From the back window, two beaming teenagers waved at him. One wore a Peter Rabbit tee shirt. His girlfriend's bosom was emblazoned with a picture of Jeremy Fisher. On either side of the lane, grey-fleeced sheep gazed down at the vehicles with yawning indifference. Daniel couldn't identify with the Herdwicks' utter lack of curiosity, but perhaps it helped to explain their gift for survival. And he'd also been told that when they were hungry, they ate their own wool to stay alive.

Touching his brake, he stole a glance across the valley, knowing that the scene was much as it had been a hundred years before. Two hundred, three hundred, more. Brackdale might once have witnessed a murder, but at least it had escaped the plague of foot and mouth that a few years earlier had left hundreds of burnt and blackened corpses on smoke-shrouded Lakeland hillsides.

He found a space to park by the church and bought a few provisions in Tasker's, where an elderly man and the proprietor were sharing a moan about the labyrinthine complexities of the latest traffic scheme in Kendal. Shopping done, he headed to the baker's on the other side of the square. Godfrey's was fast becoming a favourite haunt. The smell of bread freshly baked on the premises was as enticing as the scones that accompanied an unexpectedly adventurous selection of coffees. He was becoming addicted to a blend from Helsinki that made it easy to understand why the Finns are supposed to consume more caffeine than anyone else in the world.

'Hello again.'

He recognised the musky perfume at the same moment as he placed the voice, then looked up from the menu to find Dale Moffat smiling at him. She was kitted out in the regulation Godfrey white blouse and black skirt. On her curvy frame the uniform had an unexpected allure.

'I didn't know you worked here.'

'I only started last week and it's just part-time. A month's probation to see whether I can satisfy Mr. Godfrey.'

She gave him a cheeky wink and he laughed as he ordered. 'I bet you will.'

'So you're settling in?'

'Fine. I guess it takes years to feel that you're part of a place.'

'Decades, more like. I'm not even sure I feel I belong, and I was born a stone's throw away. Trust me, Brackdale's stuck in a time-warp. I live on my own, same as Leigh, but I have a boy and there aren't too many single mums around here. Trouble is, I make waves, people think I'm dangerous to know. Most of the good folk of Brack don't approve of me, never did, even when I was a skinny teenager. My skirt was always a bit shorter than all the other girls'.' A candid grin. 'Some things don't change, eh? At least I give them something to talk about.'

She bustled off and he indulged in a little people-watching. He always chose the table in the front window if it were free, so that he could see the villagers come and go. This was so different from Miranda's favourite café bar in Islington, where everyone in the streets outside was constantly rushing somewhere, too busy to take in the world around them. The pub door opened and Joe Dowling came out to water hanging baskets crammed with purple, white, and yellow pansies. He was wearing a bright blue sports shirt, tight trousers and mocassins of a sort that had been in vogue a couple of years ago. A fair-haired woman with a heavy shopping bag stopped to speak to him, but he gave a lascivious grin and said something that seemed to embarrass her. Cheeks flaming, she turned on her heel and scurried away across the square.

'That's Tom Allardyce's wife.' Dale was back with the coffee and scones. 'She and her cousin are chalk and cheese. Joe's as bad as her husband, in his way. And he's got the dirtiest mind of any man I've ever met. Which is saying something.' She sighed. 'Poor woman, no wonder she looks like she has the cares of the world on her shoulders. She'd be better off getting out of here. She's not bad-looking, she'd never be short of someone to share her bed when she was in the mood. I once made the mistake of telling her so to her face, but she looked at me as if I was mad. Or a trollop. Or both. Some women, they need a man in their lives, however mean he is to them.'

'But not you?'

She smiled. 'Oh, I don't mind having a man in my life every now and then. But on my terms, not his. I keep saying to my sister, there's no point in spending your days waiting to find Mr. Perfect. Even if he does come along, you can guarantee he's already spoken for.'

'And what does Leigh say?'

Dale tossed her hair. 'Oh she worries too much, does my big sister. God knows why, I've known her literally all my life and I've never understood what goes on inside her head. One thing's for certain, she's too fussed about doing The Right Thing. After we spoke to you in The Moon, she started fretting that she'd been unkind when she spoke about Tom Allardyce. They say he saw his best mate killed in front of his very eyes on the Shanklin Road. I ask you, does that justify behaving like a brute?'

He said carefully, 'So Marc Amos lives with this police officer, Hannah Scarlett. Can you tell me if she…'

'I don't know anything about Hannah,' Dale interrupted. 'I only ever met her the once, just after the murder and—well, it wasn't a happy time.'

Her reticence was as disappointing as it was improbable, and he wasn't sure he believed her anyway. But he'd better move on; if he pressed her about his father's sidekick, she might clam up altogether.

'So what did you make of Barrie Gilpin?'

'Same as with Allardyce. Barrie had problems, we all knew that, but some things you can't excuse.'

'Like murder?'

'And being a Peeping Tom.'

'Really?'

'So the story went. There was talk about it after he died. Gossip. Don't ask me for the details. And I can't say that he ever peeped at me, though I don't always remember to draw the curtains. Maybe I scared him, maybe the girl who was killed led him on. It wouldn't surprise me.'

'You knew Gabrielle Anders?'

'She was staying at The Moon when I worked there as a cleaner. Oh yes, I could tell you a thing or two about her.'

'I'm all ears.'

She treated him to a teasing grin. 'Not just ears, I hope.'

'What was she like?'

Someone coughed noisily. The stout and long-suffering Mrs. Godfrey was standing behind the counter with her meaty arms folded. She was trying to direct Dale's attention to an old lady at the next table, waiting patiently for the éclair she had asked for.

'Just coming!' Under her breath Dale added, 'I knock off in half an hour. You can buy me a quick drink in The Moon if you like.'

◇◇◇

As Lynsey, the prospective Mrs. Dowling, served him with a second orange juice, he tried his hand at gentle inquisition, but she turned out to be a native of Penrith whose parents had moved to Whitmell eighteen months earlier and she'd never heard of Barrie Gilpin. Within a couple of minutes he'd concluded that, whatever talents she might possess, Joe Dowling wasn't marrying her for the benefit of sparkling conversation.

Dale was very late and he amused himself by moving to a table in an alcove with a poster from *The Lady Vanishes*. When at last she arrived, complaining that Mrs. Godfrey was a slave-driver and predicting that her employment in the baker's would be short-lived, he supplied her with a Bacardi and Coke and said,

'So you've never found it claustrophobic, spending your whole life in an enclosed valley like Brackdale?'

'Never known any different, have I? It must seem peculiar to someone like you, someone who's appeared on television and travelled the world. Unsophisticated, what's the word...parochial?'

'One or two of Oxford's most sophisticated people are utter shits, in my experience. As for parochial, I find that kind of appealing. The Lake District is so small. I never realised an invisible line was drawn between the lakes in the north and those in the south.'

'Dead right. There's an invisible passport control at Dunmail Raise.'

He laughed. 'When I went into the paper shop next door it dawned on me, they stock *Le Figaro* for the tourists, but not *The Keswick Reminder*. So...you were going to tell me about Gabrielle Anders.'

'Not much to tell, really.'

'Give me a hint.'

'Well, she was supposed to be touring the area, but my impression was that she wouldn't have minded settling down, if she could have found a man to hitch up with. Provided he had a few bob. She knew Tash Dumelow, maybe she wanted to follow her example and team up with someone like Simon. Though I don't think she was as choosy as Tash.'

He drained his glass. 'She wasn't interested in Barrie Gilpin, then?'

'You must be joking. If she did give him a come-on, it would just have been for fun. She had bigger fish to fry.' As if led by a particular train of thought, her gaze travelled to the bar. Joe Dowling had appeared and slung his arm around Lynsey's waist. 'Maybe not that big, though. Look at that slimy toad, thinks he's such a charmer. It'll serve him right when the girl's forty and the size of an opera singer. It's a fat family, cellulite's in the genes, you mark my words. She's put on a stone since Christmas. Ten to one, she's pregnant and he hasn't even realised yet. Joe's not the sort who believes in doing the decent thing.'

Daniel refused to be diverted by her pleasurably malicious speculation. 'Did he fancy Gabrielle?'

'He'd fancy the creature from the black lagoon if it wore a thong and was into leather and handcuffs. Trust me, Daniel, there are things about Joe Dowling and his tastes you really don't want to know. Yet he fancies himself rotten, thinks he's God's gift to women. At least he met his match years back when he tried to flirt with Tash one night at closing time. In the nicest way, she gave him the brush off good and proper, made him look such a fool in front of everyone. For once in my life I felt like flinging my arms round the woman.'

'But you don't care for her?'

'Oh, she's not so bad, isn't Lady Muck. But obviously, I'm jealous as hell.' She gave him an unexpectedly disarming smile. 'Our paths haven't often crossed, but she tries hard to fit in around here, to act like a native. She's always wanted to be One of Us, I think. Maybe it's the foreign ancestry, something in the blood, I've never known anyone so single-minded. Let's face it, it's paid off. If ever a woman had everything she wished for, it's Tash.'

'And her husband's a property developer.'

'Who knows better than to shit on his own back doorstep, if you'll pardon the expression. He's never tried to build on Brackdale's green and pleasant, even his farm is a bit ramshackle. All you need to know is that he's absolutely loaded and he worships the ground Tash walks on. Sickening, really. Mind you, I used to be cynical about her motives, but even I'm prepared to admit, it can't just have been Simon Dumelow's bank balance that was big enough to catch her eye. The clincher is, even after all these years, they still seem besotted. Matter of fact…'

'Yes?'

She guzzled her drink. 'Tash is lucky in more ways than one, trust me on that. Simon might not mind a bit of mild flirting, but give a hint of going any further, and he backs right off. Worse luck. Whenever I meet a decent bloke, he's always spoken for. By the way, I didn't catch the name of that pretty wife of yours.'

'Miranda. And we're not married.'

She stretched and yawned, in a seen-it-all manner. 'Don't tell me, let me guess. You're not into long-term commitment? Even though you've both run off from the city to live together in a tiny place like Brackdale?'

He shrugged. 'Miranda and I haven't known each other that long.'

'Early days, then?'

As he nodded, she stood up. 'Better stop at one. Alcohol goes straight to my head, terribly. I start talking out of turn and after three drinks I'm an utter disgrace. Anyway, I'll rack my brains, see what else I can remember about Gabrielle Anders, if you're that interested in a dead lady. My number's in the book, by the way. If you ever want to get in touch.'

He watched her walk up to the bar and speak to Joe Dowling and his fiancée. Whatever she said succeeded in causing Lynsey's face to flame and the landlord's vulpine smile to dissolve into a hard line of anger. But Dale didn't seem to care. On her way out, she threw Daniel a smile. As if to say: *see, it's like I said, I do make waves.* She was no fool, he thought, but she liked playing a part, was turned on by the idea of being dangerous to know.

Chapter Nine

It might be too late to put things right with his old man, but Daniel still needed to put his own mind at rest. Achieve closure, as Miranda liked to say. She often wrote about the importance of achieving closure. Of course he must tread with care. In Brack, it would be as easy for a newcomer to put a foot wrong in conversation as to stumble off a fellside track in the fog. He and Miranda would have to work hard for a long time if they were ever to become part of this community. Bad enough to be an off-comer, far worse to be disdained as a ghoul.

Did they even *want* to become part of the community? As they drove to Brack Hall on the Saturday evening, Daniel asked Miranda and she had no doubts.

'Of course. This is what it's all about, isn't it? Forsaking the city for village life.'

'We're a mile from the village. Days could pass without our seeing a single soul, if it weren't for all the workmen tramping in and out.'

'Doesn't that bother you?'

'Not in the least. All I ever wanted was to run away with you.'

She put her hand on his thigh. 'That's a lovely thing to say, but I don't want to be a hermit. Okay, we have our writing, but we can't want to hide away from the world forever.'

'Round here, it takes a generation before people really accept you as one of them.'

'Relax, we can always bond with the other off-comers. How about the people in that mobile home park in the next valley?'

He grinned. 'So this is our first toe in the water, so far as integrating with the community goes? A dinner party with the local squire and his wife. Very traditional. Except that he only keeps a farm as a write-off against tax and she's a townie who plays at being an artist.'

'Tash is in love with the Lakes. She rang up this afternoon, while you were outside, to check we were still okay to come. We talked for a couple of minutes and she told me she could never bear to leave. She was trying to persuade me that coming here was the best decision I ever made.'

'Did she need to?' he asked. 'Aren't you sure?'

The hesitation before she replied chilled him more than any simple nostalgia for city life. 'It's just that—sometimes I wonder. What will we do when the cottage is sorted?'

They pulled up outside the electric gates guarding the Hall and he forced a smile. 'Why worry? After everything that's gone wrong this past few days, we'll be old and grey before all the work is finished.'

◇◇◇

'Feel that wall,' Simon Dumelow said. 'See how thick it is?'

After greeting them with champagne, Tash's husband had insisted on taking them for a guided tour. He was a bluff Lancastrian with an extravagance of grey hair, expensively cut. His black short-sleeved shirt and matching designer slacks probably cost twice as much as Daniel's best suit. Daniel guessed he was in his mid-fifties, but he had the boyish enthusiasm of a kid showing off his model railway set.

First stop was the Virginia creeper-festooned pele tower that had once provided a refuge from Border raiders. Underground were the cellars, air-conditioned and lined with racks crammed with vintage wine. Now they had arrived in the tunnel-vaulted room occupying the ground floor. In the fourteenth century a windowless and fetid home to the livestock, today it was a games room with dazzling overhead lights. The only battles it saw were fought on a full-sized Thurston billiard table. A dutiful guest, Daniel thrust his hand against the stone and murmured with appreciation. The wall was undeniably solid.

'Six feet,' his host said. 'Six feet of Cumbrian sandstone, would you believe? They don't build them like this any more.'

'Dumelow Properties don't,' his wife said sweetly, 'that's for sure.'

Simon Dumelow smirked at his guests and patted his wife on the rump. 'She likes to bite the hand that feeds, does Tash. Keeps forgetting that without Dumelow Properties she wouldn't be the lady of Brack Hall.'

'It's a wonderful home,' Miranda said. 'Like a castle.'

'That's exactly what it was,' Simon said. 'Pele towers were scattered on either side of the border in the days when the English and the Scots were always fighting. Come to think of it, have they ever stopped? Inside a place as well-fortified as this, you could withstand a siege if ever the Reivers came to call.'

Tash clicked her tongue, as if embarrassed. 'Darling, aren't you forgetting? Daniel is the historian, he'll know far more about what went on in the old days than we do.'

Daniel felt, as he often did when history was mentioned, rather like a divorce lawyer expected to have an intimate knowledge of the subtleties of probate. 'It's not really my period,' he said. 'I'm a nineteenth century man.'

'You look perfectly modern to me,' she said.

Simon slipped an arm around her. 'Hey, no flirting. Daniel's a respectable academic. You behave yourself in company, do you hear?'

'Okay, darling,' she said, pecking him on the cheek. 'Anything you say.'

He raised his eyebrows. 'Anything?'

'Behave.'

Simon opened a door that gave on to a flight of steps. Half way up, he tripped and barked his knees on the stone. He gave a brief cry of pain but rapidly assured his wife that no harm had been done. The first floor had been turned into a cavernous living space stuffed with antique furnishings. One wall was covered from floor to ceiling with expensively framed watercolours of lakes and mountains, bathed in endless hues of purple and orange. Next to the door, a longcase clock was chiming the hour.

'Jonas Barber senior of Winster,' he announced with pride. 'One of his finest. Not often you find his clocks with a yew case. Of course, Tash chose the antiques, planned all the décor. She's the one with artistic flair. Not only that, she painted all the pictures. Every single one.'

'That's Tarn Fold and the cottage!' Miranda exclaimed.

Tash was no Turner. In fact, Daniel thought, her daubs were no better than average village art group standard, but she'd at least captured the tranquility of the setting, with the cottage slumbering under the midday sun and a gleam of water beyond. As they contemplated the picture, Tash lifted it from the hook and handed it to Miranda.

'Take it, please. A housewarming present.'

'Oh no, we couldn't possibly...'

'Don't say another word, it's yours,' she insisted. 'I'll ask Jean to make sure it's safely packed with lots of bubble wrap.'

'Very determined woman, my wife,' her husband said. 'Knows what she wants to do and goes and does it. You may as well give in right now.'

The clock ticked relentlessly until the argument ended with the present being accepted with profuse thanks. As they headed up the stairs again, Miranda asked, 'How long have you lived here?'

'Ten years.' Simon spoke deliberately; he was taking special care not to miss his footing a second time. 'I was coming out of my first marriage when I looked round this place. I'd always hankered after living in the Lakes, ever since I read *Swallowdale* as a kid.'

'I suppose I liked *Winter Holiday*,' Miranda said as they reached the next landing. 'Wasn't there a girl who liked making up stories and wanted to be a writer?'

Tash nodded. 'Dorothea?'

'You're right. Pure escapism.'

'Yes—well, anyway.' Tash was blushing, as though the Ransome books were an illicit passion. 'You two weren't like Simon, were you? You never harboured a dream of moving to the Lakes.'

'No,' Miranda admitted. 'We moved here pretty much on impulse. Another kind of escapism, if you like.'

'That's the Lakes, they put a spell on you,' he said. 'The same weekend I set eyes on the Hall, the estate agent invited me to a party and I met Tash. So I fell in love twice within the space of twenty-four hours.'

The upper floors of the tower had been converted into offices and a library. As they climbed to the roof, Daniel thought that the Dumelows were not like a couple who had been together a decade. They kept touching each other, brushing against each other, like lovers in the early days of infatuation, still acclimatising to each other's bodies. He took it as a good omen for his new life with Miranda. Maybe Brackdale really was a Shangri-La for lovers, removed from the everyday world where romance died all too soon.

The evening air was cool as they stepped out on to the flat roof of the tower, and Miranda shivered as she peered over the edge of the battlements. The ground seemed such a long way down. 'So this was where the locals stood to fire arrows or hurl missiles at their enemies?'

'That's right,' Tash said. 'Simon has this fantasy that he might do the same if ever any of his business rivals turn up outside our front door.'

'They'd never be fast enough to catch up with me,' her husband said. 'Now, how about that? Beautiful or what?'

Daniel surveyed the panorama beyond the cobbled courtyard and grounds of the Hall. From the gravelled drive, a track led to the farmhouse and a string of outbuildings. A separate lane linked the farmstead to the main road into the village. From the point where the lane petered out, the coffin trail led past fields where the sheep grazed quietly, towards Underfell. His gaze travelled along Priest Edge. The Sacrifice Stone, there was no getting away from the Sacrifice Stone. It stood on top of the ridge, an anvil awaiting a giant blacksmith.

'I met Tom Allardyce in The Moon under Water,' Daniel said.

Simon chuckled. 'Let me guess. He didn't buy you a pint and make you feel welcome.'

'Someone said he likes animals more than people.'

'That's about right. Although maybe it's not such a bad fault in a farmer. If foot and mouth had touched Brackdale, I'm sure Tom would have shot the men from the ministry rather than see his beasts destroyed. Allardyces have farmed in Brackdale for centuries, but he'd do better if he was less bloody-minded. We've had a few run-ins over the years. At least his wife's a treasure. We appreciate her even if he doesn't.'

'I gather he has a temper.'

'Poor Jean,' Tash said. 'She's such a decent woman. You'll meet her soon, she's cooking a wonderful meal for us. They're chalk and cheese, the Allardyces. Jean wouldn't say boo to a goose. As for Tom, one of these days I'm sure he'll square up to Simon, and then he'll have gone too far.'

'I've coped with worse in the building trade,' Simon said.

'Let's not talk about him,' his wife said. 'Welcome to Brackdale. I only hope you two will be as happy here as Simon and I have been.'

◇◇◇

'So how are you settling in to Tarn Cottage?' Tash asked as Jean Allardyce served blueberry swirl cheesecake.

The farm manager's wife kept scuttling in and out of the dining room like a nervy mouse. She was an excellent cook with a predilection for dishes that made Daniel put on weight simply by looking at them. That Tash retained her lithe figure was a tribute to her gym regime. The workouts must be ferocious to compensate for such a calorie-laden diet.

'Fine,' Miranda said. 'Of course, there's so much to do and we keep debating the choice of décor. Our tastes aren't exactly the same, but it would be boring to live with someone who had identical tastes. Like putting yourself through a Xerox machine.'

Daniel said, 'At least the place is habitable, after weeks of builders coming and going. God knows how the old woman who used to live there coped. It was so primitive.'

'Mrs. Gilpin spent all her life in the valley,' Tash said. 'A trip to Lancaster would have been like a visit to a foreign country. She didn't like change, did she, Jean?'

The housekeeper shook her head. 'She—she liked to keep herself to herself.'

'You grew up in the valley?' Daniel asked her.

'Yes, but we never had much to do with the Gilpins. The father died when Barrie was a baby. Barrie was a few years younger than me. His mother doted on him but tried not to let it show. She didn't want him to grow up spoiled and anyway, he had…problems. Everyone thought he was a weirdo, kept a distance. Though I couldn't help feeling sorry for him.'

Daniel nodded. 'He was likeable, once you got used to him. And no fool, just a bit naïve.'

Tash's eyes widened. 'You talk as though you met him.'

'I stayed here when I was a boy,' he said. 'For a couple of weeks, Barrie and I became friends. I enjoyed his company. He was gentle, wouldn't hurt a fly. I find it hard to imagine how he could ever have committed any act of violence. Let alone such a barbaric killing.'

'Coffee?' Jean Allardyce asked. Her voice was croaky, as if the mere mention of the murder was enough to bring back distressing memories.

'Black for me, please,' Miranda said. 'So you knew the Gilpins too, Tash? Before the girl was murdered, I mean?'

'Well.' Tash nibbled at her lower lip, as if regretting having said too much. 'We've tried to become part of the local scene.'

'It's taken ten years to make our neighbours realise that we don't want the place bulldozed to make room for a leisure centre or hypermarket,' her husband said. 'Even if only for selfish reasons, there's no way we'd ever want to spoil the valley.'

'And Barrie Gilpin,' Daniel said, dragging the conversation back. 'You came across him?'

'An oddball,' Simon said.

Tash frowned. 'That's unfair, darling. He was different, that's all.'

'Oh yeah? I remember you saying…'

'Look, I admit I found it difficult when you were away and there was no one else around here but Barrie. He could be scary.'

'He was a voyeur. He made you feel uncomfortable.'

Tash coloured. 'Even so, I didn't dislike him, not at all. He was—well, naïve. Child-like. I felt sorry for him. That's why I was happy for him to work here.'

'He worked for you?' Daniel asked. 'Doing what?'

'This and that,' Simon said. 'Painting and decorating. Helping Tom to clear out the pond every now and then. You could call it cheap labour, but it suited us and it suited him.'

Tash shook her head. 'You could say the murder was my fault.'

Daniel stared at her. 'What do you mean?'

'Listen, the truth is that Barrie Gilpin was pretty much unemployable, but I persuaded Simon to find him work to do. Big mistake. If he hadn't been hanging around here when Gabrielle Anders came calling, she'd be alive to this day.'

'Gabrielle was a friend of mine.' Tash gave a little shiver. They had moved from the dining area into the sitting room that adjoined the tower and were washing down a splendid meal with strong coffee. 'Even now, I hate to think about what happened to her—up on the fellside.'

'Sorry if I'm raking up bad memories,' Daniel said. 'It's just that I don't know the full story and from the fragments I've heard, I'm bound to be curious.'

Simon produced bottles of Drambuie and Irish Mist. When Miranda said that she was driving, he laughed and said, 'Don't worry. You won't find any speed traps or lurking panda cars in

Brackdale. The police are putting up cameras on all the main roads, the bastards. One more way to take money from us. But you're safe in the valley.'

'No thanks,' she said. 'I need my wits about me if I'm to negotiate all the bends and narrow lanes on the way home. I've already developed a habit of catching my wing mirror against the dry stone walls.'

'You'll keep us company, Daniel?'

Daniel hadn't tried to keep pace with his host's consumption of booze during the meal. Even so, he could feel his eyelids drooping. But alcohol might loosen tongues.

'Sure.'

As he filled each glass to the brim, Simon said, 'Tash hadn't seen Gaby for years until she showed up here.'

'Gabrielle.' His wife corrected him firmly. 'She always wanted to be called by her full name.'

'Sorry, darling. Well, Gabrielle had been living abroad and then she came back to England on holiday. She didn't give us any advance warning at all, even though…'

'Darling, that was just her way,' his wife interrupted. 'She loved to do things on the spur of the moment. I suppose that was one of the things I liked about her. Poor Gabrielle, she was so much fun, always.'

'It was a pleasant surprise when she turned up,' Simon said with a grin. 'I was working at home one afternoon. Tash had driven up to Ennerdale for a day's painting. The doorbell rang and I found this gorgeous lady standing outside. She told me she used to know Tash back in Leeds.'

'We both shared the same dreams,' Tash said. 'We fancied ourselves as actresses. Failing that, as models. Magazine front covers, television, you name it. Of course it never happened. We both did plenty of photo-shoots, but the big break never came.'

Miranda said, 'So you moved to Cumbria?'

'Gabrielle and I both drifted out of the business and we drifted apart as well. We were both sick of city life. I fancied moving to the countryside, Gabrielle decided to emigrate. Last time I heard from her, she was leaving for America. She wasn't good at keeping in touch, I didn't have an address or phone number for her. To be honest, I'd almost forgotten about her. So I hardly expected to come home one day and find her telling Simon all the embarrassing stories about the way I used to fluff my lines whenever I had an audition, even for the simplest voiceover.'

'Just think,' Simon said lazily, 'if your acting career had taken off, you could have a part in a soap instead of living out here in the middle of nowhere.'

'I know which I prefer,' Tash said. 'It was a wonderful surprise to see Gabrielle again. And so heartbreaking that she died such a cruel death.'

'Did she stay with you?'

Tash took another sip from her glass. 'We offered, but she'd booked into The Moon under Water for a few days and she didn't want to put us to any trouble. Or so she said. I did wonder if she liked having Joe Dowling follow her round with his tongue hanging out. When you've lived in Brackdale a while, Miranda, you'll find out what he's like. Anyway, Gabrielle was just bumming around, stopping off in the Lakes on her way further north. She said she'd seen more of America than her native country and she wanted to put that right. Later on, I couldn't help thinking, if only she hadn't looked me up on the off-chance…'

'You can't blame yourself,' Simon said.

'But Barrie met her through me. You can't deny that.'

Her husband shrugged. 'He didn't have a history of violence. Nobody could have foreseen the murder.'

'How did you come to introduce Barrie to Gabrielle?' Daniel asked.

'We'd asked him to varnish the pergola. He'd finished for the afternoon just as I came home from Ennerdale. When I drove into the courtyard, he was filling the bins. He always liked to chat and we were having a word when Simon came out with Gabrielle. When I saw her, I couldn't believe my eyes. There was so much to catch up on, but of course I introduced Barrie before the three of us went back inside. His jaw dropped at the sight of her. I could see at once that he was smitten, but it never occurred to me that there might be any harm in it.'

'He used to watch you,' Simon said. 'I guess he fancied Gabrielle just as much. I suppose there was a resemblance. Two tall, glamorous blondes, both totally out of reach so far as he was concerned.'

'Perhaps he didn't realise that Gabrielle was out of reach,' Miranda suggested.

'In his own funny way, he was rather sweet.' Tash nibbled at her lower lip, casting her mind back. 'Always trying to do little kindnesses for me. Trouble was, he was so clumsy that he usually made a mess of things. He made sure he bumped into her the very next morning. When he offered to show Gabrielle round Brackdale, it sounded like a ham-fisted chat-up line. She turned him down nicely, but I could tell he was upset. Unfortunately, he wouldn't take no for an answer.'

'It's a fault of our sex,' Simon said lightly, giving Jean Allardyce an affable nod as she returned to clear the coffee cups. 'Let's not spend the whole evening discussing the murder. Too depressing. Take it from me, Daniel, Tarn Cottage is a bargain, even with all the work it must need. I saw the price the agents were quoting and I'd have put a bid in myself, if it hadn't been for the memory of Barrie Gilpin.'

'So you believe he was guilty?' Daniel asked.

Simon drained his glass. 'He was the obvious suspect.'

'The obvious suspect isn't always the right one.'

A dismissive wave of the hand. 'Don't let it worry you. By the time you want to consider selling the cottage, his name will be long forgotten and there won't be any need to factor a discount into the price.'

Tash said quietly, 'You'd like to think that Barrie didn't kill Gabrielle?'

'I'm not convinced he was capable of it,' Daniel said.

There was a clatter as one of the cups slipped off Jean Allardyce's tray. Simon picked it up off the carpet and said, 'No harm done, Jean, it was empty already.'

Turning to Daniel he said, 'This is nothing to do with the fact that you're making a big investment in Tarn Cottage, by any chance?'

'Nothing whatsoever. I don't like trial by innuendo, that's all. Barrie Gilpin is everyone's favourite suspect, but he never had the chance to defend himself. It seems unjust.'

'He was never charged because he fell into a ravine before the police caught up with him, simple as that.'

'Maybe that was very convenient.'

'Who for?'

Jean Allardyce banged the door shut after her. Perhaps alarmed that the conversation had acquired a prickly edge, Tash said, 'I've been wondering, Daniel. I suppose it's pure coincidence, but...'

'What?'

'When Gabrielle was killed, Simon and I both talked to the police, as you'd expect. They needed to check on her movements and how she came to know Barrie Gilpin. I'll never forget the stink of the mortuary when I had to identify her poor broken body. I remember being comforted by the detective in charge of the case, he was called Kind too. It's not such a common surname...'

'It's not a coincidence,' he said. 'Ben Kind was my father.'

'I don't think it's the best way to make friends, that's all,' Miranda said an hour later. She'd driven back to Tarn Fold with an elaborate caution intended to compensate for the effects of a couple of drinks, but without any luck. In the darkness she'd clipped a jutting wall with her bumper, and her humour had suffered even more than the paintwork.

'They were happy to talk,' Daniel said as he unwrapped Tash's gift from its packaging. It wasn't a bad picture, he decided, but probably best not inspected too closely. 'All I did was ask a few questions.'

'You sounded like a bloody police officer yourself,' she grumbled. 'As for happy, I wouldn't count on it. Simon looked distinctly pissed off and poor Tash seemed quite embarrassed by the end.'

'We'd had a few drinks.'

'Even so. They obviously couldn't understand what had prompted Ben Kind's son to move to Cumbria and buy Tarn Cottage.'

'I did try to explain.'

'Well, I'm not sure they believed you,' she snapped. 'It must be very hurtful for Tash, when the woman killed was an old friend. They obviously feel responsible for having introduced Barrie Gilpin to Gabrielle. People want to forget a tragedy like that, not be cross-examined on it.'

'I spent years teaching students to challenge assumptions,' he said. 'I'm sure the Dumelows can take it.'

Miranda snorted. 'I don't want us to finish up without a friend in Brackdale. Surely you've found out as much as you need to about Barrie Gilpin and his murder? There can't be any more questions to ask.'

'There are always more questions to ask.'

'But why? It's not as if you've been commissioned to write up the case for an academic journal.'

He laid the painting on the table and gave her his full attention. 'I want to know if Barrie Gilpin really was guilty.'

'Does it matter?'

'Hey, I thought you always took the side of the underdog.'

'Yes, but…'

'Well, then. I've explained why it matters.'

'Oh yes, I understand about your dad and everything. But it was such a long time ago.'

'It's what I do, looking into what happened a long time ago,' he said patiently. 'I'm a historian, remember?'

Tears were forming in her eyes. 'You came here to get away from all that.'

'No.' He hated to see her cry, but she wasn't thinking straight. Why didn't she understand? 'Sorry, darling, but we discussed this endlessly before we even put the deposit down on the cottage. I wanted to escape from all the stuff that surrounded me in Oxford, and in the media. As well as the business with Aimee. Just like you wanted to get away from problems at work and your affair with Richard. But you weren't escaping from writing, any more than I was escaping from *history*. I couldn't do that.'

'So,' she said wearily. 'Are you going to keep on upsetting people?'

'You mean, am I going to keep asking questions?' he said. 'Well, yes. I can't stop now. Not until I start getting answers.'

Chapter Ten

Hannah was on the phone, trying to unravel the mystery of why her computer had crashed for the fourth time since lunch, when Nick Lowther strode into her room, flourishing a sheet of paper. *Later*, she mouthed, but he stood his ground. Drumming her fingers on the desk as she listened to a jargon-freighted explanation as unfathomable as it was unconvincing, she found another outlet for her frustration by glaring at her sergeant and shaking her head.

'You'll want to see this,' he murmured. 'Promise.'

At last the technical guru surrendered with a grudging promise to look into the problem. Hannah hung up and said, 'What have you got?'

He handed over the sheet and she saw it was a typed note of a telephone conversation. A dedicated telephone hotline had been set up with some fanfare, as part of the awareness campaign surrounding the launch of the cold case review unit. Members of the public with information about any unsolved serious crimes in Cumbria had been urged to call. Predictable as rain on a bank holiday, the response had been a deluge of crank messages and hoaxes. Baseless hints, malicious allegations and wildly improbable confessions to felonies both known and hitherto unimagined had flooded in. The team had anticipated this in discussion before the media conference. The tedious task of sifting out time-wasters was the price to be paid for soliciting the community's help. Infinite patience was essential when panning for gold.

The hotline was a direct dial-in straight to the Cold Case Review Team's office. The only snag was that the team wasn't big enough to man the phone 24/7, so anyone calling outside normal working hours found themselves talking to an answering machine. Each morning the tape was studied and calls returned by one of the DCs. If the phone rang during the day, it would be picked up by whoever was nearest. Because the calls didn't go to the main station control room, routine taping was out of the question. Too much grief under the human rights legislation. The DC had to scribble notes during the conversation and then decide whether they deserved to be written up.

'So Maggie took this call,' Hannah said to herself as she scanned the notes.

'And she decided it was worth a further look, even though the woman didn't give her name.'

Typical Maggie, Hannah thought. Of all the DCs in the team, she was the most painstaking. So much so that Bob Swindell regarded *her* as a pain. Even her typing, every comma in the right place, was so meticulous that it put full-time secretaries to shame. Whereas Linz and the two men tended to rely on instinct, Maggie Eyre didn't believe in taking chances. She was a hoarder by nature: rumour had it that she'd never thrown away a school exercise book, recipe, or knitting pattern. In the course of an inquiry, she never discarded any scrap of information until she could be sure that it wasn't viable as evidence. Better safe than sorry, she argued, although Hannah feared that if everyone were equally cautious, the investigation would become even more cluttered than Marc's book-stuffed attic room.

According to the note, a redial established the call as having been made from a phone box in the square at Brack.

Caller: I read in the paper about those…cold cases. Something has been on my conscience all these years, although I never said a word to a living soul. Not even…well, I was just afraid of what would happen and besides, I didn't want to believe…maybe I'm wrong anyway, wrong in what I think. There could be an innocent explanation for what I saw. I've always hoped so. All the same, it's been weighing on my mind.

Eyre: Take your time.

Caller: Thank you. I'm sorry. I shouldn't be doing this.

Eyre: There's no need to worry. You're doing the right thing. I'm not going to hang up on you. This is all in strict confidence.

Caller: Well, you say that, and I'm sure you're trained about confidentiality. But how can I be sure? This is serious. I don't even think I ought to be talking to you at all. It's not right. Oh God, all this time and worry and I'm still not thinking straight.

Eyre: One thing at a time. Can you just give me a few details? If you could just tell me who you are…

Caller: I can't give my name. I'm sorry, I really am, but I don't want to get involved, not any more than I am already. I shouldn't even be making this call.

Eyre: You have some information about a crime, a crime that wasn't solved?

Caller: Yes, a girl was killed here in Brackdale. Murdered. Her name was Gabrielle.

Eyre: When was this?

Caller: Seven years ago, it must be. You'll have the records, anyway. The papers were full of it. The thing is, your people thought they knew who did it.

Eyre: Someone was arrested?

Caller: No, he died. An accident, I think, but some folk say he killed himself out of shame. Couldn't live with the guilt.

Eyre: What was his name?

Caller: Barrie, Barrie Gilpin.

Eyre: And you say that Barrie Gilpin…

Caller: Everyone blamed him, said he'd murdered her because he was a pervert. But he wasn't, he was kind, he just had problems, that's all. It was so—so *unfair.* What I saw...oh God, I felt so terrible when I...

Eyre: Please don't upset yourself. It's all right, it's not...

Caller: I'm sorry. I just can't do this.

Eyre: Don't cry, madam. You can take a break, we could speak later on, when you've had a chance to calm down. Please, would you just tell me this. How can I get back to you?

Call terminated.

'Now you see why I thought you'd want to know straight away?' Nick asked. 'I remember you telling me how Ben Kind obsessed about the case. He didn't buy the official line, that Gilpin was responsible.'

Hannah nodded. 'He always said that our job in a murder case is to see justice done for the victim. It plagued him like an ulcer, the thought that he'd failed her.'

'He was waiting for a call like that.'

'One piece of information, that's what he reckoned, we just need one little titbit of evidence to show that Barrie Gilpin couldn't have been the culprit. Marc and I were talking about Barrie only the other night. And now a call has come, but Ben wasn't here to take it. Question is—is this *the* call? Or just a red herring?'

'What do you make of what the woman has to tell us? She doesn't exactly give much away.'

'She says *here* in Brackdale, which suggests she lives there. If Maggie's note is accurate.'

'It will be. And we're told that the woman *saw* something.'

'Which she may have misinterpreted. Or invented.'

'Okay, it's not much, but Maggie thought...'

'She was right to make the note. What else does she have to say? You and I both know that most anonymous callers are just out to cause problems. Either for us or someone they have a grudge against.'

'Maggie said the woman seemed genuine. Genuinely worried, anyway.'

'Age?'

'Maggie thought thirtysomething. Flustered, but then plenty of people are when they call us. She spoke slowly, the sentences were nervous and broken. At least it helped Maggie to make a good note.'

'She did well. Even so, the woman couldn't have given us much less to go on.'

'True.' Nick nodded at the note. 'Bin?'

'Of course not. Listen, I'm not jumping to any conclusions. This may be a dead-end, probably is. Fingers crossed, she'll ring again. Brief the team, just in case anyone else answers the phone if she rings back.'

'Already done.'

'And we need to dig out the old files on the case, see whether anything jumps out at us.'

'I asked Maggie to set the wheels in motion. You'll have them on your desk first thing tomorrow.'

'You can read my mind.'

He winked at her. 'Spooky, huh?'

She grinned. 'Scary.'

After Nick had left, Hannah tried to finish entering up her replies to a diversity monitoring questionnaire. Impossible: the memory of Gabrielle Anders' dead face blotted out everything else. She had been pretty once, even her passport photograph couldn't conceal that, but someone had hated her enough to destroy her looks as well as her life.

Gabrielle had been killed a fortnight after Hannah's promotion to sergeant. It was the first time she'd ever worked with Ben Kind on a murder. Until then, she hadn't known him well. People tended to be wary of him, and although she'd been advised to keep her distance, she couldn't help being intrigued by his reputation. Everyone reckoned he was a good cop, tough and relentlessly honest. Too honest, Hannah decided, to make it right to the top. You needed to be a bit of a diplomat if you wanted to build a brilliant career. Professional competence could only take you so far. His Achilles heel was that single-minded focus on catching criminals. It didn't allow time for winning friends or influencing people. Worse, he was famous for not suffering fools gladly, even if the fool in question was responsible for his annual performance review.

She would never forget that first day up by the Sacrifice Stone. The picture remained as vivid in her mind as a snapshot stuck down in an album, and at the same time as unreal as a dream. Even by mid-afternoon, the mist had not quite cleared. She remembered the cold bite of the winter on her cheeks as she patrolled the crime scene perimeter, watching scenes of crime officers in their white suits, moving along the slope of the fell like ghosts. She had to watch every muddy step. The downpour was washing traces of the crime away and yet the gathering of evidence could not be rushed, lest something was missed. Walkie-talkies hummed, above the valley a helicopter droned. Whenever the photographer's flashbulb popped, she shut her eyes, but each time she opened them again, the corpse was still there. Anger stabbed her like a knife in the ribs, at the sight of the naked limbs splayed across the top of the boulder. The victim's face had been hacked at and her head almost severed at the neck and now the poor creature was exposed to all these prying eyes. She was being photographed and probed and measured while her sightless eyes stared up to the heavens. No one treated her any more as a living and breathing human being. She had become an exhibit, a problem to be solved.

It didn't take the forensic specialists long to break the news that the victim hadn't died here. Trouble was, this information provoked more questions than it answered. Most murderers move their victims for the purpose of concealing their crime. Not this one. If fell-walkers hadn't been deterred by rain and the thick morning mist, Gabrielle's body would have been found even sooner. So what was the purpose of bringing her here? A symbolic ritual? An ironic nod to the myths of a godless past?

Hannah remembered wild conjectures jumping in her brain like fire crackers. She knew better than to voice her ideas. Ben Kind was a Puritan amongst detectives, addicted to facts and scathing about enthusiasts who got off on theories. Speculation was a dangerous self-indulgence in his book, draining an investigation of time and resources, leeching all the energy out of it. No one ever solved a crime by guesswork. You might as well hire a psychic or peer into a crystal ball.

As Hannah exchanged a word with the DC recording the scene on video, she kept an eye on Ben Kind. He was standing on the fell-side, arms out-stretched, directing his team to their tasks as though conducting an orchestra. Nothing about his gestures was flamboyant, but his self-assurance was unmistakable. She didn't see anyone to whom he gave an order hesitate or ask questions. They did what they were told, not out of fear, nor even out of unthinking self-discipline, but because they knew that he was very good at his job. Although he might not have made it quite to the top of the greasy pole, Ben Kind commanded loyalty from those who liked him and respect from those who didn't. His face was a mask; you would lose a lot of money playing poker with him. But as Hannah moved away, she caught a hint of suppressed fury in the set of his mouth and jaw.

Within hours it emerged that Barrie Gilpin, who lived in the nearest dwelling, had disappeared from home. He was the obvious suspect and before long his body was found. Mystery solved? The powers-that-be were content: the press climbed off their backs and turned their attention to other stories. Ben Kind was unhappy, but there was little he could do. The inquiry ground to a halt. Barrie's death had cheated them all.

◇◇◇

Hannah hauled herself out of her chair. While wading through the reports about the most promising calls to the hotline, she'd missed her lunch and now the hunger pangs could no longer be ignored. Maybe she'd cope better with the bureaucracy if she had something in her stomach.

In the canteen, she bit into a Cox's orange pippin. In her head she could hear Ben's voice.

'*Everyone remembers who was in charge of an undetected murder.*'

He never spoke a truer word. Failure to trace a murderer gnawed away at any senior investigating officer who cared about the job. Sometimes he'd talk to her about it, and once she asked how he squared his doubts about who had killed Gabrielle with his mistrust of intuition.

'Don't take this the wrong way, but is it just because your son played with him as a boy?'

Without flinching, he said, 'I never said that there's no room for a detective's instinct. Gut feel, based on experience, it's the most valuable asset we've got. When you analyse it, a sound instinct is always based in fact. Like Barrie's record of violence.'

'He hasn't got a record of violence.'

'Shades of the dog that didn't bark in the night-time. A crime like this doesn't come out of the blue. Ask any profiler.'

'I thought you loathed profilers.'

'The ones who let their imagination run away with them, sure. Barrie Gilpin was a mystery to most folk in Brackdale. He could seem cold and he was often rude. It's the nature of the condition, I've read up on it. But none of that makes a young man a murderer.'

'We know that he fancied Gabrielle.'

'And that he'd made a play for a number of girls in the village, most of whom turned him down flat. Sometimes mockingly. Each time he crept away with his tail between his legs. He must have felt wounded, but he didn't threaten any of them, let alone harm a hair on their heads.'

'One witness said he was a Peeping Tom.'

'Okay, so he might have liked to hide in the bushes and wait for a pretty woman to take her clothes off without bothering to draw the curtains. Not very nice, but it doesn't mean that he was a murderer.'

'His body was found near the scene.'

'He was the sort who was always likely to be in the wrong place at the wrong time. If that's what happened here, someone took advantage of him to get away with murder.'

◇◇◇

'Penny for 'em.'

Lost in the past, she hadn't even heard Les Bryant march up to her table. He plonked down his polystyrene cup and sat down opposite her without asking if it was all right. As yet she hadn't made up her mind how to play things with him. He was leaving it to her to speak first. Elbows on the Formica surface, jaw cradled in his palm, studying her face as if it were a cipher that he'd been tasked to decode.

Pushing her plate aside, she said, 'We had a call about a case I once worked on.'

'Yeah, I heard. You and Ben Kind.'

'You knew him?'

'Our paths crossed a long time ago.' Bryant pondered and for a moment she wondered if he was teasing her, making her await his verdict. Had he—somehow—picked up on gossip about her and Ben? It seemed unlikely, but after all, he was a detective. 'Yeah, he was all right. So—what do you think he would've made of Sandeep Patel?'

The question knocked her off balance. She took a breath, telling herself not to let this man rattle her. That was his game, for sure. He'd been asking questions, checking up on the woman he was supposed to report to. He meant to see what stuff she was made of, test her out. No way would she let him walk all over her.

'He'd have wanted to see him put behind bars. If you mean, would he have taken the risk of staking so much on Ivan Golac's confession, God only knows. I think he'd have done the same as me.'

Bryant shrugged. 'Maybe.'

The smart thing was to leave it there. She didn't want to be forced on to the defensive, but he'd succeeded in needling her.

She couldn't help saying in a cold, flat tone, 'Hindsight's wonderful, but someone had to take a stand. No regrets.'

Swinging on his chair, he said, 'Suppose that's right. Tell you the truth, I'd have done the same myself.'

He had this knack of taking her by surprise. 'You reckon?'

'What was there to lose?'

'Vast amounts of public money.' She hesitated. 'Credibility. Career progression.'

Did she detect the glimmer of a smile? 'So you think that this new job is all about keeping you out of harm's way?'

'The thought's crossed my mind.'

'Mine too.' He shrugged. 'Doesn't matter. It's still an opportunity.'

'You'll be telling me to think positive next.'

A bite of cynical laughter. 'I don't give a toss for all that motivational crap.'

'Well, then.'

He jerked a thumb in the direction of his heart. 'If you ask me, a detective's either got it *here* or he hasn't. You wanted Patel locked up. It didn't work, but I'll bet you had him wetting himself for a few months.'

'That's not the object of a prosecution.'

'No, but it's not a bad consolation prize.'

She laughed as she thought back. 'You should have seen his face the day he was arrested. Sheer panic. That's when I thought—*yes, you're guilty!* For a while I believed, I actually believed, we were going to get the right verdict.'

'You know what they say about the judicial process.' He made a face, as if spitting something out. 'A system designed to find out which is the better of two lawyers. Tell you this, though. I don't see it as a game.'

'Meaning what?'

'Meaning, I don't see this as a way of competing with the poor sods whose inquiries got nowhere in the past. Like your old boss and that murder up on the fells. We've not been put on this review team to see how clever we can look, thanks to all the modern forensic stuff. That's not what I'm about.'

'Nor me.'

He belched comfortably. 'Thought not. You ask me, this is more like a chance for us to put things right. I've never been keen on loose ends. Let alone the thought of people getting away with murder.'

Chapter Eleven

Driving home through a spring storm, Hannah wondered about coincidences. First, Ben Kind's son had moved into Barrie Gilpin's old cottage; then a nameless woman had suggested that Barrie was innocent of murdering Gabrielle Anders. Hannah could not imagine what might connect the two events, could not conceive what had brought Daniel Kind to the Lake District now that his father was dead.

Rain pounded her windscreen. She swore and screwed up her eyes as the lights from an oncoming heavy goods vehicle dazzled her. As the lorry lumbered away into the distance, she pictured Daniel in her mind. Although she rarely watched television, she'd caught a couple of his programmes. She'd been curious about the boy she'd heard Ben speak of. The physical similarities between father and son were subtle, the resemblance more apparent in their quick, urgent movements than in physical build or shape of jaw. They shared a sharp sense of humour and she guessed that they would laugh at the same jokes. Daniel's thesis that a historian was a sort of detective intrigued her. He must care as passionately about uncovering secrets of the past as Ben had about solving crimes.

Passion. Yes, that was the word that came to mind when she thought of Ben. He was a tough, demanding boss but fiercely loyal to his team. Hannah had been devoted to him. The drift of thought made her shiver, even though the inside of the car was warm. She and Ben had never had an affair. There had been times when she'd speculated about what it might be like, moments when he'd given the impression that he thought of her as a woman, rather than just as a loyal and industrious subordinate. Once or twice he'd touched her on the arm or back. Maybe it was accidental, but she'd found the *frisson* scary as well as exciting. He'd never gone further and she'd never given him any encouragement; Marc's jealousy of the time she spent with Ben weighed her down enough without an additional burden of guilt to bear. Besides, Ben already had one broken marriage behind him, and Cheryl back at home. She had Marc. Why spoil everything for the sake of a quick fling?

Sometimes she wondered whether the careful way in which they avoided flirting with each other was in itself a sign that their relationship might easily trespass beyond the professional boundaries. But nothing ever happened; after he retired she kept in touch, but didn't often find the time to see him. When she'd heard of Ben's death, she'd sat cross-legged on the staircase at home and surrendered herself to a good old-fashioned cry. Thank God Marc had been out that day. He'd have been sure that he'd had good cause to suspect her of infidelity. Even now, in lonely moments she interrogated herself, wanting to know if it really would have hurt anyone, if she had just slept with Ben once or twice. She still wasn't sure of the right answer.

She slowed to a crawl as the lane bent first one way and then another. In this downpour it would be so easy to skid and go through a hedge or smash into a stone wall. At last she could see lights in front of her and she knew that she was almost home. Marc would be absorbed in his catalogue; it was her turn to cook their meal. Not so many years ago, she'd ached to see him even after the shortest separation, and to this day she loved to stroke his fine hair, to run her fingers along the smooth contours of his naked back. This evening, he was more likely to fall asleep in front of the television than to start kissing her all over as a prelude to making love. The trouble was that life kept getting in the way. Her job, his job, pointless arguments about who had more time to deal with a flooded washing machine or a blocked drain. Maybe every couple went through these phases, but it reminded her of being stuck in a traffic jam. No sign of movement on the road ahead.

Over coffee, she decided to tell Marc about the anonymous call. In their early years together, whenever she talked about her latest case, he'd been as rapt as if she'd been describing the discovery of a fabulously rare first edition. Sometimes she worried that she said too much to him, but a couple shouldn't have taboos, and she had to trust the man she loved.

'Attention seeker,' Marc diagnosed after she recounted the conversation between Maggie and the woman. 'Craving the limelight but too frightened of being found out as a liar to go through with it.'

Even if he were right, Hannah was sorry that he wasn't intrigued. The Gabrielle Anders killing had been the first murder case she'd been involved with after meeting Marc. They had only been sleeping together for a few weeks and she hadn't yet moved in here, the house that he'd been born in and inherited after his parents' death. She'd confessed to him—and to no one else, certainly not Ben Kind—that blended with her horror at the brutality of Gabrielle's killing was not only a grim resolve to see justice done but also a shivery excitement from being at the heart of the investigation.

Taking advantage of his knowledge of the area, she'd speculated aloud about the significance of the draping of the body over the Sacrifice Stone the night after its discovery. They'd stayed up most of the night while he recounted all he knew of the history of the ancient landmark and the obscure legends about virgins slain each year in return for a guarantee from the old gods that the valley would remain fertile forever. Life coming out of a death, he'd told her, is the most potent myth of all.

'Maggie's not soft,' she said stubbornly. 'When I quizzed her, she was convinced the woman was genuinely wanting to help, and genuinely afraid.'

'What would she be afraid of after so long?'

'Suppose she'd seen a husband or a lover behaving in a way that made her suspicious. Or a *former* husband or lover, someone who's fallen out of favour in the meantime. How about a work colleague or neighbour? That's the upside of cold case investigations. Witnesses may be tempted to come out of the woodwork when they wouldn't have contemplated talking to us at the time of the original investigation. I'll never forget the sight of poor Gabrielle Anders and comparing the photographs of her when she was alive. She'd been so pretty once. Not too difficult to understand why our caller might be frightened, is it?'

'Where do you go from here?'

'To the old files, and the original exhibits. I'll crawl over the statements while Nick sees if any of the evidence can be improved forensically with the new techniques.'

'I thought you never had much luck with forensic stuff linking Gilpin to the crime?'

'Clothing fibres were found at the scene. A few hairs. He'd been up by the Sacrifice Stone on the night of the murder, we were confident we could prove that. The fact he'd gone missing and his body turned up nearby seemed like a bit of a giveaway.'

'To say nothing of the murder weapon.'

'The most damning evidence we had. If you remember, the pathologist reckoned that Gabrielle was killed by a blow to the head and then post-mortem her face was struck and her neck cut by the axe we found.'

Marc nibbled at a hangnail. 'He'd hidden it near a cairn on the fell-side, hadn't he?'

'*Someone* had hidden it. Even Mrs. Gilpin couldn't deny that it was Barrie's axe. The only question was whether it had been stolen to commit the crime. Not impossible.'

'But unlikely.'

'Stranger things have happened. Ben kept pointing out that if you wanted to frame someone for a murder, Barrie was an ideal candidate.'

'He didn't like to be proved wrong.'

'Nothing was proved either way,' she snapped. At once she wished she'd kept her mouth shut. Why must she always rise to the bait whenever he had a dig at Ben? In a calmer tone she added, 'He wanted everyone to keep an open mind, that's all. Which is precisely what we ought to do now.'

He yawned and stretched out a hand for the TV remote control. 'Best of luck.'

'You might like to rack your own brains.'

'What do you mean?' he murmured.

'Well, you were walking in Brackdale yourself that day, remember? Gabrielle was staying at The Moon under Water. Was there anything you noticed, anyone you saw, that was a little out of the ordinary? You might not have paid attention at the time, but with hindsight...'

The theme tune of his favourite quiz show was playing on the television. 'I'm sure I'd have mentioned it,' he said absently, his eyes shifting to the screen. 'It was just a normal afternoon as far as I was concerned. Nothing out of the ordinary at all.'

What if she'd been my sister?

Half a dozen file photographs of Gabrielle Anders were fanned out on her desk, but instead of inspecting them, Hannah was staring through the rain-streaked window. In her head she could see her father's pale face as he bent to whisper bad news in her ear. On the morning of her fourth birthday, her mother had miscarried. Years later, Mrs. Scarlett told her that the baby had been a girl. Hannah had longed for a younger sister, not least as an ally in the daily skirmishes with her insufferably superior elder sister, but Mum had never been able to carry a third child to term. Had the lost child lived, she would have been the same age as the dead woman.

That thought had sneaked into Hannah's mind during the dreadful afternoon up at the Sacrifice Stone. Gazing at Gabrielle's ruined face, she'd dug her nails into her palms, fighting to suppress her anger at such cruelty. A detective needed to remain detached. Soon she would have to attend the post-mortem, when the cold flesh would be cut to the bone, when organs and tissues would be explored with relentless attention to forensic detail. But Hannah could not bring herself to think of Gabrielle Anders as an exhibit and a source of clues. A few hours before, Gabrielle had lived and breathed.

She might have been my sister.

Who was she trying to kid? Turning back to the photographs, Hannah was forced to admit that she and Gabrielle were scarcely lookalikes. No point in bitching that it was wonderful what you could do with make-up, subtle lighting, and cosmetic dentistry. There was a gulf between them in *attitude*. You could see it in Gabrielle's almond eyes and in her high cheekbones, you could see it in the way she held her head. She was a predator. In one of the studio photographs, taken when she'd been an aspiring model, she gazed straight into the lens while her tongue peeped out and touched her upper lip. This was a woman savouring power, the power to stop a man in his tracks and make him do her bidding.

Hannah had always lacked that confidence. She could never tease men into watching her every move, and the thought of screwing her way to the top made her gorge rise. Anything that she achieved in her career would be thanks to her own efforts. The wild life hadn't been kind to Gabrielle in the long run. Easy to imagine that she had acquired the dangerous habit of thinking herself irresistible and that in the end it had cost her life. If the two of them had ever met, they'd have had nothing in common. Probably loathed each other on sight. They weren't sisters at all—yet Hannah could never quite rid her mind of the notion that fate had forged a bond between them. Victim and detective, thrown together by sudden death.

The door swung open, rocking on its hinges as Les Bryant strode in. As usual, he dropped into a chair without being asked. The little discourtesies were a habit, gestures to make the point that she might be in charge, but he had no intention of tugging his forelock to her. Fair enough, as long as he stayed on-side.

'Nice bit of stuff,' he muttered with a nod at the photographs.

'Not when I saw her,' Hannah said, sliding out of a plastic wallet a set of photographs taken at the post-mortem and shuffling them on to the desk. The corpse's face was scarcely recognisable, the lovely hair matted with blood.

He winced at the wounds on the swollen face. 'Vicious bastard. If Gilpin did kill her, what happened to him was poetic justice.'

'And if he didn't, then he's another victim.'

'You're not suggesting he was thrown into the ravine?'

'We never found a scrap of evidence that suggested his death was anything other than an accident. Suicide was an outside bet, so was murder. But the verdict at the inquest was accidental death and Ben Kind didn't disagree. He wondered if Barrie might have had a close encounter with whoever had killed Gabrielle. There were traces of her blood on his hand and sleeve…maybe he'd come across the body during a nocturnal ramble and fallen to his death while he was running away in panic.'

'Speculation,' Bryant said.

'Yeah, Ben had to admit he was pissing in the wind. Apart from any other consideration, Barrie was a strong, fit young man. Even if he'd stumbled across someone armed with an axe, he'd have had a good chance of showing him a clean pair of heels. But if Barrie was set up, we never came close to showing who did it, or how. We couldn't argue against the decision to run down the inquiry.'

'So what's changed? Yesterday's phone call doesn't take us too far.'

Us. At least he was thinking as a team member, not a devil's advocate whose first priority was to scoff at any fresh initiative. 'All I'm doing is taking a second glance. Nothing more. I can't justify devoting too much resource to something as nebulous as the message that Maggie took.'

Les Bryant leaned back in his chair. 'Time to look at the case from a different angle, then?'

'I think so.' Hannah pointed to the photographs. 'Starting with the victim.'

'How much do you know about her?'

'Not a lot.' Hannah sighed. 'Born and raised in the East End. Home a tower block, mother an occasional prostitute. She was one of four kids with three different dads. Before her tenth birthday, she was bunking off school. At fifteen she moved out and no one kept in touch. She seems to have followed a boyfriend up to Yorkshire.'

'The Promised Land,' Bryant said in his broadest West Riding accent.

'If you say so. She modelled a bit, tried a little acting. She'd ditched the boyfriend early on and he went back to London. We checked and he died of a drugs overdose a year before Gabrielle was killed. She mixed in bad company. The old story, plenty of men were keen to take a pretty girl to bed in exchange for a slap-up dinner and a few quid to help with the rent.'

Les Bryant plucked at a hair growing from his nostril. 'My daughter wanted to be an actress. Christ, the day she signed up with an agency, I hit the roof, but would she listen? They ripped her off something rotten. At least she finished up with an Oscar.'

'Really?' Hannah was startled.

'Yeah,' he said, deadpan, 'while she was resting, she took a job as a dental hygienist in Batley. Finished up marrying the dentist. Oscar Padgett.'

She laughed. 'There are worse fates.'

'Obviously you've never been to Batley.' He saw her glance at the post-mortem photographs. 'Matter of fact, I spoke to Jenny on the phone only last night, but you know something? It's six months since I last saw her face to face. Kids, bloody hell. You have any?'

His conversational swerves kept catching her on the back foot. She was starting to like the crusty old bugger, but she'd hate to be interrogated by him.

'Never got round to it.'

He puffed out his cheeks. 'Not bothered about the ticking clock?'

She shrugged and said, 'Neither of us is exactly desperate to start a family.'

Bryant said, 'Take it from me, there are more important things than the job.'

'Actually, I worked that out a while back.'

'Well, then.' His dour features were expressionless. Challenging her to get uptight, but she wouldn't be provoked.

'We were talking about Gabrielle.' She cleared her throat. 'While she was in Leeds, she met up with Natasha Litvinov. Tash Litvinov, as she was known. They had plenty in common, both struggling for a break.'

'Many are called, but few are chosen.' Bryant grunted. 'I told my Jenny, but would she listen?'

'Both of them became disillusioned, they decided to start again. Tash came up to this neck of the woods, met a rich man and settled down. Gabrielle wanted to get right away. She fancied trying her luck in the States.'

'Hollywood?'

'She never seems to have made it beyond Las Vegas. For a couple of years she lived with a croupier from one of the casinos. Most of the time she spent as a waitress, serving free booze to gamblers to keep them at the tables or the slot machines. The pay was nothing special, but a pretty girl can make a good living out of tips from the punters.'

'Why come back to England?'

'According to Tash, her relationship had broken up and she was getting homesick. She'd earned a few quid and had this idea of travelling around Europe. Britain was her first stop.'

'And her last.'

'Uh-huh. She'd only been back a week when she turned up on her old mate's doorstep. Tash had done well for herself, she'd married a property developer called Dumelow. He bought a mansion in Brackdale and played the local squire. After all those auditions, she finally landed the part of lady of the manor.'

'How thrilled was Tash to see a face from the past? A reminder of the dark days, before she met her sugar daddy?'

'She told us she was thrilled to have someone around she could gossip to about the past. She does her best, but the truth is, she doesn't exactly have a lot in common with the good folk of Brackdale. Though she did introduce her friend to an odd-job man who worked on the estate.'

'Don't tell me. Barrie Gilpin.'

'Got it in one. Barrie took a shine to Gabrielle from the moment he set eyes on her. He kept turning up at the pub in the village where she'd taken a room. According to the landlord, he was a bit of a nuisance. Constantly offering to buy her a drink, not taking no for an answer.'

'Did she show him up in public? Take the piss?'

'As far as we could establish, she humoured him, let him buy her the occasional orange juice.'

Bryant groaned. 'You can't help wondering if it would have been safer to be rude. He might have felt encouraged. Stalkers are like that. They take the slightest pleasantry as a sign of lust.'

'*Men* are like that, never mind stalkers.'

'You know what I mean.'

'I don't think he was stalking Gabrielle,' she said. 'He was just lonely and out of his depth. This glamorous woman with a Nevada tan had turned up out of nowhere and she didn't make him feel small when he tried to make friends. Of course, he was excited. That doesn't make him a murderer.'

'Easy for him to have become carried away. If he tried it on and she lost patience with him, who's to say that he wouldn't have snapped? He had access to the axe that killed her.'

'There's more. All the evidence pointed to the body having been moved. The Dumelows had a four-wheel drive that was stolen the day before Gabrielle's murder. We found it burned out in a remote wooded area. Barrie could have killed her and then used the vehicle to transport her up the coffin trail, within spitting distance of the Sacrifice Stone. Headlights in the dark can be seen for miles in a valley like Brackdale, but we couldn't find any witnesses. No big surprise, at that time of night, probably nobody was looking. Afterwards, so the official theory went, he hid the axe, dumped the four-by-four, and set off over across the fell-side. In the dark, he slipped into the ravine. He broke his legs in the fall and in any event the sides were too steep for anyone to climb out if they weren't kitted out with the proper gear. Death by exposure, everything neatly tied up.'

'Why go back up the fell? Why not go home and tuck himself up like a good mummy's boy? If Ma Gilpin was besotted by her only child, she might even have come up with an alibi.'

'Not her. She was so honest it hurt to take her statement. Trust me, I interviewed her. From the word go, she admitted that he'd been out most of the evening.'

'Do you think she was afraid he'd killed Gabrielle?'

'No way. She was convinced of his innocence, she never wavered for an instant. He wasn't capable of hurting anyone, she was adamant about that.'

'Not exactly evidence to stake your reputation on,' Bryant said with a weary sigh. 'I can see why pinning the crime on Gilpin was the only game in town.'

'But it wasn't,' Hannah said. 'Ben Kind was no fool. He'd have faced up to reality if nobody else was in the frame, but there were other candidates for the murder of Gabrielle, men with access to the four-by-four and the axe...'

'Tash Dumelow's husband, for one?'

'Simon Dumelow's made a lot of money in a rough business and when he was twenty, he picked up a conviction for actual bodily harm. But he's much older and apparently more civilised now. For a long time he's been paying other people to do his dirty work for him. We wondered if he'd made a pass at his wife's mate and reacted badly to rejection. But by all accounts he's always been genuinely crazy about Natasha, and even though she was laid up with flu at the time, she swore he never left the house that night. Then again—what if she was lying to protect him?'

'Who else?'

'Tom Allardyce, the tenant of Brack Hall Farm, Ben's suspect of choice. Tash had introduced him to Gabrielle Anders, just as she had Barrie. Eight years before Gabrielle was killed, he was charged with raping a girl he'd met in a nightclub in Carlisle. But the prosecution fell apart.'

'The way prosecutions do,' Bryant said grimly.

'Yeah, tell me about it.'

'Did he have an alibi for Gabrielle's murder?'

'You bet, again conveniently provided by a mate of his, the local publican. Man called Dowling. The investigating officers couldn't shake him and the CPS advised that if the case went ahead, Allardyce would walk out of court without a stain on his character.' A tinge of bitterness entered her voice. She couldn't help it; she was thinking not so much of Allardyce as of Sandeep Patel. 'Actually, those were the very words the lawyer used. I looked up the file.'

Chapter Twelve

'Why are you doing this?' Miranda's cheeks were crimson, her eyes packed with tears. 'What do you want to speak to her for?'

He placed the receiver back in its cradle and turned to face her. Sun was streaming into the kitchen through the narrow blinds, making him blink in the glare. The most beautiful morning since they'd moved in—and all of a sudden she'd lost it, absolutely lost it. He wanted to say *what's the problem?* but his mouth had dried. This was a landmark, as striking in its way as the Sacrifice Stone: their very first row. It had flared without warning, an explosion from an unsuspected spark. She'd walked in to the kitchen as he was dialling and when she asked, he said he was calling Hannah Scarlett. Thinking nothing of it, so that he was rocked on his heels when she cried out as though he'd smacked her. A mug of coffee slipped from her hand and crashed to the floor, splintering in jagged fragments, brown liquid eddying across the new diamond-shaped tiles.

Upstairs, Wayne had stopped hammering. He must have overheard. Daniel could picture the young builder's coarse features wrinkling with prurient amusement. He swore to himself. His shoulder muscles tightened with tension; he'd never seen her like this before. How to calm her down? He might have been a junior doctor, asked to diagnose from symptoms he'd never encountered before.

'You can't keep on with it,' she said, 'this constant…reaching back in time.'

But I told you, it's what I do, he almost said. *I'm a history man.* He ground his teeth, forcing himself not to throw more coal on the flames.

'We were supposed to be starting all over again,' she said. 'Clean sheets for both of us.'

'That's right. Of course. I never meant…'

'Then why hark after what's gone?'

'This isn't about Aimee. You're right, we agreed we had to get over everything that had gone wrong. Aimee, Richard. And it's working, we're doing fine. Talking to Hannah Scarlett is different, it's about…'

'It's about Barrie Gilpin! Your precious Barrie, the suspected murderer! You know something? It's finally dawning on me. You'd never have wanted to live here if it wasn't for *Barrie.*'

She was leaning towards him, pointing her finger. During the small hours, he'd been dimly aware of her restlessness. The smell of paint lingered in the bedroom and neither of them were sleeping well. In the early hours, she'd climbed from under the duvet and disappeared downstairs to make herself a drink.

She's overwrought, he said to himself. *All this work on the house, living 24/7 in a building site, it's enough to exhaust anyone. The noise, the dirt, the dust, they'd test the goodwill of a Mother Teresa clone. This isn't about me, or Barrie, or Hannah Scarlett. I just need to give her space.*

'Sorry, I know I've harped on about the Gilpins. This is our place now, not theirs. I never meant to hurt you.'

He reached out for her, but she stepped backwards, evading his grasp. Her foot slid in the pool of coffee and she gave a little yelp as she clutched at the table to keep her balance.

'Are you okay?' he asked. Not a clever question, but the best he could manage.

'No, I'm not okay.' As her head shook, her hair flapped in front of her face so that he couldn't make out her expression. 'I just feel I can't shake it off, this thought that a murderer lived here, in my house. I thought if we cleaned and painted and everything, the place would become ours. But Barrie Gilpin's clinging on like—like some sort of incubus.'

'Miranda…'

'There's no escaping him. Not when we go out to The Moon under Water. Not when we're invited to dinner by the Dumelows. We had the chance to make new friends and then you started asking about Barrie Gilpin and the evening was spoiled.'

'I'm sorry,' he said again.

'This isn't healthy, Daniel. You need to let go.'

'I don't care so much if Barrie was a murderer.' He surprised himself by saying this, but as soon as the words left him, he knew it was the truth. 'I liked him, but you're right, it was a long time ago. If he killed the girl, he deserved his fate, as everyone says. But I need to speak to Hannah Scarlett.'

'What for?'

'Dad and Cheryl were drifting apart, and his work meant everything to him. Maybe he confided in Hannah Scarlett. She can tell me about him.'

'But what do you want to know?'

'What he was *like*.'

Arms folded, she said, 'He's dead, Daniel. I hate to say it, but you need to move on. Start writing again, we can't live on fresh air.'

He swallowed hard. 'You're right. But first I want to talk to someone who knew him well. All I want to do is to fill in a few of the blanks…'

'Don't even try,' she said. 'Some mysteries aren't meant to be neatly solved, some questions don't have any answers. Leave them be.'

'I can't.'

She snorted with exasperation. 'I give up. There's no reasoning with you. All right, but don't blame me if you end up hurt. He did walk out on you, remember.'

'I remember.'

'A man who's capable of that is capable of anything.'

There was a knock and Wayne put his face around the kitchen door. As usual, he made it obvious that he was drinking in the sight of Miranda. In her clinging Levis, she always looked good, for all the blotchiness of her complexion and the rings around her eyes. Trying not to smirk—but not trying too hard—Wayne couldn't keep the *schadenfreude* out of his voice.

'All right, folks? Any chance of a cuppa, if you're not too busy?'

◇◇◇

'Hannah Scarlett.'

Her voice was low and cautious, as though he was calling to sell uPVC windows or a time share in Spain. As he'd waited to be put through, he'd wondered if she would instruct a minion to fob him off. He watched the sun play on the surface of the tarn as he pressed the mobile to his ear. Miranda had retreated to the bedroom with a headache but that hadn't stopped Wayne humming "Yellow Submarine". Daniel didn't have a game plan, other than to hope that curiosity would get the better of her when she was given his name. So far, so good.

'We've never met, but you worked with my father, Ben Kind.'

'That's right.'

'I moved to the Lake District recently and…'

'Yes, I heard.'

'I met Marc when I visited his shop.'

'He mentioned it.'

The conversation was becoming a ritual dance, the participants invisible to each other and unwilling to risk a false move. What might she look like, he wondered irrelevantly: another peaches-and-cream blonde, a younger Cheryl—or more like his mother, angular and dark?

'I suppose you're puzzled about why I should call you.'

'The thought's crossed my mind,' she said calmly, 'but I'm sure you're intending to explain.'

'You'll be aware that we've bought Tarn Cottage.'

'Uh-huh.'

Too late, he realised that he should have planned what he was going to say. He'd never give a lecture without adequate preparation and rehearsal, so why had he blundered into this without proper thought?

'It's just that…I'd love to talk to someone who knew my old man.'

'You could try his wife.'

'Been there, done that, come away with a flea in my ear. She's moved on.'

'I bet she has,' Hannah Scarlett said drily.

'She doesn't want to be reminded of the past. Or that I was part of his life before she took over.'

After a pause she said, 'He talked about you.'

His skin prickled with embarrassment. 'Not tediously, I hope.'

'Ben was never tedious,' she said. 'He was proud of you and of what you'd achieved. You should be proud of him.'

'I suppose so,' he said, 'which is precisely why I'd love to talk to you about him. Not over the phone, but face to face. Sorry, I know it's an imposition—but would you mind?'

Another pause. He guessed she was weighing up pros and cons. When she spoke again, her voice seemed to shrug.

'I don't see why not.'

He almost stammered out his thanks but something stopped him, an intuition that if he became effusive this woman would draw back into herself. Ben Kind had prized loyalty; that was why his desertion of his family had come as such a shock. Cheryl had been—well, an aberration. If Hannah Scarlett had earned his father's trust, she must be dependable and discreet. She'd keep her emotions on a tight leash and have little time for people who lacked the same control.

'When would suit you? Of course, I'll fit in with your diary. My time's my own and you must be rushed off your feet. Leigh Moffat told me that you've taken on a new project.'

'Oh, she did, did she?'

He discerned a touch of scepticism. Maybe she and Leigh didn't hit it off? None of his business, anyway. He said, 'You're in charge of a cold case team. It occurred to me that you might want to take a second look at the murder of Gabrielle Anders.'

'Now why would you think that?'

No surprise at his suggestion, he noticed, just a dead-bat response, a professional refusal to give anything away. Interesting.

'No reason, really. The party line was that Gilpin was the killer, but nothing was ever proved. So—when can I see you?'

He hated sounding like a bashful suitor, trying to fix up a date, but her reply was measured. No hint of playing hard-to-get.

'Today I'm busy, but I have a space in my diary tomorrow. Mid-morning in Kendal?'

'I could offer you lunch if you have time.'

'I'm not into social lunches, but I can spare you twenty minutes. I like to get out of the office for a breath of air every now and then, maybe we can meet by the river? Say half ten on one of the benches near St George's, overlooking Stramongate Weir?'

'How will I recognise you?'

'You don't need to, Daniel.' He noticed her use of his first name. 'I've seen you on the box, remember?'

'Fine, I'll look forward to it.'

'See you there.'

For a moment his skin tingled. It was almost as though they were arranging a secret tryst.

◇◇◇

Returning to the cottage, he scribbled a conciliatory note for Miranda and propped it up on the breakfast bar. There was still no sign of her downstairs and he didn't want to court trouble by disturbing her. Unseen, Wayne continued to slaughter the Beatles' repertoire and was embarking upon a tuneless rendition of "Can't Buy Me Love".

If he wanted to clear his head, there was no better way than by climbing up to Priest Edge. He made himself a sandwich which he put with an apple and a can of Bud into his rucksack. He changed into a zip-up jacket and the pair of virgin Timberland hiking boots kept by the kitchen door. He and Miranda had been so busy with the renovations and decorating out the cottage that they'd neglected more than their writing. As he'd tidied up loose ends in Oxford, he'd pictured them spending long afternoons of exploration on the fells, but so far it hadn't happened. Time enough for that, she said, once their home ceased to resemble a builder's yard. When that would be, he dared not guess.

As he stepped out into the garden, a bird flew out from the rhododendrons and dipped over the tarn before vanishing into the trees. At first he assumed it was a blackbird, but a glimpse of the crescent of white at its throat persuaded him that he'd spotted a ring ouzel. Uncommon, according to his RSPB guide. He'd make a twitcher yet.

Quickening his stride, he headed for the path that wound up the hillside to the Sacrifice Stone. After seeing its dark outline against the sky so many times, he'd decided it was time for another look from close quarters, time to retrace the steps of that first trek with his father, the day he'd met Barrie Gilpin. He would return to the valley by way of the corpse road, following a circular route past the Brack Hall farmstead before branching off on to the lane that led to the disused corn mill and ultimately Tarn Cottage.

By the time he was home again, with any luck not only would Wayne have departed but Miranda should be back to her usual self. They could make up after the quarrel. Talk, maybe watch the DVD he'd picked up in Kendal at the weekend.

Her usual self. As the path climbed, he reminded himself that they'd met such a short time ago. What *was* her usual self? Might the Miranda he thought he knew be someone of his imagining, might he have misled himself about her true nature? Even with the sun beating down on his forehead, the question chilled him. He told himself not to be stupid, that it was absurd to allow a single quarrel to provoke such doubts.

The path was sticky with mud after the rain of recent days, but even though the new boots were pinching, he made steady progress. Despite the fall-out with Miranda, he felt energy surging within him. He liked the sound of Hannah Scarlett. As he neared the top, the climb became steeper. He tripped over a twisted tree root and came to rest on a spiky clump of purple heather. When he looked up towards Priest Edge, the strange boulder was looming above him. With the ground falling away all around, it seemed like an island in the sky. From this perspective, it seemed that a single gust might topple it over and send it tumbling down the slope, crushing him and everything in its wake. But this was an illusion: nothing could shift the Sacrifice Stone.

In his head he conjured up images of silent worshippers trooping along the hillside, bearing the young girl to be surrendered to their deity when they reached Priest Edge. In return for a death, they hoped to be granted fruitful living. Daniel could not conceive what prayers might run through the high priest's mind as his acolytes laid the girl upon the rock and he unsheathed his knife, readying himself to slit her throat. And what of that other killer, who had mimicked the ceremony: had a current of cruel pleasure rippled through him as he brought the axe down on his unconscious victim?

Too much imagination could seriously damage your peace of mind. Time to move on. He picked himself up and five minutes later was scrambling over the last rough patch and clambering on to the summit of the fell. At last the grey bulk of the Sacrifice Stone squatted in front of him. At close quarters, the rock was smaller than in his childhood memories, but it occupied much of the narrow ridge, allowing space for no more than a couple of people to squeeze past on either side. He ran the tip of his index finger along the jagged rock. The Stone was a table resting on a base that lifted it clear of the ground. Finding temptation impossible to resist, he hauled himself up, so that he could sit on the smooth hard surface.

At once he experienced the adrenaline rush of being on top of the world. Scanning the panorama below, his heart beating faster, he might have been a king on his throne, surveying his realm. From his vantage point he could see the neighbouring valley of Whitmell, look over to the narrow cleft of High Gill and hear the rushing water of Brack Force. Shading his eyes, he gazed over Brack's green and pleasant land towards a distant strip of water that he recognised as Windermere.

Here it was much cooler than down in the valley; the breeze made his cheeks tingle. A couple of greying fell-walkers, kitted out for all weathers, approached from the direction of Old Scar. He guessed that they were traversing the Brackdale Horseshoe, an arc formed by the crags that enclosed the valley.

'Beautiful day,' he said.

The woman paused mid-stride to wag a finger. 'Better watch out for yourself, young man. You know the old story? If you climb on to the Sacrifice Stone, you'll look Death in the eye before the month is out.'

'I'll take care,' he promised. 'And if all else fails, I'll increase my insurance cover.'

She gave him a fierce glare before hurrying to catch her husband. Daniel recalled that his sister's book had mentioned the dire fate foretold for those who defiled the Sacrifice Stone. Of course he shouldn't have climbed it anyway. He scrambled off the boulder and, unfastening his rucksack, pulled out his makeshift lunch. There was nothing he could do to mitigate his breach of pagan protocol except, perhaps, to make sure he took his litter home.

The sun slipped behind a cloud and he found himself shivering. His fault for being beguiled by the brightness and neglecting to wear enough layers. After taking a couple of bites at his apple, he opened the can. The taste of the beer revived his spirits. He was wiping the foam from his mouth when a walker in a wine-red wind-cheater came into view. As the man trudged onward, his slender build and slightly jerky gait seemed familiar. So was the thick fair hair, flapping over his eyes.

'Well, well.' Marc Amos smiled as he neared the Sacrifice Stone. 'Do you come here often?'

'First time since we moved in,' Daniel said with an answering grin. 'What about you?'

'As often as I can make it. If you want to get away from it all, where better?'

'Shouldn't you be minding the shop?'

'We're closed today. If I were a good boy, I'd be checking inventory or visiting a couple of people with collections to sell, but frankly I was in the mood for a treat. After spending all weekend at a book fair up in Carlisle, I was longing for the chance to clear my head and get some fresh air into my lungs. What better way to do it than by walking the fells?'

'This place is hard to beat, I agree. So much crammed into—what, less than a thousand square miles?'

'Much less. I'm ashamed to say it's months since I last walked the Horseshoe from beginning to end. It's my favourite trek in the southern fells. Wainwright preferred the Kentmere Round, but even Homer nods. I like to linger on the way and soak up the atmosphere. When Wainwright was sketching the fells, he used to picture Roman legions on the march. I try to put myself in the shoes of the people who were here before the emperor's men. The hunter-gatherers and then the Celts.'

'Ten minutes ago, someone reprimanded me for climbing up on to the Stone in defiance of the old superstitions. All I wanted was the luxury of a magnificent view whilst I picnicked. I'd forgotten that I was taking my life in my hands.'

'You don't mind making waves, do you?'

'What makes you say that?'

'Leigh Moffat mentioned that you caused a fuss a few nights ago in The Moon under Water. When she went to the bar, the landlord and Tom Allardyce were discussing the way you'd been talking about the girl who was killed here. You'd riled them, they were saying it was none of your business. Although they didn't put it as politely as that.'

'Storm in a teacup,' Daniel said lazily. 'All I said was that Barrie Gilpin's guilt had never been proved. It's harsh to be condemned as a murderer when you've never had the opportunity to defend yourself.'

'You know better than most: history is written by the survivors.'

'Yes,' Daniel said. 'That worries me a lot.'

Marc gave a brittle laugh. 'Surely you can't expect people here to be thrilled at the prospect of stones being turned over? The girl's long buried, Barrie Gilpin, too. Time to let them rest in peace.'

'Will they be at peace if they've been cheated of justice?'

Pushing the hair out of his eyes, Marc said, 'If Barrie Gilpin was innocent, someone else must be guilty. For all we know, someone who is still living and working in the valley down there.'

Daniel gave him a long look. 'Having claimed two victims, Gabrielle and Barrie. Would it hurt to give that someone a wake-up call?'

Marc cleared his throat. 'Can I offer you some advice?'

'Feel free.'

'This isn't Oxford. With so many tourists clogging up the car parks, the Lakes might seem cosmopolitan, but under the surface a place like Brackdale is introspective. Claustrophobic. There's a lot of prejudice against people who come here from elsewhere and try to shape their surroundings to suit themselves. The locals have developed a carapace, it's a way of preserving their identity. As for Tom Allardyce, you don't want to get on the wrong side of him.'

'Our paths aren't likely to cross.'

'You don't understand.' The urgency of Marc's tone took Daniel by surprise. 'The man has a reputation for violence. Jean Allardyce has sported plenty of bruises over the years and they haven't all come from walking into doors. The army threw Tom out for brutality, and I'd guess that says it all. He beat up Barrie Gilpin more than once and from what Leigh tells me, he's taken a serious dislike to you. I hate to sound melodramatic, but you'll find you've made a dangerous enemy.'

Daniel watched Marc Amos striding off into the distance, his wind-cheater a red blob dipping between the rocks and eventually vanishing as Priest Edge fell away towards the depression of Far Gate. Below the fell's steep flank lay Whitmell Vale, a ravine-scarred trench watered by a meandering beck. The sheep-crowded fields and the isolated stone cottages scattered along the floor of the valley presented an inviting prospect. He'd save Whitmell for another day and keep to his plan to follow the coffin trail back to Underfell, that part of Brackdale that lay between the Hall and the slopes.

Centuries had passed since, with no consecrated ground in the Vale, Whitmell folk had strapped their dead on packhorses and taken them over the fell to a final place of rest in the graveyard at Brack. Eventually a small church boasting a neat spire was built to serve the tiny community, and thereafter the coffin trail served no useful purpose. For those travelling from Whitmell to Brack, the lane that curved between the jaws of the Horseshoe provided a quicker route from one hamlet to the other. Yet the coffin trail boasted an enduring virtue in its glorious views of Brackdale, and fell-walkers had never allowed the track to fade away through disuse.

The descent was easy and it did not take long for him to reach the foot of the fell. He crossed the beck that provided the grounds of Brack Hall with a natural boundary and skirted the Dumelows' land on his way to the village. While he looked over to the farmhouse, the front door opened. Jean Allardyce emerged, shopping bag in hand, and hauled herself into an elderly Land Rover parked on the hardstanding beside the house. As Daniel reached the end of the driveway, the vehicle pulled up beside him.

She put her head out of the window and called, 'Can I give you a lift?'

'That's good of you.' He was happy to walk, but as usual curiosity got the better of him. No harm in a short detour: Miranda wouldn't be counting the minutes until his return. 'If you could drop me off in the village?'

'No problem, I'm just on my way to Tasker's. Jump in.'

He clambered in beside her, taking in a faint freesia fragrance as she bent towards him to move a sheaf of travel brochures off the passenger seat. He hadn't taken much notice of Jean Allardyce until now and hadn't fully realised that, although timid and inconspicuous, she was a pretty woman with full lips and porcelain blue eyes. He found himself clenching his fists at the thought of Allardyce beating her.

'Booking your holidays?' he asked as she tossed the brochures into the back.

She smiled. 'Just weighing up the options. A harmless fantasy. Ever since I was a child I've had this dream of journeying across the Prairies, seeing the hidden corners of Indian Country. I blame Laura Ingalls Wilder, I used to love her tales about the pioneers.'

'You wanted to explore a different world?'

'Yes, it would be a dream come true. Places with names like Plum Creek and Silver Lake always seemed more enticing than Grizedale and Ullswater.' After looking each way with an unnecessary care that, he suspected, was a habit, she eased the Land Rover out into the lane. 'I suppose you find that hard to understand.'

'We all need a change, once in a while.'

'You're right. I've spent my whole life around here. I've seen nothing of the world. *Nothing.*' Her voice faltered. 'You won't believe this, but I've only ever been to London once, and that was on a school trip to see Madame Tussaud's and the Tower.'

'Miranda will tell you that you haven't missed much.'

'They say that familiarity breeds contempt.'

'Maybe not contempt, but...'

'I think contempt is the right word,' she said, unexpectedly fierce. 'Never mind, you've both taken a risk, leaving your jobs and your friends, starting all over again. It's very brave. Sometimes I wish I'd had that kind of courage.'

'I don't think we were brave. Rash, yes.'

'I suppose that at least you knew Brackdale. You were friendly with Barrie Gilpin.'

'That's right. He was a good companion.'

She said tightly, 'It's a shame that everyone remembers him—the way they do.'

'Your husband is very sure that Barrie killed the girl.'

'Tom's very sure about everything.' She added, as if it was an explanation, 'He was in the forces, you know.'

Daniel kept quiet, guessing that she hadn't picked him up out of mere altruism. She needed someone to talk to. He was aware of her trembling in the seat beside him, as if she were worrying that it was a step too far even to hint that her husband's judgment might not be perfect. Her eyes were locked on the road ahead, although even when it straightened, her speed did not exceed twenty miles an hour. Her natural caution was, he suspected, allied to a conscious fear of the consequences of doing the wrong thing. Anger welled up inside him as he contemplated the ways in which the strong may subjugate the will of the weak. But even if Allardyce used his fists to cow his wife, at least he had failed to rob her of the capacity for independent thought.

After a few moments she said, 'I felt sorry for Barrie, but after he died, there was nothing more anyone could do for him. Tom said it was all for the best.'

'Not if Barrie weren't guilty.'

'No, no.' Her voice broke. 'It ruined his mother's life, you know. Wrecked it. The way people turned from her, if she went into the village. No wonder she hid away. She was almost a hermit, by the end. The innocent always suffer, don't they?'

'Yes,' he said. 'They suffer most.'

'And yet, that's Tom's point. He says it's better to let sleeping dogs lie.'

'Do you agree?'

'I don't know,' she said unhappily, slowing as they approached the market square. 'I simply don't know.'

Joe Dowling, his tan apparently replenished by a spell under the sun lamp, came out of The Moon under Water, watering can in hand. He smirked at Jean Allardyce, but treated her passenger to a scowl. Jean edged around the marked-out spaces, but there was no sign of a gap in the rows of cars. A yellow Alfa had double-parked opposite Tasker's, and Daniel saw Tash Dumelow checking her rosy lipstick in the rear view mirror. As she caught sight of them, a broad smile spread across her face and she waved energetically in greeting.

Daniel waved back and said to Jean, 'What's she like to work for?'

'Over the years, Tash has been very kind to Tom and me.' To his surprise, Jean's reply was neither perfunctory nor dutiful, but oddly elegiac. 'We don't see that much of Simon, but they make a lovely couple. Tash may not have been to the manor born, but you couldn't wish for a nicer boss.'

Remembering the bitchiness of the Senior Common Room, he said lightly, 'So life in the Lakes isn't all bad, then?'

'Probably not,' she said. 'You really shouldn't take any notice of me. I'm—not myself at the moment.'

'Thanks for the lift, anyway. If you could drop me off around here…'

Greatly daring, Jean halted the Land Rover precisely over the double yellow lines. Daniel wouldn't have been surprised if she'd told him it was the first time in her life she'd flouted the parking regulations. Perhaps he was a good influence on her. She'd be farting in public next.

'Will this do?'

'Perfect. It's very good of you.'

'Think nothing of it,' she said absently. He could tell that her thoughts had flown away. To the little house on the prairie? 'I suppose it's true what they say. All good things must come to an end.'

Chapter Thirteen

The cottage was quiet as he reached their new front gate. His legs and back were aching after the long walk: too many years sitting in libraries, hunched over old manuscripts. He glanced at his watch: quarter past five, a later return than he'd intended. At least Wayne's rusty white van had disappeared, so there was no one else in the house. Pausing on the threshold, he took in a draught of air. Time to put things right with Miranda.

She was curled up on the living room sofa, in her white gown, listening to Sheryl Crow. As he walked in, she glanced up and gave him a little smile. He sat down beside her, so that their legs touched, and put his arm around her shoulder, feeling the bone beneath the towelling.

'I was about to have a bath,' she whispered.

Something was bothering her, he knew her well enough to be certain of it. Wanting to let her share it in her own time, he said nothing and waited.

'I feel dirty.' She bent towards him, so that her face nestled against his. He felt the dampness of tears on his cheek.

'What is it, Miranda?'

'It's—well, it's Wayne.'

A cold apprehension fingered him. 'What about Wayne?'

'After you'd gone, I went to bed. I felt so drained, I needed some sleep. When I woke up, it was after three o'clock and I had a headache. I came downstairs for something to eat and an aspirin and he was in the kitchen, making himself a drink. We were chatting, it was all very friendly, I didn't even mind that he'd stopped work. He was telling me that he was a keen angler, describing the excitement an angler feels when he catches something. I told him a bit about life in London. And then, just as I was starting to feel okay—well, he made a pass.'

Daniel tightened his grip on her. 'What did he do?'

She closed her eyes. 'He put his hands around me. I think he must have gone into the village for a drink at lunchtime whilst I was asleep. He pulled me towards him, his breath smelled of beer.'

Daniel could picture the young man's leering face, as he decided to take advantage of his opportunity. So many *if onlys* were passing through his mind.

Miranda kept talking, the words coming out faster as she remembered. 'It was just as if I was a carp he'd caught and he was reeling me in. I screamed and slapped his face. Daniel, I was out of my mind, I didn't know what he was going to do to me. He and I were all alone here and I didn't have a clue when you'd be back.'

Daniel swore. He didn't trust himself to speak.

'Thank God, he—he backed off, as though he couldn't believe I wasn't surrendering. His cheek was bright red where I'd hit him. It looked so absurd, I'd have laughed out loud, if I wasn't so scared. He turned on his heel, jumped into his van and drove off down the lane. Brakes squealing as he rounded the bend and disappeared. I called his firm straight away and told his boss what had happened. He promised to sack Wayne and asked if I wanted to tell the police, make a charge of assault. I said no, as long as I never have to see him again. The man said of course not. Eddie can finish the work.'

'Never mind the work. As long as you're all right.'

She took in a breath. 'I think so.'

'We must hire a different builder.'

'Don't make a fuss, I just want to forget it ever happened. Everything's sorted. It was awful, but it only lasted a few seconds. Now it's over.'

'Oh God, Miranda. I'm so sorry.'

'It's okay, darling. It's not your fault.'

'The bastard, the utter bastard. I shouldn't have left you here with him.'

'I'm a grown-up. Besides, he's a chancer, not a rapist. There was no real harm done.' She took a breath. 'He simply jumped to conclusions—about you and me. He thought he was in with a chance.'

'He was eavesdropping when we quarrelled.'

'I've been thinking about that,' she said, wriggling away from him so that they were standing face to face. 'Perhaps I was mean.'

'No, I shouldn't keep harping on Barrie Gilpin.'

'Like you said, it's about your father. If you do want to talk to this woman, this police officer, I can understand. If it's important to you, it's all right. You can go ahead.'

She was looking at him expectantly. The thought sneaked into his mind: *she wants me to say that I won't ring Hannah Scarlett, that nothing else matters to me but her.* At once he dismissed it as shameful and wrong.

'I didn't mean to upset you.'

'I shouldn't have ranted,' she said. 'It's just that…well, you know.'

'Things will be fine.'

'You're right,' she said eagerly. 'Let's put it all behind us. Wayne, the argument, everything. Let's forget all about them.'

'Sure,' he said. 'Go and have your bath. It'll do you good.'

'I was wondering,' she said. 'Do you want to join me? My hair needs a wash and I remember that time in Oxford, you did it so well, it really turned me on. Afterwards, we can make up properly, if you like.'

Doubts stilled, he brushed his lips against her cheek. Already the tears had dried. 'Yes, I would like.'

◇◇◇

In his dreams, he was lying at the foot of the Sacrifice Stone. His hands and legs were tied with rope and there was a gag in his mouth. Twilight cloaked the fells, but he didn't feel cold. He was trembling because he was afraid what would happen next. As he waited, a blurred face entered his line of vision and a knobbly finger wagged at him.

'I warned you not to come up here.'

The woman he'd met walking on the fell had turned into a witch. Her nose was beaky, her cheeks speckled with warts. She began to cackle, baring huge yellow teeth.

'You only have yourself to blame, young man. You did not heed the legend.'

She glanced beyond him, as though something had caught her attention. He strained hard so that he could turn his head. The muscles in his neck were sore and tears stung his eyes.

A small crowd of people was approaching along Priest Edge. Tom Allardyce was at the front, manhandling a naked girl towards the Sacrifice Stone. Her hair was long and blonde and he knew that it was Miranda, Miranda in her teens. Some of the faces in the gathering were familiar: Wayne the builder was there, and the Moffat women, Tash and Simon Dumelow, and Joe Dowling and his wife-to-be from The Moon under Water. Their faces were alight with excitement, but on the fringe he saw Jean Allardyce weeping quietly. Her husband grinned at Daniel, then ran his hands down Miranda's sides. Her legs were matchsticks, her breasts mere buds.

'Tonight she is a virgin once again,' the witch hissed in his ear. 'It is as if you'd never touched her.'

Miranda's face turned to him. Her complexion was pale and flawless, her eyes wide with terror. As he tried in vain to move, she cried out in despair.

'Why did you have to do this? Why couldn't you let well alone?'

He wanted to answer, to explain and to apologise, but the gag made it impossible to speak. Exhausted, he could do nothing but watch as the mob lifted Miranda up on to the top of the Sacrifice Stone. Wayne and Joe Dowling stepped aside and a man garbed in a flowing robe emerged from the middle of the crowd. A shaft of moonlight fell on him and Daniel recognised Marc Amos. In one hand he held an open leather-bound tome and he was chanting something incomprehensible. In his other hand a sharp blade glinted.

Miranda screamed, shattering the night.

At once he was awake, clutching her warm bare body, saying a prayer of thanks under his breath as he ran his fingers over her back and thighs, proving to himself that they were safe together after all.

'What is it?' she murmured dozily.

'Nothing,' he said, 'just a bad dream. Everything's going to be all right.'

Next morning he headed off towards Kendal before eight, stopping on the way at the builder's. He'd told Miranda about his meeting with Hannah Scarlett, but she seemed more bothered about Wayne losing his job as a result of her complaint to his boss. She even said that, having slept on it, maybe she'd over-reacted, perhaps she should have been flattered.

The yard was an Aladdin's cave of timber, bricks, and breeze-blocks, overseen from a hut in the corner by the proprietor of the firm, Stan Mustoe, a stout and balding Geordie in outsize denim jeans and a gravy-stained tee shirt. Over the racket made by two brawny youths loading a pick-up truck with planks, he proffered apologies for Wayne's behaviour and said he'd given him the sack by way of a text message the previous evening.

'Tell you the truth, I was glad of an excuse to get rid. He's bone idle, leaves all the graft to Eddie.'

'We noticed.'

'Trouble is, reliable labour's like gold dust round here. He'll walk straight into another job, if he wants one.'

'So what did he have to say for himself?'

'You know what these lads are like, Mr. Kind.' The builder shook his head sadly. The image of social responsibility was marred by the faded words tattooed on the knuckles of either hand. *Love* and *Hate*. Shades of *Night of the Hunter*; in his younger days he must have fancied himself as a latter day Robert Mitchum. 'Ten minutes later, he called back and said he was only messing. Having a laugh with the lady of the house, that's the way he put it. Cheeky bugger. In fairness, though, there's no real harm in him.'

'So he didn't deny it?'

Mustoe's meaty shoulders rippled in a dismissive gesture and he took a swig of tea from a chipped Newcastle United mug. 'Must have read the signs wrong, he said, the stupid sod. Mind you, speaking as one bloke to another, we've all read the signs wrong in our time, haven't we, Mr. Kind?'

Reading the signs wrong. Men did it all the time. Very often, there weren't even any signs to be misread, but that didn't stop them. There was nothing more to say. As he reversed out of the yard, Daniel couldn't help asking himself if Gabrielle Anders had died because Barrie Gilpin had misread the signs.

He drove down the hill into Kendal and squeezed into the last vacant parking space on top of the Westmorland Shopping Centre. Outside, a straggly-haired, dungaree-clad Joni Mitchell wannabe plucked at a guitar and wailed about the big yellow taxi that had taken away her old man; presumably he wanted to flee from her singing.

On the opposite side of Stricklandgate stood the Carnegie Library, where an affable assistant found him copies of the local papers from the time of Gabrielle's murder. The reports told him little he did not already know about the case, but carried a couple of photographs of his father that he'd never seen before. One was a close-up, a head and shoulders shot revealing tired eyes and a fleshiness of the jowls that suggested too many nights in smoky bars. The other was taken at Underfell, close to the crime scene, and showed Ben Kind issuing directions to his subordinates.

At his side was a slender young woman officer with a pageboy haircut, paying close attention. Hannah Scarlett?

At ten fifteen he set off for their rendezvous. Kendal was a fiendish maze of courtyards and ginnels, but he was learning his way around the grey limestone buildings. Stramongate was a couple of minutes from the library, an ancient thoroughfare leading from the main shopping street over a bridge crossing the Kent. As soon as he'd spotted the church, he identified the benches that Hannah Scarlett had mentioned, scattered around a stretch of grass by the bend in the river. On a hillock overlooking the scene stood fragments of a ruined castle. It was starting to drizzle as he sat down facing the *no-fishing* signs by the weir.

A woman in a leather jacket was striding along the path from the bridge. Medium height, short brown hair damp from the rain. The pageboy cut was no more, but he was certain this was Hannah Scarlett. As she came nearer, her gaze locked on him. In his stomach he felt an unexpected jab of apprehension. Maybe Miranda was right. This woman might know stuff about his father it was better for him not to know.

She came to a halt a couple of yards short of the bench. 'Daniel Kind.'

It was a statement, not a question. Her face had a few freckles and was faintly tanned by the wind and sun. She wore no make-up or jewellery and didn't have a single ring on her long slim fingers. He couldn't detect a perfume. He guessed that her attitude was *take me as you find me.* When they shook hands, her grip was firm. Her gaze was intense as she weighed him up. Her dark eyes gave nothing away. It would be no joke, being a suspect under interrogation by Hannah Scarlett.

'It isn't every day I get to meet a television celebrity from the soft south.' Her voice was husky, not easy to hear against the crash of water cascading over the weir. He caught the faint undertow of scepticism in her words. Not a woman who was easily impressed.

'All that is history,' he said with a grin.

She winced. 'So a flair for lousy jokes runs in the family? Did he train you in the art of card tricks, too?'

He waved her to sit down. 'I used to think my dad had a pretty good sense of humour. As for conjuring. he always used to enthrall my sister and me. I never did figure out how he could make the King of Diamonds turn into the Ace of Spades. Then again, I was only twelve years old.'

She joined him on the bench, leaving a gap between them. 'Presumably there was a lot of resentment when he left, as well as unhappiness.'

'For my mother and Louise, yes. Both of them very bitter, his name became a dirty word. Me, I was just dazed. His running off with Cheryl was a disaster that came out of the clear blue sky. Being told that he'd walked out was like being hit by a falling tree.'

'You had no warning?'

'I suppose Mum realised something was up, but we never discussed where and why they went off the rails. Talking about the time when we were family of four, not three, was absolutely off-limits.'

'He hated hurting you all.'

'You think so?'

'I know so. Of course, he and I didn't talk about what had gone wrong between him and your mother, that was private. Over a lager one night after we'd wrapped up a case, he told me that not a day passed without his conscience nagging him. Your sister was—what, fifteen at the time? Studying for her exams? He had a lot to feel guilty about and it didn't help when he phoned her and tried to explain.'

Daniel leaned forward. 'Louise never mentioned to me that he called.'

'Did she not? She told him that he'd ruined the lives of all three of you. Swore at him and said some vicious things about Cheryl. She made it clear she never wanted to speak to him again. That cut him up, and yet he had to admit that it was his own fault.'

Daniel's eyes settled on a board by the river. *Dangerous Water.* 'All through my teens, I had this recurrent dream. The settings varied—home, school, my uncle's house—but the plot-line was always the same. The phone would be ringing and I knew it was Dad, wanting to talk to me, to say that one day we'd be together again. I never made it to the phone in time. It would fall silent the moment before I picked up the receiver, and all I'd ever hear would be the dialling tone.'

'Now you know why he didn't call you sooner. Once bitten, twice shy. But he was thrilled when you eventually made contact with him.'

'Whenever we did speak, he came over as a bit of an old curmudgeon.'

'That was just his way. To survive as a detective, you need a hard shell. But if you harden up all the way to the heart, maybe you've got a problem.'

For a moment, he wondered if Hannah Scarlett might be talking as much about herself as about his father. She seemed cool and collected in person, as she had on the phone. Whatever might lie beneath the surface poise, she could hardly be more different from impulsive, vulnerable Miranda. This was a woman who kept her feelings under lock and key.

'Deep down, he was as compassionate as any cop I've met. Not that he'd thank me for saying it.' She paused. 'You deserve to know what he was really like. I don't blame his wife and daughter for judging him harshly, but there are two sides to every story.'

Daniel said, 'I haven't come just for you to tell me what you think I'd like to hear.'

Her eyes narrowed. 'I wouldn't do that.'

'It's good of you to spare this time to talk to me.'

'The least I can do. I owe your father a great deal.'

She told him how Ben Kind had taken her under his wing and about how much she'd learned from him. How he'd taught her that showing empathy for the victims of crime must not stop her from detaching her emotions from the case. How often he'd urged her to keep her eye on the ball; every investigation was full of crap that could distract even an experienced detective. The secret was never to lose focus.

'As the years passed, he gave up on amateur magic, concentrated on playing the gruff sceptic. A popular act with the older men, a chap on my team plays that game. You have to look past the scowls and grumbles, try to make out what they really think and feel.'

'And what did Ben Kind really think and feel?'

'He was a decent man, Daniel. The only wrong thing he ever did that I know of was leaving you and your family in the lurch so that he could run off with Cheryl. I suppose he felt cornered.'

'Meaning what?'

She studied her unvarnished nails for a moment, as if making up her mind how much to say. 'He did once let something slip. Whilst he was still living at home, Cheryl gave him an ultimatum. Although she made most of the running, after they'd slept together a couple of times, she insisted that if he didn't make an honest woman of her, the relationship would have to end. Forcing him to make a choice.'

'He told you that?'

'And one other thing. Long before the end, he was afraid he'd made the wrong choice.'

For a little while, Daniel didn't speak, just studied the ground at his feet.

'Are you okay?' she asked.

'I spoke to his neighbours,' he said, looking up again. 'They told me that Cheryl started an affair before he died.'

'It wasn't her first,' Hannah said shortly.

'I take it that you weren't a member of her fan club?'

'Sorry, I shouldn't have said that.'

'I'd rather you tell me the truth.'

'Even if the truth is uncomfortable?'

'Historians expect it to be.'

'Just like any police officer, then?' she said with a glimmer of a smile. 'Don't get the wrong idea. Cheryl and I scarcely knew each other. The two of us had nothing in common, apart from Ben. Besides, I don't think Cheryl had many women friends.'

'But men friends?'

'Men she liked. She was a flirt. And once or twice she went further.'

'My father told you that as well?'

She cleared her throat. 'In this job, when you work together for a long time, you share a lot. Grief, disappointment. Confidences get shared too.'

As he considered this, he didn't look at her, kept his eyes on the river rushing past. For all the warnings, he couldn't help dipping his toes into that dangerous water. Presently, he said, 'So you and he were very close?'

'We weren't lovers,' she said shortly, 'if that's what you mean. Very good friends. The best, I'd say. But no more than that.'

Her candour startled him. 'Sorry. I...'

'No need to apologise. Cheryl made the same assumption, apparently, but I'm not sure she gave a damn. On the contrary. If Ben was getting his oats elsewhere, he wouldn't be troubling her, would he? I suppose that's the way her mind worked. Of course she was wrong. As you've discovered, I share a house with Marc Amos.'

'Owner of one of the best bookshops north of Manchester.'

'So he tells me,' she said with a crooked smile.

'Small world, huh?'

'That's the Lakes for you. Everyone is connected to everyone else.'

'Sort of appealing.'

'Some people find it suffocating.'

'Even with all the hills and meres and open spaces?'

'Sure. I love the beauty of the Lakes, same as you or any other tourist. But even here, people lie and cheat and commit crimes, same as everywhere else.'

Same as you or any other tourist. He cringed inwardly. Her instinct was to bracket him with the sightseers who clogged the lanes and car parks around Bowness and Grasmere.

'Did Marc tell you, he and I bumped into each other yesterday?'

'Uh-huh. I gather you were up on Priest Edge by the Sacrifice Stone. Where Gabrielle Anders' body was found.'

'My first time there since that family holiday.'

She said softly, 'I confess, I'm intrigued. As I understand it, you've thrown up your home and your career to come and live in this neck of the woods. It may not seem that far from the madding crowd if you've ever been stuck in a traffic jam on the way to Windermere, but it's a different world from Oxford and Television Centre.'

'What's so strange? There's nowhere more beautiful in England. For once the tourist brochures aren't a pack of lies. Even though I don't believe what I was told, that it rains less here than in Devon.'

'It's a fact. Even so, they say if you can see High Gill through the mist, it's going to rain. If you can't, it's raining already. Tell me this, though. Of all the properties on the estate agents' books, how did you happen to end up with Tarn Cottage?'

'It's a long story.'

She pulled back the leather sleeve and glanced at her watch. 'You have ten minutes.'

'And there I was, thinking I'd be asking the questions. Finding out more about him.'

'Are you saying you came up here just to explore your past?'

'No it was more a matter of getting away from the present. For Miranda, as well as me.'

'Miranda's your wife?'

'My partner. She's a journalist.'

'So you're a media couple,' she said lightly.

'No,' he said, more vehemently than he'd intended. 'Absolutely not. From the moment we got together, one of the things we had in common was that we both needed a change in our lives. She'd split up with her boyfriend and was having problems at work. I'd stopped enjoying teaching and television is a treadmill. Of course, I won't earn as much based here, but money isn't everything.'

'In my experience,' she said drily, 'people who have no money never say that.'

'Ouch. Then let's just say, I was sick of academic in-fighting. And there was something else. My ex-girlfriend had died and suddenly my old way of life had too many sour memories.'

'I'm sorry.'

'In an odd kind of way, I wanted some good to come out of Aimee's death. I guess that at one time or another in our lives, all of us have the urge to make a new beginning.'

She knitted her brow. 'You reckon?'

'Yes,' he said gently, 'I reckon. Why, have you never found that?'

'Marc and I have been together a long time. We're set in our ways, soon we'll be like Darby and Joan.' For a moment she seemed to be talking to herself rather than to him. Forcing a smile, she added, 'Also, we care about our jobs. I can't imagine life outside the police and Marc is crazy about books. Your situation was obviously different.'

'Miranda and I were fortunate. Not everyone has the opportunity to start again, but I suppose that sometimes it's a mistake to surrender to the temptation.'

'Like Ben?'

'We weren't abandoning anyone, that's the difference. We saw a way out. So we took it. '

She gave a brisk nod, as if to say: *that's enough small talk.* 'All right, then, the Gabrielle Anders case. Have you been talking to people about the murder since you moved to Tarn Cottage?'

'What makes you think that?'

'Is it true, have you been making waves?'

He noticed that she'd dodged his question by asking another. 'You could say so. I'm an incurable nosey parker. There are lots of loose ends connected with the case, don't you agree?'

'Occupational hazard.'

'Isn't that rather defeatist?'

'My job isn't an academic exercise,' she snapped.

'Touché.' For the first time, he saw a spark of temper in her eyes. She wasn't quite as controlled as she wanted him to believe. It gave him a buzz that he'd managed to pierce her defences, if only for an instant. 'Sorry, I didn't mean to offend you. Too many years in an ivory tower, I guess.'

'Police work isn't as neat as a thesis, nicely typed and bound. It's all about the messiness of reality. We don't have endless time to toss around theories or ponder over psychological whys and wherefores.'

'You're not immune from curiosity, though? Barrie Gilpin was an oddity, but why would he kill Gabrielle?'

Hannah's mouth became a tight line. 'Why does any man commit an act of violence? Why does a teenager rape a defenceless old woman, or a father suffocate his kids? Barrie was a voyeur and he'd taken a fancy to Gabrielle. Who knows what may have happened between them? We can't make up the evidence to fit our preconceived ideas. Or preferences. Don't historians base their work on hard facts, too?'

'With some of my former colleagues, you might be surprised. But you're right. Historical research isn't intuition, it's detection.'

'I heard you say that on the telly, so it must be true,' she mocked. 'All I can say is that the original investigation turned up nothing that exonerated Barrie Gilpin. Not a thing.'

'Guilty till proved innocent, then?'

'I didn't say that.' She sighed. 'Listen, I didn't mean to be glib about the loose ends after Barrie's body was found. They bothered me, just as they bothered your father.'

'He knew the real Barrie. He'd played with him, even performed a few magic tricks, much to old Ma Gilpin's disapproval. I can't believe he saw Barrie as a murderer. So—why not review the old file?'

She nibbled at her lower lip. 'All right, I'll tell you something. In strict confidence, okay?'

'I'll respect it.'

'If you're your father's son, I'm sure you will. Mind you, this won't stay confidential for long. If I know the Lakes and the way people talk, it'll be common knowledge by this time tomorrow. The Gabrielle Anders case is one of those we're taking a second look at. Starting this afternoon, we'll be talking to some of the people who gave statements, seeing whether memories can be jogged.'

'That's good news.'

'I don't suppose everyone we speak to will be quite so positive.'

'But if it helps the truth to come out…'

'Daniel,' she interrupted. 'Just be clear about this. One thing you learn in my job is that the truth is usually the last thing people want to emerge. Guilty or innocent, it doesn't matter. Everyone has something to hide.'

'Everyone?'

For a moment he thought she was about to say something else, but instead she stood up and brushed droplets of rain from her coat. 'I'd better go.'

He scrambled to his feet. 'Thanks for your time. I appreciate it.'

She offered her hand. Her flesh was cold. As they shook, another question struck him.

'Hannah.' Using her first name felt strangely intimate. 'Why did you ask if I'd been making waves?'

She opened her mouth and he thought: she's about to say *no particular reason* and it will be a lie. This woman doesn't ask questions without reason.

But she paused and seemed to have second thoughts. 'Daniel, I'm already running late. I'm sorry, you wanted me to tell you more about your father. Maybe one of these days we can talk again.'

'I'd like that.' He took a slip of paper from his pocket and scribbled two numbers on it. 'Call me any time at the cottage or on my mobile.'

She didn't reply, but gave a quick nod and walked swiftly away towards the bridge. He watched her go, while the questions she hadn't answered swirled across his mind like ripples on the river.

Chapter Fourteen

'Nipped out to do a bit of shopping, then, ma'am?' Nick Lowther asked.

He was kicking his heels outside the door to Hannah's office, looking for all the world like a sardonic teenager. A creased sheet of A4 was in his hand. Somehow, what would have been insubordination from anyone else she found acceptable from Nick. In the job, you had to trust someone, and he'd never let her down. Feigning to cuff his ear, she waved him to follow her into the room.

'If you must know, I've been talking to someone with a personal interest in the Anders killing.'

'I wondered where you were hurrying off to. You seemed rather cloak and dagger about it.'

Hanging her coat on the hook, she hoped she wasn't blushing. She always worried that her cheeks reddened easily, even when she had nothing to be embarrassed about. Nick often had that effect on her. He might get above himself sometimes, but he was scarily perceptive. So far she hadn't told anyone that she'd arranged to meet Daniel Kind. It had taken long enough for the rumours to fade about her and Ben. Neither of them had ever done anything to encourage gossip that they were having an affair, but that made no difference. Nobody enjoyed indulging in wild guesswork more than supposedly trained detectives—not when it came to prurient speculation about other people's sex lives. Not that Nick would have given her any grief. Perhaps she should have confided in him earlier, but if Daniel had proved a waste of time, what would have been the point?

'I talked to Ben Kind's son. Daniel, the historian, who's moved into Tarn Cottage.'

Nick's face was as inscrutable as though they were on opposite sides of the table in an interview room. How easy it was to stumble into the trap of sounding guilty and defensive; just as well there'd been nothing incriminating about her encounter with Daniel.

'What's he like?'

'All right,' she said, groping for the right words. He wasn't bad looking, but that was irrelevant. 'Pretty bright, I'd say.'

'That's a relief, ma'am. We'd hate to think that Oxford's standards are in decline, wouldn't we?'

'That's your quota of sarky backchat used up for the week,' she said. 'In one way he reminds me of his father. Ben was never content with obvious explanations.'

'Sometimes the obvious explanation is right.'

'Yes, Ben could be a pain,' she said with a grin. 'Daniel Kind isn't as tough, but I'd guess he's no pushover. Once he starts something, I don't believe he'd give up easily.'

She gave him a quick run-through of the conversation with Daniel. 'I'm keeping an open mind about whether there's a connection between his arrival and the call we had about Gilpin. He's fascinated by the case and my guess is that he's not hidden it when he's been talking to people in Brack. Maybe something he's said caused that woman to call. I suppose she still hasn't rung back?'

He passed her the sheet of paper. 'You suppose wrong, ma'am. Which is precisely why I was trying to find you.'

She scanned the note. This time Linz had answered the phone. In large, voluptuous handwriting she'd recorded the brief conversation. The woman had identified herself as having rung earlier and then said that she had made a mistake.

I didn't mean to cause any trouble, I just got confused. I wouldn't want you to waste any more time. That's all. Better let sleeping dogs lie. It's right, what people said at the time. Barrie Gilpin did kill the girl, must have done. I'm so sorry. Please forget what I said before. Please. Goodbye.

She'd rung off before Linz could put a question.

Hannah sighed. 'Thanks a million, whoever you are. What do you make of it?'

'According to Linz, she sounded panicky. Chances are, she's a neurotic with time on her hands.'

'Or someone has leaned on her. The update briefing is at twelve. Let's see where we're up to before you and I set off for Brack.'

'Finally, the Gabrielle Anders murder.' Hannah pointed to the scrawled agenda on the whiteboard. 'We don't have enough material to justify a full-scale review. DNA hasn't thrown up any new leads. But there has been a development that makes it worth spending a little time on the case. Linz, can you take us through it?'

Lindsey glanced round at her colleagues. Making sure that she had everyone's attention, Hannah thought: that always mattered to her. So far she'd had less than her customary share of the limelight. The other pair of DCs were working with Les Bryant on the review that was progressing fastest, an inquiry into a series of rapes coupled with the attempted murder of a prostitute. The crimes had been committed in Workington, Whitehaven, and Cleator Moor, and an interesting new name had come into the frame. The only snag was that it belonged to someone who had left Britain for Australia six years back.

'Mobile switched off, Gul?' Linz asked. 'Or are you still waiting for hot news from the Chief Constable?'

Everyone laughed; even Gul mustered a sheepish smirk. His phone-dependency was a standing joke and he took at least one allegedly urgent call in the course of every briefing. The rest of the team reckoned it was less to do with his receiving a flood of vital information than with trying to polish his image for Linz's benefit. The ace detective, with a range of contacts the envy of the Cumbria Constabulary. Hannah was sure that Linz, like everyone else, knew that half of his calls came from a much more extensive network, comprising past and present girlfriends.

When her audience had settled, Linz talked them through her note of the call about the Brackdale murder. 'To my mind, she was fibbing. This crap about making a mistake, I don't buy it. She was scared stiff. Age, mid-thirties, maybe older. Local accent.'

'You'd go along with that, Maggie?' Hannah asked.

'Uh-huh. Same woman, must be.'

'Just because she's scared,' Les Bryant said, chewing his gum, 'that doesn't mean she has any evidence to give us that's worth tuppence.'

'How do you mean?' Maggie asked. She never disguised her enthusiasm for learning from the guru, but Hannah couldn't decide whether Les was flattered or irritated by her attention.

'She might just have got hold of the wrong end of the stick. What if she was full of sympathy for Gilpin and couldn't believe he was guilty? If the man she suspected has got wind of it, he may not be best pleased. He may even have threatened her. Doesn't mean he did for Gabrielle.'

Bob Swindell murmured assent and Hannah made a mental note that he and Les were chumming up. Better keep an eye on them to make sure that knee-jerk cynicism didn't become corrosive and start to demoralise the whole team.

'Good point, Les. We won't know, of course, until we catch up with her. Are we any further forward on identifying who she is?'

'Even if we only look at the people interviewed at the time of the murder, there are several candidates,' Nick Lowther said. 'I've prepared a simple profile of our caller.'

Les Bryant grunted. He rated psychological profilers on a par with old ladies who pronounced on their friends' fortunes after reading patterns in their tea leaves. She wondered if Nick had used the phrase deliberately to wind him up.

'We're looking at a Brackdale resident or visitor,' Nick continued, 'probably a woman born and bred in the valley. Someone who knew Barrie Gilpin and had come across Gabrielle Anders while she was staying at the pub. Possibly connected with someone who featured in the original inquiry, maybe as an early suspect before the spotlight fell exclusively on Gilpin.'

'And what are you doing now you've drawn up this...'—Les Bryant couldn't even bring himself to utter the word—'what d'you call it?'

'I've prioritised three women who were spoken to during the original investigation for re-interview.' When Les cleared his throat loudly, Nick added, 'Obviously, the list isn't cast in stone. We have to start somewhere, but remember that our caller may be someone who's never blipped on to the radar screen.'

'And the three are?' Bob Swindell asked.

'Jean Allardyce, wife of Tom. We spoke about him before. She gave her husband an alibi for the murder.'

'Maybe it wasn't kosher?'

'Maybe. Even so, we can't rule out the Moffat sisters, Dale and Leigh. The DCI and I are proposing to see Allardyce this afternoon, after we've talked to Dowling. Bob and Linz, can you make arrangements to interview the Moffats?'

'For those of you who don't know,' Hannah said, 'Dale Moffat worked at the pub at the time of the murder and so did her sister. Dale was a cleaner, Leigh looked after the kitchen. Nowadays Leigh runs the café in my partner's bookshop. He's known both of them since way back. That doesn't affect in any way how you two conduct your inquiries. No soft-pedalling because of it, okay? I simply wanted you to be aware.'

'What about the lady of Brack Hall, Natasha Dumelow?' Les Bryant asked. 'Doesn't she fit the—*profile?*'

'She's an off-comer. As far off as Moscow. She's lived in England a long time, she speaks the language fluently, but you wouldn't say she has a local accent. A long shot, at best.'

'All the same, I wouldn't mind interviewing her,' Bob said with a lascivious grin. 'I remember seeing a photograph of her in *The Westmorland Gazette* when she put on an exhibition of her paintings a few months back. Very tasty.'

'Sorry to disappoint you,' Hannah said, 'but the bad news is, DS Lowther and I are scheduled to interview the Dumelows tomorrow. The husband's not available today, doing some deal to make himself even richer, I suppose. The good news is, the Moffats are both attractive ladies. See how much we look after your welfare, Bob?'

'I owe you one, ma'am.' Bob treated Gul to a wink. He'd been playing the field ever since coming home early from a shift because of a migraine and finding his wife in bed with her best friend's husband.

'Happy with all that, Les?' Nick wasn't above having a dig at the team's guru, and Hannah made a note of something else she would have to watch. The team couldn't afford to splinter into two camps, believers and sceptics.

Les Bryant scratched himself under the armpit. 'Police work's all about making choices. Only snag is, the choices need to be right. Bear in mind, if our mystery caller is frightened for a reason, she may be at risk herself—even if Gilpin did kill Anders.'

The room fell silent. Already, people had acquired the habit of listening to what Les Bryant said with close attention. He seemed to take it for granted.

'Most of all,' he muttered, 'we don't want another body turning up, do we? Whether or not it's draped over some ancient monument.'

◇◇◇

In the car on the way to Brackdale, Nick asked, 'You think he could be right?'

Hannah exhaled. 'If the woman was telling the truth the first time she called, the answer's bound to be yes. Talking out of turn may have alerted the man she suspects. If he's violent…'

'Allardyce, in other words?'

'Let's keep an open mind.' How many times had she heard Ben Kind say that? And how many times had she thought about him since his son had introduced himself on the phone? 'Don't forget that Joe Dowling has a record.'

'Thumping a lad who'd broken into the pub he used to run in Penrith, ten years back? Plus a not guilty verdict on a charge of fiddling his VAT? It's not quite the same.'

A thin drizzle was falling as they rounded the bend between the fells and followed the road into the valley. Brackdale was lush, although Hannah knew that the farmers would start worrying at the first hint of a dry spell. Yellow poppies bloomed on the grassy verge. Ahead lay the whitewashed cottages that marked the outskirts of the village. Easy to see why Marc loved Brackdale, but she'd never wanted to spend time here since the death of Gabrielle Anders. By day it was peaceful enough, but in her memories it remained a crime scene sheeted in darkness. Try as she might, she'd never been able to rid her own mind of the glare of the arc lights, cutting through the night to illuminate the bloody corpse on the Sacrifice Stone.

As the wipers thrashed across the windscreen, she said, 'I remember taking Dowling's statement. Another thing I remember is that I didn't take a shine to him. He fancied himself, but he had a face like a fox. I can still picture it, fixed in a permanent leer as he studied my boobs.'

'It's just the effect you have on red-blooded Englishmen, ma'am.'

She shot him a sidelong glance. 'Very funny. Don't forget, he was a red-blooded Englishman who had this gorgeous young tourist staying under the same roof. When he said he'd barely noticed Gabrielle since her arrival, I wanted to smack him, just for insulting my intelligence.'

'He admitted talking to her. The landlord and the guest, he was doing the hospitality bit to perfection. You can't criticise him for it.'

Hannah said stubbornly, 'I wouldn't like to be a chicken caught by that particular fox. Like Allardyce, he's someone we'd have looked at more closely, if it hadn't been for the hue and cry over Barrie Gilpin.'

'Is that why you want to talk to them both yourself?'

She stretched in the passenger seat, as if flexing her muscles. 'You disapprove?'

His gaze was fastened to the road. 'Course not. But you must admit, this is a tad unorthodox.'

'So what? The way I see it, this is a lucky break.'

'Best to make the most of it, then.'

'Too right. How often in this job do we get a second chance?'

'She was a sweet girl.' Joe Dowling's eyes kept darting between Hannah and Nick. He might have been a bookmaker, calculating odds. *What can I say that will put me in the clear?* 'What that lad did to her was—unspeakable.'

'You got to know her well, then?' Hannah said.

'No, no, I wouldn't say that,' he said hastily. 'Like I told you at the time, in a place like this, guests come and go. We see so many of them. You chat to everyone, try to make them feel at home. I mainly remember the complainers, to be honest.'

Hannah doubted that honesty was second nature to Joe Dowling. 'The people who make trouble?'

'Yeah, the world's full of them. You must find the same, in your job.'

'Too right,' she said.

'The typical guests, now, they become part of the furniture. We've had people stay here half a dozen times or more over the years and yet I wouldn't recognise them if they walked through that door. The only reason Gabrielle Anders stood out was...'

As his voice trailed away, Hannah said, 'Because she was murdered?'

'I hate to say it, but that's right.'

Dowling fiddled with the zip on his fleece. It bore a picture of a submerged moon. Hannah had him down as a man who cared about appearances, yet never managed to capture quite the right look. Sad, really.

'So glamorous young women are constantly stopping off here on their own?' Nick's eyebrows went up. 'Only to blend in with the mahogany in the snug?'

They could hear Kylie Minogue warbling on the saloon bar jukebox, the dance rhythms thudding through the thin partition. The three of them were closeted in a cubby-hole piled high with cardboard boxes full of potato crisps, perched on stools around a Formica-topped table that might have been at the cutting edge of contemporary design forty years earlier. The air was ripe with the aroma of cheese and onion and smoky bacon.

'I can't understand why you're asking these questions.'

'As I explained on the phone,' Nick said, 'we've been tasked with reviewing the original inquiry.'

'Everyone knows Gilpin killed her. Your boss was involved, weren't you, love?'

'I'm not your love, Mr. Dowling,' Hannah said in a frozen voice.

'Well, anyway, there's nothing more I can tell you now. It's old news as far as I'm concerned. Gilpin's dead and buried, but he killed her, you mark my words.'

'Pure speculation,' Nick said. 'Barrie Gilpin was never charged, let alone convicted. And now further information has come to light.'

'What information?'

Nick returned his gaze. After a few moments, Dowling lowered his eyes.

'This is all down to that Daniel Kind, isn't it?' he grumbled, turning to Hannah. 'His dad was your boss, wasn't he?'

'Why do you mention Mr. Kind?'

'He's stirring up bother.'

'What sort of bother?'

'He was in here the other night, insinuating that Gilpin was set up. Which is another way of saying that the girl was killed by someone else. Maybe someone who's still around in the village. That's not very nice, is it? And no good for my business, either. People take offence.'

'People?'

'Tom Allardyce, for one. This Daniel Kind was pulling his plonker, so to speak. Big mistake, in my book. Not a good idea to get the wrong side of Tom.'

'He has a violent temper, doesn't he?'

He shrugged. 'It's no secret, cousin Jean's felt the back of his hand more than once. Though maybe sometimes she asks for it. Not the brightest button in the box, isn't our Jean.'

Hannah strove to keep her tone civil. 'It isn't impossible that Barrie Gilpin was innocent.'

'Oh, for Chrissake,' Dowling said. 'Ask yourself what game Kind's playing. You know he bought Mrs. Gilpin's cottage for a song? Nobody wanted it, because of what happened. Now he's aiming to up the value of the place by persuading everyone that Gilpin didn't kill the girl.'

'You seriously believe that?'

'Yes,' he said, all righteous defiance. 'I seriously do. He's having you on. All this isn't about sorting out some old miscarriage of justice, it's about a property speculation.'

Nick said, 'You haven't told us anything about the girl yet. What was she like?'

'Pleasant enough, as far as I can remember.'

'She was a looker.'

Dowling shrugged. Over-elaborately, Hannah felt. 'Plenty of good-looking women come to the Lakes, Sergeant.'

'She'd spent time in America, hadn't she?'

'Las Vegas. I recall we spoke about the weather one morning at breakfast, when it was pissing down outside. The city's slap bang in the middle of the Nevada desert, isn't it? She loved the year-round sun, said it made such a change from the long, dark winter nights she'd grown up with.'

'So why come back to England?'

He picked at his nose, as if as an aid to thought. 'She'd made a few quid working on the Strip and she said she wanted a holiday. The climate here may be lousy but at least you don't keep tripping over Elvis Presley impersonators. As far as I know, she was touring round and looking up friends.'

'Did she tell you anything else?'

'We talked about slot machines. At the time I was thinking of hiring a couple of one-armed bandits for the saloon. She'd worked in bars and hotels, she'd even trained as a croupier at one point. The tips they get are unbelievable. I remember asking if she thought Blackpool would ever take off as a casino resort, but she laughed fit to burst. Said it would need more than a spot of global warming for the Fylde Coast to match Vegas.'

'Apart from that?'

'Nothing springs to mind. She'll have chatted more to the staff than to me. I was rushed off my feet, since my wife wasn't around to share the load.'

Nick made a show of leafing through papers on a clipboard. 'You said in your statement that Mrs. Dowling was on holiday. Did she not return?'

'Oh aye,' Dowling said. 'I suppose there's no harm telling you now. Glenda had got herself mixed up with a bloke who owned a bed and breakfast in Coniston. Don't they say love is blind? No sour grapes, but the man was built like a brick shit-house and he looked like one and all. She came running back here in the end.'

'This was after Barrie Gilpin's death?'

'Yeah, a fortnight later, maybe. It didn't work out. In the end she moved in with a salesman from a car showroom in Barrow. I'm well rid of her, to be fair. 'Sides, I fell on my feet with Lynsey. Lovely girl. Very giving.'

'You told us before that on the day of the murder, you didn't see Gabrielle Anders after breakfast.'

'Right. I served her, that I do remember. She asked for hash browns, said she'd developed a taste for them in the US of A. I said we only did a full English. It was like a little joke we had going.'

Hilarious, Hannah thought, a real rib-tickler. 'Did she say what she'd be doing that day?'

'Let me see.' He made a pantomime of trying to collect his thoughts. 'I think she was going to see the Dumelows. As you know, Mrs. D was an old pal. I don't recall anything else.'

'And what did you do later that day?'

'I was here all the time, as far as I can remember. Matter of fact, I wasn't feeling well.'

'You told me last time your stomach ulcer was troubling you.'

'Been a martyr to it for years,' he insisted. 'Off and on. Too much to worry about, that's my problem.'

'You served behind the bar from half-five to six, according to your statement. After that, the pain was too much and you had to go up to bed. You said you left the staff to look after everything downstairs.'

'As far as I can remember.'

'So you don't have a witness who can account for your movements after six o'clock?'

'I don't need one. I never touched that girl. I was in bed.'

'Alone?'

He treated her to the foxiest grin in his repertoire. 'Unfortunately.'

'So no one can vouch for where you were or what you were doing?'

'Trust me, you're barking up the wrong tree.'

'Trust you, Mr. Dowling? All right, which tree should we be barking up?'

Dowling pursed his lips, as though measuring the likelihood of being penalised for what he intended to say. They could almost hear the grinding of cogs in his brain.

'Far as I'm concerned, Barrie Gilpin killed that girl, end of story.'

'But if he didn't?' Nick asked.

Hannah watched as he wavered before speaking, like a poor swimmer hesitating on the edge of a deep, deep pool.

'If he didn't…then my money's on the chap who was pouring vodka and lime down her throat the night before she died.'

'Tom Allardyce?'

A throaty chuckle. 'No way, that girl was out of Tom's league. Whatever he may have liked to believe.'

'Who, then?'

Joe Dowling's face folded into a nervous smirk. 'His lordship.'

'His lordship?'

'Well, that's how he'd like us to think of him. The squire of Brack Hall, I mean. Simon Dumelow.'

◇◇◇

'Diversionary tactic?' Nick asked as they strapped themselves back into the Mondeo. 'The stuff about Dumelow, I mean.'

'What else? The first time Dowling told me about his ulcer, I wasn't convinced. Second time around, it sounds more convenient than ever.'

Nick looked over his shoulder as he eased the car out of its parking space and into the road. 'Do you reckon he killed her?'

'Part of me wishes he had. I'd love to read him his rights, see that sly little grin wiped off his face.'

'And Simon Dumelow?'

'The first question is whether Dowling has any reason to hold a grudge against him. Besides, what was he saying? Not that she took her friend's husband up to her room. Simply that she let him buy her a few drinks one night when Natasha was under the weather.'

'Any evidence that Dumelow fancied Gabrielle? Or vice versa?'

'Nothing that I recall. He struck me as pretty uxorious.'

'Sorry? You forget I've not swallowed as many dictionaries as you.'

'A man who loved his wife,' she said with exaggerated patience.

'Blimey,' Nick said. 'We don't come across many of them, do we?'

'Except for you.'

When he didn't come straight back with a smart rejoinder she was disconcerted. Maybe she'd been tactless, perhaps for once he and Becky had quarrelled. Better carry on talking.

'After Gabrielle turned up on their doorstep, the three of them spent time together, but whenever Simon was working, Natasha took her touring around the Lakes. She had no family here and probably not too many real friends. She said she was thrilled to see Gabrielle again. At one time they'd been inseparable.'

'Gabrielle didn't have any close ties either, as far as I can tell from the file.'

'No. During her time in the States, she'd had plenty of boy-friends, but nobody even semi-permanent. She wasn't the type to settle down, according to Natasha, she liked to drift from one place to another. At the funeral, the saddest thing for me was that there wasn't anyone to mourn her, *really* mourn her, other than Natasha.'

'The two of them were very close?'

'No suggestion they had a lesbian affair, if that's what you mean. But while they were in Leeds, they'd fought together to make headway in a tough business. Not that either of them achieved much success. Pretty faces and blonde hair aren't every-thing, even in that game.'

'What do we know about their time as models?'

'Not a lot, that's why I asked Les Bryant to make enquiries via his own contacts in West Yorkshire Police. See if we can pick up anything in Gabrielle's past that might have a bearing. Natasha admitted that they saw the seamy side of life while they were struggling to make ends meet.'

'Modelling was a euphemism for prostitution, then?'

'The way Natasha put it, they preferred the company of gen-erous men. She implied that Gabrielle may have gone the extra mile, but where do you draw the line between being nice to a rich bloke and screwing for money? In the end, they both decided to get out.'

'And lucky old Natasha found herself a cushy billet with a millionaire property dealer.'

'Maybe Gabrielle had the same idea. Let's face it, there are plenty of potential sugar daddies in the big villas overlooking

Windermere. Whatever the truth, I'd bet the key that unlocks this case is here in the Lakes.'

'It may have been buried with Barrie Gilpin,' Nick said.

'Unless our mystery caller has it.'

'Jean Allardyce is Dowling's cousin. Possibly she has something on him, something she's ready to share with us.'

'Or on her husband.'

'What if their marriage has just gone pear-shaped?' Nick suggested. 'She might be more willing to talk to us this time.'

'We'll find out soon enough.'

They turned into a narrow lane marked with a worn board proclaiming *Brack Hall Farm only: no public right of way.* As their route meandered through well-kept fields in the direction of the farmhouse, Hannah wrinkled her nose. No matter how long she lived in the countryside, she would never learn to love the smell of manure.

The sound of the car engine set a dog barking. From behind one of the out-buildings, a collie appeared, in belligerent mood. More evidence, she reflected, that animals reflect the personalities of their owners. As they neared the farmhouse, they could see Tom Allardyce, in waterproof jacket and gumboots, washing his Land Rover in the cobbled yard. When he caught sight of them, he spat on the ground.

Nick pulled up alongside the Land Rover and they both jumped out. The air was rank with the smells of sheep and dogs and disinfectant. Allardyce put down his bucket of dirty, foaming water and nailed them with a long hard stare.

'You're early.'

'Sorry, Mr. Allardyce,' Nick said. 'We'll sit and wait, if you're busy. Or perhaps it would be convenient to have a word with your wife?'

'What do you want to speak to her for?'

'Oh, you know. Background.'

'Hard luck,' Allardyce said sourly. 'You'll have to try another day.'

'Isn't she around?'

Allardyce shook his head and started buffing the nearside front door.

'We can wait, if she won't be long. When will she be back?'

'No idea.'

'Has she gone far?'

'Dunno.'

Hannah said urgently, 'Can you tell us where your wife is, Mr. Allardyce?'

He didn't even face her as he said in a negligent tone, 'Search me.'

'No, I'm not searching you. I'm asking you. Where is she?'

'Your guess is as good as mine. I'm not her keeper. She's gone away.'

'Gone away? Don't you know more than that?' Hannah stepped forward to eyeball him. 'What sort of a husband do you call yourself?'

He gave her a crooked grin and said, 'Long-suffering?'

Chapter Fifteen

After parting from Hannah Scarlett, Daniel had a sandwich lunch at a café in the Master's House before returning to the library. This time he was searching out archive materials about Lakeland corpse roads that might provide background for the article he'd suggested to the editor of *Contemporary Historian*. For the best part of three hours, he lost himself in research. He hadn't brought his laptop: a conscious decision. It had remained locked in its case and hidden under a pile of magazines at the bottom of a cupboard ever since his arrival at Tarn Cottage. Instead of tapping details into his computer in the manner that had become second nature, he jotted longhand notes in a school exercise book he'd picked up at the branch of WH Smith just down the road, much as he had when revising for his A Levels. It was a nostalgic indulgence, but when he checked his watch and realised that he'd spent longer than he'd intended, it dawned on him how much he'd enjoyed his afternoon's work. *Enjoyment*. He'd yearned for it during his sabbatical and been disappointed. In Oxford it had eluded him but here, in a modest provincial library possessing a fraction of the resources available in the Bod, he'd rediscovered the pleasure of historical research for its own sake. At last he wasn't racing against a deadline for a script or a book, or trying to find a new way of presenting old facts for a tutorial or seminar. He felt as though by chance he'd bumped into a childhood sweetheart and found that she was as much fun to be with as when they were both seventeen and first in love.

The sun made a belated appearance as he started back to the cottage. His mood was light and he followed a roundabout route along leafy back lanes, catching glimpses of Windermere every now and then, and of the chain-guided car ferry chugging across from Bowness to Sawrey. Low branches kept caressing the roof of his Audi. Whenever a vehicle approached from the other direction, one or other of them had to reverse as far as the nearest passing place. But the peacefulness of the Lakes amply compensated for any trivial inconveniences. He could understand why his father had fallen in love with this place, just as he could understand why the old man had liked Hannah so much. He liked her too; he felt sure he could trust her. With a little prompting, she would help him to get a handle on his father's life after leaving home and to understand at last what had made the man tick.

Turning into Tarn Fold, he saw a flash of yellow shining through the trees. Tash Dumelow's car was parked close to where he and Miranda had stopped that very first morning when they had found that Tarn Cottage was up for sale. The Alfa came into full view a moment later. It was carelessly parked, making it difficult for him to pass, and it was empty. She'd left the driver's door open.

What had happened to her?

Puzzled, he pulled up behind the Alfa and jumped out. He had a half-formed idea of going in search, but maybe he was over-reacting. Besides, he didn't know which way to head.

Might she have left the car here and set off on foot for the cottage?

The sun had disappeared again and he felt a chill on his back as he wandered beneath the canopy formed by the trees, trying to decide what to do for the best. He heard a rustling and then footsteps, coming from behind.

'Hi, Daniel, how are things?'

He spun around and saw Tash emerging from a path that led between the trees and down to the beck. An artist's pad was in her hand. Relief flooded through him.

'Are you okay?'

She was breathing hard, as though from the exertion of the climb. As she approached, he was conscious of her perfume. Although she was casually dressed in white tee shirt and blue jeans, a second glance revealed that, despite the lateness of the afternoon, they both looked as crisp and freshly laundered as if she'd just put them on. It may have been a long time since Tash Dumelow went slinking on the catwalk, but old habits died hard. Even when she came out to do a little sketching on her own in an unfrequented corner of the valley, she took care to keep up appearances.

'I'm fine, how are you?'

Rather than answer directly, she asked, 'Stopping for a stroll along the banks of the beck?'

He pointed to the open car door. 'Curious, that's all.'

'Sorry. I didn't mean to distract you.' She gave him a teasing smile, but he thought he could detect tiredness and strain behind it. 'I should have taken more care to park prettily and lock the car up. But one of the nice things about this part of the world is that there's so little crime. In the pay-and-displays at Bowness or Ambleside it's different, but I don't think many car thieves venture this far off the beaten track.'

'You're here to paint a picture?'

'Not today. I'm just working up an idea for my next exhibition. Even though it's on my own doorstep, I've never tackled the old corn-mill. I've been wandering up and down and on both sides of the beck, trying to decide on the best viewpoint. Thinking out the composition, seeing how the shadows of the trees fall on the brickwork. On second thoughts, I ought to come back early tomorrow morning, catch the freshness of the light when the sun first comes out.'

'I never realised watercolouring was so complicated.'

'Well, sketching out a scene soothes my nerves whenever I'm a bit flustered. Some people chill out with music, others with sport. For me, the ideal escape involves heading off alone with just a few sheets of paper and a piece of charcoal for company.'

'You don't look flustered to me.'

'Thanks.' A brief smile faded. 'It's nothing, really.'

'Glad to hear it.' Instinct told him that she wanted to say more, but was holding back. She shifted from one foot to another and he was reminded of his time in college, when students wavered before confessing their latest cause for angst.

'As a matter of fact, I'm worried about a friend of mine.'

'Sorry to hear that.' He wasn't sure that it was a good idea to encourage a confidence. Especially from an attractive and very married woman. But he could hardly walk away without another word. 'Nothing serious, I hope?'

'I hope not. With any luck, I'm over-reacting, making a fuss over nothing.' Head bowed, she seemed to be deliberating whether to say more. 'Actually, it's Jean. You know, Jean Allardyce? She may work for us, but she's also one of my closest friends. I rely on her a lot. She's a lovely lady.'

'As it happens, I saw her again yesterday. I'd been walking along the old coffin trail and she gave me a lift into the village.'

'Of course, I saw you both. She and I had a cup of coffee in the baker's after she'd dropped you off. '

'What's the matter with her?'

Tash glanced over her shoulder, as if anxious that someone might overhear. But they were alone, and Tarn Fold was peaceful and silent. Daniel couldn't even hear the sound of distant hammering from the cottage.

'She's—well, she's gone.'

'Gone?'

'Left home. At least, that's the way it seems. We haven't seen her at the Hall since this morning. She'd said she wanted to have a private word with me about something and we'd arranged to get together at one o'clock, but she never showed up.'

'Perhaps she forgot?'

Tash shook her head. 'One thing about Jean, she never forgets.'

'There's a first time for everything.'

'Mmmm...' Tash was plainly unconvinced. 'I waited for three-quarters of an hour. By that time, I was very concerned. It was so out of character. I walked over to the farmhouse, but there was no sign of her, inside or out. Tom wasn't there, either. When eventually I tracked him down, he denied all knowledge of where she might be.'

'Maybe she's set off on another shopping trip.'

'I don't think so. She's due to go to the supermarket tomorrow to stock up.'

'There are other shops besides supermarkets.'

'But she hasn't taken the Land Rover and Jean wouldn't even walk to Brack, let alone any further. She's suffering from an ingrowing toenail... And there's something else.'

Gently, he said, 'Tell me.'

'When we were in the house, I saw a suitcase, stashed behind the umbrella stand. It bulged as though she'd filled it to overflowing.'

'It may have been there for ages.'

'Maybe.' Plainly she was unconvinced.

'What did Allardyce have to say about the suitcase?'

'I—I bottled out of asking him.'

'But why?'

'He may be our tenant farmer,' she said slowly, 'but he's his own man. And he has a dreadful temper, not just violent but irrational. He's always been like that, but lately, he's seemed worse than ever. You should hear him ranting when Simon complains about the fencing or the fact that the covering on the sheep dipper wouldn't pass muster with the health and safety people. I keep expecting him to burst a blood vessel. God knows how he'd react if I suggested that his wife might have been preparing to move out. He's—on the edge.'

He remembered his conversation with Jean Allardyce the day before. 'She kept a stack of tourist brochures in the Land Rover. Only yesterday she was telling me that she'd like to travel.'

'Did she give away any clues?' Tash's tone was urgent. 'What else did she say to you?'

'Very little.'

'Think back. Was there anything? Anything that might explain what's happened?'

'I gathered she was discontented, but I didn't pick up any reason why she'd choose this particular time to leave home.'

'You're sure?' When he shook his head, she gave a lavish sigh. 'Thank God for that. I'm sorry, Daniel. I shouldn't have loaded this on to you, and for no good reason. After all, we hardly know each other.'

'It's not a problem.'

'I have this awful feeling I've led you and Tom on a wild goose chase. I suppose Jean will turn up any minute now, safe and sound, wondering what all the fuss has been about. Much to my embarrassment. What's the betting, she's back at the farm already?'

'She's your friend,' Daniel said. 'It's only natural that you should be concerned. Especially given Tom's reputation.'

A wary look came into Tash Dumelow's eyes. 'That's not fair. Don't forget, Jean's stuck by him all these years. Deep down, he's not really an ogre. She always said his time in Northern Ireland cut him up very badly.'

'But?'

'No buts,' she insisted. 'I'm really grateful for your support, Daniel. You've helped to set my mind at rest.'

'I'm glad.' He was tempted to clasp her hand, but thought better of it. 'I only want to help. If Jean isn't…'

'No, don't say another word.' She tossed her sketching book on to the Alfa's passenger seat and pulled the ignition key out of the back pocket of her jeans. 'You've been very kind. And so patient. It's something we women do, isn't it? Simon's always saying I worry unnecessarily. Until we started talking, I'd persuaded myself that something dreadful had happened to Jean.'

'We still don't know where she is.'

But Tash had climbed into her car. As she switched on the engine, he realised that he was talking to himself.

'What is she like?' It was half an hour later.

'Who?' Daniel wanted a few more seconds to compose his answer. He hadn't told Miranda about his meeting with Tash Dumelow, but he'd been speculating about Jean Allardyce's unexplained absence and why Tash was quite so concerned about it.

'You know. Hannah Scarlett.'

'Oh. Pleasant enough.'

'Is that all?'

A suitably neutral adjective occurred to him. 'Business-like, I'd say. Yes, definitely business-like.'

'Did she help you to fill in the gaps about your father?'

'Sort of. She said he was a decent detective, but I didn't learn much more. She was pressed for time.'

'Pity.'

'I gave her my number. She said she might be willing to meet up again for another chat. In the meantime, she'll mull over the questions I've asked, see what she can do to give me chapter and verse.'

'I see.' Miranda took another sip of wine. 'Well, do you think there was a romance between her and your father?'

'She said not.'

They were lazing out on the paved area, glasses at their elbows, watching a kingfisher that had become bold enough to emerge from its home in the vegetation on the far side of the tarn. It perched on a low branch of the willow that stretched its claws over the water. Every now and then the bird took flight, skimming over the surface of the tarn in a dazzle of blue and green before flying in a circle around the trees and returning to land on its perch. There it remained, undisturbed by intermittent outbreaks of Eddie's hammering, a joyless clatter suggestive of sporadic bursts of gunfire in the face of an overwhelming enemy.

'You mean, you actually asked her?'

'No, she volunteered it. Perhaps she read my thoughts.'

'Interesting. Doth the lady protest too much?'

'She struck me as honest,' he said icily.

'Darling, she's a police officer. They are trained to gather information, not to give it away. And not above telling a few porkies when it suits them. Trust me, I'm a journalist.'

Stung, he almost retorted: *Hannah isn't like that.* But really, how would he know?

'You were never a crime reporter.'

Miranda raised her eyes to the heavens. 'Daniel, I don't need an apprenticeship in the magistrates' courts to have an inkling about how the police behave.'

'Don't forget, my father was a policeman.'

'You rarely give me a chance to forget it,' she retorted. 'But you never saw him again after you were twelve. As for me, my first boyfriend after university was a DC in the Met.'

'I never knew that.'

'There's a lot you don't know about me,' she snapped. 'Or me about you, for that matter. Anyway, Iain and I had been going out for a fortnight before I discovered he was married. Not just involved, actually married to another woman.'

'God,' he said softly. But what really struck him was Miranda's choice of words. *There's a lot you don't know about me. Or me about you.* They'd made a new life together on a whim. It was so out of character for him, he couldn't quite believe he'd taken things so far. Thank God their love for each other was so strong.

'Anyone at home?'

Leigh Moffat was peeping over the makeshift barricade created by the tarpaulin-covered pile of timber, destined for the bothy, that Eddie had dumped at the side of the cottage. To Daniel, her auburn hair seemed to have lost its lustre and her earnest features were pale and drawn, as if she'd missed out on a good night's sleep.

'I did ring the bell, and knock at the front door,' she said apologetically, 'but...'

A renewed onslaught with the hammer finished the sentence for her. 'Can you squeeze past the stuff?' Daniel waved at his glass. 'I've just opened a bottle of Rioja. Care to join us?'

She shimmied between the cottage wall and the barricade. 'I knew I'd regret that cream cake for elevenses. Back to the diet tomorrow, strict rations. But a drink would be lovely. Only one, mind, as I'm driving.'

She took a seat on the wooden patio chair that he'd unfolded for her. Her figure didn't suggest any need to diet: she'd poured herself into charcoal jeans and a purple jersey with a generous v-neck. Lucky Marc Amos, to have this woman as a workmate and Hannah Scarlett to come home to. For a few minutes the three of them sipped from their glasses and chatted idly about the cottage renovations and shared complaints about the unreliability of tradesmen. Miranda didn't mention Wayne, of course; the previous afternoon's trauma seemed already to have faded into the faraway past.

'I hate to intrude on you like this,' Leigh said. 'I don't mean to presume on such a brief acquaintance.'

'We're glad of any visitors,' Miranda said. 'It's so lovely here, but I've not acclimatised to the isolation yet. When the workmen finish for the day, the place is as quiet as a cemetery. One of these days, when we're sorted, we'll have a housewarming and you can consider yourself invited.'

'That's kind of you.' Leigh put her glass down on the paving. 'Although your hospitality isn't making it any easier for me to ask the favour that brought me here.'

'Ask away,' Daniel said.

She cleared her throat. 'The police have been questioning my sister and me this afternoon. Just because we were both working at The Moon under Water at the time Gabrielle Anders stayed there. I finished early at the bookshop so that I could meet them at home. Two constables, they'd already brow-beaten Dale. Resurrecting the past. Talking about the statement she gave after the girl was found murdered.'

'It's a cold case,' Daniel said. 'You've seen the publicity about this new team the police have set up? I'm sure the questions are merely routine.'

'Dale and I were wondering why they'd chosen to dig up that particular cold case. Cumbria isn't exactly a hot-bed of crime, but surely there are plenty of old inquiries that failed to produce an arrest or conviction. Why pick on that one?'

'They're not focusing simply on the Anders murder. It's one of several they are reviewing.'

With a sharpness he hadn't heard from her before, she snapped, 'Then you're already aware they are looking at the case?'

He drained his wine, barely noticing the flavour, just relishing the lift that the alcohol gave him. Miranda's face had creased with anxiety but he could see no good reason to dissemble.

'It's no secret, I did talk to Hannah Scarlett.'

Leigh leaned forward so that their faces were close together. 'Have you any idea of what you're doing?' she said bitterly. 'Any *idea* about the can of worms you're opening?'

For a split second he thought about Tash's fear that Jean Allardyce had gone missing. Even if she had, it couldn't be down to him in any way. Could it? 'Sorry, I don't follow.'

'Can't you imagine the disruption and upset this kind of thing causes?'

'Hang on a moment,' he said. 'When we talked in the pub, I thought you agreed that Barrie was an unlikely killer.'

'Barrie's dead.'

'Does that make everything all right?' Miranda gave him a baleful glance, but he plunged on. 'His reputation doesn't matter, is that it? It seems to be a widely-held opinion in Brackdale, If he wasn't guilty, fine, no problem. He was an oddball, anyway, a loser. So who cares?'

'That's not fair.' Leigh flushed. 'Okay, Barrie was one of life's scapegoats, but it's not the real issue. By encouraging the police to dig over old ground, you're opening a Pandora's box. Who knows what may fly out?'

'The police are perfectly capable of turning up stones without my egging them on. Hannah Scarlett is a good detective.' *A good detective.* He realised that he'd borrowed the phrase she'd used to describe his father and added quickly, 'A woman her age doesn't make Chief Inspector without being quick on the uptake.'

'You're right,' Leigh said slowly. 'She is a good detective.'

'Well, then. What are you afraid of?'

'Daniel,' Miranda said. 'This isn't helping...'

'It's all right,' Leigh said. 'I'm not offended. In fact, you're absolutely right. I am afraid, though not for myself. Afraid that innocent people will get hurt. People I care for. That's why I came to ask you a favour.'

'You can always ask.' Daniel ventured a smile to take the chill off his words.

'The favour is this. Can't you give up on trying to fight Barrie's corner? You know and I know what he was really like, why not leave it there? If you insist on re-opening old wounds, even more innocent people will suffer, and how can that help Barrie? I know your heart's in the right place, and I don't mean to be patronising when I say that. The truth is, though, you're simply making matters worse. If you have any influence with Hannah, please try and persuade her to concentrate on something more worthwhile.'

'Even if I wanted to do that,' he said, 'why should she listen to me? My only connection with her is that she worked with my dad. She strikes me as very much her own woman. You can bet she'll make up her own mind about what she does.'

'I suppose you're right.' Leigh swallowed the rest of her wine. 'She is her own woman.'

'In any case, if there's one man who has a chance of talking her round, surely it's Marc Amos. Or have you talked to him and got nowhere?'

When he'd met her previously, she'd seemed poised and self-confident, but now her voice was low with despair. 'You don't understand a thing, do you? Oh God, I should never have blundered in here. I've only made myself look ridiculous.'

Miranda reached out an arm, as if to offer consolation, only to find herself clutching at air as Leigh scrambled to her feet.

'I must go. I've said too much already. Thanks for the drink. I shouldn't have disturbed your evening. Sorry.'

Daniel watched as she pushed and shoved her way blindly past the makeshift barricade, scratching her arm on a protruding length of timber as she made good her escape.

'Leigh,' he called, 'can we talk about this? Please?'

She didn't look back, just shook her head and hurried around the corner of the building and disappeared from view. He was about to follow, but Miranda's shaking voice halted him in his tracks.

'Happy now? Or won't you be satisfied until your obsession with what happened all those years ago has antagonised every single person in this bloody valley?'

After Eddie finished, they ate a scratch meal together in silence. The food tasted of dust. Whilst Daniel was filling the cafetiere, Miranda announced that she had a migraine and was going to bed. Left to his own devices, he swallowed a couple of mouthfuls of coffee, slung the crockery in the new dishwasher, and decided to go for a walk. The evening was mild and another hour's exercise before darkness fell might help to set things in perspective. He felt a sort of kinship with those sci-fi movie heroes who slay the wicked alien only for the creature to spring back to life, more fearsome than ever, in the final reel. This new life was turning out to be even more complicated than the old.

Their bedroom door was shut. He tapped gently and said, 'I'll be out for an hour. Going to clear my head.'

No reply.

He padded down the stairs again and put on his jacket and boots. He'd decided on a circuit of the Fold, taking in the pack horse bridge, a stretch of the beck and the disused corn-mill that Tash Dumelow was planning to paint. An undemanding ramble, a chance to sort things out in his mind.

A bright red tea rose was coming into bloom by the side of the path. The memory came back to him of his grandmother, who had stayed with the family the Christmas before she died.

He would have been ten years old and he always associated her with the aroma of cigarette smoke blended with talcum powder. She was a shrewd Lancastrian who must by then have realised that her life would soon be destroyed by the cancer eating at her lungs.

'Promise me this, you two,' the old lady wheezed one night while he and Louise were reducing each other to tears of rage over some petty juvenile dispute. 'Life is shorter than you realise. You must remember to stop and smell the roses.'

It was the last conversation he could recall having with her. Time to take her advice, he thought, pausing to inhale the rich scent. As he unfastened the gate, he turned over in his mind the conversations he'd had with Jean Allardyce and Tash Dumelow and Leigh Moffat. So much for being a stranger in Paradise. As a boy, life had seemed simple to him, no more than a steady and straightforward ascent of a mountainside to gain greater and greater heights. And then his father had deserted them and he'd discovered that the way forward was barred by crevasses as deep as they were dangerous.

From out of nowhere came the muffled blare of Elmer Bernstein's theme from *The Great Escape*, wildly incongruous in the calm of the clearing. He hadn't even realised that he'd left the mobile in his jacket. By the time he'd finished fumbling in his inside pocket and fished it out, the ringtone was silent.

Who could have called him? It was late for one of the tradesmen to get in touch and there weren't many other possibilities. When they'd moved here, they'd bought each other new mobiles, ditching the old numbers that former colleagues knew by heart: all part of the plan to cut themselves off from the past.

As he pressed the button to check, the phone rang again.

Chapter Sixteen

'So you've nothing further to add?' Nick Lowther asked.

Tom Allardyce's expression remained impassive. Except, Hannah thought, for a hint of scorn in the way the corners of his lips turned down. Grudgingly, he'd led them into the kitchen, a large well-proportioned room commanding a view of Underfell and the coffin trail that wound down from the slope beyond. At least he was house-trained to the extent of leaving his boots in the back porch before venturing on to the well-scrubbed green linoleum tiles. Half a dozen towels were hanging over a huge old-fashioned wooden clothes horse to dry, and the rich smell of baked bread lingered in the air. Before taking a seat at the table occupying the centre of the room, Hannah had run her fingertips along the rims of half a dozen Port Meirion plates displayed on a tall pine dresser. Not a speck of grime. Whatever Jean Allardyce had done with herself, she hadn't forgotten the dusting before her departure.

'Don't reckon I have.'

'And you can't tell us when we may be able to speak to your wife?'

'No.'

Hannah stood up. 'In that case, Mr. Allardyce, we won't be troubling you any further.'

'Thank Christ for that. I can get back to my work.'

'For the moment, I should say.' Hannah forced a sweet smile, hoping to provoke him. 'For the time being, you're quite free to carry on cleaning your car.'

'It's a job to be done,' he said, as if stung. She exulted inwardly at having dented his calm. So that was his weakness. He didn't like it to be suggested that he shirked his duties. 'One of the many. I was up in the fields before six this morning. And you ask me where Jean is! I haven't got the bloody time to be looking after her as well as everything else.'

'When your wife gets back,' Nick said, 'can you ask her to give us a ring?'

'Assuming she does get back,' Hannah added.

Allardyce glowered. 'And exactly what d'you mean by that?'

Hannah didn't reply, just allowed her gaze to settle on the farmer, letting him exercise his imagination.

◇◇◇

'What do you reckon?' Nick watched as the collie raced after the departing Mondeo, barking furiously.

'I'd say the dog's marginally preferable to his owner. At least with our four-legged friends, what you see is what you get. Allardyce gives nothing away.'

'He stuck to his story about the night Gabrielle was killed. Hear no evil, see no evil. Backed up with a convenient alibi from his good lady.'

'Not quite so convenient for him if she's vanished.'

'What do you make of that? Something or nothing?'

'I wish we had tapes of those calls. Perhaps we should have set the hotline up differently. Run it into the main switchboard so that we could have automatic recording. Then we'd know if Jean Allardyce was the woman who phoned us.'

'Wisdom of hindsight,' Nick said. 'Don't reproach yourself. It's an utter waste of energy.'

'All right, if she is our caller, then why would she go missing? That's what bugs me.'

'Early days yet. According to Allardyce, it's only a few hours since he last saw her. Barely long enough for a serious shopping trip, never mind anything more life-changing. Maybe she's playing hookey for once in her life. For all we know, she has a secret lover lurking in Staveley or Troutbeck or somewhere.'

'She's not the type.'

'Is there a type?'

Hannah gave him a sharp glance, but he was concentrating on the road ahead. 'Anything's possible. As I remember, she wasn't bad looking, in a bloodless sort of way. Good complexion, I rather think she had an enviable pair of boobs, but her cardigans were so shapeless, it was hard to tell. If you ask me, the mere thought of an assignation with a lover would have scared the living daylights out of her. Quite apart from fear of what hubby would do if he found out. Did you see that dog-eared Mills and Boon next to the coffee machine? My guess is that she got her fix of romance strictly secondhand.'

'What would have prompted her to ring the hotline, if she'd kept quiet about something important the first time around?'

'Allardyce gave us one interesting titbit. She served Daniel Kind and his partner when they came to dine with the Dumelows. Could be Daniel said something that pricked her conscience. Especially given that she didn't share her husband's hostility to Barrie Gilpin.'

'So that's why you asked him about Ben Kind's son?'

'Elementary, my dear Lowther. Even though Allardyce says he's sure that Barrie killed Gabrielle, she may have suspected there was more to the murder than met the eye. Don't forget, if she has been keeping back important information about the case, it may have nothing to do with her husband.'

'Her cousin Joe Dowling, then?'

'Or Simon Dumelow.' As their car rounded a bend, Hannah caught a fleeting glimpse of the Sacrifice Stone outlined against the sky. 'Consider this. If she caused strife for her employer, it wouldn't only be her job on the line. Her husband would finish up right behind her in the dole queue. That's the sort of prospect that may have been weighing on her mind. It could explain why she told Linz that we should forget about her earlier call.'

'Isn't Dumelow supposed to be in a business meeting today?'

'With his accountant in Manchester, or so he told his wife. If Jean Allardyce hasn't turned up by tomorrow morning, I'll ask Maggie to check him out. Has he really been closeted in some high-powered boardroom wheeler-dealing? He wouldn't be the first man to lie to his wife about his whereabouts.'

'You don't think he and Jean Allardyce…?'

'It seems unlikely he'd leave his gorgeous wife for her. But who knows?'

'Maybe she's just so sick of Allardyce that she's decided to jack the marriage in.'

'With no clue or warning? She hasn't left any note or word of explanation. Unless he's found one and is keeping mum.'

'Which isn't impossible. Anyway, in her shoes, would you want to provoke a man like Allardyce any further if you were running out on him?'

'It might be the best chance I'd ever had. Revenge is a dish best eaten cold and all that. On the other hand, I don't think I'd hang around to wash his towels and the kitchen floor, let alone start baking bread before I packed my bags and left.'

◇◇◇

The minute she walked through the door of their cottage, even before she set eyes on him, she knew that Marc was in a temper. No Poirot-like powers were required to reach this conclusion; it was enough to hear her partner stomping around on the creaky upstairs floorboards. The slamming-shut of the bathroom door merely confirmed her deduction.

In the early months of their relationship, when she'd first encountered his propensity for acting like a spoiled teenager each time something didn't go his way, she'd allowed his moods to rattle her. Eventually she'd realised this was the reaction he sought, whether or not consciously. Her most effective retaliation was to feign indifference. These days, pretence wasn't often required; ignoring him and getting on with what she wanted to do was becoming easier all the time. As she made herself a toasted cheese sandwich, she wondered if this pattern was common to all couples. Perhaps it was a sign of maturity, that one could still love a man whilst finding his habits and behaviour a source of recurrent irritation.

She couldn't be sure, though; this was by far the longest and most intense relationship of her adult life and she didn't have much first-hand experience to measure it by. Her father had succumbed to prostate cancer when she was eleven, and although her hazy memories suggested that her childhood belief that her parents were devoted to each other was not far off the mark, her mother had re-married within twelve months. The step-father had proved to be an alcoholic and Hannah and her elder sister hadn't shed many tears when his liver had packed up permanently. While she'd been at university, her mother had died of pneumonia and her sister had emigrated after meeting an Italian on holiday. Isobel had divorced Silvio after a couple of years but had stayed on in Rome, teaching English as a foreign language, leaving Hannah to make her way in the police force. Apart from a couple of fellow students and (a big, big mistake that made her go cold simply to recall the gleeful gossip that her surrender provoked) a handsome but boastful fellow police cadet, she'd slept with no one but Marc. Listening to fellow women officers, she'd sometimes wondered if she was missing out. Too late to worry now. She was doomed to respectability. She was a Detective Chief Inspector.

Upstairs, the shower was roaring. Presumably Marc was trying to sluice away the troubles of the day. He'd already tried one solution; a bottle of Glenfiddich stood on the breakfast bar alongside an empty glass. While munching the toastie, she channel-hopped with the TV remote. True to form, when she fancied half an hour's escape, the screen was filled with soap opera actors shouting at each other, demanding *Do you have any idea how that makes me feel?* The alternatives included a documentary about AIDS in Africa and a close-up of a bowel operation in a hospital drama renowned for its gritty realism. She'd moved into the kitchen to wait for the espresso machine to finish gurgling, when she heard heavy footsteps bumping down the stairs.

'Fancy a drink?' she called. Perhaps his mood had nearly run its course. If not, she could always retreat into the bathroom herself and relax with a long soak in the tub while the aromatherapy candles gave the steamy atmosphere a tang of rosemary and juniper.

'I'll have a whisky. Neat.'

He was framed in the doorway and as she turned to face him, it struck her yet again what an attractive man she shared her life with. At least she hadn't become indifferent to him, at least he still had the ability to turn her on. His features were smooth and regular, his gaze clear and penetrating, and she knew that if he touched her in a certain way, she would melt: not a matter of choice, not a decision to be made, he could still do it for her.

She gave him a conciliatory grin. 'Bad as that, huh?'

He replied with a grunt and wandered off to the living room. When she followed with a well-filled tumbler and the bottle of Glenfiddich, he was watching the TV without the sound. The documentary had finished and been replaced by a football match. Two European teams she'd never heard of. She switched off the set and put on the CD player. Erik Satie; not her sort of music, too ethereal, but Marc was a fan. He gulped the whisky down without uttering a word. The coffee was still too hot, so she went to sit cross-legged on the rug, right at his feet. She caught the whiff of alcohol on his breath as he poured himself another generous measure.

She pushed the glass to one side with a firm shake of the head. 'If you drink much more of that tonight, you'll be no good to me later on.'

He still didn't say anything as she eased off his socks and began to stroke his soles. Foot massage was something he liked, something that often formed a prelude to making up after an argument or a period when they'd been too busy to spare enough time for each other. Suddenly she realised how much she wanted this to end in their making love, to magic away the troubles of the world.

'Want to tell me all about it?' There was no hard skin anywhere on his feet, no callouses, no corns; he just didn't have physical blemishes, this man. Already she was getting into a rhythm, moving her hands up and down, up and down.

'I don't think that would be a good idea,' he said hoarsely.

She could feel the tension in his body. He hadn't closed his eyes yet in surrender to her caress, let alone made a move to unfasten her blouse or jeans.

'Come on, talk to me,' she whispered.

'It won't help.'

'Hey, relax.' She ran her nails lightly over the surface of his feet. 'You're not the only one who's had a difficult day.'

It was true enough. They were no nearer to finding their anonymous caller. Bob Swindell had reported that Dale Moffat in particular had been hostile and unco-operative when questioned, but Linz didn't recognise the voice of either of the sisters. The likeliest candidate remained Jean Allardyce and she'd gone AWOL. Tomorrow they'd have to try again. How much did Marc care about that, or about anything other than his own preoccupations? Increasingly of late, a sceptical voice kept quizzing her: *Just how tough can it be, running a bookshop, for God's sake? Opening and shutting pretty much as you please, answerable to no one but yourself?*

'Is that so?' He lifted his legs, pulling out of her grasp. 'Sorry, it keeps slipping my mind how much more arduous your job is than mine.'

'I never said that.'

'You were thinking it, though.' With a defiant glare, he picked up the tumbler and took a mouthful of whisky. 'Don't deny it, Hannah. I know you too well.'

Her cheeks started burning and that made her angry, with herself and with him. She hauled herself up and said, 'For God's sake, what's got into you tonight?'

His eyes were glistening. For a few seconds she was afraid she'd gone too far and that he would dissolve into tears. 'All right. If you really want to know, it's to do with this inquiry your people are running. Leigh called me earlier. She and Dale have each been given the third degree by a pair of your DCs.'

She was baffled. 'Is that all?'

'It's enough.'

'Leigh's getting it out of proportion. The team was only conducting routine follow-up interviews.'

He tossed back the remainder of the whisky. 'Is this simply because Daniel Kind has turned up on the scene? Because his father never accepted Barrie's guilt, you want to keep the son happy by going through the motions, is that it?'

'This has nothing to do with Daniel Kind.'

'You've not spoken to him?'

When she hesitated before replying, she saw a gleam of satisfaction in his eyes. 'He and I have talked, yes. What about it?'

'There's no need for your sidekicks to go around upsetting people all these years later.'

He poured himself another finger of Glenfiddich. In some bizarre way, he seemed to regard himself as having scrambled on to the moral high ground. With no bloody justification at all. The sheer unfairness of it made her skin prickle.

'What's the problem?' Her voice was rising; she couldn't help herself. 'I don't get it. For God's sake, Dale and Leigh aren't kids who need to be seen in the presence of an appropriate adult. They're mature women, they can cope with a few questions.'

'Leigh told me they pretty much reduced Dale to tears. Don't they realise she's a lone parent? That she's…vulnerable?'

'Vulnerable? Don't make me laugh, she's about as vulnerable as Cruella de Ville.' Hannah softened her tone as she added, 'Don't worry, I haven't forgotten that you and she used to see each other. Fair enough if you still want to look out for her. But there's nothing to fret over. Bob and Linz were only doing their job. No one's accusing her of murdering Gabrielle Anders.'

'Easy for you to say,' he snapped. 'Routine investigations are all in a day's work for you, but the sisters aren't used to being interrogated. Made to feel as though they are being secretive, holding stuff back, obstructing the police in the course of their inquiries.'

'Dale and Leigh were both working at The Moon under Water at the time. It was possible that either of them might have been our anonymous caller.'

'Ludicrous.'

'Or they may have seen something, without even realising its significance. We have to cover all the bases.'

He took another drink of whisky. 'This is so typical. You people do anything you want.'

'*You people?*' She reached out and seized his wrist. 'Hey, this is me. Your partner, remember? I'm not *you people.*'

He drained his glass and poured again. 'It's true, though, isn't it? Police work is all about trampling over lives, regardless of the consequences.'

Without a word, she took the tumbler out of his hand and put it down on the rug. 'Marc, I can't believe you're saying this. It's so over the top. Look, we're both tired, you've obviously had plenty to drink already. It's not even dark yet, but never mind. Why don't we have an early night for once?'

'You always have to have the last word, don't you?' he said bitterly. 'I will go up, but maybe I'll spend the night in the spare room. You can get on with your work as late as you like without any disturbance.'

His words were like needles entering her flesh. 'Why are you doing this?'

He gave a curt nod in the direction of her briefcase and laptop. 'You'll have brought work home, presumably? As always. You're forever saying you need to catch up with the paperwork. Well, here's your chance.'

'I don't need to…'

He sprang to his feet, although the decisive effect was compromised by a slight stumble which caused him to knock over the glass of whisky. As Hannah let her voice trail away, she watched an amber stain spreading out over the rug. Reaching out for the music system remote, she brought an abrupt end to *Trois Gymnopedies.*

He stopped at the door, seemed to waver for a moment. 'Goodnight, then.'

She didn't answer. Tonight there wasn't anything more for them to say to each other.

She'd never asked Marc directly about his love life in the years before they got together. It wasn't that she was incurious; far from it. But there were some questions—a lot of questions, actually—that it was better not to ask. You never knew how easy it would be to live with the answers.

Unlike her previous lovers, he seldom talked about himself. Except at their most intimate moments, when he gave himself to her without reservation, there remained something unknowable about him, something other-worldly and remote. In those heart-stopping weeks after she'd first slept with him, she'd vowed that she would suppress her natural inquisitiveness and concentrate on the here and now. All that mattered was that she never lost him.

Of course, she couldn't resist playing the detective game. As time passed, she became assiduous in picking up crumbs that he dropped. Marc was no monk in his earlier days, that was for sure. He'd lost his virginity to an older woman whom he'd met while working in a hotel during his gap year. Maybe from her he'd learned the patience and technique that made him as different from her previous lovers as Mozart from Meatloaf. He'd taken lovers at university, but out of term time he kept going back to a Brackdale girl he'd first courted as a diffident, acned schoolboy. Dale Moffat.

Hannah sat in the living room, rifling her memory for the bits and pieces of information he'd let slip about Dale. After consigning the Erik Satie CD to the bottom of a box of their least-played music, she'd put on Diana Krall and gone in search of comfort food. In a corner of a kitchen cupboard she'd discovered a forgotten box of Belgian chocolates. The legend boasted that the contents represented an exquisite combination of refined taste and time-honoured tradition: how could she resist? She'd worry about her weight in the morning. In the absence of sex, chocolate wasn't such a bad substitute.

As for sex, every community had at least one Dale. Pretty, vivacious, narcissistic; smart enough not to cheapen herself by spreading her favours too thinly but not quite smart enough to do a Tash Dumelow and hit the jackpot. When Marc was sixteen, she'd dumped him for the star centre forward of the school football team. By the time he came back as a student on his first vacation, the acne was long gone and the soccer player wasn't scoring any more. Hannah gathered that Marc and Dale liked each other's company and liked going to bed together even more, but it was never a grand passion. Long before Marc took his degree, Dale caught the eye of a married man and, in time-honoured tradition, finished up pregnant. She'd kept the baby but not the boyfriend.

When the child was a little older, she and Marc had resumed their affair on a sporadic basis. As far as Hannah could figure out, it was a fallback position in more senses than one. If Marc was ever without a girlfriend for the night and Dale wasn't otherwise engaged, they usually finished up in bed together. In the unlikely event that matrimony had ever been on the cards, Hannah had no doubt that the presence of Dale's boy, Oliver, was enough to deter Marc. For a lifelong commitment-phobe, taking on a stepson in addition to a wife was too much to ask. Perhaps that was why he insisted on surrounding himself with books. The dusty tomes never threw up or got toothache, they never made demands.

'She does know about you and Dale?' she'd asked when Marc said that he'd invited Leigh Moffat to run the café at Amos Books.

'Of course, those two don't have secrets.' The question seemed to amaze him. 'But it's not an issue.'

She'd thought about joking that it would be different if the boot was on the other foot, and she was proposing to set up with

the brother of an ex, but she let it go. It would never occur to
him that she might suffer a pang of jealousy. In a way, she felt
flattered that he regarded himself as incapable of betraying her.
Only in the darkest moments of self-doubt did she wonder if
she was fooling herself. Or if he was fooling himself.

Leigh was less blatantly alluring than her sister, but to
Hannah's mind more attractive. Like Dale, she'd never married;
Hannah didn't have a clue why not. There had been relationships
with men, Hannah gathered, but nothing that lasted, and she
seemed content to spend a lot of time with Dale and Oliver,
upon whom she doted. Apparently she'd been on her own for
years, making a modest career in catering while Dale drifted from
job to job. Both were intelligent women, but neither seemed to
possess any burning ambition. Hannah couldn't relate to such a
lack of drive. To her, it was an article of faith: any woman with
talent owes it to herself, and to her gender, to make the most of
her potential. From childhood, she'd been determined to make
her own way and never to be beholden to a man.

Leigh wasn't the type to worry without good cause. Whenever
Hannah met her, she radiated a calm assurance that verged on
the intimidating. Impossible to imagine that in her entire life,
she'd ever allowed a soufflé to sink or stepped outside her front
door without the benefit of a discreet touch of blusher and eye-
shadow. If neither she nor Dale was the anonymous caller, why
so much angst over what they remembered of the day when
Gabrielle Anders had been murdered?

Unless, Hannah supposed, they remembered something
about Marc that they didn't want anyone to know.

◇◇◇

The choice was simple. She could imitate Marc and take refuge
in booze to stop worrying herself sick. Or she could *do something*. No contest. She found herself reaching into her case for
the personal organiser, and then for the phone.

She was halfway through dialling Daniel Kind's mobile
number when she asked herself what she was doing. Already
it was mid-evening; soon it would be dark. He would be busy

with his work or doing whatever he did in the company of his partner, the journalist. They weren't even friends. It was—well, Lauren Self's phrase would be *quite inappropriate*. What would he think if she called him out of the blue, without an excuse? As his phone rang, she cut off the call. Perhaps he was out. Besides, she wasn't sure what to say if he answered. The impulse to dial his number was inexplicable: why not Nick, or even Les Bryant? It wasn't as if she fancied him. That morning, she'd taken care not to look straight into his dark eyes, so reminiscent of his father's. The trouble was, all he had to do was to check who had called in order to discover that she'd called for a couple of seconds, only to think better of it. Embarrassing.

Given the option, it's always better to do something than nothing.

How many times had she heard Ben Kind say that? As a piece of philosophy, even he'd admitted its limitations, but right now it was apposite. What did she have to lose?

She dialled the mobile number again.

Chapter Seventeen

'This is Hannah Scarlett.' A long pause. 'Have I called at a bad time?'

'No, no,' Daniel said hastily. 'It's fine, absolutely fine.'

'I felt guilty about rushing off this morning, after I'd dragged you over to Kendal.'

'No need.'

'I really didn't give you much of an insight into Ben as I knew him. I'm sorry if you thought it was a wasted journey.'

'Of course not.' He didn't want her to hang up without agreeing to talk to him again. 'If sometime you could spare…'

'Tell you what. I'm not far away at the moment. Are you busy this evening?'

'No.' He groaned inwardly: why keep saying *no*? 'I'm just taking a walk in Tarn Fold, that's all.'

'Do you know The Slow and Easy?'

'On the road into Whitmell?'

'That's it. If you'd like to drive over, I can meet you in the lounge bar for a chat. Not for more than half an hour, mind. I mustn't get back home too late.'

'Are you sure?'

'Sorry,' she said abruptly. 'You're breaking up. I'll see you there in twenty minutes.'

The Slow and Easy was an old coaching inn by the side of the road connecting Brackdale with the neighbouring valley. A blackboard outside bore the legend: *I wandered lonely as a cloud and then I thought—sod it, I fancy a pint.* The lounge boasted slate tiles and an inglenook with a smoky fire and there wasn't a jukebox or pinball machine in sight. According to a magnificently bearded old man leaning on the bar, the carved oak bar had been made from a four-poster bed. Hannah wanted a tonic water and Daniel opted for half a pint of Jennings' Sneck Lifter as a treat to celebrate her unexpected call. On the way here he'd speculated what lay behind it. He wasn't naïve enough to believe that a senior police officer would indulge in spur of the moment socialising with someone she'd only met once. Presumably her sudden enthusiasm for an early second meeting was linked to the interviews that Leigh Moffat had complained about. He was glad to see her, whatever the ulterior motive.

'It was good of you to phone,' he said, handing her the glass. 'So—you were working late?'

'I'm off duty now,' she said carefully. 'As you may have deduced from the change of outfit.'

In sweatshirt and jeans, she looked even slimmer than when they'd met in the morning. Smaller, too. Almost fragile. He pulled his eyes away from her and took a draught of beer.

'Since we spoke this morning, I've heard I'm not the only one making waves. Your detectives have been quizzing Leigh Moffat and her sister.'

Cradling her chin in her hand, she smiled and said, 'I told you, news travels fast in these parts. So you're already plugged into the Brackdale grapevine?'

'Not exactly. In fact, I suspect I'm in danger of becoming *persona non grata* the length and breadth of the valley. Leigh came round to the cottage specially to rebuke me for making a song and dance over my Barrie-Gilpin-is-innocent campaign.'

'Did she now? I suppose you wouldn't like to tell me more?'

He made a show of weighing up her request, but could see no good reason to refuse. 'Why not? It's not as if we spoke under the seal of the confessional.'

'Fire away, then.'

As he recounted the conversation with Leigh, her face remained a mask. When he'd finished, she just said, 'Interesting.'

'Why do you think she's so worked up?' he asked.

'Oh, women are strange creatures,' she said with a faint smile.

'Thanks, but I already knew that.' He finished his drink. 'I presume you're not going to take me into your confidence?'

'Nothing to tell.'

'That I doubt, somehow.'

'Can I buy you another drink?'

He glanced at his watch. 'You said you don't have long.'

She gave a lazy shrug and picked up their glasses. 'Half of bitter, was it?'

'I'll settle for an orange juice this time. I'll need all my wits about me if you're going to interrogate me any further.'

She laughed. 'I hope you don't feel I've lured you out here on false pretences.'

Settling back in his chair, he said, 'Am I complaining?'

Unexpectedly, she blushed. 'I will talk to you more about your father. If not tonight, then soon. Promise.'

He watched her thread her way through a crowd of burly young men in hiking gear. If she was aware of their admiring glances, she gave no sign of it. The bearded Methuselah at the bar leered at her shamelessly but she took no notice. She moved with a purpose; he guessed that everything she did, everything she said, had a particular direction in mind. Many bosses might feel threatened by a subordinate with drive, especially a woman subordinate with drive, but he was sure his father would have encouraged her. He'd have been a good mentor. Might even have been a good father, given the chance.

When Hannah returned with the drinks, she asked how he was acclimatising to life in the Lakes. 'Missing the dreaming spires yet?'

'Not me. These days they dream too much about tuition fees and graduate debt. This place suits me fine, even if I have ruffled a few feathers.'

'How about your partner? Miranda, did you say?'

'Yes, Miranda.' He took a taste of his drink. Fresh orange, not the carbonated crap he'd become accustomed to at his local in Oxford. 'Funny thing is, if it weren't for her, we wouldn't have moved here. She was passionate about it. But it's not been easy for her, living in a lonely cottage surrounded by nothing but trees and water and building materials. Very different from Islington. Less happening, fewer people to talk to. She's not as anti-social as me.'

'I can't believe you're anti-social.'

'Seldom happier than when I'm on my own, lost in a book. Miranda loves company. Apart from a not totally successful dinner at Brack Hall, we haven't mixed much.'

'But you've become friendly with the Dumelows?'

'I bumped into Tash in the village and she invited us over to the Hall. I blotted my copybook by arguing Barrie's case. Miranda wasn't best pleased. I guess she's hankering after the social whirl.'

'The other man's grass?'

'Something like that.' A bawdy joke caused the hikers to erupt in an ear-splitting guffaw; perhaps a jukebox would have been preferable, after all. 'We always want what we haven't got.'

'You're right.' A faraway look had come in her eyes and he wondered what was passing through her mind.

'No one's immune, I suppose. I was talking to a woman yesterday, a farmer's wife. She's spent all her life in the Lake District, the place must be part of her body and soul, and yet she was telling me how she yearned to get away. She has this romantic notion about the old pioneers, travelling across the prairie.'

Suddenly he had Hannah's full attention. She leaned across the table and said, 'Can I ask who that was?'

He blinked. 'She's called Jean Allardyce. I met her at Brack Hall. She and her husband…'

'I'm acquainted with her husband. He and I talked this afternoon.' She hesitated. 'His wife wasn't at the farm and he didn't seem to know when she'd be back. What exactly did she tell you?'

Taking his time, he repeated as much of what Jean had said as he could remember and told her of Tash Dumelow's concern about her apparent disappearance. As he talked, he was acutely aware of Hannah's intense concentration upon him. In other circumstances, he might be flattered that an attractive woman was hanging on his words. But he didn't fool himself: what interested her was the information he had to impart.

'You'd make a good witness,' she said when he'd finished.

'I'll take that as a compliment.'

'You should. So how would you describe Jean Allardyce? Thirties, timid, quietly spoken? Local accent?'

'Yes, she has fair hair and blue...'

'It was her voice I was especially interested in.'

'May I ask why?'

She swirled the water around in her glass. 'Let's just say that a woman has made a phone call to us and we'd like to talk to her again. Snag is, we don't know her name, but Jean Allardyce is a candidate. She's not available for us to interview, though Tom Allardyce reckons he expects her back any time. But ask him where she's gone or when she's likely to return and he doesn't have an answer.'

'Shit.' He bowed his head.

'What's wrong?'

'What if something's happened to her?' He swallowed hard. 'What if...someone has decided she knows more than she should?'

'From what you say, she was toying with the idea of getting out of Brackdale. Tash Dumelow's story backs that up. She'd packed a suitcase.'

'She wanted to unburden herself to me. Sounds like she was seeking for help. If I'd spent more time talking to her...'

'You're not reproaching yourself?'

'Why not? If only...'

'Stop it.' She reached across the table and laid her hand on his. Her palm was warm. 'You mustn't blame yourself, it's ridiculous. For all we know, she's checking in at Heathrow at this very moment. Destination: the Little House on the Prairie.'

'You really think so?'

'Well…'

'The truth is, I could have done more.' His voice had become hoarse. 'Should have done more.'

She withdrew her hand and looked him in the eye. 'You take things seriously, don't you? So did Ben. Too seriously, most people used to say. I'm not criticising, the same people would say I suffer from the same fault. But it is a fault, make no mistake. You can't take everything to heart. If you're not careful, it becomes unbearable. You're not responsible for Jean Allardyce. Okay?'

When he nodded, she stood up and said, 'Good. That's settled, then. Look, I really have to go. I'm sorry, but I never intended to stay this long. You've been incredibly helpful and I do appreciate it.'

'One of these days,' he said wryly, 'you must tell me more about what it was like, working with my father."

'It's a deal,' she said. 'I'll be in touch. Goodnight.'

She turned and strode towards the door. They'd shaken hands when she'd arrived, but not on parting. Somehow it didn't seem necessary. He could still feel the warmth of her palm.

'You mustn't blame yourself.'

The words echoed in his brain as he drove home. How many times had he heard them before? After his father's desertion, Daniel had confided in a teacher that in a way it was down to him that the family had split asunder. During their holiday in the Lakes, he'd spent too much time with his new friend Barrie; if he'd paid more attention to his dad, the old man could never have brought himself to leave. The teacher had gone to inordinate lengths to make sure the family had support and to reassure her star pupil that he had nothing to feel guilty about. It all became too much for Daniel, who finished up wishing he hadn't said a word. With Aimee, it was far worse. Once again, everyone was kind, but this time there wasn't much doubt that he had something to blame himself for. He could have saved her.

As he peered through the windscreen, trying to make out the bends in the road, pictures from the past kept flipping through his head like the leaves of a photograph album. When he reached Tarn Fold, he parked in the spot that had been occupied by Tash Dumelow's Alfa earlier in the day. He wasn't ready to return to the cottage and see Miranda. Since moving to the Lakes, he'd pretty much managed to stop tormenting himself about Aimee, but tonight there was no escaping her memory.

Outside he could see nothing but darkness. With the windows wound up, he couldn't hear the sounds of the unseen creatures in the trees and undergrowth. Here in the heart of the country, he was remembering Aimee's death in the city.

Familiar images jostled in his brain. At breakfast on the last day of her life, Aimee had been monosyllabic as she nibbled at a few cornflakes, but that was nothing out of the ordinary. She'd been back home from the Warneford for a fortnight, following treatment for severe depression. He'd never found rhyme or reason for the sense of hopelessness that she confessed to in her bleakest moods. She was a senior research fellow with a growing international reputation in the field of comparative labour law, and although her parents' divorce had left her sceptical about marriage, she and Daniel had been lovers for a couple of years. They hadn't moved in together—she said she wasn't ready for that sort of permanence—but neither of them ever looked at anyone else. She had everything to live for, people would say. But what did people know? Depression never respected logic; the illness ran in her family and her mother had taken a fatal overdose when Aimee was only sixteen.

Before going into the Warneford, she'd made a botched attempt to slit her wrists. After a morning's research in the Bodleian, Daniel had called in at her flat close to the Parks. When there was no answer, he let himself in and found her in the bathroom, lying face down on the floor with nothing on. Her flesh was the colour of chalk, a contrast to the curly chestnut hair spilling on to her shoulders. A lilac smell from pot pourri in a basket on the windowsill masked the sourness in the air. The razor blade was lying where it had fallen, near her toes. A dark stain was spreading over the green vinyl floor.

At first, the belief that she was dead robbed him of movement, but when belatedly he checked for a pulse, he realised she was still breathing. She'd simply fainted from the loss of blood. As he phoned for an ambulance, relief of an intensity he'd never experienced before swept over him like a tide. She was safe.

When she returned home from hospital, he was reluctant to leave her alone. But she insisted that she couldn't forever use him as a crutch and although he protested, deep down he knew she was right. He took to working in the college library, a ten minute walk from her flat. His favourite corner was beside a window overlooking the small quadrangle. Out of term time, the quiet was disturbed only by the rustle of the leaves on the horse chestnut trees outside. He could sketch out synopses for a new book to his heart's content. One September afternoon he emerged from the library staircase into the blinding sunlight and bumped into Theo Bellairs. When Theo invited him up for tea, he checked his watch before accepting.

'I really should be getting back to Aimee.'

'Nonsense, my boy.' Theo laid a hand on his shoulder. 'In the modern jargon, you must let her have a bit of space. Didn't you say last week that she was on the mend?'

'I said she has good days and bad days.'

'There you are, then. My dear fellow, do take that worried look off your face. Tell me about your latest plans over a cup of Darjeeling and you can inspect a Macaulay first edition that I've picked up at Sotheby's. Candidly, it's a better investment than the college pension. Come on, I promise not to detain you for long.'

Of course he'd said yes and after half an hour of civilised conversation, he'd made his excuses and left. Having switched off his mobile on entering the library, he found he'd forgotten to switch it back on.

Aimee had left a voicemail message. She spoke almost in a whisper and he had to strain to catch the words.

*Daniel, I'm so sorry. I've tried hard but it isn't any good. I'm going
to the tower. Please don't think badly of me. I do love you. I do.*
He felt dizzy, unfocused, as though in a moment his legs
would buckle and he'd crumple on to the gravelled path. She
meant to kill herself, he was sure of it. He had to find her, to
rescue her for a second time.

The tower. Oxford had plenty, but he was sure she meant St
Michael's, in Cornmarket. It was part of the Northgate Church
and its Saxon origin made it the oldest building in the city.
Aimee loved the church and sometimes slipped in to pray, though
Daniel was never clear what exactly she was praying for.

He found himself running through the college gate, ignoring a porter's cheerful greeting, brushing past a baffled SCR
colleague in the lodge. Cornmarket wasn't far away. How long
would it take her to reach the top of the tower? A student on
a bicycle nearly collided with him as he raced across the road
without looking and a woman with a double buggy containing
two red-faced infants clipped his ankles as he plunged through
the mass of shoppers.

Breathless, he turned into Cornmarket. As he raced along the
pavement, he could see a crowd that had gathered a little way ahead.
Around the foot of St Michael's Tower. As he found his progress
blocked, he turned to a diminutive Asian man who was standing on
tip-toe, trying to see what had captured everyone's attention.

'What is it?'

'Someone threw themselves off the tower,' the man said. 'A
young lady, I heard. And on such a beautiful day, as well.'

Blinking away tears, Daniel pushed through the onlookers,
telling himself that the worst might not have happened. This
wasn't the first time that someone had chosen St Michael's for
a suicide attempt. It might not be Aimee.

'Hey, mate, who d'you think you're shoving?'

'Yeah, this isn't a peep-show, you know.'

He took no notice of the angry exclamations and didn't
mutter an apology as he elbowed in the ribs a couple of young
shop assistants. They didn't seem to notice; they were just excited

by the enlivening of their afternoon. In the distance he could hear a siren keening.

'The ambulance will be here in a minute,' someone said.

He pushed his way through to the front of the crowd. Stretched out on the pavement not far from the foot of the old tower was the body of a woman. A tall man was bending over her. He'd taken off his tweed jacket and slipped it over the corpse's head. It was a corpse, Daniel was sure of that. The fall from the top of St Michael's would kill anyone. Her skull must have been smashed on the unyielding concrete.

Daniel couldn't see the dead woman's face, thank God, but he didn't need to. He recognised the Aran sweater she'd knitted for herself, the navy blue corduroy jeans, the strands of chestnut hair that had escaped the covering jacket. And he recognised the end result of a despair too deep for him to touch. No second chance this time. He'd failed to save her, after all.

You mustn't blame yourself?

Absurd. How could he not?

Chapter Eighteen

A light was still on in the spare room when Hannah got back to the house. When she opened the front door, she heard Marc's footsteps on the landing. As she hung up her jacket, he padded down the stairs.

'You're out late,' he said as they turned to face each other in the hall. In the harsh light his pale face was haggard. She'd bought his red silk dressing gown last Christmas, but beneath it his shoulders seemed to slope in defeat.

'Interviewing a witness.'

'With Nick Lowther?' When she groaned, he repented at once. 'Sorry, ignore that. None of my business.'

'No, I wasn't with Nick. I am capable of making a few enquiries on my own.'

She didn't say that she'd been talking to Daniel Kind. In days gone by, Marc had made even more of a fuss about Ben than he did about Nick. She didn't want to create a new object for his absurd jealousy. And it was absurd, of course.

'Sorry, I didn't…'

'Oh, forget it,' she said. 'Look, I fancy something to eat. Can I tempt you?'

'Hannah, we need to talk.'

'Not tonight we don't, Marc. It's been a long day.'

She made as if to move past him and head for the kitchen, but he folded his arms and stood in her way. The smell of whisky on his breath was unmissable.

'Please, Hannah. It must be tonight.' He wasn't quite slurring his words. Not quite. 'This is very important, not just for me, but for—for us.'

She stared at him. 'Living room?'

He led her to the sofa and they sat facing each other, wary as two dogs encountering each other in the park, uncertain whether they are friends or foes. For once he didn't reach automatically for the remote control to put on classical music. God, she said to herself, this must be serious.

'What's on your mind, Marc?'

'I need to tell you something. Make a clean breast.'

The central heating had been programmed to switch itself off half an hour earlier, but that wasn't why she suddenly felt cold. The expression in his eyes, on his face, was not familiar. For a few moments she couldn't place it, but then she realised that he was ashamed. *Marc, ashamed?* Well, well, talk about a first time for everything. All of a sudden, she was listening in her head to the cool voice of Ben Kind

'When the suspect is about to confess, it's the most delicate moment of all. You're walking a tightrope, you mustn't rush. One false step—and you're finished. Don't give a clue what's going on in your mind. You may be winning, but no game is over until it's over. Never let the initiative slip.'

She stretched out her legs. 'Okay, Marc. I'm listening.'

'You're always so calm,' he said, in a tone of nervous wonder. 'What must be going on in your head?'

'Not a lot,' she said. 'It is late. But like I said, I'm listening.'

He took a breath. 'There's a reason why Dale and Leigh were stressed-out by the interviews today.'

'Other than brutal police interviewing techniques?'

Ben would have fumed, but she couldn't resist scoring a cheap point; it helped release the tension. Marc waved a hand, a tired gesture of surrender.

'I'm sorry about earlier on. Forget what I said. I was overwrought, okay?'

Hearing him say *sorry* so often was a novelty. She'd never known him give the impression of being fearful of her. She was in charge, but it didn't feel good.

'Carry on.'

'After Gabrielle Anders was killed, I told you a lie.'

She fought to keep her voice from trembling. 'What did you lie about?'

'I was out in Brackdale on the day of the murder. But I told you that I walked the Horseshoe. It wasn't true. I made a detour and went down the coffin trail and into the village.'

Her gaze didn't flicker, but her thoughts were jumping. Had he seen something relevant to the murder inquiry and kept his mouth shut?

'I headed straight for The Moon under Water.' The booze must have given him courage; the story started tumbling out like a stream in spate. 'Dale was in charge of the cleaners there. Sometimes she took advantage and invited a boyfriend round. If a room wasn't occupied, she could make use of it. She said Joe Dowling didn't know, but thinking it over, I'm not so sure. The slimy toad had his eye on her and I bet he knew what she was up to. She never admitted it to me, but I'd lay odds that he made sure there was a payback. Probably that's why she stopped working there.'

'Go on.' Hannah scarcely trusted herself to say any more.

He coughed. 'Anyway, on this particular occasion, I was the one she invited.'

After a long pause, she said, 'But we were seeing each other at the time.'

'I know.' His face had aged with misery; it had lines and flaws that she'd never noticed before. 'I shouldn't have said yes. But you'd just started working with Ben Kind...'

'And you were jealous?'

'Yes!' Tears brimmed in his eyes. 'I can't help it, Hannah, it's the way I'm made. I hate it when men fancy you, but it's even worse when you fancy them.'

It was a mistake to respond, but she couldn't let it pass. 'Are you suggesting that I fancied Ben Kind?'

'I don't want to argue about it,' he said thickly. 'Deny it if you want, that's fine. But I thought you did.'

'So you decided on tit for tat?'

'You could say…'

'And when the chance of a quick shag came along, you couldn't say no?' Her voice was getting louder.

'I've regretted it ever since.'

'Not as much as I regret it! Oh shit, Marc, how could you do this?' She was almost choking with anger and despair. 'When we started going out together, you told me you and Dale were finished. Over. Done.'

'It was true!' he insisted. 'And then I bumped into her one evening when you were working and she was lonely and so was I and—things got out of hand.'

'How many times?' she demanded.

She'd seen the same hunted expression on the faces of a hundred criminals. The panicky arithmetic: *what's the least I can get away with?*

'Twice that week,' he said eventually. 'That's how often we made love. I would close the shop and make my way to Brack. You and I were passing strangers, Ben Kind had you running errands all over the place for him. I'm not making an excuse, just trying to explain. Of course, that afternoon was the end. I swear it. Dale was as upset as me. Imagine how she felt when she heard that Gabrielle Anders was dead. She'd spent part of the day in question in bed with the boyfriend of one of the detectives investigating the murder. Wouldn't you be scared stiff?'

'How would I know? I've never been in that situation.'

'She swore she'd never do anything to mess up my relationship with you, and she meant it, she kept her word.'

'By lying to the police?'

'We didn't see any alternative. It seemed to be for the best. No one saw us, Joe Dowling was out. Dale didn't harm the investigation. When the constable questioned her, she told him she hadn't seen Gabrielle since breakfast time. Perfectly true, as it happens. The room we used was on the same corridor as Gabrielle's and we didn't see her on the way in or out.'

Hannah said nothing.

'The truth is,' Marc said, 'Dale and I have both moved on. We'd pretty much forgotten what happened.'

'Oh yeah?'

'Honestly, I swear it. Then your team re-kindled the investigation and Dale found herself being quizzed again. She panicked. How could she know whether you knew or had guessed about her relationship with me?'

'Did Leigh Moffat know that you two were sleeping together at the time of the murder?'

He shook his head. 'They look out for each other, but Leigh has enough sense not to be her sister's keeper. Over the years, she's learned that there are some parts of Dale's life it's better for her not to know about, and that suits Dale. Leigh's obviously aware of our original relationship, when we were kids. But the first she learned about The Moon under Water was this afternoon. Dale didn't have anyone else to turn to.'

'And?'

'Leigh was bloody furious with both of us. Most of all, she wanted to protect our relationship. You have to believe that.'

'At this precise moment, I'm inclined to believe anything of the Moffat sisters.'

'Hannah, please. Leigh is so honest, it's painful, but she doesn't want our lives to be wrecked by an old indiscretion. She didn't want me to tell you, but it's not simply a matter of protecting me. She hates the thought of me hurting you.'

Hannah considered. 'Is that it?'

His eyes widened. 'Isn't that enough?'

'Anything else you want to tell me? Additional offences to be taken into consideration?'

He tried out a tentative smile and reached towards her, but when she flinched, he thought better of it. 'I'm so sorry, Hannah. What more can I say? I wish we'd never…it was wrong. Better for you not to know. But with a root and branch cold case review…'

'You were terrified I might find out anyway?' Hannah interrupted.

'Well, yes.'

She stood up. 'Thanks for telling me.'

He stared at her. 'Don't you want to say—anything else?'

'Not right now. It's late and I'm dog-tired and tomorrow will be as busy as today. Unlike you, I don't have the option of putting up a *closed for business* sign whenever the mood takes me. Or whenever I'm made an offer I can't refuse.'

'I suppose I deserved that.' He gnawed at his lower lip. 'Do you still want me to sleep in a separate room?'

'Right now, Marc, I don't give a fuck what you do.'

She strode out of the room and headed up the stairs. As she reached the top, she heard him calling from the hallway.

'There's more. I have to tell you.'

If he's slept with anyone else, that's it. I'm out of here.

'Don't you think you've said enough?'

She could hear him breathing hard. When she turned, he was standing at the bottom of the stairs. Tears filled his eyes.

'No, these are things you should know. Not about me.'

'Go on, then.'

'When Dale was questioned, it brought so much back.'

'I bet.'

He blew his nose. 'You need—the police need—to have this information. I don't know if it's relevant…'

'Tell me.'

'Two things. First, Gabrielle Anders slept with Joe Dowling. At least once, maybe more often. Dale opened Gabrielle's door once and saw her with Joe. She was lying on her back on the bed, letting him climb aboard. They were so engrossed they never knew they'd been seen.'

'You never mentioned this before.'

He hung his head. 'At least now you can understand why. Besides, I thought everyone agreed, Barrie Gilpin killed Gabrielle. There didn't seem any point in complicating things.'

She said coldly, 'And the second thing?'

'Gabrielle had a lot of cash in her possession, but it seems to have vanished after she was murdered.'

'How do you know this?'

'Dale surprised her in the room one morning. This time Gabrielle had remembered her *do not disturb* sign, but Dale didn't notice it in time.'

'Oh really?'

'So she told me. Anyway, Gabrielle had all this money spread out over the bed. Dale didn't have the chance to count it before she made her apologies and left. When she came back to clean the room, the cash had vanished. But she reckoned it was thousands.'

Hannah hushed the mutterings in the briefing room and said, 'During the original investigation into Gabrielle Anders' murder, the initial focus was on finding Barrie Gilpin. That isn't to say that other lines of enquiry were neglected. Ben Kind took care to keep an open mind about the case, even though the ACPO wanted a quick result.'

Her throat was dry and she took a sip of water. Apart from coffee and the maximum dose of paracetamol, she'd had nothing all day. She'd woken up with a fierce headache, and the thought of eating even toast and marmalade was enough to make her heave. She couldn't have felt worse if Marc had clubbed her on the skull. Come to think of it, he had.

'We all know two things, don't we? One, we don't need to prove a motive to secure a conviction for murder. But two, if we can't figure out the why as well as the who, we may struggle when the case comes to court. Juries look for complete narratives. They want to know whydunit, before they decide on whodunit. So Ben looked at several angles. For instance, was the site where the body was found significant?'

'The possibility of pagan ritual.' Gul Khan wasn't quite licking his lips, but he did sound hopeful. He preferred his work to be enlivened by a touch of the bizarre.

'We couldn't find any evidence to support any meaningful link to witchcraft or Druids or any of that garbage. The likeliest scenario involved Barrie Gilpin's well-documented fascination with the legends of Brackdale. The smart money was on his having a warped idea of sexual fulfilment. Maybe that caused him to lay out his victim's corpse on the Sacrifice Stone.'

'Gabrielle wouldn't be the first young woman to be murdered because she led a man on and then turned him down,' Nick Lowther said.

'Sure,' Hannah said. 'But Ben Kind didn't leap to the conclusion that nobody other than Barrie could have killed her. Joe Dowling's wife was away that night and there was nobody to back up the story that he took to his bed because of illness. Tom Allardyce, we've spoken about. His wife gave him an alibi, although her disappearance is a cause for concern. Has there been a rift between them? We need to speak to her urgently.'

'Yeah,' Gul said. 'Marital discord doesn't half give us some opportunities.'

Hannah cringed inwardly. In her flattest, least emotional tone, she explained that fresh information had come to light. Joe Dowling and Gabrielle might have had a fling, and a large and unexplained sum of cash had been seen in her room shortly before she died. No need to reveal the source of the leads at this stage, even though Dale would need to be re-interviewed. One thing was for certain: it wouldn't be wise for Hannah to question her, even if she could bring herself to do so.

'Could the killer have wanted to conceal his victim's identity?' Linz suggested. 'Or did he think she was someone else?'

'We didn't devote much time to those possibilities,' Hannah said. 'There wasn't any doubt who she was. Plenty of people had talked to her during her few days in Brackdale. And despite the damage done to her face, once she was tidied up, she was still

recognisable. Tash Dumelow didn't have any trouble in identifying her.'

'What about Gabrielle's previous life?' Maggie asked. 'Anything in it that might cast light on her murder?'

'Tash Dumelow helped us to build a victim profile. The long
and short of it was, Gabrielle Anders was a drifter. A sexy drifter,
but a drifter all the same.'

Les Bryant said, 'Which is why I thought we should take a
fresh look at her past. We don't have anything new on her time
in the States and I can't believe it would help us anyway. But
her years in Leeds—that's another story.'

'As I mentioned yesterday,' Hannah said, 'Les has been speaking with former colleagues in Yorkshire. This morning, he's come
up with something fresh. Over to you, Les.'

He joined her at the front of the room and cleared his throat.
'Tash Dumelow was a good friend of Gabrielle, and for a couple
of years she seems to have been closer to her than anyone. But
she had to admit that Gabrielle was less successful with acting
than with taking big money from rich businessmen in city
centre hotels.'

Linz said, 'You're not suggesting all this cash she had was
payment for services rendered from Joe Dowling?'

'Unlikely,' Hannah said. 'He's famous for his tight fists. I can't
believe he'd part with his life savings, however good she was. Free
board and lodging would be closer to the mark.'

'Maybe he saves up for the little treats that girls like Gabrielle
can provide,' Bob Swindell suggested.

'And the money was never found?' Maggie looked up. 'Could
we have stumbled across a different motive for murder here?'

'Good question.' Gul was eager. 'All along, we've assumed
this is a sex crime. The nature of the killing, the place where the
body was found, everything points in that direction. But what if
someone killed her for the cash and then laid a false trail?'

'Did she have a criminal record?' Linz asked.

'Of course we made a routine check at the outset,' Hannah
said. 'Only to draw a blank.'

'I blame the bloody Data Protection Act,' Les said. 'All this European shit about human rights and civil liberties. People are scared stiff of putting anything down in black and white. Everyone's afraid the written records will come back and bite them when the bureaucrats find out. Result: you have to rely on word of mouth. So I talked off the record to people who worked in vice ten years ago and more, just to see if the name meant anything to them. Guess what? A DS I used to work with remembered her vividly.'

'That's the trouble with being drop-dead gorgeous,' Bob Swindell said. 'Too memorable. No use for undercover work. Aren't you glad you're not a blonde, Linz?'

Linz stuck her tongue out by way of reply, but when Les glared at them, they shifted uncomfortably and shut up.

'Now then,' he said. 'Gabrielle was seeing a crooked business-man by the name of Webber. He was half-Jamaican, half-Tyke, and he had his finger in various pies, if you'll pardon my French. Including a brothel in Bradford and a night club in Leeds. He made his money as a small-time builder and he kept the business going mainly as a convenient way of laundering drug profits. He was implicated in a number of serious assaults and at least two murders of business rivals, but there was no evidence. Surprise, surprise, the CPS wouldn't dream of prosecuting without being presented with a cast-iron case, and the CID would never have found anyone willing to testify. People used to wet themselves at the prospect of crossing Eldine Webber.'

He paused for effect, building suspense like a West Riding Hitchcock. Linz shuffled her feet impatiently, prompting Maggie to frown a rebuke.

'And then one day, Vice got a lucky break. Webber was found dead in his penthouse near City Square. A cocktail of booze and drugs had done for him. Sad to say, he choked on his own vomit.' A melancholy smile. 'The verdict was accidental death, but the circumstances of Webber's passing were a tad mysteri-ous. He was alone when he was found, but rumours began to surface that Gabrielle had been seen with him on the night he died. By the time of the inquest, she'd disappeared.'

After the team had digested this, Gul asked, 'So did she murder her sugar daddy?'

Les shrugged. 'Everyone had their own conspiracy theory. She'd killed him deliberately, she'd killed him accidentally, he'd died during a sex game and there'd been a cover up. One suggestion was that his enemies had paid her to kill him while his pants were down.'

'West Yorkshire never got to the bottom of it?' Bob smirked.

Les's dour expression didn't flicker. 'Let's just say, not many tears were shed about his passing.'

'Simon Dumelow is in the property business too, isn't he?' Maggie asked.

Hannah nodded. 'These days he plays the local squire. Opens the village fete and pays for the bouncy castle at the primary school sports day. His buildings win awards and he has a high ranking in the North West rich list. It wasn't always that way. Construction's a rough industry and most people in it get their first leg up the ladder by breaking a few rules. Occasionally a few heads. But Dumelow's never been convicted of anything worse than speeding.'

'That's a hanging offence, mind, if some chief constables are to be believed,' Bob muttered.

Linz said, 'Any connection between him and Webber?'

Hannah said, 'There's no evidence whatsoever to suggest it, but then we didn't know about the rumours of Gabrielle's involvement with Webber's death. Simon Dumelow maintained that the first time he met Gabrielle was when she turned up on his doorstep to renew her acquaintance with his wife. At the time we had no reason to doubt that. And his wife gave him an alibi for the night of the murder.'

'But?'

'But she was ill in bed with flu, so how watertight was that alibi? Worth our taking a closer look at Mr. Dumelow, especially in light of what we've learned about his movements yesterday. Maggie?'

'He was supposed to be attending a business meeting with his accountants in Manchester yesterday,' Maggie said. 'That's what his wife thought. But he cancelled, said he'd gone down with a stomach bug. We do know for sure that he wasn't laid up at home. So—where was he?'

Chapter Nineteen

'We should call at the farm first,' Hannah said as they passed the sign saying that Brack was just a couple of miles away. 'See whether Jean Allardyce is back at home.'

'You don't sound optimistic.'

'Are you? She may have told Daniel Kind that she fancied getting away from it all, but I can't see her being brave enough to take the plunge.' Hannah's stomach rumbled. She still hadn't eaten anything today, but at least the headache had faded. 'Besides, if Tash Dumelow's right in saying that Jean left a suitcase behind, it doesn't look good. After we've checked the story with her, we may have to consider a search of the premises.'

'And finish up with egg on our faces if she's safe and sound and sunning herself on the front at Morecambe?'

The walls of the cottages on the approach to Brack glinted in the sun. Hannah and Nick were both wearing their dark glasses. On a day as lovely as this, she reflected, there wasn't so much to choose between Morecambe and the South of France. Except maybe ten degrees Celsius.

'Yeah, that's the snag. I can picture Lauren's face if I say we need a warrant. And hear all her arguments against. Jean Allardyce is a grown woman, she has every right to up and leave at a moment's notice, blah, blah, blah. '

'It's true, we don't have any evidence that her husband wished to harm her.'

'Even so, I'm worried.'

'Maybe you worry too much,' he said gently. 'Everything all right?'

'What do you mean?' she asked.

'You look shattered. Didn't you get any sleep last night?'

She brushed a stray hair out of her eyes. 'That bad, eh?'

''Fraid so.'

'It's nothing, I'll be fine. Things are complicated, that's all.' She hesitated, debating whether to say more. They were driving into the village, close to The Moon under Water, where her partner had betrayed her in a squalid upstairs room. 'Dale Moffat is Marc's ex.'

'Ah.' He was looking at the road ahead, braking to allow an old woman with a wicker shopping basket, heedless of the zebra crossing thirty yards away, to make arthritic progress across the market square. She seemed oblivious to danger, as if the motor car had never been invented.

'No big deal,' she said. 'It was all a very long time ago. Water under the bridge.'

'Fine.'

She cursed inwardly for having protested too much. 'I thought you could talk to her, get more info about this money she saw in Gabrielle's room. Tomorrow?'

'No problem.'

'Thanks.'

The old woman gained the pavement outside Tasker's and acknowledged their presence with a toothless grin. Nick winked in response. That was what Hannah liked about him. No impatient revving of the engine, no fuss, no hassle.

'This Daniel Kind,' he said, as they started up again. 'You talked to him again last night?'

The question disconcerted her. 'Yes, that's when he told me about meeting Jean, and what Tash Dumelow had said.'

'You think it's coincidence that soon after Ben Kind's son shows up, we take the anonymous call and Jean Allardyce disappears and we start to find out all sorts of things about the case?'

She thought this over. 'No, I don't.'

'Because he's poked his nose into the case?'

'Once the snowball starts to roll, it develops its own momentum. That's the nature of cold case work. It's what we hope for, isn't it?'

Nick wouldn't be distracted. 'Is Daniel a wannabe detective?'

'What makes you say that?'

Keeping one hand on the steering wheel, Nick ticked points off on the fingers of the other hand. 'Well, he was estranged from his old man and may be trying to make some sort of connection with him. I caught one of his television programmes. He likes to draw comparisons between historical research and detective work. Already he's had a couple of conversations with his dad's old sergeant.'

'Not so much of the old, thank you. Daniel's doing his best to help, that's all.'

'Maybe he ought to take care.'

'What do you mean?'

Whenever Marc or Nick spoke about Daniel, she felt defensive. Silly, because there was no need, she didn't have any skeletons in her cupboard. It wasn't as if she and Daniel had a thing going.

'Hey, don't bite my head off,' he said calmly. In the distance they could see the pele tower of Brack Hall and the signpost pointing towards the farm. 'Let's assume Barrie didn't murder the girl and the real culprit is still around. How will he react to the man who's stirring trouble for him? Perhaps you ought to have a quiet word.'

'Warn him off?'

'Yeah, his idea of a fate worse than death is probably poor TV ratings. Maybe he needs reminding that a murder case isn't an intellectual exercise.' Nick's voice tightened. 'Picture in your mind what the killer did to Gabrielle.'

'And she hasn't been in touch at all?' Hannah asked.

They were back in the Allardyces' kitchen. A mound of unwashed crockery rose from the sink, the floor had become caked with mud, and the air was thick with the smell of burnt bacon. In the space of twenty four hours, the ideal home had transformed into a greasy bachelor pad.

Allardyce shrugged. 'Not a dickey bird.'

'She's never done this before, has she?' Nick asked. 'I mean, it's completely out of character.'

'You know what women are like.' Allardyce gave him a hard stare. 'Or maybe you don't, eh?'

To Hannah's surprise, Nick coloured at the cheap dig. He wasn't often so easily nudged off his stride. She said, 'We're not talking about any woman, Mr. Allardyce, we're talking about your wife. You've been married a long time. She's vanished without any explanation and you're unconcerned. It seems strange.'

'Aye, well,' he grunted. 'There's plenty around here that you might find strange.'

'So you don't care what may have happened to her?'

Now it was Allardyce's turn to flush. Rising to the bait, he said, 'You're talking bollocks. She might be anywhere. With her stupid sister in Carlisle…'

'Have you called her?'

'I did ring up,' he said grudgingly. 'No answer. Typical.'

'Can we have the number?'

He nodded at a pine notice board on the opposite wall. 'It's pinned up over there.'

'What about her cousin, does he know anything?'

Allardyce shook his head. 'They've never been close, but I did ask. Joe hasn't a clue where she might be.'

While Nick made a note, Hannah said, 'So you *are* worried?'

Allardyce plucked at one of the thick hairs sprouting from his nostril. 'No need for you lot to interfere. I'll deal with this in my own way.'

'By giving her a good slapping once she turns up?' Nick asked. 'Just to show her who's boss?'

Fists balled, Allardyce took two swift paces towards him. The men were eyeball to eyeball. Hannah's stomach lurched. The farmer was a man on the edge, she thought. Unpredictable and dangerous. She didn't want to see Nick hurt.

'I don't recommend you to vent your temper on DS Lowther, Mr. Allardyce. You'll finish up spending the night in jail. Maybe quite a few nights.'

Both men were breathing hard. Allardyce raised a grimy finger and wagged it in Nick's face. 'Next time you try to be a smart-arse, I'll make you regret it.'

'Mr. Allardyce…' Hannah began.

He turned on her. His face had reddened with fury. 'Now you listen to me, missus. I don't know what's happened to Jean, but it's my business, no one fucking else's. You leave me to sort it out. All right?'

'So you've been checking up on me, Detective Sergeant?' Simon Dumelow said.

Nick stretched his arms in a semblance of a yawn. He'd regained his composure after the brush with Tom Allardyce and, like Hannah, had made himself comfortable in one of the vast armchairs in the drawing room of Brack Hall. Meanwhile Tash Dumelow was busying herself in her studio, sorting out pictures to be displayed in a forthcoming exhibition.

Simon hadn't seemed troubled when they'd asked if he'd been drinking with Gabrielle in the pub the night before her death. According to him, Tash had complained of flu symptoms and had insisted that he keep her friend company in the pub while she got an early night. Simple as that. No question of Tash being kept in the dark, or being jealous. She had nothing to worry about: Gabrielle couldn't hold a candle to her. Nor was he fazed by mention of Eldine Webber's name. He just shrugged and claimed it meant nothing to him.

'Purely routine, sir.' Nick didn't disguise the relish in his voice; he always loved mimicking Dixon of Dock Green.

'My bean-counter was on the phone within five minutes of your calling his office. His secretary said more than she was supposed to and he was flapping about client confidentiality.' He seemed, Hannah thought, to falter over the longer words. Had he been drinking? She sniffed the air, but could smell nothing other than Simon's tangy after shave. 'To say nothing of the risk of losing my audit work. I know for a fact that it pays for his mistress and her cosy apartment opposite the Lowry in Salford Quays. Of course, I told him not to worry. You weren't seeking corroboration of my whereabouts for any sinister reason.'

'Quite right, sir.'

'I take it…' Dumelow began. For a few seconds the sentence seemed to lose its way. 'I take it that you're looking into the fact that Jean Allardyce went AWOL yesterday.'

'We are aware that she isn't at home, sir, although Mr. Allardyce hasn't reported her officially as a missing person.'

Dumelow shrugged. 'Chances are, she decided she couldn't take any more of Tom. Between you and me, sometimes I feel the same. Not a bad farmer when he's so inclined, but stubborn. And he cuts corners. When I pick him up on it, you can be sure he's got an answer. Everything's my fault for penny-pinching.'

'You have no idea where she might be?'

'None whatsover. It's a bloody nuisance. My wife's beside herself with worry.'

Hannah wondered if Tash Dumelow's anxiety was motivated partly by a fear that she might have to dirty her pretty hands with the housework. An unworthy thought: no doubt Tash was genuinely concerned. Daniel seemed to think so, and he struck her as a good judge of people. Did he fancy Tash? Most men would. But he didn't seem the sort to cheat on his partner. Ben hadn't been that sort, either. Although, she had to remind herself, he had cheated, and with Cheryl of all women.

Dumelow said, 'So you've discovered that I lied to Tash about what I was up to yesterday. I suppose you wonder why.'

'It did cross our minds,' Nick said.

Hannah watched, trying in vain to fathom Simon Dumelow's game plan. During the original investigation, he'd struck her as articulate and plausible, and he still was, despite the odd hesitations when he spoke. But he'd been caught out in a lie and she presumed that in a few minutes they'd be listening to a confession of adultery. Yet he seemed as relaxed as if taking them on a tour of a building site rich in potential for development.

'I'll be glad to explain, but first I'd appreciate your confirmation that we're speaking in confidence.'

Hannah said, 'You'll understand, we can't sign a blank cheque. You wouldn't in your business, Mr. Dumelow. But in—delicate situations, we obviously try to be discreet.'

A wan smile. 'Thank you. If you don't mind, I'll treat myself to a nip of whisky. I don't suppose you will join me?'

She shook her head and they waited while he went over to a drinks cabinet and poured a tot from a crystal decanter. Even though he still seemed calm, she noticed that his hand was shaking.

'With each year that passes, Detective Chief Inspector, I realise how important it is to savour the good things in life. So—you're burning to know where I was yesterday. The answer is that instead of going to Manchester, I took a taxi all the way to Liverpool. I'd managed to book an appointment at short notice in Rodney Street.'

Rodney Street. Merseyside's answer to Harley Street. Like a punch in the ribs, the realisation hit Hannah that she'd got it all wrong.

Dumelow grunted. 'I can tell from your faces that you weren't expecting that. True, though. I'll give you the name of my consultant when we're finished. To cut to the chase—I've been suffering from headaches lately, trouble with my balance, and things have kept getting worse. The other day when I was driving to my office, I found it difficult to keep off the pavement. My GP was obviously bothered and referred me to a specialist. It didn't take that long to get an expert diagnosis.'

Hannah said nothing. There was nothing she could say.

Dumelow puffed out his cheeks. He was a strong man, but suddenly it seemed an effort for him even to talk. 'Well, as any Yorkshireman might say, I've had a good innings. Only sorry it's coming to an end. I rather fancied knocking up a century, but the Great Umpire in the Sky has decided to give me out sooner than I'd have wished. I have a tumour of the brain, and I'm told that it's inoperable.'

It was quite a confidence to keep while they talked to Tash Dumelow. Her husband was adamant that he didn't want her to know he was dying yet. He was determined to wait till the last possible moment before breaking the news.

'We've had a great marriage, Detective Chief Inspector. Trust me, I know. My first wife turned out to be a harpy. But Tash and I have always suited each other down to the ground. I don't want her to think of me as an invalid until she has no choice.'

Tash was chatting about the art of framing watercolours. Soon she would become a widow and she didn't have a clue. When they'd first met, Hannah had regarded her with an instinctive mistrust. Ben Kind—who had *definitely* fancied Tash—had laughed and called it prejudice. Of course he was right; it was the bias of a hard-working professional against a woman who has ended up in the lap of luxury because she shagged the right man at the right time. With a pinch of envy thrown in because of Tash's looks. Right now, Hannah wouldn't have changed places for all the cash in Cumbria. How would she feel if Marc succumbed to a terminal illness? Even after his confession of infidelity, the mere thought made her knees weak.

She let Nick do most of the talking. When he asked if the name of Eldine Webber meant anything to her, Tash's eyes widened but she took refuge in vagueness, saying simply that the name rang a distant bell. In the end, she admitted that he might have been one of Gabrielle's boyfriends, but said she couldn't be sure. It was all so long ago. Hannah was sure that Tash remembered more than she was willing to admit, but could understand her reticence. Eldine Webber belonged to a world that the lady of Brack Hall had left far behind.

Nick's questions turned to the disappearance of Jean Allardyce, and Tash confirmed Daniel's account of their conversation. Neither Nick nor Hannah was left in any doubt that she was worried about Jean's safety, but when pressed on Tom Allardyce's temper, she was evasive.

'Who can tell what goes on behind closed doors in a marriage? The two of them have been together for a long time, I'm sure there's a spark there.'

'But he did hit her?'

Tash ducked her head, reluctant to face them. 'Well, he may have slapped her once or twice. To be frank, I know he has. But anything more than that…no, it doesn't bear thinking about. I'm sure there's some innocent explanation. I just wish I knew what it is.'

Hannah said, 'Suppose something has happened to Jean Allardyce? An accident, perhaps. It's not uncommon on farms. They are dangerous places.'

Tash pursed her lips. 'Simon is always preaching to Tom about the importance of health and safety. But Tom's dreadfully careless. He doesn't seem to realise how important it is these days to comply with all the rules and regulations. He simply says they're crap, but that isn't the point. Simon worries that we might not be covered by our farm insurance if we don't obey all the small print.'

'I wonder,' Hannah said. 'Would it be possible for us to take a look around?'

'You mean—the Hall? It's not a problem, but I can assure you, Jean isn't hiding anywhere in the building. If she's anywhere…'

She stopped short and Hannah said, 'Yes?'

'No, no. Forget it.'

'Please, Mrs. Dumelow. This isn't a game. You're anxious about Jean Allardyce and so am I. What were you going to say?'

Tash swallowed. 'It's just that, if—if she is anywhere on the farm, I'd have thought he might—I mean, she could have had an accident...'

'Where do you think she might be?'

'Well,' Tash said wretchedly. 'There are plenty of outbuildings. You could have a look round those if you want.'

Subdued but holding hands, the Dumelows took Hannah and Nick on a guided tour of the farm. In other circumstances, Hannah might have wondered if the apparently affectionate husband and wife were putting on a show for the benefit of their visitors. This afternoon such cynicism would have seemed crass and offensive. She had no doubt that the Dumelows were genuinely in love.

The yard smelled of mud and dirty straw. As they walked through it, they bumped into Tom Allardyce, who was on his way back from the fields. When Simon explained that the police just wanted a quick look round the farm, Allardyce replied by striding past them without another word. Tash ran after him and murmured something in his ear, but Allardyce didn't turn to face her. He just spat on the ground and stomped into the house.

Simon turned to the detectives and cast his eyes to the heavens.

'See what we've had to put up with?' he mouthed.

Tash rejoined them. 'I just wanted to remind Tom that if there was anything he wanted to tell the police, now was the time. All you want is a bit of co-operation. You saw how he reacted.'

None of them said much as they trudged around the scattered buildings and sheds. Hannah's headache had returned and her wellingtons were tight. Despite the fine weather, there was still mud on the ground, as well as a regular quagmire in her brain. If Allardyce had killed his wife, there were plenty of places in the vicinity of Underfell for him to dispose of the body at minimal risk. This was a lonely spot; as long as you weren't careless enough to be seen by a walker over on the coffin trail, or someone watching from the Hall, you could do more or less as you pleased without fear of detection. It would take a painstaking search by a large team of officers to have a realistic hope of finding a well-hidden corpse on the farmland. If he'd buried her somewhere up on the fells, chances were that it might never be discovered.

She heard Simon Dumelow whisper to his wife, 'Are you okay, darling?'

'Yes, it's just that—I'm afraid that he's hurt her. You know what he's like. Perhaps he hurt her more than he intended.'

'Where next?' Nick asked.

Simon rubbed his forehead; his stride had shortened in the last few minutes and he seemed close to exhaustion. Hannah noticed that his wife gave him a sharp glance. Her concern was almost tangible and Hannah wondered if she had already guessed that something was wrong.

'What do you think, darling?' he asked. 'Is it worth taking them up to the sheep handling facility?'

She clapped him on the back. 'It won't take long. Then you can have a rest. You look as though you need it.'

'Working too hard, that's all,' he mumbled.

The four of them made their way in the direction of the coffin trail and the slope of the fell, towards the small field near the beck. 'This is where the sheep are gathered in,' Tash said. 'They are kept in those pens and there's a dipper behind those dry stone walls.'

'Twice a year dipping isn't compulsory any more,' Simon added. 'Unfortunately, there's been talk of an outbreak of sheep scab, so Tom dipped the animals the other week to give them protection.'

'But the dipper isn't enclosed?'

'Not in a building. Sheep dip's toxic, you know. Better to have the tank out in the open air.'

They reached a dyke and beyond it the walls enclosing the sheep dipper. It was about fifteen feet long, with a battered wooden cover. Simon said, 'We can't leave it open to the elements, of course. The tank's protected to avoid accidents and keep the insurers off our back.'

'The cover doesn't look that secure,' Nick said.

'One more job to do and to pay for,' Simon said with a hollow smile. 'I've kept nagging Tom about it. He ought to get round to it soon.'

'Mind if I lift the cover and take a look?'

Simon leaned against the wall for support. 'Be my guest. I'd give you a hand, but…'

'No problem, leave it to me.'

Nick strode to the sheep dip tank and, bending down, started to pull the cover to one side. Even in the open, the stench took Hannah's breath away. As the tank came into view, they could see the grey milky fluid. And then they saw something else.

Tash screamed and buried her face in her husband's neck. He seemed to be hypnotised. Nick's face was empty as he kept on shifting the cover.

Hannah chewed her lip so hard that it began to bleed. She'd never once been sick at a postmortem. Throwing up in the presence of death was an admission of weakness. But the sight of Jean Allardyce's fully clothed body floating in the sheep dip tank was enough to make the strongest stomach heave.

Chapter Twenty

The morning after his talk with Hannah Scarlett, Daniel over-slept by an hour, but as Eddie wasn't due to turn up until ten, it didn't matter. When Miranda opened the blinds, sun flooded the kitchen and as they munched croissants, she chatted about her plans to turn the barn into their office. It was as if they'd never exchanged a cross word.

In the course of a cold and invigorating shower, Daniel had resolved to stop worrying about Jean Allardyce and Barrie Gilpin. Hannah was right: he could do no more for them than he could for poor Aimee. If Jean had disappeared, no-one would try harder than Hannah to find her. Another decision was not to think too much about Hannah, either. Each time he remembered the way she'd put her hand on his, he felt like a schoolboy fantasising over a girl who is out of reach. Dangerous territory; better not to stray into it.

As she filled the cafetiere, Miranda announced that she was itching to write again. She still fancied producing a series of features about downshifting for a lifestyle magazine and she meant to ring every editor in London until she found a taker for it. After all, they'd have to start earning a bit of money soon. The house proceeds wouldn't last forever.

'How are you getting on with your article about corpse roads?'

'Let's just say it's making appropriately funereal progress.'

She laughed and said, 'I'm feeling guilty that I haven't walked the coffin trail myself yet.'

'You should. It fascinated me, imagining that I was treading in the footsteps of the villagers of three hundred years ago.' He mimicked the sombre tone of a fellow historian who presented on television. '"Trekking over the fell through rain and mud, bearing their melancholy burden."'

'Weird.' She shivered pleasurably. 'I was thinking, maybe I might take Tash up on her invitation to pop round for a coffee one morning. I could leave the car at the farm and walk up the fell from there.'

'It's a long haul if you go all the way to Whitmell, and you won't find a bus to bring you back.'

'I wasn't planning to cover the whole route, just the easy bit. It isn't far from Brack Hall Farm to the top of the fell and it looks like an easy climb. I could stroll along the top and take a look at the Sacrifice Stone from close quarters.'

'Just as long as you don't climb up and sit on top of it.'

When he told her about the warning words of the woman he'd met and the legend, she giggled and exclaimed, 'So you're doomed?'

'Fraid so.'

'Well, better be practical. Did I ask if you'd made a will?'

'You inherit my books.'

'Such generosity.'

Wobbling dangerously on her stool, she kissed him on the cheek. One thing led to another and a couple of minutes later she was leading him back upstairs. When she slipped off the last of her clothes and clambered on top of him, he found that sleep had washed away the tensions of the night before.

They were dressed again with five minutes to spare before they heard Eddie's truck pulling up at the end of the track. Daniel reminded himself that if he had any discipline, he'd have made use of the time to work on his article. But what was so admirable about having discipline? That was the whole point about moving out to the sticks. No more deadlines; they could please themselves.

While Eddie set to work, Daniel retreated to his computer and tapped out a few paragraphs about the coffin trail. For the first time since the move, his prose was racing. Walking the trail for himself had unshackled his imagination; until now he'd needed to hack out every sentence, like a labourer using a pickaxe on granite. After he'd completed the second limb of the route as it zigzagged down into Whitmell Vale, he would turn his attention to other corpse roads. Rydal to Grasmere was an obvious choice, but he liked the sound of the more remote corpse way across the rugged western reaches of the Lake District, from Wasdale Head to Boot.

When the phone rang, for a moment he wondered if Hannah was calling him again. On hearing Theo's voice on the other end of the line, he felt a wrench of disappointment coupled with surprise.

'How did you get this number?'

'Unlike a good historian, a good detective never reveals his sources,' Theo said smugly. 'That said, of course I would not claim to be any sort of detective, good or otherwise. Perish the thought. So I will admit to you that I spoke to Prittipaul and he let me in on the secret.'

Prittipaul was the editor of *Contemporary Historian*. Of course it had been naïve to imagine that he could stay out of reach of the past for long. Few institutions are as ruthless in tracking down their alumni as Oxford colleges, even if only so that old members can be urged to give generously to the Master's latest pet project. Prittipaul was by nature tight-lipped, but Theo had probably called in some favour. Or indulged in a little blackmail, for the chairman of the company that published the journal was a member of his coterie.

'My coming here wasn't a secret.'

'Even though your old mobile number has been disconnected and you left no exact forwarding address? You've even closed your email account.' Theo's tone was more-in-sorrow-than-in-anger. 'Such a pity that you wish to cut yourself off from your friends and colleagues.'

'So what can I do for you?'

'I just wondered how you were getting on in your leafy retreat.'

'I'm looking out through the window right now. I just saw a heron diving into the tarn.'

'So your infatuation has not run its course as yet?'

'No,' Daniel said. 'It's only just begun.'

In the pause that followed, he realised with a start that he'd been thinking of his love affair with the Lakes, not with Miranda. But in a way they amounted to the same thing, surely.

'As it happens,' Theo said at length, 'a group of us in the University have been talking about starting a new historical journal. The editorial board meets for the first time in a couple of weeks. But we are a little thin on the ground so far as your specialisms are concerned. I wondered if you might care to join us? Nothing too formal. In fact we'll be combining a little business with a spot of gastronomic pleasure. The meeting's being held in a rather splendid new bistro up in Summertown. You might like to bring along your, ahem, lady friend. Make a long weekend of it.'

'Thanks for the kind invitation,' Daniel said. 'And I'd be glad to offer the occasional article, if it helps. But I don't think I'll be coming back to Oxford yet awhile.'

'Your social calendar is already crammed?'

'What I like about this place is that I don't have a social calendar any more.'

'It'll end in tears,' Theo murmured. 'You do realise that, don't you? The world treats escapists roughly, Daniel. They learn that in truth, they cannot escape themselves.'

'Thanks for the warning, Theo. It's good to talk.'

The Master made a noise halfway between a snort and a yelp and slammed down the phone. For another hour, Daniel tried to recapture the rhythm of his writing, but it was no good. The spell had been broken. He went downstairs and told Miranda about the call, and to his astonishment, she said that it might have been nice to go back to Oxford. Just for a weekend.

'But we agreed…'

'It wouldn't hurt, would it? I mean, it's not as if a few days make any difference. The cottage is bought. We'd come straight back.'

'I've left the college behind me.'

'Well, it's up to you. But it would have given us a break.'

He blinked. 'Do we need a break?'

'Don't tell me you're not sick of the smell of sawdust. I feel like a case study for an ENT specialist. I don't believe my sinuses will ever be clear again.'

'Temporary inconvenience, nothing more. Remember what we agreed? No pain, no gain?'

'I just never thought you'd take it all so seriously.'

He couldn't help sighing. 'Don't you take it seriously?'

'Yes, but…oh, it doesn't matter. Forget I ever uttered a word.'

◇◇◇

In the afternoon, he offered to fetch supplies from Tasker's while Miranda cold-called the editorial desks of some of the magazines she'd never written for. The sky was blue, the sun high and it was an easy decision to walk. This is the life, he reminded himself as he left Tarn Fold and strolled along the lane towards the village. When talking to Theo, he'd felt no tug from the past, no harking back to Oxford and the career he had abandoned. He missed none of it: not the SCR politicking, not the interminable meetings to debate the latest financial crisis, not the city's petrol fumes, not the crowded buses, not the bicycle thieves. Walking the lanes of Brackdale, the biggest threat to your well-being came when a tractor lumbered past and you had to press yourself into the hedgerow's prickly embrace.

As the lane meandered, he eavesdropped on the conversation of the sheep and inhaled the smells of earth and grass. Lifting his eyes beyond the walled-off fields of Underfell, he gazed towards the Sacrifice Stone: sullen and hostile as ever, as though it resented the valley's loveliness and wished it nothing but harm. After staring down over Brackdale in grim silence for so many centuries, he thought, the Stone would never yield its secrets.

Who had killed Gabrielle Anders and laid her body out upon it? He needed to know everything. It was no longer enough merely to establish that Barrie was innocent of the crime. An act of wickedness had destroyed the young woman whose only crime was to visit the Lakes and look up an old friend. She'd survived the sleazy joints of downtown Vegas, only to be brutalised and killed in an area that even aesthetically challenged bureaucrats recognised as possessing *outstanding natural beauty.*

Would Hannah find the culprit? He ought to leave the investigation to her; it was absurd to suppose that he had inherited some genetic instinct for detection. Yet he wanted to do more than rely on such crumbs of information as she deigned to pass to him. He felt pangs of hunger for knowledge that a police officer, trammelled by rules and procedures, could never satisfy. At college, he'd craved information about the past like a junkie yearns for one more high. This urge wasn't such a different sensation, except that this time he sought to understand who had destroyed a fellow human being. And why.

Rounding a bend, he realised that he was within half a mile of the village. The stone houses of Brack came into sight at the same instant as a siren punctured his reverie. It was a wail that haunted him. He could never hear the sound without being propelled back to the Cornmarket and the sickening presentiment that his lover was dead, that he hadn't reached her in time to talk her out of destroying herself. The siren howled again and his stomach knotted.

Within moments he could see them thundering along the road. An ambulance, followed by a police car. Even as he watched, they skidded to the right and raced up the lane towards Brack Hall Farm.

Chapter Twenty One

Hannah took two quick strides so as to stand between the Dumelows and the sheep dipper. When she breathed in, the fumes hit her like a smack on the face. Her head was still throbbing, but she could not succumb to the horror. Fighting to keep a tremor out of her voice, she said to the couple, 'This is a crime scene now. DS Lowther will stay here while I accompany you back to the Hall.'

Simon was stroking his wife's fine hair as she wept, murmuring inaudible words of comfort to her. His eyes betrayed no expression. Hannah thought he was hypnotised by the sight of the body. Perhaps he was asking himself what death felt like.

A gull swooped over them, mewing *keee-ya*. Nick straightened his back. His face was white. Pulling out his radio, he said, 'I'll call the control room.'

Hannah led the Dumelows along the track leading to the farmhouse. The couple walked slowly; both husband and wife seemed unsteady on their feet. Hannah didn't try to hurry them; her legs too felt heavy, her shoulders tense and weighted with dismay. A hundred yards from the dipper, the path forked and they came to a halt. Tash took out a handkerchief and blew her nose noisily. Her cheeks were blotchy and there were furrows around her mouth and eyes that Hannah had never seen before.

'She didn't fall in by accident, did she, Detective Chief Inspector?'

'Of course she didn't,' her husband said. 'You saw the tank, how it was covered up. Jean didn't do that. Couldn't have done.'

'She always was afraid of him,' Tash said. 'There are things she told me, in confidence…darling, I never even mentioned them to you, for fear you'd throw him out. That was the crazy aspect of it, you see. Despite everything, she still cared for him. And now he's done—that.'

She pointed towards the sheep handling facility. Nick was standing by the stone wall, talking into his radio while he kept guard over the murder scene. And it was a murder scene, for sure; Hannah didn't need an inquest verdict to tell her that.

'The bastard,' Simon said croakily. 'I should have fired him years ago.'

'What would have happened to Jean if you had? That's what always bothered me, that's why I didn't want to rock the boat.' A thought struck Tash. 'Maybe she would be alive today if I had. Oh shit, shit, shit.'

'Don't be silly. You've always done your best to help her.'

'Much good I've done her!'

'Mrs. Dumelow,' Hannah said gently. 'It won't help to beat yourself up over this. Whoever has done this wouldn't…'

'There isn't much doubt who's done it, is there?' Tash interrupted in a high-pitched voice. 'That scumbag Allardyce…'

'We don't have proof…'

'For God's sake, how much proof do you need?' Tash was almost shrieking. 'There are so many things I could tell you. I begged her to leave him, make a new life for herself, but it was no good. He'd cowed her into submission, it was as if she didn't have a mind of her own. That's the way he operates. He's vicious, a control freak. If she dared to stand up to him, he used to rape her.'

Hannah stared. 'She told you that?'

'Yes, and it wasn't only when she defied him. He insisted on sex every night. Regardless of anything.' Tash was speaking rapidly, as if a dam of reticence had burst. 'Kinky sex was what he liked best. He used to tie her up, pretend to strangle her with her own tights. Occasionally there were threesomes, with his slimy pal Joe Dowling. Her own cousin. If she showed any reluctance…oh God, he's a wicked man, a pervert, and I turned a blind eye to it, even though it was all going on next door.'

Simon said hoarsely, 'You should have told me, darling.'

'She swore me to secrecy, said he'd kill her if he found out that she'd talked to anyone else. How could I betray her?'

Hannah said, 'We'll need to take a full statement from you, Mrs. Dumelow.'

'What if he denies it?' Tash's pupils dilated with horror. 'He's a hardened liar and Jean is dead. Joe won't admit his part in it, he'll be too scared. I can't prove any of this. Nothing.'

'Leave us to worry about that.'

'You know Tom's past. He's got away with things before. But I'm not sure you know the whole of it.'

'And you do?'

In a whisper she said, 'I think he may have killed Gabrielle Anders. God forgive me, I thought Barrie was guilty. But now I'm not so sure.'

'What?' Hannah stared at her. 'What's your evidence for saying that?'

'Jean told me she gave him a false alibi. She never believed that he'd murdered Gabrielle, but that's because she didn't want to.'

'That doesn't prove he murdered Gabrielle.'

'Come on.' Tash was weary as well as scornful. 'If Barrie didn't stab her, who did?'

'That's pure speculation.'

'She told me she phoned the police about it, although she didn't dare give her name. You know about that, you must do.'

'Yes,' Hannah said. 'It took us a while, but we suspected Jean Allardyce made the call.'

'I thought that was why you'd come back here. To check up on him.'

'Well…'

'Listen.' Tash's voice faltered as she gestured to the farm-house. 'That man killed her and it's my responsibility. Jean was my friend. I'm the one who let her down. I have to make amends.'

'Darling...' Simon said.

As he started speaking, Tash broke away from them and started running towards the farmhouse. Hannah hesitated. If she gave chase, what was she going to do when she caught up with her quarry—rugby-tackle her to the ground? Hardly the way to treat a key prosecution witness. But she had to do something. Suppose Allardyce tried to hurt Tash, maybe even attempted to kill her?

'Mrs. Dumelow, come back!'

Tash kept running and so Hannah started after her. But the other woman was lithe and fit and she'd opened up a gap. Soon she reached the yard and Hannah saw her carry on until she was standing a few paces away from Allardyce's front door.

'Jean's dead!' she shouted. 'You killed her!'

A siren wailed not far away. The paramedics were turning into the rutted lane.

'Mrs. Dumelow!' Hannah panted. 'Please. Come back.'

Tash seemed to spot a movement at an upstairs window. 'You murdering bastard!'

'It's not safe, Mrs. Dumelow!'

'Put that down!' Tash bellowed at the figure in the window.

Hannah was nearly at the yard. The siren had fallen silent. Tash Dumelow was waving her fist at the man in the farm-house.

'You'll never get away with it!'

'Mrs. Dumelow, please!'

A rifle shot rang out and Tash Dumelow screamed.

Out on the main road, Daniel heard a crack shattering the stillness. Just like the shot he and Miranda had heard at Tarn Cottage. For Christ's sake, surely Allardyce wasn't firing at the ambulance or at the police? He could see a police car parked near the front of the Hall. Was Hannah at the farm, checking on Jean Allardyce's whereabouts after he had passed on the information from Tash Dumelow? He offered up a prayer that she wasn't indulging in any heroics.

'Hear that?' A cyclist pulled up beside him, a tubby man whose voice wobbled with excitement. 'Sounded like someone's trying to pot the panda car that just whizzed past. Or maybe even the ambulance. For goodness sake, what's going on?'

Daniel spread his arms. 'Your guess is as good as mine.'

The bullet had kicked up a spray of dirt close to the barn, ten yards away from where Tash was standing. She'd covered her face with her hands, but hadn't moved. It was as if the shot had paralysed her. Allardyce hadn't aimed at her, Hannah was certain. A marksman trained by the army, however rusty his aim, would have come much closer to his target.

No time to deliberate. She raced into the yard and seized Tash by the wrist.

'Come on—quickly!'

Tash stumbled as Hannah dragged her across the cobbles. Her face was glowing, as if being shot vindicated her. By hazarding her safety, she'd induced Allardyce to give himself away. Hannah ducked her head as they moved. At any moment the farmer might fire again.

At last, they reached the barn and safety. Hannah pressed her back against the stone wall. The windows of the farmhouse were out of sight, so they were out of Allardyce's range. The main risk now was that he might emerge from the front door, rifle in hand.

'What do you think you were doing?' Hannah gasped as she let go of Tash's wrist.

'I had to confront him. You can see what his temper is like. It was the only way.'

'You might have been killed.'

'So might you,' Tash said. 'You didn't have to come and save me.'

Hannah was still trying to catch her breath. 'What else could I do?'

Tash blinked away tears. 'I'm sorry, I shouldn't have exposed you to danger.'

'At least we're both still in one piece.'

'What are you going to do?'

'Back off and call for help. I've had my ration of excitement for the time being.'

She called the control room and told them where she was. 'We have a firearms situation here. Can you get a couple of ARVs over soonest? Along with dog patrols?'

Tash said, 'ARVs?'

'Armed response vehicles.'

'Why dogs?'

'We don't want anyone hurt. Or any thing.'

Tash raised her eyebrows. 'But if he does shoot again, it's better for a dog to stop a bullet?'

Hannah grunted. Tash had a knack of putting her at a disadvantage. 'I don't want to lose one of my fellow officers.'

Tash paled. 'I guess you're right. Tom's crazy, I've thought that for a long time.'

Hannah glanced over her shoulder. In the distance, Simon Dumelow was edging along the path that led to the Hall. He should be safe; not even an SAS veteran could shoot round corners. An unworthy thought flashed into her brain: *does it matter to him?*

Nick Lowther was approaching. He must have deserted the sheep handling facility on hearing the shot. The ambulance and a police car had pulled up nearby and their occupants were clambering out. She put up a hand to show that she was all right, then waved him back. He still had a job to do with the SOCOs at the crime scene and she didn't want him to stray into the line of fire.

'Listen, Mrs. Dumelow. I need to keep you out of harm's way, but we'll also need information from you, just in case this mess doesn't sort itself out as quickly as we'd hope.'

'Anything,' Tash said. 'What do you need to know?'

'The layout of the farmhouse. Apart from the front and back doors, are there any other exits? And what sort of arsenal does Allardyce have in there?'

'You only need worry about the two main doors. Unless he takes his life in his hands and climbs out of the landing window on to the roof of the lean-to. As for guns, I'd guess he has a stockpile.'

'Jesus.'

'He owns a rifle, I think it's a .22. I remember him showing it off to me.'

'For killing vermin?'

'That's his excuse,' Tash said. 'He has a Kestrel shotgun as well, for rabbits and pheasants. But I'm sure he has several other weapons he's never told us about. He loves just holding them. Caressing them almost, I've always found it creepy. It's like other people collect antiques. Of course, he won't have them licensed. But I don't have a clue what might be stashed away inside the house.'

Hannah cursed under her breath. A peaceful backwater in rural Cumbria, and she was facing someone who might possess more firepower than a vanload of Yardies in the East End of London. And who had the training to make use of it. She scanned their surroundings, assessing the available cover between the farm and Brack Hall. The good news was that there was plenty. The bad news was that most of it was soft cover: rhododendrons with their last purple flowers and the spiky hawthorn hedges lining the track between the farm and the Hall. From the first floor of the farm, Allardyce might not be able to see someone hiding behind the greenery, but that wouldn't stop a stray bullet from doing a lot of damage if you happened to be in the wrong place at the wrong time. Apart from a scattering of sycamore and horse chestnut trees, hard cover was scarce between the barn and the Hall.

At her side, Tash Dumelow was shaking. Her skin was taut over her cheekbones and she looked as though it was a long,

long time since she'd been a pin-up model. Hannah put her arm on the other woman's shoulder, felt her tension. Why trust to luck? It wasn't worth the risk of making a dash for it. The first ARV would be here in another ten minutes, fifteen at the most. They would tough it out until the cavalry arrived.

The tubby cyclist screwed up his eyes and squinted across the fields towards Brack Hall Farm. 'If you ask me, the shot came from the farmhouse.'

The combination of rifle fire and the sirens had prompted a small crowd to gather at the end of the lane leading to the farm. People were gossiping with perfect strangers, relishing the camaraderie. Daniel felt a stab of embarrassment as he lingered; they were worse than rubber-neckers slowing down to gape at a motorway pile-up. Of course, he ought to keep on walking into the village to perform his errand at Tasker's. But he was worried about Hannah Scarlett and it would require more self-discipline than he possessed to tear himself away. A drama was being played out at the farm and he couldn't imagine what was in the script or how the final act would end.

A harassed woman who was failing to calm a neurotic Jack Russell terrier said to nobody in particular, 'You're not safe any-where, these days, are you?'

'Who lives at the farm?' the cyclist asked.

'Tom Allardyce,' an elderly man in walker's kit replied. 'Surly bugger. Take it from me, he'll be behind this. That feller's made trouble all his bloody life.'

The woman shushed her yelping dog again and murmured, 'It's all gone very quiet over there.'

'*Too* quiet,' the cyclist said solemnly.

Daniel decided that he couldn't bear much more of this. He detached himself from the little group and wandered along the road towards a gap in the hedge. From there he could see both the emergency vehicles. Beyond, police officers and paramedics were conferring. Allardyce was nowhere to be seen; nor was Hannah Scarlett.

The silence was ruptured by another shot.

◇◇◇

'Are you all right?' Tash hissed.

'Fine,' Hannah said.

All she'd done was to bob her head round the corner, to see if she could still make out the bulky shape of Tom Allardyce at the upstairs window. The movement had provoked him into firing against the wall of the barn. The roar as the shot ricocheted off the brickwork was deafening.

No wonder he's twitchy, she thought. Nothing seems to be happening, but he'll be starting to fear the worst. If he carries on like this, it'll become a self-fulfilling prophecy.

If only she had a clear sight of him. What if he moved, or decided to come out of the house? She was tempted to edge back into the farmyard. Perhaps she could try to initiate a dialogue. Not about his wife's murder, far less that of Gabrielle Anders, just in an attempt to persuade him that he had nothing to gain from a stand-off, and a great deal to lose. But that was madness. Bargaining with an armed criminal was a job for a particular kind of person. A few years ago she'd flirted with the possibility of becoming a negotiator, had studied the literature about the training on offer at Hendon. When she confided in Ben Kind about her idea, he was quick to talk her out of it.

'You're not boring enough.'

What he meant was that a negotiator confronted with potential suicides or hostage situations needed infinite patience. An ability to sustain endless, monotonous, soothing conversation was a key part of the job spec. Once he'd pointed out the pitfalls, she didn't need much persuading that she was better off with real detective work. In the CID, if a tricky interview wasn't going well, you could terminate it there and then. No such option when you were negotiating over life and death.

She said to Tash, 'Promise me you'll stay out of the line of fire.'

Tash closed her eyes, seeming to collect her thoughts. When she opened them again, she said, 'You saved my life.'

'It's not an issue. I just don't want you to…'

Tash put up her hand. 'I shouldn't have done it. I don't know what prompted me to challenge him. It was stupid.'

'It was pretty brave, actually.'

'I'm so angry about what happened,' Tash said fiercely. 'To see Jean—floating like that, just as he left her. Covered up. God only knows whether she drowned or was poisoned by the sheep dip. How could he do that to his own wife? It shows you what he's like.'

'Sure, but leave it to us now, okay?' Hannah squeezed the emotion out of her voice. 'We'll deal with him.'

'These people in the—the ARVs. If he fires at them, will they try to cripple him? Shoot him in the legs?'

'It won't come to that,' Hannah said.

'But if it does?'

'The firearms officers would only fire in self-defence.'

'To wound him?'

'No,' Hannah said. 'If they do fire, it's because life is in imminent jeopardy. When these guys shoot, they shoot to kill.'

Daniel rejoined the throng as a couple of young constables were setting up a cordon at the end of the lane that led to the farm. Another police car had just driven through. The officers stonewalled every question and shooed the onlookers back down the road. In the absence of authoritative information about what was happening, the elderly walker was proving to be a real knowall. He announced in strident tones that the latest arrival was a second armed response vehicle.

'Looks just like an ordinary traffic car to me,' the cyclist protested.

'They keep their weapons locked in the boot,' the smartalec informed him. 'My daughter-in-law works for the police in Carlisle. Some of her stories would make your hair curl, I promise you. Joe Public doesn't know the half of it, I can tell you that for nothing. Not the bloody half of it.'

◇◇◇

'Armed police,' the officer shouted into a loudhailer. 'Mr. Allardyce, we have the farm surrounded. Come out of the house slowly and put your weapon on the ground.'

Silence. Tom Allardyce evidently wasn't in the mood to give himself up for arrest. He was downstairs now, stationed at a window close to the main doorway. Hannah knew there were two contrasting interpretations of his change of position. One, he was preparing to wave the white flag. Two, he was steeling himself to come out in a blaze of gunfire.

Hannah had paused in her briefing of the negotiator, a bald DCI whom she'd never met before. He spoke in a Lowland monotone and was obviously well-suited to his job. Ben had been right, she thought. Ten minutes talking to this man and you'd be bored into submission.

At least now she could see the farmhouse. They were crouching behind the stone wall on the other side of the path from the barn. Nick had joined her but Tash Dumelow was safely back in the Hall. So far as Hannah could see, everything was in place for the conduct of a containment situation. The first priority was to keep the lid on everything; no need for shock and awe. Time was on their side, thank God. If Allardyce had emerged from the house before back-up arrived, Hannah would have been at his mercy. At least the arrival of four authorised firearms officers, together with a couple of dog patrols, had pretty much boxed off that risk. Hannah would never want to argue with the huge glowering Alsatians, but the sight of the AFOs' guns was heart-stopping. Each man was built like a prop forward, each carried serious weaponry: a Glock 9 mm. machine pistol and a Hechler and Koch carbine machine gun.

Somewhere inside the farmhouse, Allardyce's collie started barking. Outside, the AFOs' radios were crackling. The men had spaced themselves out around the farmhouse, covering each aspect of the scene as best they could. Hannah saw that they were keeping a wary eye on arcs of fire. For good reason: no matter how long you practised your skills in video-shoots, nothing could prepare you one hundred per cent for the reality of armed response. At least as scary as the unknown quantity inside the house was the possibility of one AFO firing towards another.

'Let's see if we can put a lid on it.' A shaft of sunlight was glinting on the top of the negotiator's scalp. 'Talk him out.'

'Even at the best of times, Tom Allardyce wasn't a smooth conversationalist,' she said. 'His wife's dead now. Presumably he's thinking he has nothing to lose.'

'Everyone has something to lose.' It sounded like something the negotiator had read in a manual.

Hannah held her tongue, but she wasn't convinced.

As the sun slipped over the horizon, the crowd kept growing. A team had arrived from regional television, and a young reporter with Morticia Addams hair and a winsome smile was conducting an impromptu vox pop. An opportunistic snack van, usually to be found selling burgers and hot drinks from a lay-by on the Whitmell road, was doing terrific business. Rumours were fluttering around like leaves in a gale. The excitable cyclist assured Daniel that Tom Allardyce had barricaded himself in the house after murdering his wife and taking the Dumelows hostage.

When Daniel called Miranda on his mobile to let her know why he hadn't returned from his errand, she decided to come and take a look for herself. She turned up equipped with Mars Bars and a thermos flask.

'It's just like being back in London,' she said gleefully as a policeman waved away a boy who had approached the cordon for a dare.

Daniel gazed across the fields. Overhead, a helicopter circled; its din was deafening. As it banked, he heard sheep bleating in panic. On the ground, the police were setting up lights in the vicinity of the farmhouse.

'You could say that.'

'I mean, I know we wanted to get away from it all, but I suppose I never realised how quiet the countryside is.'

Daniel couldn't think of an answer that didn't trouble him.

'Jesus,' Nick Lowther breathed. 'He's coming out.'

'Let me see.' Hannah pushed past him and fixed her eyes on the farmhouse. Her palms were sweaty. She could see the front door opening.

'Armed police!' the senior AFO screamed. 'Come out and put your weapon on the ground!'

Hannah could see Tom Allardyce, framed in the doorway. In his hand was a rifle. She was too far away to see the look in his eyes, but his body language wasn't encouraging. He was rocking back and forth on his heels like a B-movie gunslinger.

'Armed police! You are surrounded!'

Allardyce shut the door behind him. The unseen collie barked again, as if in warning. The farmer lifted his rifle, then brought it down again. He began to move, as if in a dream.

'Armed police!' Hannah could hear the AFO's desperation. He sounded young. This might be his very first containment. 'Drop your weapon!'

Allardyce kept walking. He seemed to be looking around, as if in search of a target.

Hannah retreated behind the wall. She was aware of Nick's warmth behind her, she could hear his breathing quicken.

'The stupid bastard. Surely he must realise…'

'Don't go any further! Armed police! If you move forward, we will shoot!'

For a long, terrible second there was silence. Hannah held her breath.

And then she heard machine gun fire.

Chapter Twenty Two

'Suicide by cop,' Hannah said. 'A fashionable way to die these days.'

'I read up about it.' Daniel savoured his last mouthful of lasagne. 'Allardyce matches the profile. People who provoke armed police officers to kill them are usually white males of a certain age who have recently suffered an emotional trauma. And if murdering your wife doesn't qualify as an emotional trauma, what does?'

She pushed her plate aside and leaned across the mahogany table. 'You're always very well informed, aren't you?'

Off duty this evening, she was wearing a white fitted shirt and black trousers. Nothing glitzy, that wasn't her style. They were nearing the end of dinner in a hot and crowded Italian restaurant in Kendal. There was nothing furtive or secret about their meal together; he'd even asked Miranda if she wanted to come along and be introduced. But she'd said no. A glossy lifestyle magazine had commissioned her to write eighteen hundred words on the pleasures and perils of downshifting and the deadline was first thing tomorrow.

Hannah hadn't said whether she'd invited Marc—she hadn't mentioned him all evening. Otherwise, she'd been more forthcoming than he'd dared to hope. It wasn't down to alcohol; she'd only drunk sparkling water. He'd learned about Gabrielle's dodgy past and her fling with Joe Dowling. About the money on her bed, which Dowling had no doubt pocketed when he learned his guest was dead, though nobody would ever prove it. About how Allardyce had avoided being tried for rape. And about how Jean Allardyce must have secretly feared that her husband was a murderer and how her inability to keep silent any longer had cost her life and ultimately her husband's. It was as though, now that the case had come to an end, Hannah needed to sign it off in her own mind before moving on to the next cold file. Perhaps it was her equivalent of his habit, childish, but satisfying, of typing THE END in bold 24-point capitals whenever he finished a manuscript. He hadn't expected her to speak so frankly about the investigation and its horrifying climax. Nor had he needed to do more than give the occasional prompt. A remark of his mother's lodged in his memory; she'd once told him that all women love men to listen to them, really listen to them—because it doesn't happen often enough. For a long time he'd assumed it was a sideswipe at his father, but in time he'd concluded she might just be right.

Yet he didn't believe that Hannah would disclose so much merely because he was willing to pay attention. She trusted him to be discreet and he found that flattering, even if he did owe it to the trust she'd had in his father. And, maybe, she enjoyed his company nearly as much as he relished hers. When he'd heard the rifle shot that ended the siege, his stomach had lurched with fear. Allardyce had murdered Jean; he wouldn't scruple at gunning down a police officer. When the news filtered through that the farmer was dead, he had to restrain himself from punching the air. It wasn't the right reaction and it certainly wasn't something he could confess to Hannah. He didn't want her to misinterpret him, to jump to the conclusion that he wanted something more from her than friendship.

Savouring the last of his wine, he said, 'That's one thing Oxford gives you, a love of information. Of course, being a mine of facts and trivia is so much easier than being a man of action.'

'Believe me, it's no great shakes being a man of action.' She sighed. 'The poor sod who shot Allardyce has been suspended from duty. Routine procedure, but no joke. Neither was being stripped and debriefed. Now he has to wait to see whether the CPS decide to prosecute him for homicide.'

'Surely they won't do that?'

'The smart money says you're right, but with the CPS, you can never tell. The kindest thing to say is that they move in mysterious ways. The lad's pretty traumatised, bound to be. He says he fired in self-defence, and who can blame him? Sometimes you have to make your mind up in a split second. He was afraid that Allardyce was going to kill him. Section Three of the Criminal Law Act says that's a good defence. Even so, you wouldn't want your whole career to depend on it. That's the trouble with the laws in this bloody country. Everything's weighted in favour of the wrongdoer and against the ordinary decent guy just trying to do his job.'

'You sound like my father. That's the sort of thing he used to say.'

She bit her lip. 'Sorry. You think I'm ranting.'

'Don't apologise. We're all allowed a rant every now and then. I can see why you and he got along, that's what I'm saying.'

'Yes,' she said softly. 'We got along pretty well. I only wish you'd had a chance to get to know him properly.'

'Thanks to you, I have a clearer picture of what he was like.'

She let a bustling waiter clear their plates and take an order for coffee before saying, 'And what do you see in the picture?'

'A mass of contradictions.'

'Same as the rest of us, then?'

He laughed. 'Let me try again. No villain could ever bully him, but he let Cheryl twist him round her little finger. He was a highly disciplined officer who kept getting the wrong side of his superiors. An emotional man who bottled things up and never let his feelings show. A rationalist who relaxed by performing magic tricks.'

She smiled. 'He never did tell me how he managed to transform one playing card into another, however many times I pleaded to be let into the secret. An awkward cuss, that was your dad. And a true friend, a man you could rely on.'

Daniel folded his napkin; much easier than ordering his thoughts. 'Despite the fact he betrayed his wife and abandoned his family?'

'I told you. He was racked with guilt, but as for moving away, his take on it was that he sacrificed what he wanted for the good of you and your sister.'

'Yeah, I still can't get my head around that.'

'I'm not pretending it was the shrewdest judgement of all time. He made mistakes, like the rest of us. Picking Cheryl to run off with wasn't exactly a stroke of genius. Without wishing to be bitchy, he could have done better.'

'Where Cheryl is concerned,' he said with a grin, 'anyone's allowed to be bitchy.'

'I suppose she loved him, at least to begin with. But by falling for her, he gave up so much. Your mother wanted him out of her life completely. Gone, finished, never to return. He hated that, but he was terrified that a battle royal would wreck your life and your sister's. I saw him face danger, many times, and he never flinched, but he wouldn't put his kids through any more pain. He said you had a wonderful mother, he admired her strength of character. She was more than a match for him. He was only sorry he'd been such a lousy dad.'

At the table next to theirs, a family birthday party was in full voice. Amidst much merriment, a white-haired great-grandmother was flapping leathery hands and pretending to be embarrassed as whooping children urged her to blow out the candles on a huge cake.

Daniel grunted. 'He should have fought harder.'

'Maybe, but I can promise you this. If he gave up too easily, it wasn't for lack of guts.'

'Come to that, if he'd fought harder with his bosses, maybe the truth about Allardyce would have come out at the time.'

Hannah paused as the old lady's candles were extinguished with a little help from the younger generation and a couple of waiters led a raucous serenade of 'Happy Birthday to You.'

'He did his best,' she said. 'Don't they say that politics is the art of the possible? Well, it's the same with police work.'

'His best wasn't good enough, was it? Sure, Barrie's death was a lucky break for Allardyce, but if Jean had been interrogated more intensively, she might have admitted that the alibi she gave him was false. How could she bear to keep on sleeping with a man she knew was a murderer?'

'Women,' Hannah said softly, 'will put up with a lot. More, very often, than can possibly make sense.'

'I still can't help wondering…'

'Don't wonder,' she said. 'It's not a recipe for contentment.'

He wanted to argue, but something in her voice made him hold his tongue. Needing to cool down, he loosened his collar. Candle-light reflected in her eyes as she traced a finger around the rim of her glass.

'You were complaining earlier on that you couldn't figure out certain things about the murder,' she said. 'Why Allardyce left his wife's body in the dipper, for instance, instead of burying it out of harm's way up in the fells before it was found.'

'He knew you were asking questions about Jean's where-abouts, but the cover he put on the dipping tank was never going to fool anything but the most casual inspection. Are you suggesting that subconsciously he wanted the corpse to be dis-covered, that he realised he was losing it?'

'God knows, Daniel. How do you read the mind of a man like that, even supposing you want to? Your father used to say that a police officer's case-bag is packed with strange things. Unexplained mysteries, all kinds of…unfinished business.' She lingered over the last phrase. 'People talk about life's rich tapestry, but it's not always crafted in elaborate satisfying detail. Pieces go missing, odd bits of the pattern seem out of place.'

'History is like that too. It can't be wrong to work at making the patterns fit.'

'Not so long as you don't treat detective work as a guessing game or a lottery. To make a charge stick, you need evidence strong enough to convince the court.'

'Which doesn't arise here. The accused is dead. Like Barrie Gilpin.'

'Listen,' she said as the cappuccinos were served. 'We didn't want Tom Allardyce to die. No one did. He brought it on himself. He knew exactly what he was doing when he provoked that AFO to shoot him, believe me. But even if we'd brought him to trial and secured the convictions, the odds are that we wouldn't find out everything. Think of Fred West and Harold Shipman.'

'Sure, but why not at least try to make sense of the fragments you don't understand?'

She lapped the chocolate topping off her drink and gave her mouth a quick wipe. 'History's one thing. Nobody's going to make too much fuss if you guess wrong about whether Queen Victoria ever dropped her knickers for John Brown. Murder cases change lives forever. We trespass enough into private grief when we focus on what the courts need to know. It's impossible to do more.'

Stung, he said, 'History matters more than you think. There's a saying in the States that says history is fiction with the truth left out. Not entirely unfair, but to my mind history is all about searching for the truth. Like police work, or so I assumed.'

'It seems to me,' she said calmly, 'that you have a secret yearning to be a detective. My sergeant thinks so too. Trust me, it's not as much fun as you may think.'

He swallowed some coffee. It was scalding, but he scarcely noticed. 'Sorry if you think I'm naïve.'

She reached across the table and brushed the tips of his fingers. Her touch was warm, but he didn't respond and she put her hand back on her lap. 'Hey,' she said softly. 'Don't be cross with me, Daniel. I do understand. Your dad was a hero and then he let you down. Of course you're bound to be fascinated by the work he did.'

'No psychiatric analysis, please,' he said. 'I get enough of that at home when Miranda combs through the horoscopes.'

'Sorry,' she said again. 'This has been a lovely evening and I don't want to spoil it with some pointless argument. Yes, history's important, and so is finding out about your father. All I'm saying is that it isn't a good idea to worry away at problems that don't have answers.'

'I don't agree,' he said, signalling for the bill. 'It's the only way we ever achieve anything.'

◇◇◇

'How did it go?' Miranda asked when he joined her in bed at midnight. He could still smell the fresh paint.

'All right.'

Her body wriggled against him. 'I finished the article.'

'Terrific.'

'Guess what? Suki, the editor, emailed me to suggest lunch next time I'm down in London. If I move quickly, there could be a chance of a regular half-page. You know, confessions of a city girl who's found herself plonked down in the countryside without a pair of green wellies to her name.'

'You make it sound as though I dragged you here kicking and screaming.'

She poked him in the ribs. 'Nothing wrong with a bit of poetic licence. I rather fancy writing a funny column. Misadventures in the middle of nowhere, something for readers to chuckle over while they sit under the hair dryer. There can be something very po-faced about beauty tips, aerobic exercises, and feng shui. Anyway, I'll see what she says.'

'So you'll take her up on the lunch?'

'Why not? I only need be away one night, two at most. I might look up one or two people whilst I'm down there. And I happen to know that Suki likes to lunch lavishly, so I'm hoping for something swish and champagne-laden in Chelsea. What was your pizzeria like?'

Absurdly, he felt defensive, as if she'd impugned the quality of restaurants the length and breadth of Cumbria. 'It was fine. And it wasn't simply a pizzeria.'

Her breasts were pressing into him, her legs were rubbing against his. Finishing an article always gave her a high and he knew she'd want to celebrate by making love. But he wasn't in the mood.

'So,' she whispered in his ear, 'you were adventurous enough to go for a Michelin-quality lasagne, then? Don't deny it, I can smell the garlic. Not that you've quite managed to put me off, though. You lucky, lucky man.'

He felt her hair on his cheeks as he kissed her gently on the lips. 'Eddie's here early tomorrow, we need to get to sleep.'

'Don't think you're getting off that lightly. Not when you've spent the entire evening with another woman. Is she gorgeous, by the way?'

'She's a police officer.'

'That's not an answer.'

Her hands began to roam as he said, 'She told me a lot about my father that I didn't know. And plenty about what happened to Tom Allardyce. But she obviously believes that history is bunk.'

Miranda giggled. 'She's out of date. Julian Barnes says that it's burps. We keep tasting the onion sandwich it swallowed centuries ago.'

He spent much of the next day in the garden, scything down brambles. Left to spread unchecked, they would choke the begonias that he'd planted to add a splash of colour while he weighed up the garden's long-term potential. It was the sort of job apt to induce myocardial infarction in the fittest, but at least it offered the reward of fast and visible progress. The lavender bushes filled the soft air with their scent, every now and then a squirrel scuttled up and down a tree and made the leaves rustle. The tarn was still and the heron invisible, but in the distance he could hear the tumbling waters of Brack Force.

In mid-afternoon, Miranda returned from an expedition to Tasker's and they sat on the paved area, eating Magnum ice creams. She was agog with the news that Simon Dumelow was seriously ill with a brain tumour. According to rumour, he only had days to live.

'Hannah Scarlett told me he was sick,' he said. 'But I didn't know...'

'He looked so fit when we went to dinner there. But remember when he stumbled on the stairs? I suppose it was a symptom and we never dreamed...'

He said slowly, 'We talked about escapism.'

'That's right. *Winter Holiday* and all that.'

'Yes.' He remembered Tash blushing as they shared memories of the children's book. Out of nowhere, a thought slapped him. 'You're right, she did understand.'

Tash Dumelow had aged ten years in the week since their encounter in Tarn Fold. She answered the door herself in tee shirt, denim jeans and trainers. Her pasty complexion had become a make-up free zone and the red-rimmed eyes were dull and expressionless. Daniel thought she'd put on weight. He could smell gin on her breath.

'Hello, Daniel,' she said hoarsely.

His throat was dry and he was wishing he'd prepared a script. Too late now. All the way over here, a voice in his head had nagged like a termagant.

You should be ashamed of yourself. The woman is grieving and you're making a terrible mistake. Why didn't you wait and think this through, instead of letting yourself be bowled along by excitement? What will you say if you are proved wrong? You're ruining everything, not just for you but for Miranda as well. Why didn't you listen to Hannah and mind your own business?

'I—we were sorry to hear the news about Simon.'

'Yes,' she said. 'Not good, is it? The nurse is with him now.'

He coughed and shifted from one foot to another. 'I don't want to intrude...'

It was a lie; he'd driven over here precisely because he was determined to intrude. But he didn't know what else to say. If she said she wasn't up to talking or slammed the door in his face, he didn't have a Plan B. He would have to go away and decide whether he dared share with anyone the idea that had leapt unbidden into his mind. It was a credible idea, it made his spine tingle just like the comparison between nineteenth-century historians and Sherlock Holmes that had become the springboard for the book and then his television series. But as Hannah Scarlett said, there was a world of difference between academic theorising and building a case on the granite of evidence.

'You must excuse me,' Tash said. 'I've forgotten my manners. What are you doing out on the doorstep? Come in for a few minutes. The nurse will be a while yet.'

'I'm sorry to disturb you at a time like this,' he said, following her along the hallway. Their footsteps echoed on the floorboards. 'It must be very difficult for you.'

'It's outside my experience,' she said, not looking over her shoulder. 'The man I love is dying and I'm being forced to watch.'

Brackdale folk had never understood the Dumelows' relationship, he told himself. Glib and easy resentment of a glamorous trophy wife missed the point. So did envy of the rich man who'd dumped his childhood sweetheart for a younger, prettier model. For once the truth was tinged with fairytale romance. This couple really were truly, madly, deeply in love with each other. But it wasn't a fairytale with a happy ending.

'Would you like a drop of something?' she asked as they entered the living room. A half-empty bottle of Gordon's stood on a silver tray next to a solitary glass.

And Tash herself, people had never understood her. The snide remarks that they exchanged behind their hands were ludicrously mistaken. This woman wasn't a city sophisticate who regarded slumming it in the valley as the price to be paid for a cushy lifestyle. Look at the watercolours that covered the walls, the shimmering dawns and the purple sunsets, the blue meres and the mist-fringed mountains. They weren't masterpieces, but they were painted from the heart. She was infatuated with Lakeland, still crazy after all these years. Brackdale was her special place, a private refuge, an oasis of safety.

'No?' She nodded at one of the vast leather armchairs. 'Do take a seat. You won't mind if I pour myself another?'

'Of course not.'

Lifting the bottle, she said, 'I know I've had enough. Too many, in fact, but who's counting? This is the best anaesthetic I know. Kind of you to call by.'

'I'll be honest with you, Tash.' He took a deep breath. 'I came to ask a couple of questions.'

Until this moment, she'd seemed dazed. Dazed by the drink and the fate of the man who was dying in this house. But something in his tone seemed to slap her into watchfulness.

'Questions?'

The warning voice whispered in his brain: *You're going to regret this. Keep quiet, make your apologies and leave her to weep. There is still time.*

'As a matter of fact, when I was a student, I spent a few months learning Russian, just for fun.'

'And?'

The longcase clock was ticking in the background. He focused on Tash's white face, so beautifully structured. Cheekbones to die for. They were so high; a Slavic inheritance, he'd assumed.

'There was a proverb I came across. I don't know if you're familiar with it.' He took a deep breath. If only his translation skills weren't so rusty. 'It goes something like this. *Skazhi s kem ty drug, a ya skazhu kto ty takov.*'

'Sorry,' she said. 'I'm way out of practice.'

He raised his eyebrows. 'Your native tongue?'

'It's a mistake to live in the past,' she said with a tight smile. 'I think of myself as English now.'

'Yes, that's one thing everyone admires. The way you've assimilated yourself into the English way of life. You speak the language like a native, no one would ever imagine that you came from Russia. The proverb, by the way, means *Tell me who your friend is and I'll tell you who you are.*'

She sipped at her drink, watching him in the way a zoo keeper might watch a tiger with a reputation for unpredictability.

'In case you needed a translation,' he said. 'Some things cling on in the memory more than others, don't they? Like the stories we enjoyed as children.'

It must have been his imagination, but the clock was getting louder. *Tick, tick, tick.*

'Sorry, Daniel,' she said coldly. 'It must be me. Perhaps I've had a drop too much, maybe it's all the—stuff that's been going on lately. My head's throbbing and I'm afraid you're not making it any better.'

He stood up. They were a yard apart, facing each other. 'You reminded Miranda of the name of the character in a book by Arthur Ransome, didn't you? A girl called Dorothea.'

'Sorry?' Her face was a mask and he guessed she was trying to freeze-frame the conversation in her mind and identify what exactly she might have said.

Tick, tick, tick.

'You both identified with the escapism in the story. But what matters is that you were familiar with the name.'

Tash spread her arms. 'I must have come across it somewhere.'

'Not as a child in Russia, though. My sister was devoted to those books, she couldn't get enough of the fun and games with Captain Flint, even though it was a fantasy world. Totally different from life at the local comprehensive. Mind you, Arthur Ransome was married to Trotsky's secretary, wasn't he? One of my favourite bits of Lakeland literary trivia.'

She stared at him. 'You're not talking sense.'

'It comes down to this. I can't believe that when you were a kid, *Swallows and Amazons* and *Winter Holiday* were recommended reading for Moscow schoolgirls. But—maybe I'm wrong. Or maybe you read Ransome after you came to England.'

'Maybe I did. What are you talking about, for God's sake? I invite you in as a friend and now you are practically persecuting me.'

The voice hissed: *This is your last chance. Stop now.*

But an almost sexual exhilaration was blazing within him and he knew he could not let go. No stopping now, he was past reason. Like when he and Miranda stripped off inhibitions along with their clothes and made love to each other that first time in Tarn Fold. Had his father felt this hot excitement, when he closed in the solution to a case? At last he knew why detecting crime had meant so much to Ben Kind. It kidnapped you, this burning urge to rip away all the wrappers and reveal the truth. It consumed you, it was everything.

Tash's hands were on her hips. Inside, for all he knew she was breaking apart, but her lips were pressed together in a defiant line. He'd never seen eyes so cold and empty. She would not yield.

He took a step towards her. With each bit of flotsam, each snippet of information swimming into his mind, he could feel himself gaining strength. The strength he needed to confront her with the truth.

You'd never imagine she was a foreigner.

He turned the King of Diamonds into the Ace of Spades.

Tell me who your friend is and I'll tell you who you are.

Tick, tick, tick, tick, tick.

'So Eldine Webber was the first?' he asked.

'Eldine Webber?' Her voice broke. No mistaking her alarm.

She was playing for time, he could see it in her eyes. Making calculations. How much did he know, how much was guesswork?

'Surely you haven't forgotten him?'

'He was—he was a friend of Gabrielle's.'

'Yes,' he said quietly. 'And Gabrielle killed him, didn't she?'

Her face was ashen. 'What are you saying?'

'Gabrielle killed Eldine Webber. And you know that better than anyone, don't you? You never were Natasha. You were always Gabrielle Anders.'

Chapter Twenty Three

'This is absurd,' she said.

'So much is absurd,' Daniel said. 'Including the idea that you and Gabrielle could exchange identities and get away with it. No offence, but neither of you exactly made a success of your acting careers. Even so, it worked. You played your part as if you were up for an Academy Award, but this performance carried on day in, day out. No one had the faintest idea that you weren't who you claimed to be. Not even Simon, am I right?'

Tash—he couldn't help thinking of her as Tash—stared at him. 'You haven't any proof of this.'

'Come on, we're past that stage, aren't we?' He spoke as patiently as any counsellor, but how could you counsel a recidivist murderer? 'Webber was a brute and somehow you killed him. From what I'm told, no one could blame you. I suppose it was an act of despair. But it meant you were in danger. Webber had plenty of enemies, but he also had ruthless friends. So you did a deal with your friend Natasha. In return for the money Webber had lavished on you, she agreed to swap identities. Why not? She was sick of the low-life in Leeds and she had an incurable wanderlust. It was a chance for a fresh start, for both of you. Something we all yearn for. Believe me, I know.'

'If you say so.'

'It was a conjuring trick.' He mimicked his father's jokey tone, that wet afternoon with Barrie Gilpin. 'Hey presto! and you became Natasha. Before our very eyes! she became Gabrielle.'

The clock was still ticking. So loud now, he could scarcely hear himself speak.

'You took her passport, everything. She headed for America and you ran off across the Pennines and fetched up in the Lakes. Where you couldn't resist trying your luck with another rich man. Had you heard of Simon through Eldine Webber? Doesn't matter. You crossed his path and the rest is—well, history.'

'I love him.'

'I know,' he said. 'And you love the Lakes. "The most perfect place in the world." Which is why Gabrielle's return was such a catastrophe. She threatened your security, she could destroy you with one careless word. You gave her money, lots of it, but that didn't work. She was enjoying herself too much to be bought off so easily. You were terrified, thought you'd never be free from danger.'

Tash didn't speak. Her expression had frozen, as though all the muscles in her face had ceased to work. If she was still making calculations, he could not guess what they were. Right now, he didn't care.

'You're keen on scapegoats, aren't you? People to blame make things so much simpler, so much safer. Changing places with Natasha got you off the hook with Eldine Webber's associates. When you decided that she had to die, you didn't have far to search for a fall guy. Poor Barrie Gilpin. I suppose you made up the story about his being a Peeping Tom and started all the gossip?'

She moistened her lips. 'Call it artistic licence.'

'You persuaded Natasha to meet you. An offer of more money, something like that? But then you killed her and made it look like the work of a maniac. You lured Barrie out on to the fell and then you had a stroke of good fortune. In his panic he lost his footing and plunged into the ravine.' He paused, trying to stifle his bitterness. 'It must have been a horrifying way to go. Slow, painful, inescapable death. But so what? Who cares, as long as you are free?'

'Listen, he may not have peeped through my bedroom windows, but he loved getting an eyeful of my cleavage whenever he could. Whenever he worked well, I wore a low-cut top and no bra, that was his reward.'

'Talk about performance management, huh?' Daniel said mirthlessly.

A bleak smile. 'I never saw anyone so motivated. He wasn't exactly subtle, your friend. He fancied Natasha like mad, I could tell that from the start. The way he tried to chat her up, it was pitiful to watch. I rang him up that night, pretending to be her. I took her mobile from her bag, so the call couldn't be traced to me. It was scary, becoming Gabrielle again after so many years, a few minutes after I'd hit her over the head and then—used the axe. I didn't enjoy that, I promise you, but it had to be done, it was part of the narrative. Just like bundling her body into the four-by-four and taking it up the fell. When I called Barrie, I could almost hear him salivating as I suggested getting it together on the Sacrifice Stone.'

'He'd have seen it as the chance of a lifetime.'

'He was a man. Utterly predictable.' The smile flickered, then died. 'Don't look at me that way. It was a matter of survival. Him or me.'

'No contest, then.' Anger raged inside him. 'After you'd dumped the body, I guess you drove back down the fell along the coffin trail. You still had work to do. Clothes to destroy, evidence to eliminate. How much did Simon know, or guess, about what you'd done?'

'Not a thing, thanks to a sedative. The most terrifying moment was when I thought I'd given him too much and he'd never wake up again. I hated being the cause of the terrible headache he had the next day. But what else could I do? Simon always wanted to protect me and make sure I had everything I wanted. I almost took him into my confidence, but it was too great a risk. Better for only one of us to have to keep the secret. And it all worked out so beautifully.'

There was a dreamy look in her eyes. Almost self-congratulatory. She had the chilly detachment that he presumed was the stock-in-trade of any successful murderer. But in the end, it hadn't been enough. Maybe Theo had been right that escapists can never escape their fate.

'Only one thing went wrong. The farmhouse windows look out towards the coffin trail and Jean Allardyce saw you.'

'I didn't even realise.' She shook her head sadly. 'Jean was often subdued when we were together, but that was her nature. Hardly surprising, when she was sleeping with a man like that. I never guessed she had a clue. No hint of blackmail, all she wanted was for the pair of them to keep working here until it was time to pick up their pension. She was genuinely decent in an old-fashioned way. One of life's victims, what more can you say? We got on well, of course, she wasn't too bright. I think she was happy to persuade herself that Barrie was the killer, even if she didn't believe it deep down. She told me it had preyed on her mind, seeing me bumping down the coffin trail late at night when I was supposed to be tucked up in bed with the flu.'

'So you hit her on the head, threw her in the sheep dipper, and pulled the cover across to hide her from view.'

'You make it sound so cruel,' she said, pouring herself another drink. 'I didn't have much choice, did I? From the moment she told me she'd rung the police—she actually apologised—it could only end one way. I tried to allay her suspicions, said I'd been worried that Gabrielle was missing and had gone out looking for her. She was so relieved, said she knew she must have misunderstood. She promised she'd call them again and say she'd made a mistake. But how could I trust her? My life was in her hands, that's no way to be. Then, when I saw the two of you chatting in her car, I was afraid she'd said something to you.'

He shook his head. 'You misjudged her. She was confused and unhappy, she didn't know what to think. But she never betrayed you.'

'So you told me, but I couldn't be sure what might happen in future. Suppose she talked to her husband?'

'You spun her some yarn over tea in the baker's shop and arranged to meet her the following day. You're stronger than Jean, she didn't have a chance once you'd decided to kill her.

After that you wanted to point the finger at Allardyce as well as checking that she hadn't blurted out too much while she was giving me a lift. So you parked up in Tarn Fold and waited for me to show up.'

'You scared me,' Tash said, taking a sip of gin. 'Even before we met, when I heard someone had moved into the Gilpin cottage, someone with the same surname as the detective who interviewed me about Natasha.'

Softly, he said, 'You fooled my father.'

'Did I? I was never sure. All the other police officers were sympathetic because I was a kind of victim, I'd lost my friend. And they liked casting sidelong glances at my tits. Your father was different. Gruff and guarded. He intrigued me, because he gave nothing away. I used to lie awake at nights, wondering whether he'd add up two and two. However much care I took over my statements, he never seemed satisfied.'

He cleared his throat. 'You were lucky with your scapegoats. Barrie fell, quite literally, into a trap. Tom Allardyce you managed to push over the edge in an entirely different way.'

'One thing Natasha told me about the high rollers in Vegas,' Tash said. 'The guys who make the big money make their own luck. They take risks, yes, but they make their calculations first. Good advice, I kept it in mind when I was working out how to get rid of her.'

'And now,' he said, 'your luck's run out.'

Tick, tick, tick.

'It ran out the day Allardyce was shot. There I was, thinking the whole mess was sorted and then Simon broke his news. The only man—the *only* man—who ever understood how to treat me. And I've lost him. Twenty minutes before you arrived, I said goodbye but I'd left it too late. He didn't recognise me. It's almost over.'

'I'm sorry about Simon,' he said awkwardly.

'Yes, well.' She pursed her lips. 'Of course, you're taking a risk yourself. Killing can become an easy option. A habit. Why should I scruple at one more death?'

Even as she spoke, she put down her glass and walked away from him, towards the corner of the room. He recalled Simon bragging about the thickness of the walls in the tower. Behind closed doors, someone could scream like a dying pig and nobody outside would hear a sound. Tash halted next to a bookcase. On its top, a pair of heavy brass bookends in the shape of lions enclosed a row of Wainwrights. She lifted one of the bookends and a couple of the books tumbled on to the floor.

'Because it's pointless,' he said. 'You'd never get away with it.'

'What's happened to Simon is pointless,' she said. 'I could make a sort of statement by killing you. A grand theatrical gesture. Show how pointless our whole fucking lives are—when you get down to it all.'

He felt himself tensing. The living room had two doors, one leading up to the tower, the other linking with the main part of the Hall. He could run if he chose, run back the way they had come. Indecision paralysed him. He'd never talked to a murderer before. What would his father have done?

Tash took a stride towards him. He caught the whiff of alcohol on her breath as she ran her finger along the edge of the bookend. She was caressing the lion's mane as if fondling a pet.

'Dusty,' she said, wrinkling her nose. 'That's what happens when you don't have a housekeeper to keep things nice and tidy.'

Daniel took a breath. Hannah had told him that the m.o. in the killings of Gabrielle and Jean were the same. They'd both been bludgeoned first, rendered insensible so that the killer could destroy them at leisure.

He could hear Hannah speaking of his father. *I saw him face danger, many times, and he never flinched.*

So: was he his father's son?

Neither of them moved.

Tick, tick, tick.

Presently, Tash shook her head. Turning, she replaced the brass lion on top of the bookcase.

'I think it's time to go.'

As he watched, she spun on her heel and walked out through the door that led to the tower. The heavy key rattled in the lock. For an instant, he thought he was trapped.

Wrong, wrong, wrong. He could walk back into the main building and she was no longer there to stand in his way. So why would she lock the door?

Shit.

Images suddenly poured into his head, as if someone had opened a sluice-valve. He could hear Aimee's message on his mobile phone, feel the pounding of his heart as he realised what she meant to do. He was back in Cornmarket, temples throbbing as he raced along the pavement. He could hear excited whispers, see fingers pointing up into the sky. Up to the top of St Michael's Tower.

Not again.

His limbs unfroze and somehow he stumbled through the door and into the corridor. As he flung open the door that led out to the courtyard, he told himself that he was already too late.

But she was still there, gazing down from the battlements. He was staring into the sun, screwing up his eyes as he tried to focus on the slight figure outlined against the sky. She'd waited for him. He had a chance, a last chance to save her. He cried out:

'Tash!'

Her reply drifted away in the breeze. He thought she said:

'*Gabrielle.*'

His stomach clenched. He was powerless to do anything but watch as she climbed on to the parapet and stepped off into the air.

Chapter Twenty Four

Hannah pointed to the grey bulk of the Sacrifice Stone looming before them. 'So the legend had a grain of truth. You did look Death in the eye.'

Daniel followed as she picked her way along the narrow track on Priest Edge. The ground was bare underfoot. In the distance he could see the coffin trail winding down the fell. Since the drama of the previous week he'd made his apologies to the editor of *Contemporary Historian* and abandoned his article about corpse roads. Only last night he'd dreamed of Tash Dumelow jolting down the coffin trail in an exultant mood, unaware that in the farmhouse below, a curtain was twitching.

When they reached the Stone he said, 'I've learned my lesson. I won't be climbing up it again.'

'Glad to hear you say so,' she scolded. 'The Lakes aren't a theme park. People ought to leave its monuments alone.'

'Sorry, it was an aberration. Put it down to the ignorance of an off-comer. It'll take time for me to behave like a native. Even longer to feel like one.'

'Thirty years minimum, no reduction for good behaviour. Never mind the tourism and the twee craft shops, Daniel. This is a private corner of the world. You can't just march in and hope to belong.'

'I guess you're right.'

'Still happy you moved here?'

'No regrets.'

'Despite all that's happened?'

He brushed his fingers against the Stone, feeling its roughness. 'Somehow the Lakes have got under my skin. Besides, at least one good thing's been achieved. Barrie's name has been cleared. Even if not by a court of law.'

'What's so wonderful about the judgment of a court of law? I've seen a few dodgy verdicts in my time, I promise you.'

'When we had dinner, you mentioned that case about the man who hired the hitman, Golac. Still rankles that he got off scot free?'

'You bet. Unfinished business.'

He'd heard her use the phrase before, it seemed to have a resonance for her. 'Like my father and the murder of Gabrielle Anders.'

She was glaring at him. 'Why didn't you talk to me about Tash instead of confronting her?'

'It would have been the sensible thing to do.'

'Too right.'

'Leaving Oxford and coming here wasn't sensible, either. Trouble is, I'm sick—yes, I'm so *sick*—of doing the sensible thing.'

'You should have trusted me.'

'I realise that,' he said quietly. 'It wasn't about not trusting you. Please believe me.'

She swivelled, as if wanting to change the subject, and gazed down the slope towards Tarn Fold. 'How's the work on the cottage going?'

'On bad days, it feels as though it will never end. As though I'll never get the dust out of my sinuses and the wood shavings out of my hair. On good days, well, things are taking shape.'

'And Miranda, is she glad she made the move?'

He looked at the traces of his footprints on the track. Soon, he thought, the farmers would be praying for rain. People were never satisfied for long.

'Most of the time, yes,' he said eventually. 'Whether she will still be so glad after she gets back from London, who knows?

I'm not sure—not convinced any more that she really thought this through. When the excitement fades…'

'Sorry, I shouldn't pry. None of my business.'

'I'm turning my attention to the garden. It's a wilderness, yet there's something that puzzles me. As if it were laid out according to a strange, lop-sided design. The only snag is, I can't make any sense of it.'

She put her head to one side, weighing him up. 'Mysteries fascinate you, don't they?'

'History is stuffed with them. Every historian wants to find answers to the puzzles of the past.'

'You said something earlier, about the moment Tash threw herself from the pele tower. You had a flashback.'

'Uh-huh.'

'Do you want to talk about it?'

He sighed. 'Why not?'

He didn't look at her as he talked about the death of his lover, but he was conscious of her intense scrutiny. When he'd finished, he said, 'My old boss thinks that by moving to the Lakes, I'm running away from what happened to Aimee. If he's right, it certainly didn't work. I've spent all my life hungering after knowledge. I'm never satisfied until I understand. That's fine for a historian, but it causes trouble in the real world. If I hadn't confronted Tash, she'd be alive today.'

'Do you wish she'd lived?'

He shrugged. 'What matters is that she didn't want to.'

A few moments passed. Hannah checked her watch. 'I'd better be going.'

'Marc will be getting back from the book fair soon, I guess.'

'Maybe.'

Something in her voice caused him to look up. 'Something wrong?'

She pushed a hand through her hair. 'Nothing that can't be sorted out, I suppose.'

He took a deep breath. 'Would you like to tell me about it?'

She hesitated. 'I—I don't think that would be a good idea.'

'Okay.'

'You understand what I mean?' Her shoulders were hunched, her tone defensive. 'I don't want to sound secretive, especially when you told me all about Aimee. But some things need to stay private.'

He shrugged. 'I'll walk you back to the car.'

In silence, they made their way along the edge of the fell and then down the coffin trail, towards Brack Hall and the farm. Hannah had parked at the point where the trail joined the lane. When they reached her car, she offered her hand. It was warm to touch.

'Perhaps I'll see you again sometime.'

He wondered if he should kiss her. Just a peck on the cheek, nothing more. He leaned towards her and her eyes widened. Something in her expression unsettled him. Shit, he thought.

Slowly, trying not to show his reluctance, he drew back.

'So how are things here?' Miranda asked as he unlocked the front door.

From the moment he'd picked her up at Oxenholme station, she'd scarcely drawn breath. The jaunt to London had been an unqualified success. She'd seen friends, lunched at the next table to a couple of hunky actors from a long-running soap, and accepted Suki's offer to contribute a regular column to the magazine. The pay was amazing and the friends mouth-wateringly envious of her idyllic lifestyle in the Lakes. A couple of people she'd wanted to see had been away, but it didn't matter because she'd soon have another chance to catch up with them. She needed to go back to Wapping to chat up an ex-boyfriend who had moved to *The Sunday Times* and might be interested in occasional lifestyle features. No need to be jealous, she'd assured Daniel; the boyfriend had finally decided he was gay and was living with a bloke who was a driver on the London Underground.

'Eddie says he'll be starting work on the bothy next week. And I took Tash's watercolour and gave it to the Oxfam shop.

Otherwise, not quite as exciting as they were for you, by the sound of it.'

'Listen,' she said as he put down her suitcase. 'You've already had enough excitement to last a lifetime. I still can't get over the idea of Tash killing her own housekeeper. Let alone this horrid picture that keeps coming into my mind of her splattered all over the courtyard. All the blood and the brains—ugh! This a beautiful part of the world, I've been telling everyone, but...weird, somehow.'

'You're still glad we moved here?'

'Of course! Let's face it, I've fallen on my feet. If we didn't have a cottage in the country, Suki would never have crossed my palm with silver. I only wish you hadn't made me promise not to write about the murders. I could have made a small fortune. All the same...'

'Yes?'

'The agent still hasn't found a buyer for my flat. Not at the price I wanted.'

'You are asking top dollar.'

'Why not? It's an up-and-coming area. But I was wondering whether it might be an idea to keep the flat. It would be so useful to have a place to stay in the city. Our very own pied-a-terre. What do you think?'

'Why would we need it?'

In playful mood, she wagged a finger. 'Don't forget what you said about Tash. She wanted to start again, but you said it was impossible. We're all the prisoners of our history.'

'God,' he said gloomily. 'I can be pretentious sometimes.'

'You're an Oxford don,' she said, punching him gently in the stomach. 'It comes with the territory.'

He shook his head. 'Oxford's in the past. I'm not going back.'

'You'll change your mind. Everybody does in the end.'

'Not me.'

'Daniel.' Her tone was patient and kind. 'The Lake District is wonderful, but it is a bit—well, remote. We don't want to cut ourselves off.'

'But that's what we agreed.'

She reached towards him and started to unbuckle his belt. 'Hey, let's not argue. I've only been home five minutes and there are far better ways we can spend the time.'

He closed his eyes as she touched him. She still had the gift of making him forget everything but the here and now. Trouble was, with his eyes shut, his brain played a trick on him. Wove a dark spell that made his body tremble.

No point denying it, no point in trying to fool himself. In his mind, Miranda too had changed places. For a few seconds before he jolted back to his senses, the wandering hands belonged to Hannah Scarlett.

CPSIA information can be obtained at www.ICGtesting.com
224206LV00001B/104/A